ARCA

Also by G. R. Macallister and available from Titan Books

SCORPICA
ARCA

THE FIVE QUEENDOMS

ARCA

BOOK TWO

G. R. MACALLISTER

TITAN BOOKS

Arca
Print edition ISBN: 9781789099348
E-book edition ISBN: 9781789099355

Published by Titan Books
A division of Titan Publishing Group Ltd.
144 Southwark Street, London SE1 0UP
www.titanbooks.com

First Titan edition March 2023
10 9 8 7 6 5 4 3 2 1

A CIP catalogue record for this title is available from the British Library.

Printed and bound by CPI Group (UK) Ltd, Croydon CR0 4YY

TO MY SON,

TIRELESS ADVOCATE FOR

THE THEORETICAL FIVE QUEENDOMS

VIDEO GAME ADAPTATION

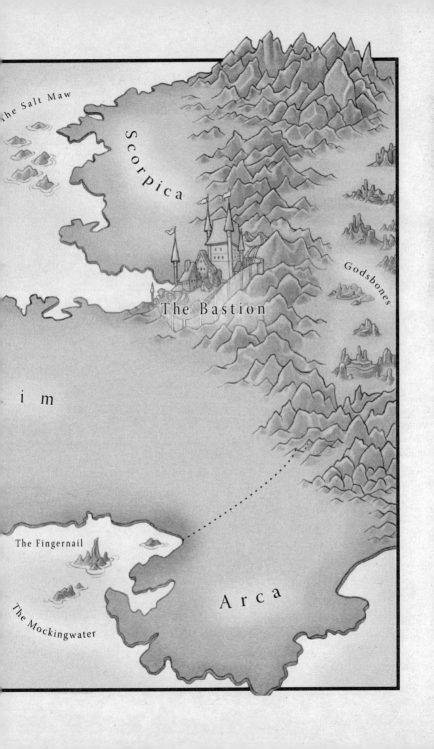

Major and Recurring Characters
Listed by Queendom

ARCA

ALISHER, a courtier of the Binaj matriclan
ARCHIS, a high-ranking courtier with all-magic
BEYDA, royal scribe assigned to Arca, a Bastionite
BONMEI, youngest courtier of the Merve matriclan
COLENA, a courtier and earth magician, mother of Dellica
DELLICA, youngest courtier of the Binaj matriclan
EMINEL, queen of Arca, Well of All-Magic, Master of
Sand and Destroyer of Fear
GOLOJANDRA, known as Gogo, an earth magician
and resident of Jesephia
ISCLA, a courtier talented at shielding minds
NISHTI, a courtier of the Binaj matriclan, earth magician
PARVAN, a courtier of the Ishta matriclan, fire magician
SARA, a courtier and air magician
SOBEK, a courtier and mind magician
VERMU, member of the Queensguard
WODEVI, a courtier and body magician
XERIO, a courtier of the Binaj matriclan
YASAMIN, a courtier of the Volkan matriclan

PAXIM

AMA, the Kingling's bodyguard (born Amankha dha Khara)

ASTER, Stellari's child

AURELI, a senior senator

BARIS, a member of the King's Elite

DECIMA, consul of Paxim, friendly with Queen Heliane

DELPH, senior member of Queen Heliane's Queensguard

EVANDER, son of the most powerful family in Calladocia, married to Stellari

FARUZEH, minister of war

FLORIANA, a military commander

HELIANE, queen of Paxim, mother to Paulus

INBAR, Queen Heliane's *cosmete*

ISOLDE, a senator

JOVAN, commander of the Swans

JUNI OF KAMAL, head of the Assembly

KINT OF KETERLI, member of the Assembly

MALIM, a senator

NEBEZ OF HAVARRAH, a talented fighter, member of the King's Elite

PANAGIOTA, matriarch of the most powerful family in Calladocia

PAULUS, kingling of Paxim, only surviving child of Queen Heliane

RAHUL, Stellari's secret lover, publicly nursemaid to Aster the Shade, a talented fighter

STELLARI, a high-ranking senator, holding the office of magistrate

TUPRAH, member of Heliane's Queensguard

YESIKA, member of the King's Elite

YUSUF, member of the King's Elite

ZOFI, also known as Zo, daughter of Queen Heliane (deceased)

SCORPICA

AZUR DHA TAMURA, an adopted Scorpican and mother to
Madazur, known as First Mother
DREE, a warrior
GOLHABI, armorer of the Scorpicae
GRETTI DHA RHODARYA, a warrior, former adviser
to Queen Tamura
KHINAR, a warrior
LU, a warrior and member of the Council
MADAZUR DHA AZUR, first girl born after the Drought
MARALE, a warrior
MARKISET, an adopted Scorpican
OLAN, a warrior
OORA, an adopted Scorpican
ORLAITHE, a warrior
PAKH, a warrior
RIVA, an adopted Scorpican
SARKH, a warrior
TAGATHA, a warrior of advanced years
TAMURA DHA MADA, queen of Scorpica
ZALMA DHA FIONEN, a smith
ZIBIAH, a warrior

$\blacklozenge$ 1 $\blacklozenge$

THE SENATOR

The fourth day of the fourth month of the All-Mother's
Year 502 Ursu, capital of Paxim
Stellari

There was nothing Stellari of Calladocia could not imagine, and once she had imagined something, achieving it was just a matter of time.

Politically, this nimble imagination was her greatest gift. From a single choice, Stellari could visualize dozens, even hundreds, of possible consequences, all of which she held arrayed in her mind's eye like the stars. Then she'd choose. If she wanted a law passed, she'd quickly puzzle out who was most likely to support it, then unspool a complex chain of favors wherein she'd persuade three or four fellow senators, no more than five, who would go on to persuade all the rest for her. She never planted a seed without envisioning the eventual tree.

Her imagination hadn't served her nearly as well outside the Senate, she supposed. Potential friends quickly tired of hearing her test out unending scenarios, breathlessly recount her victories, torture herself over the rare losses. Lovers bristled at being treated like tally marks. But for Stellari, the difference between the personal and the political grew more faint until it vanished entirely. Let strangers stay strangers, let lovers turn their backs and go. She was extremely happy with what her imagination had done for her, all told.

She was, after all, the unlikeliest of senators. First off, she was not a landholder, or at least she hadn't been. She'd come up through the Assembly. All the best families of Paxim were represented in the Senate, their wisest and strongest women handing down laws from the comfort of the capital. It had been that way as long as there had been a Paxim. The Assembly was a newer experiment, two centuries old, including members of the poorer classes. Stellari had made a name for herself initially as the Assembly's representative from Calladocia, a remote southwestern district, a position she'd gotten mostly because no one else wanted it.

But that put her on the pathway to power. When Calladocia's most important landholders fell on hard times, their female line dying out and the senatorship under threat of dissolution, the head of their household summoned Assemblywoman Stellari. The matron Panagiota offered Stellari the chance to marry her last remaining son, lay claim to their family lands, and take on the vacant senatorship. Immediately seeing the ways in which it would put greater strength in her hands, Stellari had readily agreed. She'd met Evander of Calladocia twice and he'd seemed perfectly lovely, if a bit timid. At their second meeting, the marriage contracts were signed. There-after, Evander remained at home in their district, leaving Stellari free to live as she chose in the capital.

And Stellari's climb had not stopped there. In only a few short years in the Senate, she'd already ascended to the role of magistrate. She was not yet even thirty years old. Gossips whispered that she seemed likely, if Decima stepped down, to rise to the position of consul. Once Stellari overheard a fellow senator call her consulship *inevitable*. She liked that whisper best of all.

But today Stellari was just another citizen of Paxim, kept in the dark. She hated the dark. All her cleverness and vision couldn't get her the one bit of knowledge she most needed: Would the widowed queen's coming child, almost certainly her last, be a girl or a boy? Stellari had already determined what action to take in either case, but the wait was interminable. She was better off than most, knowing what only a handful of high-ranking officials now knew: the queen's labor had begun. The rest of the truth would come when the child did. The augury had been unclear, and besides, thought Stellari, practical women did not trust auguries. Predictions were half shams and wishful thinking. Only facts were facts.

This queen had birthed two girls and two boys over the years—a stillborn boy, then a living girl, then a set of girl-boy twins—but only the youngest girl remained. A single child was bleak ground on which to stake the country's entire future, especially when misfortune seemed to covet the queen's company. The stillborn boy had been a bad omen in the early years of Heliane's rule. The arrival of a girl the next year was heralded as a sign of better things to come. As for the twins, the boy had always been sickly, quick to bruise at the slightest touch. The world proved too much for him before his first year was out. His sister Zofi was stronger, with no sign of her brother's ills; in fact, she was a daredevil of a child, willful and mischievous. Then fever flooded Ursu, a whimsical pox that carried off the healthy young—including the queen's eldest daughter—and left the elderly and lame untouched in their beds. Then, only months ago, one more misfortune struck: King Cyrus, too, sped to the Underlands, wasting with a disease not even the medical experts of the Bastion or the gifted healers of Arca could cure. Now only Queen Heliane and Queenling Zofi remained. A second heir would secure the nation's confidence. This child would determine the future.

Stellari would have to wait for the signal smoke—black for a boy, white for a girl—just like everyone else.

3

Being like everyone else was perhaps the thing Stellari hated most in the world.

She lifted her head from the pillow and stared out the high, square window toward the triple spire of the palace. The sky above the central spire remained stubbornly blue. No smoke. No way of knowing how long it would be before smoke appeared.

"Do I need to yank the child out of her wrinkled *muoni* with my own two hands? Time is wasting," she complained to Rahul, who was sprawled out on the bedclothes next to her, his back still sweat-slicked and gleaming.

"You think this afternoon was a waste?" he answered.

She turned over with a lazy smile. He was inviting a compliment and she knew it. It was one of the ways in which they were so well-matched: both delighted equally in giving and receiving flattery. Looking at his long body stretching out, tawny and beautiful against the pale sheets, she was reminded of other ways in which their match was excellent.

"Time is never wasted with you," she said. "And your dedication to distracting me was delightfully . . . thorough."

"I aim to please."

"You strike your aim." She offered her neck and he leaned over to kiss it, running his lips up its curve until he reached her jawline, then flicking out his tongue to take a light lick of salt from her skin.

He relaxed back onto one elbow, letting her take a good look at the full length of his body, and she happily indulged. He was all sinew and grace, his jaw broad and square, his thick brows low over deep brown eyes. His face was too rough-hewn to be attractive, but there was a magnetism to him she found more compelling than beauty. Any Arcan man could look good through the use of their inborn enchantments. Rahul was different. His magical talents lay elsewhere. Not one Arcan man in a thousand had his particular manifestation of magic, which was why he was the first Arcan man she'd ever chosen to share pleasures with, and she strongly suspected he would be the last. Not, of course, that she would tell him so. Complacency was a risk she didn't care to run.

Rahul raised a hand, and she thought he might use it to reach for her, but he ran it over his own head instead, exposing for just a moment the white scar dividing his black hair at the scalp.

She was the one who reached out, then, for the only thing he wore: a glass amulet dangling from a cord around his neck, resting in the curls of his lightly furred chest. The double teardrop shape remained firm under her touch, of course. It had been forged by a fire magician to withstand any force, magical or otherwise. The level of the glittering sand within, a shadowy, changeable gold in color, was what she examined.

"Running low, then?"

"Likely all right for a few months. It depends on what's needed."

She hummed noncommittally and kept turning the hourglass shape in her fingers, watching the sand tilt and settle, enjoying the charm's seamless, flawless curves. It felt warm against her fingertips. She never knew whether that was from the magic used to bind the artifact or from Rahul's own steady, welcome heat.

He prompted her, "Will you need my assistance in the wake of the child's birth, do you think?"

She tried to read his eyes, but as always, it was difficult. She enjoyed that about him. He wasn't entirely trustworthy, but he was also dependent on her, and his need was something she could trust. No one in Ursu but Stellari knew that he was Arcan; he was safe here. While some in Arca would worship him as a hero if they recognized him, there were others who would attack him on sight. He would risk it, of course, for her.

"I don't expect to," she said. "I want to save you for when I need you."

"Ahh," he sighed, and this time when he raised his hand he did reach for her, letting his nimble fingers drift down, down, down. "I expect you'll be needing me again very soon."

She let out a little gasp of pleasure as he reached his goal. This, too, she trusted.

As she shifted her body to open to him, her gaze drifted toward the window. The sound in her throat turned from sigh to squeak. Every part of her went rigid.

He opened his mouth to ask why she'd stopped, but when he followed her gaze, he shut his mouth without speaking.

Out the open window, above the skyline of Ursu, rose a twisting billow of smoke.

Stellari's throat closed. How long since they'd lit the torch to signal? How many minutes had she lost?

The smoke was black. Dark as jet. No mistaking it.

"The All-Mother's *muoni*. A boy," said Rahul, half to himself.

But Stellari was already on her feet, splashing herself quickly with water from the basin, her attention gone. Within moments she had stepped into her magistrate's sky-blue robe, wrapping and belting as she went, heading for the door. At least she'd left her hair up in the braided crown that marked her as a senator, she told herself. The interwoven plaits were disarrayed from her afternoon in bed, no doubt missing most of their pins, but there wasn't time to call a servant to replait them. She'd do the best she could in motion.

In ten minutes she would be in the halls of power, ready to whisper, *I'm sure I must be the only one who has concerns* into the right ears, settling her fingers on the arms of certain senators. For others she'd stroke the braid above her ear and peek meaningfully over her shoulder, then muse, *Of course I'm loyal to the queen above all others, the monarchy is eternal, but if something were to happen to the queenling, who would follow after? It just doesn't seem wise to allow a son to rule. Didn't our foremothers, who laid down these laws, know best?*

She was ready to sow discontent, but she needn't start from seed alone. The freshly widowed queen had many allies in the Senate, it was true. But other legislators were more like Stellari, disdainful of the very idea of monarchy, no matter who wielded its reins. These women had their own goals and ends in mind, for the nation and for themselves. Discontent was already there, in sprouts and seedlings.

6

All Stellari needed to do was help them grow.

What Stellari didn't know—because no one in the Five Queendoms could yet know—was that the birth of this royal son would usher in a new age, one beset by questions. There were girls born the same day as Paulus, but the next day only boys, and the same was true the next day and the next day and for fourteen long years thereafter.

Nor did Stellari know that three years into the Drought of Girls, in the irrepressible Queenling Zofi's seventh year, she'd ride out on a spirited sun-gold mare that had been a gift to Heliane from the High Xara of Sestia. The golden mare would return hours later, panting, with a damaged leg and an empty saddle. Heliane's young son Paulus, her only remaining child, would become the queen's sole heir, just as many had feared.

Stellari didn't know that year after year after long year would pass with no girls' names written in the scribes' official record books, the lack of girls wreaking havoc throughout all five queendoms, weakening their careful peace until it crumbled. She didn't know—how could she?—that the renegade sorcerer Sessadon would break Queen Heliane's back at the Rites of the Bloody-Handed, leaving the monarch fragile and fading. Stellari could, it was true, imagine anything. But that day, as she rushed toward the Senate, smoothing down her crown of braids and rehearsing her whispers, she didn't imagine the Drought of Girls.

Years later she would look back on the fourth day of the fourth month of the All-Mother's Year 502, on that last moment before she stepped into the Senate, as the end of something. Of innocence, for many. Of peace, in a number of ways. It was both the key moment of Stellari's rise and the seed of her eventual fall.

Ten minutes after she spotted the black smoke, Stellari took a deep breath and swept into the Senate, head high, mind already spinning in a hundred directions.

"May the All-Mother be praised!" she called brightly. "A son for our queen. And healthy, yes? How blessed she is. How blessed we are. A miracle."

THE VOTE

Eight years later
The All-Mother's Year 510
Stellari

Stellari's swollen belly preceded every step she took, her sky-blue robe stretched tight across its round, exaggerated curve. Pushing the limits of modesty was, of course, no accident. While the more conservative senators might raise an eyebrow, she'd calculated the impact on each and every member of the senate, and her clinging robe would do more good than harm. On a day this important, every advantage was needed.

She strode as quickly as she dared through the streets, thronged on every side by the busy market day, ale-mongers and cheesemakers calling for attention, shoppers haggling and scoffing to pay as few coppers as they could. She realized she hadn't eaten that morning, but there was no time to rectify it now. If she didn't press forward, she might miss her turn to speak. That would be utter disaster.

All-Mother, but these streets were awful. Crowded and close. Say what one would about the poor reaches of Calladocia, her home district, but at least the dirt and noise and ugliness there had room to breathe. There, in a hurry, one could travel by cart. On streets this narrow, feet were the only reliable transportation, and Stellari's feet were not what they'd once been. Swollen by advanced pregnancy, they constantly ached as if she'd been stung by two dozen blunt-tailed bees. Still, they got her where she needed to go.

Almost there, finally. She lifted the hem of her blue robe to her bare knees and skirted a pile of ox dung as she took the last turn to reach the Senate. She paused a moment to gather herself on the steps, smoothed the shoulder of her robe, and crossed the threshold regally, as if she had all the leisure in the world.

On any given day in the Senate, one or two dozen senators were not present in the room, their usual places left open, like missing teeth in an incomplete smile. But today there were no empty spaces, only the one Stellari stepped into, taking her position just in time for the opening bell to toll.

Still catching her breath, Stellari surveyed the room for Decima. Her gaze glided over the sea of robes in a remarkable variety of tints and shades of blue. Some senators' robes were dyed with woad, others with a heated mixture of copper and sand, still others with a rare clay found only near the border where Paxim gave way to Godsbones. Within the infinite variations, the robes had one thing in common: they'd plainly cost a great deal. And every woman of the Senate wore her dark hair in an intricate crown of braids, the higher and more complex the better, her head held high.

Stellari was ready to play her fellow senators like the strings of a harp. The outcry of the Senate was her favorite music. Without fire and passion, they were just women in expensive blue robes, passing time with no more urgency than a cluster of needle-beaked crakes foraging along the lip of a pond. She would give those crakes something to squawk about.

Ah, there, thought Stellari, finally locating Decima, who wore an elegant pale blue to flatter her deep golden skin. Quickly Stellari noted the mismatch between the consul's robe—impeccable, smooth, lavish—and her comparatively simple plaited crown. Why so few braids? Had Decima's *cosmete* not been available to dress and prepare her that day? Or perhaps Decima had passed the night in a home not her own. The smudges under her keen eyes spoke to a lack of sleep that rivaled Stellari's. Did Decima have some other plan for the day?

"In the name of the All-Mother, the queen, and the peace of Paxim," intoned the caller, "let the senators gather for the commencement of this session."

Stellari took one more look around the room, reading faces, noting looks, and braced herself to begin. Today was the day. Her committee would report its findings; she would recommend a course of action, and they would vote. On the face of it, a simple set of actions, but within that structure, a wild gambit of invention—and, if the pieces lined up correctly, reward.

Decima, in her simple plaits, rose. When the consul put forward the ritual question, "Do we agree to examine the day's business?" only the ritual answer was expected. From their first day, senators learned to open the session by nodding, slapping one's palm against the robe on one's thigh, and declaring, "Yes."

One hundred twenty-four blue-robed senators—including the consul Decima herself—nodded, slapped palm against thigh in unison, and called out, "Yes."

A moment later the one hundred twenty-fifth senator, Stellari, rose to her feet and boomed in her loudest, throatiest voice, "I speak the question all others here are thinking. Where are our girls?"

The instant outcry was gratifying beyond belief.

Stellari managed to keep a smirk from her face, but just barely. Instead she raised her hands for quiet, even though it was not her hands that mattered. What mattered was the gaze she fixed on the consul in that moment—a strong but not challenging gaze, a question and not a command, and to her gratification, the consul responded exactly how she'd wanted.

The consul said, "Magistrate Stellari, this is unusual."

One hand on her belly, Stellari feigned remorse. "We live in unusual times. I apologize. I could not keep my tongue a moment longer."

"Yet you were already first on the docket to speak today."

Stellari offered nothing but silence, and she could practically see the thoughts flitting through Decima's head. *Should I offer some reproof? Punish her? No, that's too much. The harm is already done, anyway.*

Decima said, "Next time, more care?"

"Yes, Consul," Stellari said, dipping her head.

"Then let us proceed. Our first order of business," said Decima, "is to hear our committees report. First, the committee investigating the Drought of Girls. Magistrate Stellari?"

Stellari shifted from foot to foot, her unbalanced weight robbing her of a bit of her usual grace, and addressed the crowd unsmilingly. "Thank you, Consul Decima. Fellow senators, I bring you the benefit of careful study and examination. I regret to report that despite our extensive efforts, we cannot say with certainty who is responsible. Yet we all agree on this point of utmost importance: whoever is responsible must pay."

She'd known the committee was a fool's errand when she'd taken it on; of course there was no way to know what had caused the Drought of Girls. They had explored all scientific or magical causes, with methods open and secret, for months. They'd even held a quiet, confidential discussion with a committee of Bastionite scholars who'd been charged with the same task and come up equally empty-handed. Nothing else the committee heard rattled Stellari but this. If the Bastion did not know a thing, it could not be known.

"But Magistrate Stellari," said Decima, her patience now obviously thinning, "surely you understand that sounds, well, like nonsense."

"Perhaps," said Stellari, maintaining her imperious air, though she felt a squeeze in her lower abdomen that weakened her knees. "Perhaps only the sagest minds among you can understand the paradox."

Outrage subsided into hubbub, hubbub into chatter, chatter into whispers, whispers into silence.

Stellari said, "Eight years now. Eight long years. Years we have spent in hope—yes, hope—that the swell in any given sister's belly might yield a new daughter of Paxim. Yet each time our hopes are dashed. Possibility dies on the vine. A boy, a boy, a boy, a boy."

She spread her hands wide, her tone generous, warm. "And we welcome those boys into our world with open arms. They suckle at our breasts and play at our feet. They will become the husbands of this generation, siring the next. They are needed. They are loved."

Careful now, she told herself. The next bit was the trickiest.

"But they are not girls," she said to the assembled, hushed crowd of senators. "And without girls, we will not grow. We will not succeed. My friends and fellow senators: without girls, we will not survive."

Whispers, too soft to tell whether they boded agreement.

Stellari forged ahead. "We are lucky in Paxim. We are ruled by a gracious, generous, intelligent queen, wise senators, a capable Assembly. The gods smile on us. All five queendoms enjoy a peace forged and preserved by the women of Paxim, by our hard work, our unflagging attention to our responsibilities."

She let her brow crease and lower. "But if the worst happens—a generation without girls—the nation of Paxim is doomed. And if Paxim falls, the queendoms tumble into chaos."

Whispers into muttering, muttering into shouts.

Stellari raised her voice higher, louder, stronger, as strong as it had to be to keep command. She could not fail now. Now was her moment.

"So perhaps the question is not, Where are our girls? Perhaps the question is, Who took them from us? Who stands to gain by stealing our future?"

Shouts grew louder, fists rose in the air.

A single voice rose up too loud to ignore. "But all five queendoms suffer! It is not just our girls that are gone!"

Stellari nodded, giving the other woman's statement just enough time to sink in. And then she spoke: fierce, direct. "So we have been told. But does anyone *know*?"

She waited for the ripple of excited little exclamations to make its circuit of the Senate and subside.

Something swarmed in her head, a feeling she didn't recognize and couldn't quite identify. Pain or power. Perhaps there was no difference between the two.

"All we know," Stellari went on, "is that Paxim has no girls, and we know only one nation could be responsible. Not the warriors of Scorpica, no scholar of the Bastion, no priest of Sestia. Only one nation wields the power to wreak this kind of havoc. Surely we suffer at the hands of the magicians of Arca."

Thunder. Anger. Shock.

Shouting to be heard, Aureli grumbled, "We know nothing," and Stellari turned without rushing to acknowledge her. Aureli was a notorious naysayer, but also one of the most senior members of the Senate. She had to be treated with respect.

"The esteemed Senator Aureli is right!" Stellari began.

Aureli made a loud, skeptical huff, but said nothing, opening the way.

"We know nothing. That is the truth," intoned Stellari, looking out over the worried faces of her fellow senators. "Yet this is even more true: we must be ready for anything."

"Be plain, would you?" challenged the senior senator, her arms folded under her dark blue robe, eyes bright with skepticism.

But Stellari had one more thing to say, one more brick to move into position. "I pray that this child in my belly is a girl," she began, curling an arm protectively around the swell of her belly, supporting it from underneath. If anyone had mistaken the message of her clinging robes, they could no longer deny it.

"A daughter is what I've always wanted most in the world. Every day I pray, and every day I hope," Stellari went on. "We have feared and worried these eight long years. We have also hoped. We can't live without hope. But hope is not a plan."

Now, at last, it was time to make her point. A military had to be established, even if it would be years before the senators were ready to go to war. One did not plant an apple seed and expect to eat the fruit that very season. Stellari shrugged off another pain—a sharp yet somehow lingering squeeze—when she was interrupted.

The outer doors swung open, admitting the last woman Stellari expected to see that day on the floor of the senate: Queen Heliane herself.

The queen moved into the chamber smoothly, almost as if floating, a purple island in a blue sea. The crown on her head was not only braids. Atop her ink-black hair sat a thick gold circlet, a single ruby gleaming in its center like an all-seeing eye.

"Queen Heliane!" Decima stepped forward, eyes bright, first to greet the queen. "This is an unexpected honor."

But Stellari wasn't fooled. She'd read the look on the consul's face when that door swung open. This visit was no surprise, not to Decima.

The queen inclined her head, gave the consul a measured smile. "Thank you so much for your welcome, Consul Decima. You know I would not have interrupted your business if it weren't of the utmost importance."

"But I—but we—" Stellari began, quickly pivoting to address Decima instead of the queen. Only the consul had the right to speak directly to the queen in the Senate chamber. Stellari forced herself to calm down, at least outwardly. She felt another twinge deep within, ignored it. "We have not yet completed the business underway."

"The queen has requested that we shelve that business temporarily. It can wait a few minutes." Without pausing to look at Stellari's face or anyone else's, Decima said, "Queen Heliane, the Senate is yours."

There was a movement at the back of the Senate, and Stellari focused on it. A woman whose robe was a pale, undyed yellowish-white, not blue. Stellari knew her, of course, as she knew all politicians. Juni, head of the Assembly. Not the same head that Stellari had come up with—that one had retired—but a younger woman, elevated to preside over the Assembly not half a year before. Stellari's surprise at seeing her in such a powerful position hadn't yet worn off.

Juni had been a green girl from nowhere, much like Stellari. Juni's large eyes and small mouth made her look innocent, credulous. She'd been both those things and more. Always a little awkward, too direct, never taking time for pleasantries. She had the best memory Stellari had ever heard of outside the scribes, never forgetting a fact or a face, but her endless awkwardness seemed to doom her ascent. When they'd both been new Assemblywomen Stellari hadn't befriended the girl, assuming she had no future in politics. How wrong she'd been.

If the head of the Assembly was here, that meant the queen's announcement must be related to the Assembly. Stellari realized immediately what the announcement must be. The very thought gave her a pain in her belly. But she would not let it show, in case anyone was watching her as closely as she was watching them.

At the front of the room now, her face solemn, the queen faced her senators. She didn't even raise her hands for the Senate's attention. She had it.

"We are all aware we live in trying times," the queen began. Her voice wasn't particularly loud, Stellari noticed, but in the respectful hush, she could still be clearly heard. "Unprecedented times. And as queen of this proud nation, I have felt the heavy weight on my shoulders of bearing us forward into the future."

Her voice rising now, soaring over the crowd with firm resolve, the queen said, "Even as much as things have changed, some must remain the same. The balance between old and new is absolutely vital to our future as a country. Our stability will stabilize the world, whatever may come. The wise minds in this room will continue to provide essential guidance within Paxim and beyond. The Senate remains constant."

Stellari joined in the applause, though it was mostly for form. No one could be genuinely moved by this obvious pandering. But senators were happy to applaud themselves, given any provocation or none.

"And so it is to our Assembly we look, to the representatives of the people, and we choose to open their doors wider. Again, much will remain the same. Candidates for office must be of age, and they can have committed no crime. Thus it has always been, since our first mothers gathered around the cook fires and made sure all were supported by the community, receiving gifts equal to their contributions."

Impatient, Stellari watched the faces of those gathered. The senators seemed untroubled, their faces turned up like sunflowers, genuinely curious and eager. It made Stellari want to scream. Why scrape and bow to a woman like this, whose only qualification was the family she was born into? Stellari herself had needed to be intelligent, savvy, and strong—some would say relentless—to rise to power. Her burning need to prove her worth gave shape to her life. All the queen had done was drop into the world from between the right set of royal thighs. It was appalling if you gave it any amount of thought.

"This is a proud day for our nation," said the queen. "The sign of a healthy government is to grow and change with its circumstances. With its people. And so it is with pride that I make this announcement: men of Paxim will be allowed to stand for Assembly offices. If elected, they will serve alongside the women of the Assembly as provisional members."

The queen looked out over them all, sweeping the crowd with her gaze, and gathered her breath for one more declaration. "We believe that this change to our Assembly will nurture our growing republic. We honor our citizens and trust them to choose wisely, determining the direction of our nation's future."

I'll tell you its future, Stellari wanted to scream. *Paxim will burn. Open the door just a crack to men, and we will all burn.*

Whatever the words out of the queen's mouth, whatever she claimed to do here today, Stellari saw right through this farce. Assembly offices were not the point, not at all. Two-fold citizens, those who were both male and female in one body, had already been eligible to serve for years. This wasn't an indication of greater tolerance, greater inclusion. Heliane was laying the groundwork for a *king*. A king who ruled Paxim. This woman would not be happy until her son sat on the Paximite throne after her. This was just the first course of an entirely poisonous meal.

But no one else seemed to see it. They swallowed Queen Heliane's words as if she meant them. The senators clapped politely, their faces masks of pleasant approval. The consul smiled. The head of the Assembly smiled. Stellari was not a violent woman, but she wanted to crunch her fist against their gleaming, bared teeth.

Instead she smoothed her robe over her belly, sipped at the air through her own thin smile, and readied herself to make a dazzling, eloquent objection. She braced her feet and parted her lips to speak.

But suddenly a sharp pain bent her double, stealing her breath. How odd she felt. She put one hand on her belly and one on her back to force herself upright, but she could not, another cramp bending her forward sharply. Then she felt a peculiar sensation, one she'd never yet felt. The child inside her moved, but not to kick or turn or settle. Inside her belly it felt like the child's heavy skull was shifting—pressing—downward.

No, she thought. *No*. The child couldn't be coming, not now. It must be Stellari's fury at being thwarted that made her heart race and her guts twist. Or perhaps it was because she hadn't eaten; she'd feel steady again after a midday meal. She snapped the world back into focus. The queen's business was almost concluded. After that, Stellari could force the Senate's attention back to the Drought. Then she'd call the vote on the military question. Then, victorious, she'd go home.

"Magistrate Stellari?" called Decima, though Stellari was sure she'd said nothing aloud. "Are you quite all right?"

Stellari wanted to say, *Yes, it's nothing*, raised her hand to wave nonchalantly, but her breath was even harder to catch now. She needed another moment to steady herself before speaking.

"Is her time near?" the queen asked Decima, her voice low, concerned.

"I think so," someone said, but Stellari could not tell who. The faces around her blurred. And she needed to know her allies. If she did not know where everyone stood, she couldn't be sure she had the support she needed. Everything would fly apart like a glass jar flung to the tiles.

She opened her mouth to brush off the queen's concern and the pain came upon her so sharp it drove her to her knees.

No, thought Stellari again, *no.* But for once, there was nothing she could do. She wasn't in control. All the same, she didn't have to go down without a fight.

"Magistrate Stellari!" said Decima. "Your time is obviously upon you. We will escort you from the chamber."

Stellari's hand flew to her belly, unbidden, but her voice was iron. "No. No. I call the vote."

"No vote matters as much as your child's health," came the queen's voice, loud but unsteady, a broken note underneath. "You will go."

Voices pattered in and out as Stellari tried to grip the rail in front of her, but it slipped out of her grasp. Like a bad dream, she thought. Everything she needed, wanted, taken from her. A few more minutes, that was all she needed. Just a few. She knew she had the votes, but only if she herself voted.

"No, take mine. Bearers! Now!" called the queen. "Bear the magistrate home. Hurry!"

Stellari realized there must be blood. She wouldn't look down to confirm it, but she felt wetness on her hands and the air had begun to smell a little less of myrrh and more, much more, of copper. Then another pain was on her, driving her back down as surely as if a woman twice her size were pushing down on her shoulders, holding her to the floor.

"Here," came the queen's voice, closer now, firm and strong again. Stellari felt hands, real hands now, lifting her. In that moment she had no strength to fight them. She'd thought there was nothing she couldn't fight, but cold fear flooded through her, and she went still. What if she didn't survive the birth? Was this how her story, her magnificent rise from nothing, ended? The child had made it clear that what Stellari would not give, the child would take.

As they bore her away, she twisted on the litter so forcefully and suddenly she almost fell off. She would have plunged to the ground if a quick-thinking, quick-moving bearer hadn't shifted and used his own body to block her fall.

"Don't let them hold the vote," she moaned, but it was too late. Her words, barely a whisper, couldn't reach the right ears. For the first time in her life, she couldn't think quickly enough to accomplish what she wanted. Her body had been hijacked, exactly like a wagon stolen by bandits; she'd been shoved off the driver's seat.

Hours later, as soon as Stellari emerged from an insensible haze, once her body was no longer overtaken by the animal business of expelling a child, she sent a messenger to the Senate. She was exhausted, torn, and desperate, but she absolutely needed to know what had happened after she'd been borne away.

It was exactly as she'd feared. They'd voted without her. The motion to begin the establishment of a Paxim military was deferred for later discussion, until the head of the committee returned; that was all right. She could shape that vote again. The matter of allowing men to stand for election in the Assembly, however, passed by the thinnest of margins, with sixty-seven senators for and the same number against, the consul Decima breaking the tie.

Holding her squalling infant in her arms, Stellari burned with fury. She looked down at the child and looked away again, the resentment too powerful to focus.

It wasn't really the child's fault. Even in the worst moments of her rage, Stellari knew it wasn't. It was only that, from this vantage, she saw no one else to blame.

✦ 3 ✦

CHAOS

Six years later
The All-Mother's Year 516, after the Sun Rites
Leaving Sestia for Daybreak Palace
Eminel

Eminel would never quite remember how she'd gotten from the maelstrom of the amphitheater to the silence of the Arcan queen's luxurious carriage, leaving the capital of Sestia—and the dead, broken body of the sorcerer Sessadon—behind.

The moment of Sessadon's death during the Sun Rites was clear in Eminel's mind, a perfect, painful recollection. Of what followed, though, her memory provided only flashes. She remembered the moment the blue snake necklace touched her skin, how cool it was in the heat of the chaotic crowd, but she did not remember it curling in on itself, locking into place. Something in her thought she remembered a tiny blue glass tongue flicking out to taste the air, but of course that was impossible. Ridiculous. Other images were clearer, more certain: the faces of the remaining Arcans turning toward her, their expressions full of shock and wonder. She even remembered some advancing in her direction. But had they spoken to her, put hands on her? Carried or dragged or gently encouraged her? She couldn't be sure. She'd swayed weakly on her feet, chaos crashing like waves around her, and there the memory ended.

She awoke in the gently rocking wagon, leaning against a heap of pillows in the corner, dizzied and exhausted. It might have been minutes or hours or days. She wasn't familiar enough with the geography of Sestia to know where she was or how long it had taken to get there. She only knew they'd left the city behind. Through a narrow gap in the curtains she saw a latticework of green rolling hills dotted with rams and sheep. Daylight—late afternoon?—brightened their creamy wool, painted the rams' horns golden. The sight would have been beautiful if she could focus long enough to enjoy it.

She lifted a weak hand to draw the curtain closed, then leaned back against the plush cushions. She felt like a shell, not a living young woman. But the blue snake necklace lay so heavy on her neck and chest she could not forget she was—suddenly—also a queen.

She forced herself to examine the interior of the lush carriage more closely, to see the smallest details. She turned her gaze upward to the clear quartz globes strung near the carriage's ceiling, each no bigger than the first joint of her thumb, glowing with a gentle, steady light. Like everything else in the carriage, the lights spoke of careless luxury. They matched the unspoken message of the plush cushions, the swaying curtains, the saffron-colored carpet under her feet. It took serious magic to cast a lasting enchantment on an object. Sessadon had taught her that.

Sessadon had taught her nearly everything she knew about magic, thought Eminel. Sessadon had also murdered Eminel's mother, along with countless others, and lied to Eminel from the moment they met. But before Sessadon's lies came to light, she'd been Eminel's constant companion and mentor. Some part of Eminel felt the sorcerer's absence and regretted it, even though she'd been the one to kill Sessadon. That death was the one thing Eminel did not regret.

Eminel remembered the power that had welled within her, that energy with the feel of polished wood, helping her distract Sessadon while simultaneously pushing the queen of Scorpica to break the sorcerer's neck. The moment Sessadon died, that power ebbed out of Eminel like a wave. That must be why she felt weak, she decided, like she'd been emptied out. Emptied of magic, but not just that; emptied of optimism and joy, of love and faith, of everything she'd once thought she knew.

She would rest. She needed rest. She let herself sink into the yielding pillows, let the gently swaying wagon rock her back to sleep.

And she dreamed.

The woman is as blue as a sapphire all over, from the crown of her head to the tips of her outstretched fingers. There is even something blue about her voice, its chill, the lack of warmth in her repetition of the single word she speaks. *Chaos. Chaos. Chaos.*

Eminel, in the dream, feels no surprise. *Chaos* is the thing this figure says because chaos is what she wants. Eminel doesn't seek chaos, but neither does she fear it. Eminel watches a crackling energy grow between the outstretched palms of the blue woman, and she can't help but reach out with her own fingers. Her own body is not blue, but there is a blue cast to her hands. Because of the nearness of the glowing light. The blue woman has begun to glow.

Eminel's hands touch those of the blue woman. Like lightning, the power sears its way through her, yet she feels no heat. Is she freezing? Burning? Impossible to tell, and besides, is there a difference? Temperature is pain the same as power is pain and fear is pain, and she quashes the pain inside her because she has enough power now that she can force herself not to feel anything she doesn't want to feel.

She lets the power swim through her veins, lick the underside of her skin. She soaks up the power. It radiates through her bones, her blood. Power inhabits her.

Then, in the dream, Eminel lets the power fly, cracking in the air like a whip, and she sees things fall: branches, birds, stones. She lets the power fly again, and this time the sky sings with a low, warm music, a sweet tune on the wind circling and echoing until it fades away.

Little spheres of light swirl through the air and then sink toward her, gather themselves to cluster around her ankles, her waist, her wrists, her throat. She laughs at their cool, playful touch. Thoughts flow into her head—from the blue woman?—and she strokes the motes of light on one wrist, tapping and teasing them until they dance into a new pattern and fuse together, and she wears cool, blazing blue light on her wrist like jewelry. She moves to touch the lights around her neck, but they only dance along the length of what is already there, the snake necklace that marks her as queen. A surge of satisfaction runs through her. Yes, she is a queen. The girl who hid in the back of a bandits' wagon, crouching, skulking, no longer has to hide from anyone or anything. She is wreathed in light, in power. She looks up to see what her dream-spirit thinks of her.

The blue woman neither smiles nor laughs, but the blue cast of her glow shifts and changes and Eminel knows, somehow, that she approves. This woman wants her to succeed. This woman wants her to have everything.

Eminel herself is drawing her hands away from each other, watching the power crackle in the spaces between her fingertips like dew-strung spiderwebs between tree branches, when cold air rushes down her throat and she breathes and then she is awake.

Eminel opened her eyes to the barest hint of thin sunlight peeking around the edges of the carriage's curtains. At first she felt a pleasant haze, the aftereffects of a half-remembered dream, but when the reality of cold air reached her, the soft feeling slipped away. Struggling to orient

23

herself, she shifted against the pillows, but both her arms prickled and tingled as she attempted to move. She must have been asleep, she reasoned, though she didn't feel rested in the least.

When she came fully to herself, Eminel realized she lay belly-down on the padded bench, one arm pinned under her body, the fingertips of the other dangling down to brush the carpeted floor. She must have slept the night away, now waking in the cool of early dawn. She shivered in the chill and reached for the dream. Hadn't it been a pleasant one? It felt like something she should remember. Instead the image of Heliane falling from the sky flashed in front of her, vivid and sharp, and suddenly her heart was galloping.

Visions, dreams, images in her mind. None could be trusted.

That vision of Heliane, it reminded her of something, and the next shiver that ran through her body had nothing to do with the temperature in the carriage. She'd had a vision just as vivid after her mother's death, one that had sent her scurrying in fear from the Rovers. That vision, she'd learned far too late, had been placed in her mind by magic. By Sessadon.

No. No. Sessadon was dead. Eminel was queen of Arca now, she reminded herself, chosen for the honor by a holy, magical item that never erred. She had more important matters to deal with than fleeting dreams and memories.

She was still alone, but that wouldn't last. That carriage door would open, and when it did, she couldn't be lying here like a snail without its shell. She needed to be ready.

She'd start with food. Ah, there it was. On a small round table, an elegant little thing with a double circle of wire lining its edge to protect its contents from rolling off when the carriage was in motion, she saw fruit piled high in a bowl. Apricots and figs, small oranges and large cherries. All she needed to do was stand up, take two steps to the bowl, and pluck fruit from it with her fingers. It was a relief to have a task so simple, so clear.

Her empty body didn't want to move, but she brushed that away. She didn't need to touch something to move it, after all, not when all-magic bubbled and burned inside her.

Two fingers on her right hand she raised, then crossed and uncrossed, and beckoned an apricot through the air in the hopes that it would land either in her hand or within her reach on the soft, plumped cushions.

Only it didn't move, not a bit.

She focused and frowned. She pushed her left elbow underneath her and was pleased she could raise herself on it, pressing her palm against the cushion under the pillows for better balance. She reached out again for the fruit with her mind, thinking deliberately about which of the six types of magic to call on, choosing earth. Fruit was a plant, once growing. The apricot should heed her call.

It didn't.

The sun was fully up now, daylight setting the luxurious curtains aglow. Eminel levered herself up higher on her elbow and stretched one more time, pointing two fingers as if she could spear the fruit on them, calling each fruit to her in turn. Peach. Fig. Orange. Last, a bright red cherry. *Come. Fly to me.* Such a small object, yet it didn't even quiver.

What if she'd lost her all-magic entirely? She wouldn't stay in charge of a nation of magicians long without it, that was for certain. She'd told herself, back in the Holy City, that she was willing to die in order to erase Sessadon from the world. Was Velja—a god she'd never prayed to, not until that moment during the rites—forcing her to make good on the promise?

Half-afraid, half-angry, she shifted her back against the padded seat and beckoned once more at the nearest cherry, one of Fasiq's favorite curses springing from a long-neglected corner of her mind. *Fly, you cock-for-brains.*

The cherry whistled toward her at frightening speed.

25

Eminel's eyes flew shut instinctively. The speeding cherry struck the carriage wall next to her ear with a loud, startling *thwack*.

After a long, silent moment, Eminel opened her eyes. But the silence was fleeting; she both heard and felt the shudder of the carriage as it slowed, bumped, and listed dangerously to one side. Terrified, she wrenched herself upright and clutched the padded cushions around her.

The carriage righted itself, rolling again on all four wheels. She heard a shout from outside, then another shout, answering. Both sounded more annoyed than panicked, at least through the thick swaddling of the padded carriage walls. She kept her arms braced tight just in case, but blessedly, the carriage slowed further, with no more fuss than a few creaks. Moments later she felt its wheels grinding to a halt.

Eminel shifted to inspect the wall behind her head and was stunned to see a hole the exact size of a cherry pit, ringed in a smear of red. Less than a handspan from her ear, the hole was too small to look through, but large enough to let in a stream of golden daylight, even brighter than what the curtains let through.

Eminel was still struggling to figure out what this meant about her power when she heard a hand turning the ornate handle of the carriage door.

Quickly she turned in the direction of the door and pulled herself as upright as she could, hoping her stern expression cloaked her fear.

The figure rising up into the carriage looked familiar: a young woman no more than a few years older than Eminel herself, her long dark hair marked with an unusual white streak. Eminel had seen her in this very carriage before, but somewhere else, too. The memory hit Eminel vividly: that white streak splattered with red, back in the amphitheater. The woman looked calmer now, ready for anything. She was also dressed less formally, in a simple tunic and leggings, though the quality of the fabric gave her away as no mere farmer. One of her arms was marked with a wicked scar that looked for all the world like claw marks, deep and old.

"Queen Eminel?" asked the new arrival, bowing, her voice deferential. "I'm sorry to disturb you, but we all thought it was important to let you know . . ."

When the woman lifted her head and her gaze settled on Eminel, her voice trailed off. She gave a little gasp of surprise.

What was it she was reacting to? Eminel didn't trust herself to speak yet. After a childhood spent hiding from sight as the Rovers crossed Paxim on the hunt, her natural inclination was to watch and wait. She did so now.

"I'm sorry," the woman said, mumbling downward. "Queen, I—I'm here to tell you the reason the caravan stopped. One of the oxen dropped in its traces. We'll be on our way shortly. I hope—I promise it won't take too long to fix."

Eminel kept her face impassive. She couldn't give away that her power was uncertain, her body weak. She knew almost nothing about the Arcan royal court, but she knew better than to trust any of them.

"I'm sorry," the woman with the streak in her hair said again. "I didn't introduce myself. My name is Archis. My matriclan is Jale. I was—am—part of the queen's entourage, both during the rites and back home."

When she did find the strength to speak, Eminel's voice rasped. "Are you all-magic?"

The woman's demeanor changed immediately: the shift was slight, but clear. Distrust slid into her gaze, where before there had been only deference. Archis attempted to cover it with a forced giggle. "Velja has blessed us both! I should have known you could tell. Yes, besides the previous queen, there were only two of us at court with all-magic. Now there's just me."

"And what do you . . . do?"

"Anything I want," the woman said, her pride evident. She flexed her fingers, wiggled them, smiled. "Would you like to see?"

"I meant," said Eminel, trying to sound royal, "what did you do for the previous queen? Your role?"

"Whatever she needed. We don't carve our court up in little boxes, not like those pompous braid-crowns in Paxim with their ministers and magistrates and advisers to the royal cloak-weaver." The derisive note in Archis's voice was impossible to miss. "The queen tells us what she wants done and we do it. If you have an assignment for me, I stand ready to serve."

As she listened, Eminel tried again to stir her magic. If she could listen in on the woman's thoughts, she would know right away whether what she said was true. But no thoughts came to mind, Archis's or her own. Either Eminel's magic was still not working or the woman could block her powers. No way to tell which.

Eminel decided the most direct route was best, at least for now. "Were you hoping to become queen?"

Archis tilted her head, spoke lightly. "Such decisions are out of my hands. If Velja willed it, I'd be wearing that necklace. She clearly favors you." Her fingertips rose to brush her own neck, possibly unconsciously, and suspicion crept back into her voice. "Yet before yesterday, no one had ever heard of you. Or if they had, we weren't told. All-magic girls always report to Daybreak Palace. Always."

Eminel ignored the implied question and asked what she wanted to know. "Is that who decides succession? Velja?"

"It happens as it happens. There's only been one succession in my lifetime. Mirriam was slain and her daughter Mirrida woke up wearing the necklace, and we recognized her as queen."

Interesting. Either Archis was not saying or did not know that Mirriam's spirit had inhabited her daughter's body; there had never really been a Queen Mirrida, only Mirriam in a different form, up until the moment Sessadon crushed the soul out of that form, leaving an animated husk. It was moot now, Eminel realized with a pang, each death only a link in a chain that seemed never-ending.

Archis said, "Thank you for your patience, Queen Eminel. As I said, the loss of the ox was quite sudden, but the interruption should be brief. We will be back in motion shortly."

"Thank you," said Eminel stiffly, then added, "You may go."

Archis stepped down to descend from the carriage, but she paused on the bottom step, looking back toward Eminel, clearly considering whether to say something.

"What is it," Eminel said, more command than question.

Archis's eyes were hooded. "There are those—well, it was your choice, I'm sure you have your reasons—there are those who will not be pleased to see you wearing a Talish cuff. I myself respect whatever decisions you make. I'll ensure no one disturbs you until we reach Daybreak Palace. Good day, Queen Eminel."

The moment the carriage door closed behind Archis, Eminel slumped back against the cushions again. Was there any connection between the fallen ox and her use of magic? Certainly a single cherry pit could not have brought such an animal down, but the coincidence seemed so unlikely. She'd never had so much to think about at once, and her brain had never felt softer, less capable.

And then, what was it Archis had said about a cuff? That was ridiculous. She'd already found herself chosen by a piece of jewelry, the snake necklace; she could hardly have acquired a cuff without knowing it. She looked down at her hands, the right and then the left, as if to reassure herself that there was no cuff on her wrist.

Only there was.

The discovery was so shocking that Eminel let out a small yelp of surprise, shaking her left hand as if she could shake the cuff right off, but it remained. She glared at the wrist suspiciously. The substance was the same temperature as her skin, and it wasn't particularly heavy, but she still should have noticed it before now. She took stock of the cuff, less than a handspan wide, examining it in detail without putting her face too close to it, just in case. The smooth cuff looked exactly like pure, flawless white quartz.

She looked up automatically at the globes of quartz that lit the interior of the carriage—only she could see now that many of them were missing. But the quartz cuff on her wrist was as smooth as glass, with no visible seam, let alone the curve of a former sphere. How could this be? If the interior of the carriage had been invaded by a magical intruder, why hadn't she been hurt, even killed, while she lay sleeping?

Perhaps she'd defended herself through magic, but when she couldn't use her magic reliably, that didn't seem possible. She peered out at the world through the cherry-pit hole in the carriage wall. No, her magic was not gone. But neither was it *right*. Her power was not hers, not if she couldn't control it.

If she trusted her magic even a little, thought Eminel, she'd cast a spell to make herself forget. That would be a fitting end for her. Her mother had chosen to spend years fleeing from the truth, hiding her daughter's gift from everyone, including Eminel herself. Maybe Jehenit had been right all along. Eminel's all-magic was not a gift, but a curse.

Outside, now, there was movement. She closed her eyes and listened intently, as still as a nervous hare. The whispers around the closed door of the wagon were hurried, harried. Then there was a long silence.

Then, at last, the caravan slowly rumbled into motion. The journey to Daybreak Palace resumed. The luxurious carriage of the queen of Arca—Eminel's carriage, now—on its delicate wheels, rolled on.

♦ 4 ♦

FACE-TO-FACE

The All-Mother's Year 516
Northeast Paxim
Ama, Paulus

When the sharp impact of Grenthus's skull split the skin of Ama's cheekbone wide open, her first thought was confusion. *How?* She checked her own position, but she'd rolled on her mark; he was a full second too fast on the rise. A sloppy mistake.

Paxim's fledgling defense force had its flaws, but through relentless repetition, their own unit had nearly perfected their drills. Their commander Floriana, Paxim-born but as relentless and precise as any Scorpican, had often kept them on the training field past sundown, honing their dives and rolls, leaps and thrusts. Only now Ama's dive had clashed with Grenthus's leap, and her cheek was split open and pouring blood, and it shocked her how much it hurt. In her year with the force she'd been struck, slapped, cut, bruised, and knocked every which way, but she didn't remember any other pain that sent her reeling quite like this.

"Cock for brains," she muttered aloud, shaking her head to clear it.

Then she noticed that Grenthus was grabbing her shoulder and pulling her toward him, not pushing away. Even though he was in the wrong, even though he'd hurt her with his carelessness. *Wait.* What if it wasn't carelessness at all? If it were a mistake, he'd be stepping away, apologizing. No. The wound he'd inflicted on her was no accident.

Grenthus shouted, "Get off! What are you doing? Help!"

They scrapped on the ground while she puzzled it out. He was pulling on the straps of her chest buckler, shouting, "What? No! Help!" again, making it seem that she was the one attacking him. Every hair on her arms stood on end, every inch of her skin sounding the alarm. *Attack. Attack.*

Other shouts, nearing where they fought. Shadows cast by bodies moving. More hands on her, around her. Then the sun glinted off a dagger slashing in her direction and Ama clutched at Grenthus, moving his body to the left at the last minute to intercept the dagger's flash. The hilt of the dagger landed with a dull thump on Grenthus's shoulder. The person wielding it didn't want to hurt him, and that spoke volumes.

Why was Grenthus against her? They'd sparred the day before, and she'd bested him, but that shouldn't have been enough for him to betray a comrade in arms. His beetle-browed face loomed close to hers, snarling, red with fury. He was exactly the kind of man who had been hoping all his life to be welcomed into a fighting force for all the wrong reasons. He knew nothing of bravery, camaraderie, the true warrior's heart. He thought it was a lark. Ama burned to show him just how little like a lark true combat would be.

"Go on. Do your worst," he hissed, his voice this time too soft for show.

Well, she'd take that invitation. Ama spat in Grenthus's eye to disorient him, then rolled on top so her knees pinned him into the dirt at his shoulders. Her full weight on his chest held him down while she took the measure of the scene. Most of the rest of their unit was still executing the drill, diving and swooping as graceful as birds, and

Floriana had not yet noticed the few who were out of true. Four of them were off rhythm: Ama now atop Grenthus on the ground, Merika lifting her dagger for another slash at Ama, and Jorik shifting himself out of Merika's path to clear the way.

Members of her own company. People she'd thought were her swordmates. They were not fellow warriors, she realized now. They were enemies. They would damage her or she would damage them or both, and things would never be the same.

Ama rolled herself under Grenthus for protection again, narrowly dodging the unusual curved blade hanging unsheathed at his belt, and planned her next move.

Could she fight them all off? Her chances were, frankly, excellent. Even pretending not to be as good as she actually was, Ama was a swan among ducks in this motley group. Her response times were faster, her slashes cleaner, her defenses harder to penetrate. But she slowed those instincts to better match with her comrades in arms. She had her reasons. When the day came that she needed her true abilities, she'd call on them then and only then.

Today was not that day. She might have grown up in the Bastion, but she collected bits of Scorpican wisdom like a magpie. One of her favorite maxims: *The wise warrior knows that force is not the only way to fight.*

So she eyed Merika and Jorik over Grenthus's straining shoulder, and when both of them closed in, she spat in his other eye and heaved his body toward their knees, tangling all three into a heap and leaving her own body free to move.

"Cease!" came Floriana's familiar bark, sharp and clear.

Their commander neared, sword in hand but pointed down, its tip swinging in rhythm with her unhurried steps. Floriana had a round, unassuming face and an awkward, bent-kneed resting stance that somehow transformed, when needed, into a lightning-quick strike too fast to follow. She was a cow at rest and a snake in battle, but this was the first time Ama had seen her move quite this way. Deliberate, but without patience. Today she was no animal, but human, bristling with authority.

As Floriana approached, Ama watched the other three untangle themselves from their untidy pile. Their eyes were still wary, tension still obvious in their limbs. She realized it wasn't a given that they'd obey the command; this was not a real military and they did not seem to understand the importance of following orders. Jorik seemed to waver. Merika looked as fierce as ever. Grenthus stood with one hand in a ready fist, the other hand reaching for the wickedly curved blade at his waist. They might still try anything.

Ama knew, then, just how deeply these people hated her. With a single, long-ago exception, she couldn't recall caring enough about anything to hate so deeply. It was, however awful, a sort of wonder.

Curved blade in his hand now, Grenthus said over his shoulder to Floriana, "Now, see here, there's no reason for you to interfere."

The flat of Floriana's sword took him across the side of the head, smacking him off his feet, before he could even turn to counter her attack.

"I'm sure you were all just sparring," she said. "Trying a new exercise. Am I right?"

"It's not what you think! We were rushing to his aid," said Merika, the dagger in her hand still waving dangerously. "This one attacked Grenthus out of nowhere! Went wild. Can't be trusted."

"Ama?" asked Floriana, her tone quiet but sharp.

"Commander," responded Ama, planting her feet evenly on the ground. She unbuckled the sheath at her waist so the sword and belt fell, leaving her unarmed. She lifted her palms and showed them to her commander. Her message was clear: she was not fighting.

"Weapons down," Floriana said, and Merika's dagger fell next, then Jorik's. Finally, with obvious reluctance, Grenthus dropped his curved blade to the dirt. It was an odd thing, a long curve of metal in a half circle bolted to a wooden grip that arced in the same half circle, a little like a scythe in shape. It landed with a clang.

Ama turned her cheek toward her commander to display her fresh wound, not just bleeding but already bruising as well. The cut pulsed and ached with surprising persistence. Part of Ama still reeled from the sudden, inexplicable attack; a separate part mused upon the nature of the wound like a scholar, wondering if perhaps the skin there was particularly thin, or why else a wound on the face would hurt more than one on a leg or arm. Not for the first time she wondered if this doubleness, this feeling of being in the moment and out of it at the same time, came from growing up where she didn't belong. Was this how everyone raised by the precise, deliberate scholars of the Bastion turned out? Or could other people figure out how to quiet their thoughts even when their bodies were on fire?

Floriana's eyes went to Ama's cheek, then Jorik's evasive gaze, then Merika's twitching fingertips, and finally landed on Grenthus's narrowed eyes, which he seemed unable to tear away from his fallen blade.

Making a decision, the commander turned to Grenthus and said, "No."

The soldier lifted his gaze, finally seeming to surrender whatever hope he'd had of finishing what he'd started.

"Yes, Commander," he said.

Addressing the group, Floriana snapped, "We're done here."

"Yes, Commander," their voices chorused, but no one moved.

Her voice sharper now, Floriana said, "Leave your weapons. They're forfeit. And anyone who's not bunked by the time my sword's back in her sheath can have half rations the rest of the week. Maybe hunger will bring down those high spirits."

The threat did its work, and the other three retreated. Ama felt their hot glares on the side of her face, but she would not give any of them the satisfaction. She looked straight ahead into the middle distance, keeping her body rigid, her breath shallow, as a chastised warrior should.

Out of the corner of her eye she saw Floriana beginning to sheathe her sword, and Ama started toward her bunk, not eager to go but equally reluctant to bear the punishment. Half rations would hit her hard. She was hungry most of the time as it was.

"Not you," said Commander Floriana, her voice low and clear.

Ama stopped instantly, on guard, waiting.

The sword snicked into its sheath. The commander folded her arms, eyeing the young woman grimly. "We need to talk."

Under her breath, Ama protested, "I didn't—they came at me— I have every right to defend myself, Commander."

"You do," said Floriana. "This is a separate matter."

"Oh." Ama wished she hadn't dropped the sword, though it was not a particularly good sword, just one she'd been issued. She always felt better with a weapon in her hand. Iron felt so reliable, steadfast, even when everything else came apart.

The commander said, "You're going to help me solve a problem."

"Of course, Commander." She didn't know what problem Floriana meant; she was not even all that curious. If it was an order, Ama would carry it out. What it was, or why, mattered little.

"It's your lucky day, Ama," Floriana said. "You're moving out."

Because she felt like she should, Ama asked, "To where?"

"Out of here," said Floriana, her eyes flicking where the other three had gone, three people who were supposed to be Ama's swordmates but were clearly, now, her enemies. "Isn't that the important thing?"

"When?"

"Now."

"Will I need a weapon?" Ama asked.

Floriana eyed her, and there was a sparkle in her gaze that Ama hadn't seen before, a kind of recognition. The round-faced woman said, her voice full of warm urgency, "You'll *be* a weapon."

So Ama bent to the ground, to pick up not the uninteresting sword she'd been issued, but the half-circle blade Grenthus had so treasured. The grip in the center fit perfectly to her hand. The outward-facing blade was sharp as a cat's claw. Up close it looked like it could take off a person's arm or head with the slightest flick of an expert wrist. She wasn't an expert yet, but she looked forward to becoming one.

"Whose weapon will I be?" asked Ama.

Floriana only smiled.

✦

There was one place in the world that Paulus, the only surviving son of Queen Heliane of Paxim, felt truly himself: curled up on cushions in the palace library, sunken so deep into blankets he could hardly be seen, both hands wrapped around a book.

He disappeared so completely into books his mother often complained that he lost track of the rest of the world. He'd missed countless calls to evening meal over the years; last year he'd nearly missed his own birthday feast, nose buried in a massive illustrated version of *The Tale of Alev and Vela*. His mother approved of the books he read, but she did not know, did not understand, why he read them.

His favorite books were mostly histories, sagas of the brave women of old and the men who loved them. He knew what he was supposed to learn from them: the modesty and wisdom that enabled past rulers to keep the peace and broker the deals that kept these queendoms in perpetual collaboration. That was what Heliane wanted him to know. How she wanted him to be.

But that was not what Paulus read for. Within those same pages he found other things to love: the legends, the stories, the things that could not be true. The irresistible irony of the God of Plenty questing all the way to the Underlands for her consort and finding him there, already faithless. The entrance to those same Underlands sitting in Godsbones, tantalizingly close, reachable by anyone with persistence, will, and a diligent mind. The stories of great queens and politicians, yes, but not for their sage wisdom and diplomatic triumphs: for their blunders, their foibles, the ways their all-too-human foolishness changed the shape of the world.

Paulus could never find anyone in the stories quite like him. That, more than anything else, was what kept him reading. He was always trying to find a place for himself among the heroes of old.

While Paxim had never had a ruling king who ruled longer than a single day, they'd had plenty of the other kind: kings in name, kings by marriage, kings who served as helpmeet and support. None of them ever quite inspired Paulus. He didn't want to be like King Samarus, mentioned many times in many books, who stood silent and smiling for years. In the stories, Samarus only once laid a hand on his queen's arm to beg mercy for a jealous young cousin who'd plotted to have her killed. Due to the king's timely, earnest intervention, mercy was granted. After her pardon, the cousin reformed her regicidal ways and eventually took the throne as Queen Coura. A happy ending for Coura; of Samarus's ending, nothing was said.

Still, that story appealed more to Paulus than the story of the king mocked at court for spending every free hour tending his lavish and exotic garden. When the king's wife, Queen Theodora, fell ill, he saved her life with a tincture of ruby-thistle, of which there was only a single plant in the entire queendom: it grew, of course, in that selfsame garden. It was a lovely story, often told. No one but Paulus seemed to notice that not a single version of the story, no matter how short or long, bothered to record the king's name.

For all his intellect and curiosity, Paulus had no role models, no certainty, no real guiding star. In his ten-and-four years upon the earth so far, the idea that he would be the first ruling king of Paxim had never seemed real. What it had taken to get him here was absurd. The Drought of Girls had played a part, though the bones of the tragedy had been earlier laid: the years between his parents' marriage and the present day, his family's losses in those years, almost unimaginable. He hated that when they thought he wasn't listening, people gossiped critically about his mother's grief, equally appalled if she seemed too affected or too unaffected by the death of child after child. Nor could he stand that no one seemed to care that he had lost those sisters and brothers too. Granted that several of them had died before he was born, but Zofi hadn't. He'd known her. Loved her. Lost her.

He'd never forget the day when Zo, a girl for whom the word *headstrong* was woefully inadequate, had snuck away to ride their mother's most treasured mare, the golden Philomel. He was there. He could have told. But with a sly grin, Zo had raised a pointed finger to her lips to shush him. She'd promised him sweets before to stay silent, and he wasn't one to pass up an extra serving of fig cake. Three years old he'd been, chubby and toddle-legged, and he'd worshipped his sister like a hero. He'd smiled back at her and gone back to whatever toy or doll he'd been fiddling with, as any child of three might.

The next time he saw Zo she was dead, those once-smiling lips flecked with spittle, head lolling on a snapped neck. While the precious, reckless Philomel was not sacrificed, thanks to his mother's intervention, he was forbidden from ever visiting the golden horse's stable. There would be no riding for him. For more than a year he was not even allowed outside the palace's inner wall, as his mother went temporarily mad with grief, holding on to him so tightly it was hard to breathe.

He grew pale and fragile, deprived of sunlight, seeing no one but Heliane for the rest of his third year and all of his fourth. At last, it was his mother's *cosmete* Inbar, of all people, who brought her back from the brink. She'd done it with the hard truth no one else would speak to the queen: even inside the palace, there was no avoiding danger. Fevers came in through windows and doors. Children born weak, like Zofi's fragile twin, carried their fates inside them from the first. Queen Heliane emerged from the dark cloud a wiser, quieter woman. Gradually she'd allowed Paulus more freedom, paying it out in small measures, until when he turned ten, she did what he would have once considered unthinkable: sent him all the way to the Bastion for education. He wondered whether she really thought it would better him, or whether it was merely necessary to signal both her confidence in the institution and in him as a future king. But that was not the type of question one asked Heliane.

After his two years in the Bastion, which built both his knowledge and his confidence, Paulus came to know his mother again with new appreciation. He was amazed by the lightning quickness of her mind, the way she was able to appease and encourage and manage a whole populace, especially with so few words. His respect for her grew to match his love. But after she returned from the rites where she'd almost lost her life, she'd begun to cluck and fuss over him once more. It seemed as if her own vulnerability had reminded her of his.

But Sessadon, who had almost murdered his mother, also gave Paulus new hope with her death. After all, it was the sorcerer who had caused the Drought of Girls. Even before his mother had made her way back to Ursu from the rites, rumors of girls born had begun to trickle in from every corner of the queendom. In turn, each of these rumors was disproven, news of each and every baby girl a lie. Still, hope refused to fade. He woke up most days wondering if today would be the day a messenger, fleet-footed and gasping, would appear to announce that a girl had been born among his cousins. If that happened, thought Paulus, he might not need to reign. He might not break ground. He could just be himself, contentedly lost in his books, as he was today.

As he turned the next page, the door to the library swung open. Only one person in the queendom would enter a room where the kingling sat without even the pretense of a knock, and Paulus braced himself.

Bearing a golden yellow apple in her hand, the white-haired queen glided into the room. Her movements had been measured and slow like this ever since her grievous injury at the sorcerer's hands. The color of the apple was unusual but familiar; his mother was so fond of the fruit, which grew only in the royal orchards adjacent to the palace, that her gardeners had named it Heliane Yellow.

As she moved slowly in his direction, Paulus left his book open on his lap but turned his face toward her, giving her his full attention. In her younger days, if she felt he wasn't focused on her, she'd been known to snatch a book from his lap and throw it across the room. She threw things far less frequently now, but on the rare occasions she did, it was best to stand clear.

He waited patiently until she was close enough to hear him, then asked rhetorically, "Eating in the library? Don't we have rooms for that? Let me think . . . there's a name for a room for dining. . . ."

"Don't be smart," she chastised him. Her indulgent, motherly smile drained the words of any sting.

"Can't help it," he said, grinning back.

"It's all that reading, I suppose. Lucky you were born to me and not some farmer or weaver. Who knows what would have become of you?"

"Perhaps I would have excelled at farming," he answered. "Or become the best weaver in the world and caught a queenling's eye, like Amadeo, and ended up here in the palace anyway. I suppose we'll never know."

"Even if you married a queen, you'd never be a ruling king," said Heliane, drawing the knife from her belt to cut a wedge of apple, which she then ate delicately off the edge of the blade. "That only happens one way. Lucky for you, that's the door you came in."

"But you could choose an heir too, if there are any new girls to choose from?" It was unusual for her to seek him here; he'd hoped she came with news, and the birth of a girl cousin would have been the best possible news for him.

She angled the point of the knife in his direction. "*You* are my heir."

They'd been over it a thousand times; he still hoped that, as reasonable as she was on other matters, she'd eventually see reason on this one. "Mother, you know as well as I do, the country will never accept me."

"They will accept you," she said, slicing into the apple again for another bite. "They have no choice. I have decreed it so."

"Decrees are only words. They tell people what they should do, not what they will do." He hated to get drawn into the old familiar argument, but she'd raised him to speak his mind with conviction, and she'd reap what she sowed. "You think I don't hear the whispers about me? What those senators say? They don't want me to reign. I don't think I ever will."

"You are my lucky fifth child. Why would the All-Mother have granted you to me if not to reign? I say you will."

"Mother . . ."

"Hush. You remind me of your father. He worried too much about what other people thought."

"And he never ruled, did he?" Paulus had never met the man who sired him; King Cyrus had wasted away a few months before Paulus was born, already half orphan. For whatever reason, the stories about his lost siblings wrecked Paulus, yet stories about his father left him untouched. Perhaps because Cyrus had lived a full life. He hadn't been cut down, like Paulus's sisters and brothers, before they'd even really had a chance to live.

Heliane ignored his rudeness. She sliced another wedge of apple and severed it neatly between her teeth. "Eresh called him to the Underlands too soon. But he could have been a fine ruler, Paulus. An extraordinary one, even: not just regal and wise, but kind. Not every ruler is kind. I see so much of you in him. When you rule . . ."

"If."

"When," she repeated, again unruffled. "When you rule, you will show them all how capable you are. How intelligent, and yes, like your father, how kind. And they will wonder why they ever questioned you."

He'd said his piece; he sensed there was no reasoning with her today. She'd been making decisions and declarations all her life. Heliane had become queen at ten-and-two, younger than he was now—the age he'd been, in fact, when she recalled him from the Bastion two years past. Had she always been regal, even so young? He'd never heard her complain about the challenges of being a ruler, of how the people expected everything from you at all times, no weaknesses, no mistakes. She never talked about how hard it was to make everyone happy, even when they wanted mutually exclusive things. He saw the strain that ruling put on her—how could he miss it?—but she never spoke her suffering aloud, only stroked the knife at her belt and made pronouncements. Parts of her he wanted deeply to emulate; parts of her he knew were completely beyond his ken.

A light knock sounded at the door, five short, sharp taps of metal on wood: a member of the Queensguard politely requesting the queen's attention, probably with the pommel of her sword.

"Enter," called Heliane. She tucked her knife into the loop at her belt; when he was younger, he'd been endlessly fascinated by that knife. As a child, he'd thought it was a badge of her office, the way the blue snake necklace represented the queen of Arca. But later she told him it was her way of reminding herself that death was always near. It helped her feel she had some measure of control.

The first face through the door was familiar: Delph, the most senior member of his mother's Queensguard, who'd been with her since the day the Scorpicae withdrew their warriors. He'd been a child then; maybe that was why Delph still made him feel like a child, even now. She was a short woman, solid and broad, and somehow he always felt she loomed over him, even though he was a handspan taller. The force of her personality took up an outsize space.

"Queen Heliane, Kingling Paulus," she said, nodding to each with respect.

"Delph," they murmured.

"Queen, you asked that I bring . . . the newest addition to the palace when she arrived. Here she is."

Delph swept back, her cream-colored cloak swirling, and indicated the woman behind her, who stepped forward into the light. Every mote of dust in the library seemed to hang, just for a moment, in the suddenly stilled air.

Paulus's first impression of the young stranger was all wiry strength, long limbs held loose and ready. He had no doubt she could best him in a fight without breaking a sweat. Next he couldn't help but notice the livid-looking cut on her cheekbone, puffy and red, so swollen it made her right eye look smaller than her left. He wondered how she'd come by it. Then he noted the way her sharp chin and wide cheekbones, framed by hair cut short in clustered waves, gave her face the same shape as the head of a spear. Last he took note of the odd weapon on her hip, a wickedly curved blade the likes of which he'd never seen.

Just as he was always looking for his own place in history, Paulus always looked to slot new people he met into the old stories, folding them into the familiar. This woman didn't make sense in any of the stories, not at first glance. He wouldn't feel comfortable until he could find someone to compare her to.

His mother said, "Kingling Paulus, I'd like you to meet Ama."

Instead of bowing, the new arrival met his eyes.

"Ama, like Amadeo?" he blurted. He'd spoken the name of the legendary weaver not five minutes before; the coincidence seemed too much not to remark on.

"I don't know who that is," she said matter-of-factly. Her diction was as precise as a scholar's, but her words were far more direct.

"You're not from Paxim, are you?" He phrased it as a question, but felt certain of the answer.

"She isn't," Heliane interrupted. "But she has shown great promise in our army, which is how she came to my attention, and how she earned her new position."

"I was raised in the Bastion," Ama said to Paulus, still not looking away. Her gaze unsettled him. She watched him like a kestrel in a keep.

"The Bastion?" he asked, drawing closer to her for a better look. "How did you come to serve in our army, then?"

"Same as anyone else," she answered. "I volunteered."

There was something familiar about her, he felt it now, though he couldn't name where the familiarity lay. Again he sought a place for her in the stories. Perhaps she was most like Coturnix, the mythical bird-woman whose eyes could penetrate any darkness, see across any distance.

Careful not to stare too long while he thought, Paulus forced his eyes away and turned back to Heliane. "And in what position did you say Ama will be serving? A new member of your Queensguard?"

"Something like that," his mother said, and he didn't like the hint of a smile on her lips. "You might say she's the first of your future Kingsguard, actually; I've engaged Ama as your personal bodyguard."

"A bodyguard? Mother. I am more than capable of protecting myself." He gestured to the sheathed dirk at his hip. In his time at the Bastion he'd learned the rudiments of fighting, though he had to admit he'd slacked off in his practice these past two years. He'd chosen this particular dirk not for the sturdiness of the blade, but because it fit a remarkable sheath tooled to look like a furled hawk's wing, its amber-dyed leather imprinted with lines so fine and delicate they were easily mistaken for actual feathers. The queen was right to question his fitness for fighting, but in front of this stranger, he would not give away how deeply he felt the truth's sting.

His mother said grimly, "We have intelligence that raiding parties have been seen at Paxim's northern outposts."

This seemed barely relevant, so far from the capital. She was reaching, and he was curious to know why. "As if bandits could—"

"They're not bandits," intoned Heliane, in a low, firm voice. "They're Scorpicae."

This knocked him back, but again, he kept his true reaction to himself. "Still. An outpost is one thing, Ursu is another. You think a raiding party will threaten the palace?"

Ama spoke up to interrupt, her voice giving no sign of emotion. "The best time to protect you is before you're in danger."

He'd found the stranger intriguing, but if she was just his mother's mouthpiece, he could forgo the intrigue. He ignored her and addressed Heliane. "Odd to choose someone who's not even from Paxim. How do you know she can be trusted?"

Heliane opened her mouth to speak, but Ama put up a hand to silence her. Unbelievably, the queen obeyed.

Then Ama stepped forward, closer than any citizen of Paxim would dare to get to the kingling. He could smell the sweat of travel on her, a salty tang, with a bitter metallic note that he guessed came from the wound on her face. The young woman's voice was firm, steady. "You can trust me because I tell you that you can, and I'm a woman of my word. I'll keep you safe."

Her nearness disconcerted Paulus, even more than her steady gaze already had. He cloaked it with bravado. "You're that good, are you?"

"If you need proof," Ama said, this time with a hint of spark, "I'd be happy to fight you."

Paulus reached toward the dagger at his belt as if to draw on her, just to see what she would do.

She did not disappoint. Before he could even flick open the thong that kept his dirk in its marvelous sheath, she had the curved weapon from her belt up and out between their faces, her steady gaze meeting his just above the gleaming half circle of the blade. The weapon looked even more daunting up close. Her message was clear: if she'd wanted, the blade would have cut his throat.

"Ama," his mother chided, but with more humor than condescension. She must trust this young woman implicitly.

"Yes?" Ama responded, her eyes not leaving Paulus's.

The queen said, "I doubt you make the kingling feel more comfortable by brandishing your weapon."

"On the contrary," Paulus answered. "I am indeed more comfortable now that I have seen your skill in action. So you can put that away."

Ama turned to comply, her gaze finally leaving Paulus's face.

"Pfft," responded Heliane, all mock disapproval. "A reasonable person would agree with me. It's just your good fortune, Ama, that the kingling happens to be unreasonable."

"Don't worry, Mother, I take no offense," he said, amused.

"I appreciate my good fortune in finding the kingling tenderhearted," Ama said, her voice a touch warmer. "We're both of us in luck today."

"I do hope you two get along," said Heliane. "You'll be spending a lot of time together."

"Will we?" asked Paulus. "I don't remember agreeing to that."

Ama answered, "As I understand it, your agreement isn't required. It is the queen's order that I not leave your side, day or night."

A typical young woman in Ama's position, Paulus thought, would take the opportunity to smile at her new charge, to put him at ease. In this way, as in many others, Ama quickly proved atypical.

Paulus had the very strong feeling that she was dangerous, and not just because of her speed with her weapon. Perhaps she was not Coturnix the bird-woman. Perhaps she was more like Queen Theodora, who before her green-thumbed husband's milk thistle was used to save her life, had been a talented and exacting warrior. No one had much liked Theodora, the stories said, but she'd been the only Paximite queen who'd ever been called on to smother a rebellion. She'd done just that, and kept Paxim together. Her ruthlessness had been exactly what her queendom needed.

So the type of danger this Ama might pose, Paulus decided, was all right. For now, anyway. His life—a life no one before him could show him how to live—could probably use some danger.

◆

While Ama had no particular dislike for the kingling of Paxim, she wasn't ready for the pure relentlessness of his company. She was used to being alone; in a sense, she'd never been anything but. Even in the dormitories of the Bastion and the tents of the Paximite army, even as an ever-shifting cohort surrounded her, she'd always been able to shut other people out. She was on her own and that was how she liked it. Then again, she had to admit, there'd been a downside to not befriending her fellow soldiers. Her fingers went up to the faint, scarred ridge where her cheekbone had been split open by Grenthus and his cronies. It was almost completely healed now, a month after her arrival, but on wet days it still ached.

Now that she had settled into her new role as Paulus's assigned bodyguard, Ama wanted time alone to train, to rest, to think. She got none of these. She slept in the same chamber as the kingling at night, settling her bedroll across his doorframe to ensure that no assassin could pass; turning their backs to each other was all the privacy one gave the other when changing clothes or taking care of bodily needs. She didn't care for it, but he gave no outward sign that it bothered him, and she wasn't going to be a cringing little boy if he wasn't. She and Paulus were comrades, of a sort. Like her bunkmates in the Bastion, before she'd left the fortress nation behind to join the Paximite army at ten-and-three. She was paid never to leave the kingling's side, so she didn't.

In that first month, they rarely talked. When they did, their conversations were superficial. No, she'd hadn't lived in Paxim long; yes, he did enjoy books. This last question she asked him in the library, after following him there dutifully and sitting in silence while he read to himself for the twelfth day in a row. She'd meant it sarcastically; he'd answered in earnest, showing off some of his favorite tomes, clearly eager to share what he loved. She felt a little bad about it, but not bad enough to ask again.

Finally, after simply following him around for weeks, sick to death of the sound of pages turning, one day she took him by the wrist and said, "Today, for a change, you'll follow me."

Paulus looked surprised, but his nod was game, and he fell into step behind her without question. He only paused a moment to grab the book he'd been reading, which he folded to his chest with one hand while she led him forward by the other.

He must be so bored of his life, she thought as they left the library.

For a moment she felt the urge to take him on a wilder adventure. But what she really wanted was to train. Let him be the bored one for once. They had to be in the same space at all times, yes, but no one had actually said she had to let him choose the space.

Ama had seen members of the Queensguard practicing in a good-sized courtyard off the back of the palace's second kitchen, and that was where she led the kingling. She was thrilled to find the place deserted. A sack of sand dangled from a tree; weapons were lined up neatly in a nearby lean-to, none of them in excellent condition, but all perfectly fine for practice.

"I've never been out here," Paulus said, clearly intending to engage her in conversation.

Ama wouldn't let herself be distracted. She merely grunted at him and pointed where she wanted him to go. Then she hefted a double-headed staff, testing its weight in her hands. A grin crept onto her face. She could feel the scar on her cheek aching faintly from the unusual strain.

Before she began, Ama took a moment to survey the area to make sure no one could sneak up on them without being seen. The kingling's security was still paramount. She noted with satisfaction that even without being told to, the kingling turned his back to the palace wall, even while he continued to clutch his book. His whereabouts secure, she was finally free to do what she wanted.

With the staff in both hands, she leapt at the dummy, starting in full without a warm-up, just in case the kingling became impatient and time was short. To practice swordplay she would have needed a partner, but practicing with the staff and the dummy she could do alone. And even if the kingling stood mere feet away from her, she could ignore him. He was safe. She could home in so tightly on her task that everything else disappeared: the droplets of sweat on her forehead, the wheeling hawk above, a useless young man in the shade cast by the palace.

The sound of her strikes rang through the air. The staff was a versatile weapon, and Ama took it through every pace: to poke, stab, slap, swing. She thrust hard against the sand dummy and it swung back at her, returning like a dogged opponent, giving her more chances to parry, dodge, bide. The rhythm was almost intoxicating, the way it sang in her blood.

"Ama," Paulus called from his spot against the wall.

He didn't sound like he was in danger, so she ignored him. She spun the staff to strike the dummy on alternating sides, a tricky exercise that tested her dexterity, though it had no direct analog in battle. Her only meaningful opponent was herself, and she relished the fight. Ama was in the moment now, deep inside where she longed to be. She'd missed this so much.

Then Paulus stepped between her and the dummy, and though she burned to follow through with her strike to teach him a lesson, she stood down. She stared at him, impatient, panting.

"You're good," he said.

"I know," she replied, whipping the head of the staff around to strike the bag just above his waist on the right side, then spinning it to repeat the action on the other side. She was pleased to note that even as her weapon almost touched him, making a loud slap against the bag, he kept himself from flinching. She could tell he wanted to—he was hardly expert—but in quarters this close, with his inexperience, any level of control was a good sign.

"Teach me," Paulus said earnestly, eyes gleaming. He seemed to mean it. Yet she noticed he still clutched his book, mostly closed, one finger marking the page where he'd left off reading.

Ama kept the staff moving, tossing it in the air and catching it, spinning it behind her back to tap the dummy behind him again, then the ground, then the dummy. His eyes stayed on her, not the staff, and she returned the favor.

"This is advanced work," she said. "And my job is to guard you, not train you."

"My mother's directive?"

"Yes."

"She never said *not* to train me, did she?" the kingling pressed.

She eyed him frankly, trying to assess whether the boy was serious enough to bother with. "And if she did?"

Usually, Paulus's eyes were dreamy, but now they were focused, intent. He shook his head. "No. She didn't, I can tell. So it's settled. You can start teaching me to fight. Will it be tomorrow, or today?"

The set of his jaw indicated that he expected more resistance. But in life as in fighting, Ama knew, taking away resistance was an excellent way to gain the upper hand.

"Right now is fine," she said. "What will you fight with?"

Suddenly cagey, the kingling answered, "What do you recommend?"

"Your full attention." Moving the staff almost too quickly for him to follow, she knocked the book out of his hand. It hit the sand with a thud and slid a handspan or two across the ground, and she watched him watch it go.

Then he raised his head again, meeting her eyes, and smiled. "You have it," he said.

Perhaps this young man had more spirit than she'd given him credit for. "Well, then," she told him with a smile. "Let's fight."

That was how they fell into a new routine. In the mornings, he followed her to the practice field and they trained in earnest. They began with the staff, at his request. Next, the sword. Then she taught him how to actually use the dagger that he'd only ever viewed as decoration, to draw and slash and stab so quickly the naked eye couldn't follow. He asked her several times to teach him the ironheaded mace, but that was the only weapon she refused. A mace was only good for smashing, and left one vulnerable to counterattack besides. There was no nuance to a mace.

In the beginning, Paulus was awkward, lagging behind, but it didn't take him long to improve. While he lacked the natural talent Ama had always taken for granted in herself, his ability to focus was impressive.

He was humble enough to recognize what he didn't know and dogged enough to overcome it. More than once, when Ama told him she thought he'd had enough for the day, he insisted on sticking with it until he landed one more blow, mastered one more combination. She could see the difference in him when he stopped training just to prove he could and began to truly enjoy what he was learning his body could do.

When one of the largest, oldest trees on the palace grounds came down in a particularly wild summer storm, Paulus was the one who suggested they have a section of the immense trunk dragged to the practice yard. The rotten sections within were hollowed out until the slab of wood was like a tunnel, almost tall enough for either of them to stand up inside, though they chose to train atop the old trunk, not within. They climbed up and practiced their footwork for hours, shuffling forward and back to learn the feeling of working within that limitation, how it changed their sword work, their strategy. Ama lost track of how many times Paulus fell, slipping off the side of the trunk and tumbling to the dry earth, but every single time, he climbed right back up again.

Even the part of their routine that stayed the same, in those weeks, began to change. After the midday meal, Ama would follow Paulus to the library. There they would spend several hours. But instead of reading silently to himself, he began to read aloud to her.

She'd never much enjoyed reading, but in Paulus's voice, the stories came alive. Before long she found herself asking questions, demanding clarification. Paulus's answers were patient and thorough. Not long after that, instead of standing by the doorway as he read on the window seat, she took a seat of her own on a nearby cushion. They weren't close enough to touch, but she liked to lean her back against the wall and let his voice surround her like warm summer rain. Some days she could even imagine she saw the heroes whose stories he told her: brave Alev, faithful Vela, lovestruck Lottin, determined Roksana.

And when she lay her bedroll down just inside Paulus's door at night, more and more often she found herself thinking of these heroes of long ago. Especially the queens. She could have been a queen herself, she knew, if things had been different. If she'd been allowed to follow in her mother's footsteps, instead of driven into hiding. Exiled. Ama had no intention of telling Paulus—or anyone—the truth of her origins, but the stories tickled at her brain. They reminded her that her own story was not yet fully written.

If someone put her story in a book, Ama wondered, what would Paulus's place be in it? She wasn't sure she would call him a friend, but neither was she sure she wouldn't. They were so different—one pampered and dreamy, the other practical to a fault—but they shared keen intelligence, curiosity about the world, an appreciation of things earned. She couldn't deny that her opinion of him had changed since that first meeting.

And there was more to it than what they had in common. The forced intimacy of each other's constant presence threatened to bring down barriers Ama knew it would be wiser to keep in place. There was no word for what they were to each other now, something like family, but with an undercurrent that reminded her constantly that they were not related by blood.

And were heroes always wise? No. The stories Paulus read aloud for them demonstrated that, over and over. She'd have to keep her wits about her. No one could make her unwise, she told herself as she stretched out on the hard floor to rest. No one could make her a fool. She could only do that to herself.

But across the darkened room, she could hear the kingling breathe. She could tell by the pattern of his breaths that he, too, was not yet asleep. She listened for intruders and she listened for assassins, but she had to admit, yes, she also listened to Paulus's breathing so she would know when something happened to change its now familiar rhythm. She listened because she felt that, one of these nights, he might have something to say.

5

ARRIVAL

Daybreak Palace
Eminel, Beyda

Eminel had plenty of time to think about her entrance to Daybreak Palace, and whether she would, when she descended from the carriage, attempt to conceal the mysterious quartz cuff. In the end, she chose to display it. Clearly, it had struck fear in Archis's heart. Eminel didn't particularly want to rule by fear, but what were her options, without power or allies? Fear seemed her only hope of ruling at all.

When the carriage rumbled to a stop at long last, Eminel closed her eyes and stroked the smooth surface of the Talish cuff. Under her fingers the quartz felt seamless, as if it had simply grown on her wrist like a trellis-trained vine. She'd been afraid of sleep the whole ride here, and when she'd succumbed to it, her dreams had been fractured, fleeting. There was a blue woman, that much she remembered, and a few times, dancing motes of light that landed gently on her skin. When she realized the lights in her dream had resembled the enchanted quartz lights in the ceiling of the carriage, the ones that had suddenly gone missing that first night, she realized there must be a connection. But she'd been alone in that carriage, she was sure of it. Had she grown the cuff herself, somehow? It wasn't a comforting thought. If she could transform matter in her sleep— unknowingly, unintentionally—what else was she capable of doing?

She never wanted to sleep again.

The door to the carriage swung open. Hot desert air rolled in as Eminel saw Archis, dusty from the road but poised and ready. Her hair had been neatened and tied back since Eminel had seen her last.

In a voice clearly meant to carry, Archis said, "Welcome to Daybreak Palace, Honored Queen."

Eminel, for her part, kept her head high, putting on an air of disdain. Behind Archis she could see others, though she had no idea of their number. She could barely catch a glimpse of the palace behind their heads. The little she saw took her breath away. She forced her gaze back to Archis, fought back the wonder and awe and fear.

"I assume you will want to rest," Archis said.

"You assume incorrectly," Eminel said. The only thing that could keep her from panicking was pretending she was a trouper playing a role. The role was a challenge, twofold: powerful magician, haughty queen. "Tell me what you think the first order of business should be."

"Well," said Archis, "we plan to begin tomorrow with the presentation of the court matriclans."

Eminel had a thousand questions. How many matriclans were there at court? Just what did their presentation entail? But she caught herself. She couldn't help being ignorant, but she could be careful about appearing that way.

"Very well," said Eminel. "Make it today, not tomorrow. We start in an hour."

There was something deeply gratifying in the immediate bustle her words created. Even this tiny sliver of control made Eminel see, with frightening clarity, how previous queens had become addicted to their power. When a woman's mere word could ripple the world, who wouldn't want to stretch that power as far as it could reach? That put her in mind of Sessadon again. She didn't want Sessadon on her mind.

"Perhaps you'd like to visit your chambers first?" asked Archis, with a pointed look that swept Eminel's body from what was surely matted hair to sand-coated feet.

"No," Eminel replied. "Please show me to the audience chamber, or let me know if I should find my own way."

"Yes, my queen," said Archis, inclining her head. "I'll take you." She gestured toward the palace's soaring archway, dark inside like a vast, hungry mouth.

Once through the doors, striding behind Archis as if she herself were leading, Eminel tried her best not to gawk. The palace was the most beautiful building imaginable. The simplicity of the Sestian palace-temple she'd seen before the rites had been impressive, precise, gleaming. But Daybreak Palace, hewn from the earth, felt as if it had been grown, not built. It felt natural. Right.

The deeper into the palace they went, the more the feeling grew. Eminel sensed something familiar in the comforting closeness of the dug-out walls. She had only a handful of memories from her Arcan childhood, but she recalled the dug-out walls of the house she'd shared with her mother and her mother's husbands. She hadn't seen walls like this since she was five years old. She could feel tears pricking at the corners of her eyes.

Yet the palace, so magnificent, bore no more resemblance to her childhood desert home than a peacock to a wren. Tall archways led to enormous chambers of unknown purpose, more halls and rooms and spaces than she could possibly count. The audience chamber Archis led her into had a high, domed ceiling, and easily could have fit two hundred women standing.

At the front of the room, ringed by armed guards, was a throne. Eminel walked straight to it and took her rightful seat.

"I will wait here," she said. "Go make ready."

Archis's parting bow was quick, silent.

Once she was gone, Eminel beckoned to one of the guards. "A dish of dates from the kitchen, please."

"Of course, Honored Queen," he said, and hastened to do her bidding.

Her choice was not unconsidered. Sweet dates had been a rare indulgence in Paxim, but she knew they grew better in this desert climate. She was an Arcan queen. She should eat Arcan food. And when the servant brought the dish as requested, she saw only approval and deference in his gaze.

At the appointed time, the room began to fill. The noise quickly became overwhelming. To calm her mind, Eminel put a date in her mouth and slowly sucked at it, pressing the pit against the roof of her mouth with her tongue. She was afraid that otherwise she might leap up and run. As the date began to melt away, she looked out over the mass of bejeweled women in rich-looking robes, accompanied by the most beautiful men Eminel had ever seen. She reminded herself she was fully in control. This was her court. These were her subjects. She only needed to get through this ritual performance, and then she could hide and rest. No one here knew her magic had left her. Everything could still be fine.

Eminel had just spotted one woman in a long, unadorned gray tunic at the back of the room, standing out for her obvious attempt at invisibility, when her attention was caught by the call to action.

A lovely man with long lashes and hair in a thick braid to his waist called out, "Let the presentation of the clans begin! Thus we welcome Queen Eminel, Well of All-Magic, Master of Sand, and Destroyer of . . ."

Here he trailed off, his face seized with a level of concern that seemed to border on panic.

Eminel turned to him calmly. She knew only the bare facts about her native queendom, but she at least knew that each queen chose the last word of her title. She had already decided on hers. In a ringing voice, she said, "Destroyer of Fear."

Though the man's expression didn't change, even without deploying her mind magic she felt relief pouring off him like a wave. "Destroyer of Fear! First, clan Jale."

Eminel wasn't surprised that Archis's clan was the first to be presented, given that Archis was the only other woman with all-magic in the court. That power, rare as it was, had to improve the standing of her whole matriclan. A dozen women, all richly garbed, walked in a cluster behind Archis. Only Archis herself carried something in her arms. Eminel laid aside the date pit she'd been sucking on, placed another sweet, fleshy date on her tongue, and watched the young woman and her fellow clan representatives slowly advancing.

"We honor you as the chosen of Velja, Queen Eminel," said Archis, garbed in white with rich embroidery, an intricate necklace of silver twined about her neck in a way that echoed Eminel's own necklace. Eminel doubted the resemblance was an accident. "Clan Jale welcomes you to Daybreak Palace. We submit to your will and glory in your reign."

At Eminel's feet, Archis laid a pearlescent white glass bowl half-filled with water. Tiny white petals of some unknown flower danced on its surface.

"Your welcome is most gracious," said Eminel, not sure if they were the right words, but investing them with weight and sincerity.

"Queen Eminel," said Archis, her voice dropping back to a lower register, soothing. "Won't you please refresh yourself? I see sand on your face. In Arca, grime does not befit a queen."

Archis took up the white bowl and extended it toward Eminel, so close Eminel could see her own reflection in the water, interrupted by the scattering of white petals and the soft ripples they caused, floating by. The ripples were more pronounced than Eminel would have expected. She realized that Archis's hands were not completely steady.

Stalling, Eminel asked, "Lovely flowers. What are they?"

After a pause, Archis answered, "We call them 'life's fingers'. Did you not have them in your village?"

I have no village, Eminel almost said, but instead she looked down at the petals, and something clicked into place.

Though the petals were small, she could see up close that their shape was highly unusual: skinnier than a fingernail but as long as the first joint of a finger bone. The sight sparked a memory. Long-petaled flowers like this grew around certain roadside temples in Paxim, clustered by the door. Once when she was small, she'd reached out for their delicate beauty, and it was the one and only time the even-tempered thief Hermei had laid his hands on her. He yanked her back by the shoulders so sharply she'd sprawled backward into the dirt, stunned and disbelieving. That was why she remembered it still.

The temple had been made of bones, long and bleached pale by the sun, almost as white as the long petals of the small flowers. The temple of the God of Death.

"Death's fingers," Hermei had told her, his voice stern. "Poison."

Now, here: a clumsy lie, *life's fingers*, but understandable under pressure.

Holding up her palm to decline the bowl, Eminel said calmly to Archis, "No, thank you. I appreciate the gift, but I will tend to such matters in private."

The other woman's facade was beginning to slip. Eminel didn't need any magic to sense her uncertainty, her anger.

"A sip of water, then," Archis insisted, offering the bowl once more, uncomfortably close to Eminel's lips. "As a blessing from Velja."

"Thank you, no," said Eminel.

Even as she said it, she saw the other woman moving, tipping the bowl at a radical slant, preparing to dash the water into Eminel's face; whether that would be enough for the flowers' poison to do its work, she didn't know, but she closed her eyes. She had time for only a scrap of thought, incomplete—*If I could, I would*—and instinctively *pushed*.

The push didn't come from Eminel's upraised hand, but from her mind. It disrupted far more than the water and the bowl. She kept her eyes squeezed tight shut, but her ears heard everything: a crack, a thud, a snapping sound. Amid it all, one wild, awful howl, cut short.

Screams went up from nearby—the other members of Archis's clan, she assumed—and whispers from farther away. She opened her eyes and saw women began to run toward the body of Archis, flat on her back on the stones, her face an unrecognizable, pulped red. She didn't know why they ran, but she leapt up to run too, the lessons of her time on the Isle of Luck—anyone hurt needed healing—still with her. Down she came from the throne and shoved aside the nearest woman, an elder from Archis's clan swathed in robes the color of pomegranate, so the queen could put her own hand in the center of Archis's chest, searching for a sign of life.

What was left of Archis's mouth flew open in one last howl. Eminel felt something surging through her fingertips and upward. The cuff on her wrist burned with the strange sensation of cold fire. Then she heard only one thing: the crowd's collective gasp.

The light in the room transformed. Where before the chamber had been lit from its edges by flickering lamps, a steady glow had emerged, putting a pale cast on every upturned face.

Then Eminel realized what the light was. Her Talish cuff, glowing blue. No one could look away. She felt power surging into the quartz cuff, cold fire shifting into a warm, crackling energy, reminding her of the very first time Sessadon helped her explore her powers, the time Eminel had asked for *more*. She felt better than she had in weeks, maybe years. She could feel everything. She could even hear the ebb and flow of her heartbeat, quickened. The space between beats seemed to stretch out as no one, nothing moved.

One exception: the poisoned bowl Archis had borne to her lay broken on the floor, its cracked halves slowly rocking. She watched them rock slower, slower still, until they settled. From the reflected light on the other Arcans' faces, Eminel could see the glow from her cuff pulse one, two, three times. The bright blue glow subsided into a cool light too faint to cast shadows. Then it faded into nothing, the cuff just a cuff again, reflecting only the flickering torchlight.

Then Eminel rose, two opposite impulses warring within: she wanted to stammer out an apology for what she'd done, the gruesome death she'd caused, and she wanted to cackle with laughter at how far beneath her such a clumsy attempt on her life had been. She was enough in possession of herself to know either reaction would be a mistake. Everyone would remember what she did here today. She would play her part.

So Eminel turned her back on the crowd. She walked back to the throne, step by measured step, where she made a slow half-turn and seated herself. She fought back the urge to stroke the cuff, which felt lighter than it had before, somehow less of a burden. She would sort out all these feelings—guilt, wonder, fear, thrill—in her own time. She reached into the bowl of dates and plucked one out between her thumb and forefinger, but didn't yet put it to her lips.

"Let us resume, then," the new queen of Arca said, her voice steady, imperious. "Who's next?"

◆

When she finally saw the queen up close for the first time, Beyda was not impressed. From the rumors, she'd expected the woman to have a terrifying presence. Though the denizens of the court—vipers and climbers, every last one—rarely bothered speaking directly to Beyda, they spoke in her presence often enough. During Queen Eminel's first week in Daybreak Palace, they spoke of nothing else. The queen had assembled a Queensguard of five women, each from a major matriclan—everyone acknowledged that Jale had been excluded thanks to Archis's attempt on the queen's life, which had only cost Archis her own—and installed them at her door with orders to admit no visitors for any reason. Only the servants who brought the queen's meals were allowed in, and they were ordered out again the instant they set down a tray.

So no one, including Beyda, knew much about the newly arrived queen. They had only a handful of facts. Eminel had not grown up in Arca. She liked date-filled sweet buns and a cup of warm goat's milk to start her day. And upon arrival, she had killed her only serious rival for the throne, sucked the other woman's life force into the Talish cuff she wore, and calmly begun her reign.

The first time Beyda saw Queen Eminel, she didn't actually realize she was looking at the queen. Beyda had been hard at work in her favorite study room, eyes searching familiar lines of text for a new interpretation, when a blur of motion at the far end of the room caught her by surprise. What she saw first was a storage shelf that swung out from the wall unexpectedly—she'd never seen it do that, not in the three years she'd lived here—and a woman whose black hair was powdered with yellowish dust. The woman was neither particularly large or small, though broad in the shoulders, and apart from emerging from a wall that Beyda had never known was more than just a wall, she was unremarkable.

"Who are you?" demanded the woman with dust in her hair. Her sharp tone was Beyda's first inkling that she was, in fact, looking at Arca's fearsome, deadly young queen.

There was nothing to do but answer the question. "I'm your scribe."

"Aren't you young for a scribe?" Eminel asked.

"Aren't you young for a queen?" responded Beyda.

"You'd know better than I would, I suppose." Eminel's brow lowered in thought. She had large, expressive eyes, and despite her furrowed expression, they still gave the impression of openness. "Do you know much about the history of Arcan queens?"

Beyda gestured at the shelves around her, jammed with scrolls, lined with books. "Everything written down. For example, that Talish cuff you wear."

"What about it?"

"The third queen of Arca wore one just like it. The story is—" She scanned the shelves quickly, her finger following her gaze, and found the book she was looking for. "Right here." She held the book out to Beyda.

"Thank you," Eminel said. "Anything else about Talish cuffs?"

Beyda said, "What do you want to know?" She felt like they had skipped a great deal, fallen into a conversation neither was ready for. But she supposed when a queen emerged from a wall and found someone with something she wanted—information, in this case—niceties no longer applied. That was a bit of a relief for Beyda. She had never cared much for niceties.

Eminel said, "Start at the beginning, I suppose."

That was easy enough. "The third queen, her name was Dejori, didn't invent the cuff. She stole it from the matriclan that did."

"Stole? Like a thief?"

"Like an Arcan queen," Beyda clarified. "Dejori summoned the inventor, demanded the cuff and its secrets, told the inventor she'd kill the rest of the clan unless the queen got what she wanted. Terrified, the inventor complied. When she did, Dejori killed all of them anyway."

"The whole clan?"

Beyda ignored the question. The answer was obvious. "Then the queen used the cuff as a power source. She'd draw off life force and keep it there. So that way she always had quartz and she always had life force, and she could cast her magic no matter the conditions."

"And when you say 'draw off life force' . . . ?"

Beyda didn't revel in the grim details, but there was no need to sugarcoat the truth. "She harvested it from her enemies in the court. As her magic burned through what she'd banked, she'd harvest more. Sometimes leaving her rivals weak, sometimes, well, taking it all."

"I see," the queen said vaguely. "Someone did warn me that members of my court might not like seeing me wearing the cuff."

"Didn't you know what it meant when you put it on?"

The expressive eyes narrowed. "That's a long story, and not one I choose to tell today." Eminel brandished the book Beyda had handed her. "Is this the best one to teach me the history of queens?"

"It's a competent introduction," Beyda said. "If you want, I can give you one that goes into more detail."

"I want," Eminel replied.

Beyda located the book. It was heavy enough to require both hands to lift down from the shelf. She handed it to the queen, who put the other book on top of it and held both to her chest, then looked back into the passage she'd come from.

Indicating the passage, Beyda said, "Does that lead directly into your chambers?"

"Oh. I could tell it wasn't commonly used, but I didn't know—the previous queen never came to visit you this way?"

"The previous queen never visited me at all," Beyda told her. It had not escaped her notice that the queen had not actually answered the question.

"But you said you were my scribe. How could you be my scribe if you weren't hers?"

Beyda replied, "I was assigned here by the Bastion. And I worked for her, yes, I wrote things down for her. But she never came into this room. No one does but me."

"Ah," said Eminel, and it seemed to Beyda like she was grasping for something to say next. "You were raised in the Bastion! So you've always been a scribe?"

"Well, no." Beyda hadn't told the story in years, if at all; she couldn't remember if she had given a complete accounting to the previous queen. Probably not. "We're all tested when we turn eight to determine our specialty. When I was tested, my affinity for numbers was extraordinary. The Mathematicians wanted me, but the Engineers won me. The Bastion loves nothing so much as a prodigy. They say fresh, nimble minds are most likely to find doors to open that most people don't even recognize as doors."

What she didn't tell Eminel, because she knew it wasn't right to speak of to a non-Bastionite, was that the Engineers had been striving for decades, maybe longer, to find a way to extend the boundaries of the Bastion. As far as the history of the Five Queendoms went, even before there were queendoms, the Bastion had simply always been there. It was assumed the structure had been excavated and built with strong magic, carving deep into the mountain for halls and dormitories, caves and throne rooms, and an incomprehensible system of pipes through which fresh air somehow flowed even down to the deepest levels. There was even a rumor, never quashed, that a secret level existed beyond the lowest known level, a bunker that could be sealed off from the world so that any disaster, natural or made by woman, could be survived by those hiding inside. The enormity of the Bastion could hardly be recorded, let alone understood. But no Engineer had ever truly understood the structure well enough to extend it. Could they dig deeper? Build higher? Extend sideways into the mountain instead of above or below it? The Engineers had hoped Beyda would be the prodigy to crack that nut. She had not done so.

Eminel's brow creased. "The Engineers won you? But you're not an engineer."

"I was, for a time. But I hated the work and wasn't good at hiding it. They finally got so sick of me they made me a Scribe of Numbers. It didn't work. I hated that, too."

"Why?"

"Scribes of Numbers travel the queendoms, surveying and recording, and they always work in partnership with a Scribe of Names. I don't work well with others."

"So you were sent here as what? A punishment?"

Beyda nodded. It was as good a word as any. "The scribe serving at the Arcan court had disappeared—All-Mother knows what happened to him, certainly no one else does—so the Board of Scholars sent me as his replacement. I guess they thought if I disappeared too, it would solve both their problem and mine."

"That's pretty heartless."

"Bastionites aren't known to have tender hearts," said Beyda dryly. "You may have heard the expression, 'Stone outside and in'?"

"Not before now."

"Well, it's not inaccurate."

The queen sounded very young when she said, "You don't seem like stone."

"Maybe you're just not that observant."

Improbably, Eminel smiled. "I suppose that's possible. I can use someone who tells me the truth, Beyda. Will you tell me the truth?"

"I have and I will."

"Thank you for the books," Eminel said, raising them. "I'll bring them back when I'm done."

"You're welcome."

Then the queen stepped back into the passage, and with a motion Beyda couldn't see clearly, swung the shelf back into place and disappeared.

Beyda stared at the wall for only a moment before she was on her feet, trying to suss out the secret. She had come to this room for years, touching every single book on every single shelf over time, and never suspected a secret passage. Was this the only one? She ran her fingertips up and down, searching for seams, finding none. When she stepped back, the only way she could tell this shelf from the others was the rug in front of it, which had been bunched up when the shelf swung out and hadn't settled back into place when the shelf had. Beyda made note of the books that marked the borders of the shelf and then, with care, smoothed the rug flat.

For the next few days, every time Beyda came into this room—she used it frequently, as it adjoined her sleeping quarters—she glanced at that shelf first, checking to see if the rug had been disrupted. It had not. Then she searched for some way to access the passageway, methodically checking each book, pressing and sliding her fingers over every inch of both the top and underside of each shelf. She took all the books and scrolls out, put them all back in. To the naked eye, one would never know the queen of Arca had swung open that shelf and stepped into this room.

But Beyda knew. And each day after she examined the shelf, she looked at the others, too, for a different purpose. She thought of things a new queen should know. First she located the best book on the history of each matriclan. When she left the room to search them out, she always checked the rug when she returned, always disappointed to find it lying flat against the floor. She made a small stack of the matriclan histories one atop the next, lining up the spines, aligning the stack with the edge of the table to make everything neat.

When the matriclan stack was complete and Eminel still hadn't returned, Beyda thought about what else a queen of Arca might want or need to know, and began gathering some of the most interesting scrolls on the use of all-magic. Many enchantments were handed down from one magician to another, from what the scribe understood, and others were developed by each individual magician herself through instinct, practice, and trial and error. But all-magic offered so many dizzying possibilities, especially at the level of skill needed to become queen, and was not passed from mother to daughter. So some queens recorded and handed down suggestions for calling on particular types of power, building a different kind of link from past to present to future. It made sense that these incantations were stored in the most obscure, remote corner of Daybreak Palace, where two kinds of things were kept: the treasured and the forgotten. Beyda had always been the second. But if she proved herself valuable to the new queen, perhaps she could become the first.

As the stack of scrolls grew, Beyda lined them up in rows, first next to each other, then on top, always building one layer carefully before starting the next. Before she retired to her quarters for the night, she surveyed the table. After several days of activity, it was almost completely covered. As she passed under the archway back to her own room, she took one more quick glance at the undisturbed rug.

When Eminel came again, if Eminel came again, Beyda would be ready.

6

THE FIRST DROPS OF RAIN

Spring, the All-Mother's Year 517
Across the Five Queendoms

Just as there had been no lightning strike or thunderclap to announce the beginning of the Drought of Girls, nothing announced its end. No curtain lifted, no clouds parted. At first, after the sorcerer's public death, only rumors unspooled: the first girl in a generation had been born in the far west of Sestia, or the deserts of Arca, or a remote trading post in Paxim. Whispers crossed borders like a dun-colored bird, fleet and fleeting. As summer yielded her crown to early autumn, word spread from the Bastion that a long-awaited girl had come squalling into the world, but after weeks with no actual eyewitness accounts, the whispers faded. If there was no girl in the logbooks, as far as the scholars of the Bastion were concerned, there was no girl.

The rumors were as plentiful as grains of sand and as flammable as dry twigs. They were willful misdirection and honest mistakes, deceptions and wishful thinking, prayers and pretense.

Then one day, finally, as spring came hard on the heels of winter, the rumors were true.

No one knew which infant girl, exactly, was the first. Certainly the tiny warrior born to the Scorpican called Azur, who labored even as her country's forces amassed on the Arcan border, was among them. Azur named the baby to honor two women she admired: Mada, mother of her mother, and herself. Madazur's birth was witnessed by dozens of fellow warriors, who greeted her with songs of celebration. Whether or not Madazur dha Azur was the very first, she was certainly the most loudly welcomed.

In the Bastion, where the girls' nursery had been shuttered seven years before, the unexpected birth of the first girl in fifteen years occasioned a flurry of activity. The mother was an engineer named Doxre, who had been so absorbed in her work she hadn't realized she was in labor until her pains were far advanced, and barely managed to call a midwife in time. The baby was born right there on the floor of a study room, the smell of birthing blood mixing with the scents of ink and clay and pencil shavings. When Lidi of the Midwives realized who she held in her arms, the first and only Bastionite girl in so long, she nearly dropped the birth-slicked baby in her shock.

When Lidi settled the squirming, red-faced girl onto her mother's chest and there was no more danger, the midwife breathed a long sigh of relief. After that, the unnamed girl's mother wrapped her arms tight around the child's slippery form, trying to keep the baby with her, but girl or not, this child would go to the nursery. All Bastionite children did. Scholars made no exceptions for miracles.

In Paxim, a desperate traveler named Marwel, soaked to the bone in a rainstorm, stumbled and fell into the nearest shelter. She crossed the doorframe of the largest temple of the God of Rescue deep in the grip of a fever, her prayers incoherent. The priests had no midwife training but they did the best they could. For hours there was no blood, only pain, and Marwel floated in and out of consciousness. The priests prayed and prayed.

The baker's boy, who stumbled across the scene while delivering the priests their bread, did not believe in prayer. So he ran two leagues to an adjoining settlement to knock on the door of a white-haired recluse called Poppy, who the other boys had always whispered was a fearsomely powerful healer. When the woman answered his knock, the baker's boy did his best to still his anxious trembling, and offered her five loaves of bread, free of charge, to come to the temple. Poppy was not a healer, had never been, but she had been a farm girl once. She gladly accepted the promise of bread, kept up with the boy's brisk pace all the way back to the temple, and proved far more helpful than the priests had been in moving things along.

When the next day dawned, the storm clouds finally clearing, the first Paximite girl born after the Drought emerged onto the floor of the temple of the God of Rescue barely breathing, but breathing all the same. Her wide eyes opened to take in the world. She was followed moments later by the second girl, her identical twin, sputtering and outraged from her first breath.

By sunrise, word had spread so far that an audience of dozens waited outside the temple of the God of Rescue, eager to see the girls with their own eyes. The faithful but practical priests kept the pilgrims waiting, and by afternoon, the crowd had doubled in size. When the sun was three-quarters of the way across the sky, the still-feverish mother shuffled from the temple with the girls in her arms, supported by Poppy at every step. As Marwel offered the crowd a glimpse of the twins—one watchful, one discontented, as they'd prove to be for years to come—the priests wound their way through the crowd with collection baskets to accept offerings to the god, passing from one side to the other and back again.

Once the happy, satisfied crowd began to dissipate, the priests gathered indoors and counted the offerings in private. They'd collected more coppers for the God of Rescue in a single day than the temple had seen in years. At a pointed word from Poppy, the ranking priest scooped up a fistful of coppers and poured them into the white-haired woman's outstretched hands. The priest then stared at the remaining heap of coppers on the wooden table, brought both hands down, and formed two piles of equal size. He slid one pile back into the largest offering basket and handed it to the younger priest to lock away in the temple's treasury. He carefully stacked the rest into a locking wooden box that he gave to the exhausted mother Marwel, blessing her with a kiss on her hot forehead, whispering words of prayer and gratitude.

Poppy exchanged a few words with the baker's boy, handing over two coppers pinched between her fingers, and he nodded. Half an hour later he returned with the baker's wagon, then drove Poppy, the new mother, and the baby girls to Poppy's house. Before he left, Poppy caught him by the arm. He thought she was going to express her thanks. Instead she reminded him that he still owed her five loaves of bread, which she hoped to see delivered tomorrow. She liked brew-rye best, she told him.

In Sestia, only her mother witnessed the birth of the first girl after the Drought, a risky, lonely birth. No crowd of warriors, no paying pilgrims, no scholars or midwives. The shepherd gave birth alone on a nighttime hillside, only the light of a crescent moon and the far-off stars to see by. As she labored on the grass, she sang at the top of her lungs, every song she knew—love ballads and lullabies and war marches and bawdy, profane drinking songs—to keep the wolves away. The sheep had wandered off, bleating, when labor pains drove the shepherd to her knees in the pink glow of sunset. Every now and then, from the darkness, she could hear a lamb's scream cut off by a predator, even over the sound of her song. Better the sheep's children than hers, she thought, ever practical.

Once the child was born—a relatively easy labor, thank the Holy One, the path having been paved by the newborn's five older brothers— the shepherd knew what she had to do. The wolves hadn't found them yet, but they would scent the blood that soaked the hillside. She needed to leave it behind. In the light of the crescent moon, she could just see the watchtower's outline. It was less than two leagues away.

The shepherd sang as she made her way. Progress was slow but steady as she crawled across the soft tufts of lowgrass, wet with nighttime dew, until she arrived at the base of the watchtower. The ladder was the hardest part, almost harder than the labor, but she bound the newborn to her chest in a sling she fashioned from her shawl to free her hands for climbing. She had just enough strength left to untie the shawl and make a nest of it on the floor of the watchtower, settling the sleeping child into it, before she curled on her side and collapsed next to the newborn. When the mother awoke the next day and heard the newborn's cries for milk, sunlight falling on the child's open rosebud mouth, that was the moment she realized the child she'd birthed was a girl. And for once, the shepherd who always had a song on her lips was left speechless.

In Arca, the first girl was welcomed into hearthside warmth, each of her mother's husbands holding tight to one of her mother's hands, her grandmother reaching out for the child with a broad, welcoming smile. Even with the love and support around her, the first-time mother's nervous temperament got the better of her during labor, and she lost control of her magic. With the first pain, the small succulent on the household shrine suddenly put forth a brilliant yellow blossom, though it had never had flowers before. As the pains built in strength and frequency, blooms in every color appeared throughout the house, a rosebush bursting from the cookstove, ivy twining up the household ladder so fast and thick it reached the door to the outside before anyone noticed it was there.

Once the child emerged—a girl, a miracle!—the grandmother wept and praised her daughter for her strength, and one of the husbands took the opportunity to climb the ivy-covered ladder to let the fresh air in. But it took several tries to open the door, even pushing with all his strength, until there was a sound of muffled snapping and the door swung open onto a prairie of wildflowers that covered the entire roof of the house, a riot of color, already attracting butterflies and bees.

And so, in every country of the Five Queendoms, the Drought was over. Women whose bellies were heavy with child no longer knew whether that child would emerge girl or boy. What had been certain was now uncertain, but in a way that brought joy, not sorrow. Where there had once been drought, there would again be plenty.

But the Drought had not been a thunderstorm or a long night or homeward journey that, when it was over, was finished and forgotten. It had been a disaster for too long, reached too far. Once the first girl took her first breath, from that moment, the Drought of Girls itself had ended. But what the Drought had wrought—over years and years, across every queendom—was not so easily undone.

7

JESEPHIA

**Ten months after the Rites of the Bloody-Handed;
a half-month after the end of the Drought of Girls
The Arcan village of Jesephia
Gogo, Gretti, Azur**

Like most remote Arcan settlements, the village of Jesephia usually rose with murmurs, whispers, and the soft groans of tired women, but today it screamed itself awake.

The mounted Scorpicae rode in first, their ponies stomping and snorting, hooves pounding against the hard-packed sand as they plunged down the main roadway between the buried houses. It was a sound that most residents of Jesephia had never heard before. The deep desert this close to Godsbones was inhospitable to creatures of every kind, including humans. Livestock was out of the question. In desert this dry, mounts were as mythical as the venomed fox, the two-headed bull. So when a dozen shaggy ponies sprinted down the settlement's only roadway, the women who'd risen early to fetch water from Jesephia's single meager spring turned with widened

74

eyes, gulped in the warm, dry air, and began to scream.

After that, pandemonium.

Arcans near the entrances of their houses jammed their feet against the rungs of their ladders in haste, yanking down and locking the doors behind them, praying aloud to Velja that the locks would hold. The sounds of slamming and praying joined the screams, the warning shouts, and that relentless pounding of hooves on sand.

The Arcans at the spring faced a choice that was not really a choice at all. A charging column of vicious warriors astride their mounts, hot panting breath and glinting drawn swords, lay between them and their homes. No safety in that direction. But in all other directions lay the open wastes, hardly safer. Once the sun rose high, anyone in the sand, if unprotected, would burn. There were six women at the spring. Three took off running into the emptiness, knowing the action might doom them, but willing to take the chance.

The three who remained were the Sehj sisters, the oldest two-and-twenty, the youngest ten-and-six. They'd come to live in Jesephia quite by accident, having left home to journey to the famous glass castle of Bryk, diverted along the way when a Seeker from Daybreak Palace made them an offer. For just a few years' commitment, they could make their fortunes tending Jesephia's only important resource: an enchanted mine that grew new gems every season. While no one knew whose magic had created the mine, these days it belonged, as most valuable things did, to Daybreak Palace. Four times a year, a messenger appeared to trade promised gold for polished gems, simple as could be.

The sisters' magic was earth magic, their skills complementary: Nel could dig tirelessly, Bijara could facet and polish a raw stone in her bare fist, and while Gogo's skills were rarely called on, they all knew her particular talent would be essential in a true emergency. Before, dozens of hard-bitten miners had been needed to free the gems of Jesephia from the earth; now all it took were these sisters, sharp-eyed and warmhearted, easygoing as kittens in the afternoon sun. They planned to serve five years in Jesephia, then use their earnings to wander the world.

But their horizon looked suddenly, terribly, far shorter. Misfortune had found them. The stomping, snorting ponies of the Scorpicae were already forming a circle, closing in.

For the first time, the sounds of Jesephia under siege included intelligible words, spoken clearly to waiting ears.

The oldest sister, Nel, said to the middle sister, Bijara, "I suppose now we know what happened to Myr." Their neighbor been missing for days, gone without a trace; speculation had run rampant. The invaders were their own explanation.

Bijara shook her head with a frown. "Not exactly. We don't know if she went willingly."

"We know enough," answered Nel, barely loud enough to be heard over the din, and no one could disagree. Whatever had happened to Myr, whether deserter or victim, she'd let their enemies know where the true value of Jesephia lay: with the three sisters of the Sehj matriclan and the valuable gems only they could bring forth with ease.

By some invisible signal, the hard-hooved ponies slowed, and the women on their backs resolved from blurs into fearsome warriors. The youngest sister, Golojandra, always called Gogo, found she could not pull her gaze away from the warrior women's faces. There was a light in their eyes, brighter and fiercer than she'd ever seen. Some carried swords, some bows, but even those whose hands bore no weapons stared down with unmistakable menace.

"Sisters," the warrior at the head of the group addressed them flatly. "I am Dree of the Scorpicae. We are here for the gems."

Nel, always the most forward of the three, raised her chin and called back, "Warriors. I am Nel of the Sehj matriclan. The gems are not yours to take."

Gogo never saw who threw the dagger, only heard it whistle past her ear. It landed in the hollow of Nel's throat. Nel's last breath was softer than a gasp—only her sisters were close enough to hear—and the constant noises of the Scorpicae's restless, shifting animals were enough to muffle the sound of her body falling to the ground.

Then the warrior who had called herself Dree raised her hand in a motion the remaining sisters couldn't quite interpret. Was she chastising whoever had thrown the dagger, telling the rest to halt? Or was she raising a hand to warn Gogo and Bijara, as if their sister's murder weren't warning enough?

Bijara stepped forward then, in front of their fallen sister, and raised her palm in an echo of the warrior Dree's motion. In a quiet aside to Gogo, almost nonchalantly, she said, "Run."

Gogo tried to whisper back without moving her lips. "No."

"Now," said Bijara, pulling her own dagger, and Gogo turned her head so she would not see, this time, the last moment of her sister's life.

And then Gogo ran.

On the wiry young messenger's first quarterly visit, he'd asked the Sehj sisters what they intended to do if attackers came to steal the gems. They had laughed, waving his concern away. But once he rode off they admitted, only to each other, that the danger was real. That very evening they'd made their plan.

Gogo's mind refused to work, unable to believe that she was now alone in the world, so she reached back for that long-ago conversation. Nel firmly explaining, Bijara questioning, Gogo listening. They'd gone through each scenario, every way things could go wrong or right in a large attack or a small one, violence or coercion, any way they might be compromised. She remembered what had worried her the most, the unthinkable, this exact nightmare. What if she were the last one left?

And she remembered what they had all, together, decided: first, she would lead the attackers straight where they wanted to go.

Gogo turned her back on the water-spring and sprinted across the flat sand. She heard warriors grunting and yanking on reins, ponies turning to follow. She was fast and they were scrambling.

Perhaps the warriors would simply shoot her in the back, but she didn't think so. She was the last sister left. They needed her.

Long before the Sehj sisters had been found, laborers had mined the magical gems with decidedly un-magical efforts. The construction of the original mine remained. Loose rock lay scattered through long portions of the tunnel, and all along its length, wooden braces held the structure aloft. They looked far too fragile to hold up the weight of heavy rock, but Gogo knew they'd been reinforced with magic. She'd been there when Myr had reinforced them, once a year, for as long as the Sehj sisters had worked here, and probably long before. For a moment she wondered again what Myr's fate had been, but she shut down that line of thought, refocused. Her own fate was the only one she could control.

She paused at the narrow entrance to the mine, turning back to watch the approach of the mounted warriors. They neared, then slowed. The leader, Dree, glanced over her companions and seemed to make a snap judgment; in a smooth motion she whipped one leg over the pony's side and dismounted seamlessly.

Then the warrior strode toward Gogo. When Dree's feet hit the ground, Gogo was surprised to see they were the same height. Gogo could easily follow her thought process; if the last Sehj sister needed to be chased into tunnels of unknown complexity, only a person the same size could follow wherever she went. Their height was the only similarity, Gogo realized. The warrior Dree was a compact ball of muscle with broad shoulders and strong thighs. Gogo had no hope of defeating her hand-to-hand. But that was not what she intended.

Gogo spun and dove through the mine's narrow entrance, into the dark beyond.

For a while she ran silently through the darkness, careful of her footing on the loose stones, and for long minutes, she wondered if she'd miscalculated. Maybe Dree's dismount had been a distraction. Maybe the Scorpicae would just wait outside for Gogo to appear again, hoping to starve her out. But that wouldn't work, not if they wanted easy access to the gems; at least one warrior would have to follow her through the twisting tunnels of the mine to their ultimate prize.

She peered back the way she'd came. Torchlight flickered against the rough rock walls, unmistakable. She picked up a loose stone and bounced it off the wall of the mine so the warrior or warriors who pursued her would hear which path she'd taken.

"This way," said one. The voice was unfamiliar; it was not the leader, but the other one.

"Getting tight," the other replied.

"You want to go on alone?" the first said. Her voice was not loud, but still easy to hear. It seemed they didn't realize that in the mine, so close and contained, their voices carried. Did tunnels not exist in Scorpica?

Gogo didn't have time to waste wondering. Everything depended on taking all the right turns. Luckily, she knew the mine as well as her own body. She knew where the tunnels were strongest and weakest, widest and narrowest. Most importantly, she knew what would bring it all down.

She scurried around three more corners as the ceiling grew ever lower. There. She reached into a nook and grabbed the long-handled stone-headed mallet, heavy enough it took both hands to lift and carry. She set her mouth in a grim line and charged ahead.

Behind her, Gogo heard the warriors' whispers. The one who wasn't Dree tripped and swore. Dree's voice carried clear as day. "Go back, if you can't follow." More oaths, then the sound of a single set of footsteps, growing more and more faint, retreating.

Two more turns, and there. Gogo had reached the end of this tunnel's branch, her destination: a wall of earth spangled like the night sky, stones as numerous as stars. She let herself be silhouetted against the sparkling wall, waiting.

When Dree came around the corner, torchlight blinded Gogo for a long moment. As she waited, she tested the weight of the mallet in her hands.

Forcing confidence into her voice, Gogo said to the interloper,

"And here we are."

Now that Gogo's eyes had adjusted, Dree's face was now visible. The expression on her face resolved from anger into wonder as she caught sight of the stunning, miraculous gems. Dree stood still, awed. Attached to her belt Gogo saw, as she expected, a long, pale string leading back through the tunnel they'd both taken to get here.

That was it, then, Gogo told herself. Now that the Scorpican knew where the gems were, the Arcan had outlived her usefulness. She wouldn't have long to do what needed to be done.

"Come," said Dree, drawing her sword. "This doesn't have to hurt."

"But it will," Gogo replied.

Now, she thought. *Here.*

Gogo hefted her mallet and swung. Not for the warrior, but for the wooden struts above both their heads. With a howl, Gogo smashed the stone head right into the thickest part of the strut, which crumbled immediately upon impact and gave way with a near-human groan.

Dree must have realized, a moment too late, what was happening, because a sound came from her, the beginning of something, "Ah—," before the roof of the tunnel caved in.

The world above them crumbled, smothering them both in clouds of earth, wiping out the lights and the gems and the air and life itself.

Everything went dark. Still. Gone.

After long, long moments, Gogo pressed her forehead against the earth that had fallen upon her—it was warm, the collapsed tunnel— and took a long, careful breath.

Her magic was still with her. She would have muttered a word of thanks to Velja if opening her lips wouldn't have flooded her mouth with sandy grit. Her earth magic made it possible to breathe while buried, but she wasn't one to tempt fate.

So that was that. Dree was dead; if the other warrior, the one who had handed over the torch, hadn't exited the tunnels quickly, she was too. Gogo had no regrets either way. No one above could possibly know that she was still alive down here, breathing almost as comfortably as she did aboveground, listening to the vibrations of the earth all around her as she wept silent, dirt-streaked tears.

For hours, Gogo listened. She could hear the rampaging high above her; over time, the hoofbeats grew fewer and fewer, the thumping on far-off doorways less, though whether that was because the warriors gave up or because they broke through into the houses below, she could not tell from her blind, smothered vantage. Likely the warriors knew that the desert surrounding Jesephia was vicious, and at some point in the day they would need to make a choice: return to their home base, press on to attack the next village, or stay here overnight. She hoped for impatience. If they stayed, she was only putting off the inevitable. If they found her alive, they would surely kill her as dead as they thought she already was.

When she'd heard nothing but silence for an hour of carefully marked and measured time, Gogo began, slowly and painfully, to claw her way back toward the surface. She'd done it before, though not from as far down.

When she broke through into the open air, she felt no sense of relief. The heaviness of the earth was still with her. She thought perhaps now that she was alone in the world, it might always be.

She'd kept her eyes firmly closed all the way up, but when she opened them at last, grit that had sneaked under her eyelids still ground at the whites. There was no water to wash them out; she let her tears do the work, running freely as she walked slowly across the deserted landscape to her home. The air carried a sharp tang of blood, but whether the Scorpicae had slain other Arcans besides Nel and Bijara of the Sehj, Gogo made no attempt to find out.

Still caked with grime, her skin visible only where the tears streaked downward, Gogo spent the afternoon burying her sisters under the hearth of the home they'd shared. It was slow work and she took her time. At one point the door above her head was flung open and she heard a voice calling down to her, thick with kindness and pity.

"Do you want to join us?" asked the voice. It was one of their neighbors, though Gogo couldn't tell which one without looking, and her head felt too heavy on her neck to lift.

"No, thank you," said Gogo politely.

"We're making for Caroji," said the voice.

Gogo didn't point out that Caroji was twenty leagues' walk away, and even if they did most of their walking in the cool of the night, the sun would dawn upon them the next day not having reached their destination. With enough water, temporary shelter, and luck, they might make it; but they would need all three. And there was no telling whether the remaining warriors had ridden in that direction. She merely repeated, "No, thank you," and set back to digging.

There were other words but she didn't respond to them, and at last, she heard the door at the top of her ladder released, gently, into place. She wouldn't leave until both her sisters lay where they belonged, under the hearth. It took hours. There was no one left to help her with the traditional binding, but she did her best. The Arcan tradition was that nothing that still had a use could be consigned to the grave. When their mother had died, Gogo remembered, the nearby households had brought their scraps to contribute. A flap of burlap here, a worn square of wool there. From such things shrouds were made. All three young sisters had been present, but a woman whose name Gogo no longer remembered had pieced the shroud together while they sat, too stunned to even feel grateful.

Today Gogo would have to go from house to house herself to retrieve whatever the fleeing residents of Jesephia had left behind. It seemed likely they'd all joined the desperate party heading for Caroji; there was no refuge closer. In their hurry, none had been thorough. After descending and scaling the ladders of four nearby houses, she'd filled her arms with more than enough abandoned fabric to wrap two corpses, even for a young woman with eyes so full of tears and grit that she could barely see.

Despite the rule, Gogo knew that loved ones often slipped something precious—a coin, a carven image, a ring—under the wrappings, but she was unable to think of an object that either Nel or Bijara had held dear.

In a way, she thought, she was the thing her sisters had considered most precious. They were certainly all that had ever mattered to her. Their dream of the future, of traveling without care and seeing more than others would ever see, that had carried true value. That dream was dead now, but she wouldn't dwell on it. She would survive the rest of the day moment by moment, task by task. She would deal with the future only when it became the present.

After several hours, Gogo had done what needed doing. Both bodies were wrapped in threadbare cloths that served no more purpose, strips of rag glued and pasted with clay. She'd been the smallest sister, and it was impossible to move either of the wrapped figures gently. In the end she dropped them awkwardly into place, embarrassed even though there was no one left to see. She piled dirt above them and smoothed and packed it down, then moved the logs and coals of the hearth fire back into place. She murmured the words of homegoing for both sisters at once, her voice hoarse from the niggling grains of sand that clung to the inside of her throat.

No matter who we are or what we do, we return at the end to Velja. We return, at the end, to the hearth.

One last place to dig, for another purpose entirely. It took longer than it would have with Nel's help, but Nel—always practical, Nel—had been careful not to bury their gold too deep. She'd known there was always a chance one of her sisters might need to dig it free without her.

All this lovely gold, thought Gogo as she scooped the thick-edged coins into her filthy hands. She hadn't realized how much they'd accrued. For a brief moment she wished she'd had the power over earth that their mother had had, the power to lift any amount of earth comfortably, to move it from place to place. But if she'd had her mother's power instead of her own, she wouldn't be alive right now, and she murmured an apology to Velja for second-guessing the god's wisdom. *I am grateful,* she whispered, the prayer grinding against the dust in her throat. *You are She who knows best. Bless my sisters' shades in the Underlands and grant that I may have more time before I join them, if it be Your will.*

How could she carry the gold? She couldn't, not all of it, unless she hauled it on a hide between two poles, the way she'd brought her sisters' bodies back to the hearth for burial. But that wasn't practical in the outside world. She'd take what she could carry and hide the rest, though she could foresee no future when she'd ever come back to fetch it.

Almost done, almost ready. She had a few raw gems—a few moments' work from Bijara would have polished them to a gleam, but Bijara's magic had left her, never to return—and tucked those away in a small bag strapped to her belly just under her breasts. The cascade of her loose tunic rendered the bag's curve invisible. Once the gold ran out, if the gold ran out, she'd trade those, and if the lack of polish made them less valuable, it also made them less likely to draw meaningful attention. The warriors had wanted the gems, probably to purchase goods to fuel their fight, or perhaps to pay off anyone they wanted to look the other way. Gogo hadn't been smart enough to be sent to the far-off Bastion for education, but she knew that even warriors used means besides violence to get what they wanted. Strategies were best in combination. As the Sehj sisters had been.

For one last moment, she considered her path. She could stay, she realized. For, say, a month. Then the palace messenger, that lean young man, would come for the season's stones. Perhaps she could leave with him, travel all the way to Daybreak Palace, see it with her own eyes. But no. She would go mad in the meantime, here with only the memories of her sisters for company. She'd be driven to suicide by their shades; she could see it all too clearly, even from this vantage, less than a day removed from a life that had been whole, now broken.

Besides, who knew what Daybreak Palace would do? The deal they'd made had been with all three sisters. The messenger might cancel the deal, or demand that Gogo stay on to satisfy it alone. She had a one-time possibility of breaking free of the agreement, and since no one knew where she was going—including her—no Seeker would be able to find her, even if Daybreak Palace bothered sending one.

So, like the other survivors, she left Jesephia, though she chose her own direction. Only haunted Godsbones lay to the east, on the other side of a caldera on the border that no self-respecting Arcan woman would dare approach; Caroji, where the other refugees had headed, that was west. To the north, eventually, was the border with Paxim.

To the south lay the shore of the Mockingwater, and Gogo had never seen the Mockingwater. It seemed as good a destination as any for a young woman of ten-and-six laden with a fortune in gold and gems but suddenly, unexpectedly alone in the world.

Unlike the other residents of Jesephia, Gogo didn't fear the severe desert heat; she could dig down underground and rest there, breathing without danger under the sand, until the sun set. She would emerge in the cool of the evening and resume walking, league after league, until she could dip her toes in the Mockingwater and stare out over its infinite distance toward the unknown horizon. She might die of thirst or starvation once the supplies in her pack ran out, but she would not boil to death in her own skin. That, she thought grimly, would have to pass for comfort. She and her sisters had always wanted to travel. Everything had changed, but she could still take that scrap of wish, that desire, and turn it into a future.

Gogo made only one more stop—back at the meager water-spring— to briskly wash the day's dirt and her sisters' blood from her body. She secured her travel pack high on her back. Then she took her gold, her gems, and her grief, and she carried it all southward, step by lonely step.

The day before, the village of Jesephia had fallen quiet toward evening much as it had murmured itself awake in the morning: a gradual ripple of hymns, yawns, whispers. Doors at the tops of ladders swung shut. Fires in hearths hissed as their coals were banked. Even in a remote desert settlement with no crying children or ecstatic lovers, sounds skittered and rippled through the evening. Complete silence came only later in the night. Tonight, like any other night, eventually there was silence, but not because its people ended their day with a sleep.

Tonight, Jesephia fell silent because there was no one left, not a soul, to make a sound.

8

ONLY THE QUEEN

Velja's Navel, where Godsbones borders Arca
Gretti, Azur

The same sunset that saw the village of Jesephia abandoned found the warrior Gretti dha Rhodarya staring at black earth under her sandals, contemplating murder.

Gretti remembered the triumph she'd felt a year earlier, selecting this very spot as the perfect base for an invasion of Arca. The broad, black-stoned caldera bridging the border between Arca and Godsbones—something like a valley, but bowl-shaped—was easily defended by perimeter guards, and the last place their enemies would think to find them. According to warriors who'd served in the queen of Arca's Queensguard, the Arcans shunned this spot, believing it bad luck. They called it Velja's Navel. As the sun sank behind the blackened, ridged edges of the caldera, casting the day's last light over the desolate red rocks of Godsbones on one side and, on the other, over Arca's golden sands, bands of Scorpicae gathered around their fires with confidence. They were nestled snug in the navel of their enemy's god.

If she'd still supported the war, Gretti supposed she'd feel triumphant looking at this black dirt. Instead, her throat tightened. Hopeful that Tamura's ruthlessness would bring their endangered nation safely through the Drought of Girls, Gretti had counseled her, drawn up plans to penetrate Arca, done more than any other Scorpican to ready their forces for battle. Only when the Drought ended, Tamura hadn't called off the attack.

And now, her usually nimble mind blank, Gretti could think of only one way to stop all-out war: killing Tamura.

Hoofbeats sounded, accompanied by the telltale rattling noise of two-wheeled carts, heralding the return of a raiding party. Two had ridden out that morning; this one was first to return.

"We bear gifts from Chagos!" called a merry voice, and Gretti's throat tightened further, knowing what had been done to secure those gifts. Chagos was the easternmost trading post of Arca, stocked with goods for any number of far-flung desert villages. Like Velja's Navel, Gretti had chosen it herself, months ago, to target.

"Hail, warriors!" A chorus of shouts welcomed the raiders. "Hail, warriors!"

Raiders unloaded their stolen goods in the flickering firelight to cheers of admiration, sacks of grain piling high, wine in barrels forming a line like sentinels behind them. Warriors were clapping each other on the back, giving and accepting praise with broad grins. The silhouette of a warrior—Gretti thought it might be Sarkh—raised a double-handled jug high overhead with both hands. She cried, "To the Scorpion's glory!"

The Scorpion didn't ask for this, thought Gretti. *Only the queen.*

Queen Tamura dha Mada stood proudly in the firelight, accepting a slosh of hammerwine poured into her cup, then raised it high to join the toast. Her laughter turned Gretti's stomach. All around them, blood stained the arms and armor of women Gretti had grown up knowing as warriors who served with honor, ruled by reason. This was what Tamura had made of them.

Someone handed the queen a joint of roasted meat, and she smiled her thanks and hunkered down next to her sister warriors to eat, licking grease off her fingers. Gretti slipped through the shadows, avoiding the brightest firelight. In silence she stood behind Tamura's hunched form.

Dozens, perhaps hundreds, of warriors over the years had suggested that Gretti Challenge Tamura. Combat to the death had been Tamura's path to power; she could not be surprised if she herself were Challenged. Countless times Gretti had pictured herself saying the words. *To you, Tamura dha Mada, I speak the Words of Challenge.* But how would that end? Tamura would simply kill Gretti and go on being queen.

But tonight, Gretti had realized that while Challenge was the honorable choice, it wasn't the only one. She didn't have to Challenge Tamura for the queenship. She could simply kill her where she crouched, right here, right now.

Hand on her blade, Gretti let the wild seed sprout in her mind.

A knife in the side of the neck would do it. Gretti only had to step forward and drive it in before anyone stopped her, and in this situation, she almost certainly could; everyone was merry, distracted. The knives they held for cutting meat were sure to turn on her after she'd done it, but what difference did that make, if the deed was done? Tamura would be gone. Tamura, whose choice had transformed these warriors from a protective web binding the queendoms together to a hard-thrust spear that would tear them apart.

Gretti tightened her grip on the knife. She wrapped her fingers around the handle, making a fist over the hilt. A tolerable warrior at best, better known for her good cheer than her fighting skills, she could never win a fair fight with Tamura. If she'd been born somewhere other than Scorpica, what would her life have been? A scholar, a shepherd, a nursemaid? Something more unusual, more rare?

She would never know. Warriors had one life, and thirty years of hers had already been spent. There was no way to take the years back and spend them differently.

When Gretti felt five fingertips in a star shape against her back, she recognized it first as a hunter's sign. She knew what it meant: *I am here, but the kill is yours.* It almost gave her the strength to leap forward and drive her knife in—almost—but instead she hesitated. It might or might not be a sign. She turned to see who had touched her.

It was Azur, face drawn with exhaustion, fingers already withdrawing from Gretti's back. It seemed obvious she had only meant her touch to catch Gretti's attention. In her free arm, Azur held her daughter Madazur, the youngest warrior of the Scorpicae, who had brought to an end the Drought of Girls.

"Gretti," she said in a soft voice. "Could you take Madazur? I'm hungry, and she won't sleep, and I don't think I can—"

But Gretti was already reaching for the child with one hand, tucking her knife back into her belt with the other. Once both hands were free, she took the girl in her arms and cradled her against her chest. Madazur's tiny eyes were wide open, catching and reflecting the firelight.

Azur didn't even stay to thank Gretti, but moved forward to take a position next to Tamura. The warrior there moved over to make room for Azur and handed her a portion of meat, quickly and graciously deferring to the most hallowed mother of her generation. Tired as she'd looked moments before, Azur seemed to come to life quickly, answering questions in an animated, authoritative tone. She was the only mother in years who could speak to what it was like to see her daughter appear; she was asked over and over again to tell the story. She obliged every time.

Gretti rocked and joggled the child, turning her back on the firelight and the warriors basking in its glow.

How wondrous to hold a baby in her arms, a tiny warrior with open eyes and round cheeks, after all these years. Gretti realized with a pang she couldn't even recall the correct words of the lullaby that had been sung for centuries, the one she'd first heard in her own childhood, what seemed like lifetimes ago. But she knew the tune. Hastily she assembled her own version of the lullaby, just for Madazur, Scorpica's newest warrior.

When the warrior has been born among us
Opened her eyes so dark and so deep
Those same eyes must close in the nighttime
When peace comes to the land, and sleep.

Though of course, thanks to Tamura's choice to attack Arca, there would not be peace. Perhaps not for a long time.

But Scorpica was not only Tamura, Gretti told herself. Perhaps she'd been thinking about it wrong. The end of the Drought, a future that had once seemed impossible, had come; this girl was proof. There had been a time before Tamura. There would be a time after her as well.

Gretti realized with a start that now she was older than Khara had been when her daughter Amankha was born, the day Khara beat back Mada's Challenge. Sometimes Gretti felt like she was still the innocent young woman of ten-and-six she'd been that day, rarely tested, never proven. She still remembered with perfect clarity the expression on Khara's face as she emerged from the birthing tent after killing Mada, resolved and regretful. And she could picture, too, both Khara's and Tamura's faces as they'd joined in their own battle a few years later, Khara's eyes bright with unshed tears, Tamura's jaw as tight and hard as iron. Gretti felt both too old and too young when she remembered that day, which remained, alone among all her memories, undimmed by time.

In the distance, Gretti heard the faint sound of approaching hoofbeats. A raiding party returning, the group that had gone to

Jesephia in search of a cache of valuable gems. Most other warriors around the fire still laughed, but Azur cocked her head at the far-off sound. Then Azur's gaze found Gretti's. Her message was clear. Gretti handed over the child, immediately missing the girl's comforting warmth. The First Mother turned to her daughter, cradling her gently, making a cooing sound as the child sought out her breast.

Gretti faded into the shadows, watching, waiting. She was neither a warmonger nor an assassin. Despite her age, she had not yet found her purpose. But perhaps tonight had shown her something. Perhaps she could look past the present chaos of Scorpica and commit herself to the nation's future. Keep an eye on Madazur and the girls who were sure to follow. In the meantime, here in the bowl of the sheltering caldera, there would always be food to cook, supplies to manage. She could offer assistance to the smith, Zalma, or even better, to the senior warrior Eghan, who used her extensive knowledge of herbcraft to act as healer. Gretti would make herself useful in saving lives instead of taking them. It was all, for now, that she could do.

✦

In the moment, any Scorpican warrior looking at Azur would see a mother lovingly tending her child, the precious baby drawing life itself from her milk-plumped breast. But the truth was that Azur only ever fed Madazur when others were watching. As much as she hated the strained ache of her breasts heavy with milk, she hated the suckling feeling more.

She was more than this, Azur told herself angrily, silently, even as the round-cheeked predator fed on her like a foal from a mare, a piglet from a sow. On nights when others cared for the child and her full breasts ached so badly the pain woke her from a sound sleep, Azur relieved the pain by squeezing the milk straight onto the black dirt of the caldera rather than catching it in a cup for later use. She was no goat, to be milked into a pail. She was the *mokhing* first mother in a generation and she couldn't have anything she wanted, no pleasures, no fighting, because her body was no longer hers.

Azur hadn't minded pregnancy, for the most part. She'd even enjoyed the feeling as her small breasts and narrow hips swelled to shocking new proportions, noticing that even her eyelashes grew thicker and longer than they'd ever been. The bodies of others were always of interest to her, and she observed the changes in her own fondly, as a friend or lover might. But then childbirth had come, not just painful but dislocating, making her a true stranger to herself. Now, even if she might be the most admired dam in the pasture, she feared remaining only, forever, a dam.

But she performed the rituals of devout motherhood for the sake of her fellow Scorpicae. They expected the First Mother to be an enthusiastic mother, so she would show them what looked like enthusiasm. She couldn't find a way back to her true self—her independent, death-dealing, pleasure-loving self—without their support.

Azur pretended to watch the suckling baby through lowered eyelashes, but as the raiding party returned from Jesephia, she couldn't keep herself from looking up. Immediately she began to count the horsewomen to see how many had returned, trying to distinguish any spoils they'd brought back from the battle in the inconstant firelight.

Angrily, Azur realized she couldn't even count the warriors reliably, let alone see what they bore. Her vision had been compromised by the pregnancy—something the older women who'd birthed warriors told her wasn't unusual—and it hadn't yet returned to normal. She had to remind herself not to let her fury show. She stroked the baby's downy skull, forcing herself to wait for her moment.

Tall, slim Khinar rose from the circle to hail the returned warriors with a raised hand. She was a recent addition to the council, wholly loyal to Tamura, feared throughout the ranks for her ruthlessness. If

Azur wanted to build on her own power and influence, she'd want Khinar on her side. But before Khinar could speak, the queen's voice rang out.

"Welcome, returned warriors," Tamura greeted them, her voice echoing in the dark hollow of the caldera. "We are eager to hear of your victory."

"Our victory was compromised," said a warrior named Pakh coldly, her words clipped. "We mourn losses."

A murmur of prayer passed around both the circle of seated warriors and the women on horseback, asking the Scorpion to welcome the fallen to the battlefield beyond.

Tamura said, her voice somewhat sharper than it had been, "We will need more explanation than that, Pakh."

Yet Pakh looked off to the side, clearly unwilling to share the news, which must have meant it was very bad indeed. The gathered warriors looked at each other, from the greenest to the most experienced like Khinar, but no one broke the silence.

Azur saw her chance and rose to her feet, causing Madazur to squawk in protest even as she continued to suckle greedily.

Tamura's head turned at the sound, just as Azur had hoped. In a warmer voice, she said, "Ah, my granddaughter, treasured beyond price. Let us all remember that when we fight, this is what we fight for." She reached out for Madazur.

The center of attention now, Azur turned the full beaming light of her smile on Tamura, her mother, her queen. These were the moments she needed to handle perfectly; enough of them would set her free. She slid her fingertip into the corner of the baby's mouth to gently break the suction before removing her from the breast, having learned the lesson of the child's powerful latch. The wet nipple popped free. Madazur's pursed lips still moved, seeking flesh, her unfocused eyes wandering. She complained softly but did not cry. Good.

Azur settled the baby gently into the waiting cradle of Tamura's embrace, murmuring, "There, there, child, these arms are welcoming arms."

Tamura smiled down at the baby, but when she spoke, it was to the assembled crowd, continuing the conversation. "Now I will hear the news. Were the gems secured?"

"No," admitted Pakh. "And we lost Marale and Dree."

"Dree," whispered Azur, the name escaping her lips by accident. Dree had been an excellent warrior, brave and brazen, though it was not her passion for the fight that leapt first to Azur's thoughts. Still, it was not only the vivid memory of a hasty, almost desperate coupling early in her pregnancy that had made her blurt the dead woman's name. Dree had been a member of the ruling council, one of Tamura's trusted advisers. With her passing, the council would be in need of another member. Instantly, Azur recognized her opportunity. Now she just needed to figure out how to seize it.

"Yes?" asked Tamura, who had not missed Azur's whisper. She missed nothing. That was why she was the queen.

"A particularly grave loss," said Azur, nothing in her voice but respect. "We honor her sacrifice."

"The Scorpion will surely welcome her company on the battlefield beyond," said a new voice behind them, and Azur and Tamura's heads were not the only ones that turned at the sound.

There stood Gretti dha Rhodarya, head cocked and arms folded, and the storm cloud that descended over Tamura's face upon seeing her was something to behold.

"I'm sorry to have missed your arrival. I was tending the fires," Gretti said to Pakh. "I have not heard what happened. Was Dree our only loss?"

"And Marale."

Gretti closed her eyes, nodding respect. "The rest of you are well?"

"Thank the Scorpion," Pakh said, finally seeming to regain her power of speech. "We returned with our health and our lives."

"But not the victory?" pressed Gretti.

Tamura snapped, "Not even the Scorpion won every battle, Gretti. If you think you can do better, would you like to lead the charge next time?"

Perhaps sensing the queen's tension, the baby began to fuss weakly. Gretti reached out her arms for the girl. Tamura seemed to consider this for a moment, the warriors watching, and passed the baby to Gretti. Probably she was hoping Madazur would continue to cry, but the baby calmed almost instantly. Gretti had often held and soothed her; Tamura had not had time.

Cradling the quieted child, Gretti looked up at Tamura and said, "I think we all know battle is not where my talents lie."

"You have talents?" Tamura replied quietly, and the tension in her voice set Azur's teeth on edge. The strain between the two women had been obvious since the day they set up camp in Velja's Navel, and seemed only to increase as time went on. Perhaps today, right here, it would boil over.

To interrupt the impasse, Azur held up her hand. She noted with satisfaction the ripple of interest that passed through the crowd as she did so. "I, for one, appreciate Gretti dha Rhodarya's good counsel. And my daughter approves of her, clearly. I value Gretti's presence here in camp, if my opinion is to be taken into account."

Khinar said, her voice sharp and dismissive, "Thank you, Azur dha Tamura, for your opinion. But I must note that you are not on the council."

Gretti looked up, eyes bright, and said clearly, "Perhaps she should be."

The ripple of interest intensified. Azur met Gretti's gaze over the baby's fuzz-covered head. Yes, the older woman had instinctively understood what she wanted. They would help each other. Both stood to benefit.

A councillor named Lu blurted, "She's young!"

Gretti said, "No younger than I myself was when I joined the council. Youth is no argument against competence."

"And untested in battle," said Khinar, gesturing toward Lu to show her agreement, as if Gretti had not spoken.

Azur opened her mouth to say, *Test me yourself, cloudheart,* but didn't have the chance.

Gretti interrupted, "Have you forgotten so quickly, Khinar? Azur was the best archer of the young Scorpicae before she even reached womanhood. She fought proudly in the earliest skirmish in the north of Paxim, long before this war. She stood toe-to-toe with our queen, her own mother, in defense of the memory of a fallen friend. Does that sound like someone who lacks for courage? Like someone who would not storm headlong into crowds of our enemies and slay them for the Scorpion's glory?"

Azur hadn't realized Gretti had been paying such close attention. But then again, that was the woman's true talent, wasn't it? Knowing where to look, when to act.

The next voice that spoke was Tamura's. "Azur is the mother of the first warrior of the new generation. I think it more than apt that she join my council."

Khinar looked to her queen, brow lowered, and then flicked at something in her pony's mane. "If you think so, Queen. The decision is yours."

"Yes," Tamura said, the corner of her mouth quirking up. "It is."

The conversation continued, but the rest was formality. Azur knew there would be no serious challenge. The queen had spoken.

Before the group dispersed, Gretti lifted the baby—now sleeping peacefully—over her shoulder and walked over to Azur. "An eventful evening. Would you like me to keep Madazur for the night?"

"Very kind of you," said Azur, stooping to kiss the baby's head.

Gretti said, "Welcome to the council." Then she was gone.

Back in her tent, though she tried to settle herself, Azur could not rest. What she really wanted was pleasures; pent-up desire was rippling under her skin like an itch, like a fever. She'd had no pleasures at all since that hasty coupling with Dree, the last day before the Scorpicae began their march through Godsbones.

Before leaving Scorpica, the warriors had hunted game for days to build up their stores for travel. Tamura had given the order, though Azur suspected it had been Gretti's suggestion. Azur had never given much thought to Dree before; they'd been paired for the hunt at random. But then an unexpected cloudburst drove them to seek shelter in a small cave against the mountainside, and they'd laughed together, wiping rainwater from their eyes and shaking it from their short hair.

When Azur turned to look out the cave opening to see if the clouds had lifted, Dree caught her hand, tugging her gently back into the darkness. Azur had read the lustful invitation in Dree's wide-set eyes, and folding her hand into Dree's, she accepted. Moments later, Dree's compact body pressed hers against the nearest wall, her kisses fierce, almost frantic. Azur let herself be pinned and pleasured, relishing the other woman's obvious passion through lowered lashes, Dree untying the laces of her vest with such haste they threatened to rip. Even the burst of cold air on Azur's bare skin felt luscious. Dree splayed one hand across Azur's exposed rib cage to hold her in place and used the other hand to guide one of Azur's newly heavy breasts into her mouth, lips and tongue savoring every inch of skin. That was what Azur remembered best: the intense heat of Dree's mouth on that breast, hot and relentless, back when pleasure was all her breasts had ever been for.

After the hunt, they'd been assigned to different squads during the march, and Dree faded from Azur's mind as other concerns—the coming fight, the baby's nearing birth—loomed larger. Every now and then she would notice Dree at the edges of her vision, hovering nearby, but always facing away. Only last night, before the raiding party left for Jesephia, had Azur noticed Dree looking directly at her, some indefinable emotion in her lingering gaze. When Dree's eyes caught hers, Azur felt herself back in that cave again, swallowed in darkness, all hands and lips and wanting.

The mere memory sent lust surging through her. Her body was still knitting itself back together after the birth, but soon she expected to be completely recovered, and she was hungry for the full range of sensation. But there was too much at stake now to couple with just any warrior. Especially now that she was a member of the council in addition to being the famed First Mother. Watchers would associate power with her attention. No one's motives could be trusted. The only pleasure Azur could safely seek would come at her own hands, which she set to the task with brisk efficiency.

Afterward, drifting off to sleep in the blessedly quiet tent, Azur's mind was clear enough to focus on the momentous change today had wrought. A seat on the queen's council, a rare and precious honor. Azur pictured the look on Tamura's face when she'd announced it: pride, satisfaction. Elevating a daughter of hers to the council hadn't been the queen's idea, but she was fully in favor of it. Probably because she thought Azur would support her in the days to come. After all, before she had become one of Tamura's adopted daughters, Azur had been no one. Just a nameless, giftless girl her village had given over to the Scorpicae without complaint. She owed Tamura her life, her purpose, her joy, even her name. Everything.

But Azur would not be beholden. She, no one else, owned her future. She would simply have to be careful to navigate the currents, making deliberate choices at every step. Tamura's interests weren't the only ones in play.

In return for today's allyship, Gretti would want a favor, Azur was sure. Only time would tell what that favor might be.

9

CELEBRATION

The All-Mother's Years 516 and 517
Daybreak Palace
Beyda, Eminel

Beyda preferred to teach Eminel in the study room adjacent to her own bedchamber, so as not to tote fragile scrolls and books with disintegrating spines back and forth through the dusty tunnel, but the queen preferred to have Beyda come to her chambers. Which, Beyda had to admit, offered certain benefits. Chief among them was the service. The two of them sat, Beyda explaining and Eminel learning, trading books and papers, questions and answers, as they sipped tiny, fragile cups of the most delicious drink Beyda had tasted in her entire life: honeyed goat's milk. When that first sip of sweet, creamy liquid passed her lips, Beyda thought this new queen might be the best thing that had ever happened to her. She would have thanked her god for Eminel, if she'd had a god to thank.

Weeks later, when the novelty had faded but the work still needed doing, Beyda was still glad to visit every day. After all, the question she'd been researching had been there for centuries and would still be there when Beyda returned to it. The urgency was with the new, unready queen. If Eminel wasn't happy, Beyda would lose the comfortable quiet of the cellar quarters she had enjoyed ever since being assigned to the Arcan court, and the rich trove of documents dating back to the Great Peace and even before. The thought of delaying her study for a few months didn't disturb Beyda; the thought of halting it forever sent a shock of fear like lightning to her core.

The first order of business for the new queen had been to learn how the Talish cuff worked. The process had been sobering. Eminel had performed a few tasks to test her magic, simple things like lighting candles and snuffing them out again. Once she coaxed an uncharacteristic guffaw from the scribe by making Beyda's books fan out and flap themselves around the room like awkward, bottom-heavy birds. But not long after that, when Beyda explained patiently that the Talish cuff was only a reservoir, not a spring—every enchantment Eminel cast while wearing it used up life force that could only be replenished by draining something or someone living— Eminel's hands flew to her mouth. Since then, Beyda hadn't seen the new queen attempt a single sliver of magic. That was as it should be. To use magic now meant that if Eminel needed it at a crucial moment in the future, it might not be there for her. And while the rest of the court had been terrified into submission by Eminel's early displays of power, there would come a day when someone decided to test the limits of that power. Like the Talish cuff, Eminel's fearsome reputation wouldn't necessarily hold its initial strength forever.

After that, the two young women grew comfortable enough with each other that Eminel left the door between her private passage and Beyda's study room propped open with a copy of a thick book on underground building techniques so old the ink had faded beyond readability. No one had ever come into that room in the years since Beyda had arrived in Daybreak Palace, so neither Eminel nor Beyda was afraid of discovery. And if the door were closed, there seemed to be no way for Beyda to open the passage from her end. With the door propped open so she could make the journey, when she arrived at Eminel's end of the tunnel, Beyda would press her ear to the wooden planks and listen for sounds. If she heard the murmur of voices, she'd wait; hearing none, she'd rap softly with her knuckles at first, then rap louder and louder until Eminel opened the door. It was an excellent system, and Beyda became accustomed to plopping herself down in Eminel's chambers, reclining against a cushion or pillow, and passing hours.

They sometimes played a strategy game called *whishnuk*, not well known in Arca but common in the Bastion, with an extravagant set clearly gifted to a previous Arcan queen by some Bastion representative long ago. The pegboard itself consisted of seamlessly melded squares of different stones in subtle variations of tan, cream, flax. The pegs were a different matter entirely. Beyda had seen dozens of *whishnuk* sets in the Bastion, all with plain wooden pegs, but these were marvels of craftswomanship— not wood at all, but exotic stones neither of the women could identify, inlaid with complex metalwork in beautiful patterns. Half the time they were so distracted by the beauty of a particular peg that they forgot their strategy. But when they did play in earnest, Eminel always beat Beyda handily. It seemed the new queen had an intuition for how game play fit together, which pegs needed to be skipped over or detoured around, and which needed to be attacked head-on.

When they tired of *whishnuk*, though—most often, when Beyda tired of defeat—they turned back to the business of knowledge, as there was always more to ask, always more to know.

During one such session, quizzing Eminel on the history of the queens who had preceded her, Beyda popped a bite of date-filled sweet bun into her mouth and sighed with pleasure.

"Excuse me," said the current queen, "was that the last one? You told me you'd ask before eating the last one."

"I didn't know it was the last one," lied Beyda, who had avoided asking on purpose, because if she'd asked, Eminel would have claimed the bun for herself. Beyda hadn't known Eminel before she'd become queen, but the scribe suspected that the absolute power of ruling a nation of magicians was going to the sorcerer-queen's head.

Yet proud as she was, the queen was also vulnerable, and both of them knew it. So Beyda was happy to help Eminel build her strength in any practical way. Eminel certainly seemed like a better person than Mirriam had been—a low bar, that—and better than the vast majority of Arcan queens before her. Better to work with this one, Beyda reasoned, than to take her chances on whomever the blue glass snake might choose next.

"I could ring for more," said Eminel, already reaching for the bell.

"Wait. Answer a few questions first. Then another date bun can be your reward."

Eminel rolled her eyes, as she always did at Beyda's attempts to curtail her luxuries. Then she gave in, also as she always did. "Ask, then."

Beyda took no joy in lingering on the details of the violent deaths of Arcan royalty. The most recent, Mirri's death at Sessadon's hands, seemed to be actually one of the least gruesome. But Beyda knew that nearly every woman at court could recite the entire list of Arcan queens from Kruvesis through Mirriam and Mirrida to Eminel herself, including each queen's exploits and her eventual ruination, from memory. It was essential to ensure that Eminel could do the same.

"Sozan," said Beyda.

Eminel pondered. "You sure I can't have a bun first?"

"Answers first. Buns after."

Eminel stuck out her bottom lip in a pout, then considered. "Did herself in, didn't she? Overreaching spell. Turned herself inside out."

Beyda made a face and said, "Unfortunately, yes."

"Next?"

"Gizem."

"Yes. All right. Gizem." Eminel was quiet for a moment, but then her eyes lit up. "Queen only five days, if I remember right. Stabbed in the neck by her sister Keje."

"That's right. And then what happened to Keje?"

"Much luckier. Reigned five years instead of five days."

"And what brought her down?"

"Same thing, in the end. Someone else ruthless who wanted her power."

Beyda pointed an accusing finger. "You're stalling."

Eminel blew a breath through pursed lips, then smiled. "I'm not *not* stalling. Give me a hint?"

"Viyan."

"Viyan," repeated Eminel, "Viyan." She went to take a sip of milk, but the cup was empty. "Oh, and now we're out of milk, too? You have to let me call for more!"

"Two more answers, and you can call. I promise. I'll be quick."

"Better be," pouted Eminel, but with a good-natured air. She drummed her fingers on her chin, then the edge of the table, thinking. "Viyan . . . oh!"

"Yes?"

"Viyan did the rebellion."

"Well, that's one way to put it."

Eminel pulled herself up straighter, reminding Beyda of the students in Bastion classrooms, all business. "Viyan led a rebellion against Keje. Marshaled everyone together and coordinated an attack. Took out Keje herself with a spell that sucked the air from the queen's lungs and smothered her still standing. And then, during the victory celebration, with the head of every matriclan that had rebelled, Viyan toasted their shared victory. She tricked them into drinking poisoned wine. Killed every last one. So nobody had the strength to challenge her for, what was it? Fifty years or so."

"All correct." Beyda nodded.

"All right . . . so who was strong enough to bring that one down? That's the next question, isn't it?"

"Yes, that's the next question. Who comes after Viyan?"

"Easy! I don't remember her name, but it's the random one, the one who didn't even know she was all-magic, who happened upon Queen Viyan in disguise. Quarreled with her and let loose her magic, not even knowing who she was fighting. Right? That one."

"Yes, that one," echoed Beyda, holding herself back from rolling her eyes. She knew all of Eminel's procrastination techniques by now. "And what was her name?"

"Velja's lower beard," grumbled Eminel. "I remember the whole story and you're going to insist I remember her *name*?"

"I mean, do you think the head of Clan Ishta remembers her name? Clan Merve? Clan Binaj?" Beyda prodded.

Eminel flicked her fingers at Beyda and pouted again. "And she's the whole reason they started bringing every all-magic girl to Daybreak Palace! So that couldn't happen again."

"Yes."

"Yes! So—"

Beyda prompted, "And her name?"

Eminel frowned. "Starts with an *M*. Mesk-something. I don't know."

"Meskhanye."

"Meskhanye!" echoed Eminel triumphantly. "Can we have more milk and buns now?"

"We can."

The queen rang the bell merrily, looking for a moment far younger than her ten-and-five years. "At last."

This time, when the basket of date-filled buns, sweet and lush and still warm from the ovens, was nearly depleted, Beyda let Eminel have the last bite.

◆

What passed for winter in Arca had given way to spring, then to early summer, when change came. Eminel had built her knowledge with Beyda's help—what a lucky thing, finding that passage—and once the queen felt strong enough, she'd resumed her predecessor's practice of regularly hearing complaints from the court. These were generally petty grievances, and whether or not the complainants were truly happy with her rulings, at least no one tried to publicly assassinate her again, which she had to consider progress.

Eminel had set strict rules around the hearing of grievances, all designed for safety, though they also gave the appearance of formality and importance. Beyda was always there, recording the names of those who appeared before they were allowed to vent their spleen, and members of the Queensguard were always present both outside and within the audience chamber. Eminel heard these complaints in the same room where she'd slain Archis. The room was much larger than the task called for, but the throne was comfortable, and Eminel felt the setting made the point.

Even though she was conserving the life force in her Talish cuff, she'd begun to draw on a touch of magic every now and again to help resolve these disputes. A nudge, a hint, and everyone was more agreeable. But in truth she felt more of a sense of accomplishment if she manipulated their responses through other means: shame, social pressure, suggestion, threats. Everything she'd learned from working with Beyda came in handy, and if Eminel didn't always remember exactly the right fact at the right time, she hit more than she missed. The magicians of the Arcan court were like the pegs in her *whishnuk* set; highly ornamental, difficult to keep track of, but easy enough to move where you wanted them if you kept the whole board in mind.

The first time Eminel considered using her magic to defend herself bodily was a dry afternoon in early summer. She was in the middle of a thorny conference with two rivals from Binaj and Merve, each of whom believed she had been promised a certain man's hand in marriage by a highly placed member of the Volkan matriclan, and tempers were running high. It didn't help when one of the Queensguard who'd been stationed outside came running into the room, shouting, with more shouting sounds coming from the open door behind her.

Reflexively, Eminel clutched both fists, nails biting into her palms. She readied her left hand, the one with the Talish cuff, and summoned an incantation for explosive power, holding it ready.

But then the guard, tall and reedlike, stopped in her tracks and gazed up at Eminel. There was a look of stunned delight on her long, narrow face. "My queen! Such wonderful news!"

And then Eminel heard the shouts outside more clearly, and nothing could have surprised her more: they were shouts of joy and delight.

"A girl, a girl! A girl has been born in Sulinelle! The Drought of Girls is over!"

Jaws dropped. The rivals embraced spontaneously, though they drew away from each other and glared again immediately afterward. The third party to the dispute reached out to hug the only other person nearby, who happened to be Beyda, who staggered two steps back with a look on her face that might have been disgust or terror. The Volkan courtier stammered an apology and wrapped her arms around herself instead. The atmosphere of joy was contagious, and before long, they were all smiling, chattering excitedly.

Heart racing, flooded with emotion, Eminel beamed at her Queensguard and said the first thing that came to her mind. "We'll have a celebration!"

"Oh yes," said one of the rivals, who gave a charming gap-toothed smile. "A celebration!"

"Yes!" Eminel said. She'd blurted her idea, but the more she considered it, the more obvious it seemed that it was not just the best, but the only, course of action. She would be nervous to move in a crowd, but nothing less than a revel would do. She could spend some of her precious magic to put up a protective shield around herself; for such an occasion, the effort was worth it. But she would have to manage the event in the most careful way, which meant not giving any potential assassins time to plan. "It will be tonight!"

The woman with the gap-toothed smile said, "Please, our matriclan would be happy to make the arrangements. Let us take care of everything."

Her rival, smothering her irritation with a voice as smooth as butter, said, "But of course we can help as well. A representative from Merve will be here momentarily."

Then the reedlike guard spoke up, saying, "But of course our matriclan would also be happy to use our resources! I can send a message right away."

"Send them all," Eminel said, a kind of mad delight bubbling up within her. The Drought was over! If there were ever a day to go a little mad, it was today. Besides, she was the queen, wasn't she? And suddenly she was no longer queen of a slowly dying nation, but a vibrant, growing one. The occasion must be marked.

Eminel commanded her guards in a firm but joyous voice. "Bring three representatives from every clan to this room to engage in the planning of tonight's festivities. There is much work to be done. I want to be kicking up my heels before today's sun sets."

The scurrying was gratifying. Even more gratifying was the moment mere hours later when Eminel walked into the high-ceilinged audience chamber and saw hundreds of Arcans milling, laughing, dancing, drinking, and smiling. The Drought was over. A new, promising day had begun.

While she had spent the past few months in simple robes the color of sand, Eminel decided that it was time to dress the part of queen, and she allowed servants to bring her ceremonial robes that Mirrida had worn before her. There wasn't time to weave something from scratch. Besides, she would risk favoring one matriclan too much over another depending on which weaver she summoned. This was safer.

From the variety of lush garments presented, Eminel chose a clinging gown that glimmered black or green depending on the light, like the outer wings of the fast-moving beetles known as dynamos. It had a dramatic neckline, skimming the hollow at the bottom of her throat in the front and plunging in the back, everywhere else a swirling showcase for the lavish amount of fabric, which billowed as she moved. She wanted something that set her apart, and this gown would do it. She remembered from her time with Fasiq's Rovers how clothing could be protection, camouflage, declaration, performance, or indulgence. This gown was all five together.

When Eminel entered the audience chamber, everyone stared openly at her, though she supposed they would have done that no matter what she wore. The stares seemed appreciative, at least. She'd thought the attention would make her uncomfortable after so long in isolation, but it didn't. In fact, tonight's crowd reminded her of the pilgrims on the Isle of Luck, their excitement to see her and what she represented, their focus on what she could do for them. She realized that here, too, so far she had simply been an instrument. It was time for these women to see her as their monarch, the one who ruled them all, not just the judge of their disputes. If the courtiers didn't like what they saw, they, not her, were the ones who would have to change.

The Queensguard stayed with Eminel as she came farther into the room, sniffing the air to savor the sharp scent of lily wine and a warmer, creamier smell that reminded her of baked cheese rubbed with wild garlic. Music trilled and piped from an unknown source, probably magic. Any courtier might have a talent that involved drawing only a little life force; in this way, their talents varied. Absently she stroked the Talish cuff. Next to Beyda, it was her most valuable companion.

She didn't see Beyda yet, but that was not surprising. The scribe had not been excited by the idea of celebrating. Still, Eminel hoped she'd be here, both for business and as a friend.

She caught a glimpse of someone in a nondescript gray robe over on the far end of the room. Was it Beyda? Certainly no courtier Eminel had ever met would pass up the opportunity to be dazzlingly gowned. But before Eminel could get close enough to see, the woman with the gap-toothed smile from earlier stepped forward, signaling for the queen's attention.

"Firelle, isn't it?" asked Eminel politely, but her gaze was already gliding past the grinning woman to the two men who stood just behind Firelle on either side.

After the presentation of the clans upon her arrival at Daybreak Palace, Eminel could count the number of Arcan men she'd seen up close on one hand. None had brought complaints to her, and now she wondered if they even had the standing to do so. Now she saw her first two men of the court up close, dark-haired and lovely, their skin glowing with health, their expressions open and expectant. The sight left her momentarily speechless.

Firelle said quietly, "Pardon me, Queen. Now that the Drought has ended, you will need husbands. Allow me to introduce Xerio and Alisher of the Binaj matriclan. The old saying goes, 'One for the head and one for the bed,' but I think you'll find that our men are not so limited."

Taking a modest step back, Firelle ushered the young men forward. They bowed their heads while approaching, reminding Eminel of the supplicants on the Isle of Luck. Then the one on the right raised his head, and his smile was a mesmerizing treasure, so beautiful. She felt honored to have been the one to put that smile on his breathtaking face.

"I honor you, Queen Eminel," he said in a musical voice. "My name is Xerio."

What could she say? It wasn't like it made sense to say her name in return. Everyone knew who she was. Xerio himself, she was sure, knew.

Xerio's face had no imperfections, but his mouth was particularly winning, with a plump bottom lip that drew Eminel's eye. As she watched that mouth, the smile faded and shifted into something else, not a smile anymore, but an expression of anticipation, excitement. Xerio was almost as tall as she, and when he drew even nearer, he tilted his head to place his mouth just next to her ear. In not much more than a whisper, he said, "I wish we were alone, my queen."

She was glad the sudden gooseflesh on her arms was covered by the long sleeves of the dynamo-green gown. She could feel a shiver rippling across the upper half of her back, open to the room's cool air.

Xerio continued, his breath warm against the curve of her ear, "I would love nothing more than to rub your feet at the end of a long day spent ruling. If you'd allow me to visit you later, I should like to give you a demonstration."

Eminel almost bade him kneel at her feet right there, calling his bluff, but before she could respond to his bold invitation, the other man lay his long fingers on her left arm, murmuring, "I honor you, Queen Eminel."

She looked down at the floor away from both of them, trying to collect herself. She had to remember that Arcan men's magic made them appealing. This was magic, what she felt. She would be vulnerable to charm, never having developed any defense against it. When those hundreds, even thousands, of pilgrims had visited the temple of the God of Luck when she and Sessadon had served as priests there, she'd seen them as Sessadon did, not even people, really. She didn't know what it was to either resist charm or give in to it. She knew that this was a fraught moment, but she was completely unprepared to handle it in any elegant way. Where was Beyda, anyway? She would help. Eminel needed help.

But Beyda was nowhere to be seen. Eminel was surrounded, but not by allies, not by friends. She'd have to figure out a way forward alone.

And then she found it. These men were just *whishnuk* pegs, she told herself. Beautiful, alluring, but simply pieces on a board, to be moved where she, the queen, wanted. Pegs did not decide. The player decided.

Eminel turned to the man on the left, Alisher. He was still far away enough that she couldn't feel his breath on her skin. In a toneless voice, she asked, "And what are your intentions? I can find out myself, but I would prefer you tell me in your own words."

"I will never hide a single thing from you, my queen," said Alisher, his lovely face serious, his eyes dark and deep. He was more elegant than Xerio, his movements full of grace, his manner intelligent. He had the longest lashes Eminel had ever seen, ink-black, night-black. "You can always count on my complete honesty."

Xerio, still so close to her, spoke again. "An alliance with the Binaj matriclan would strengthen your position in the court. All the more so if you choose both of us. Our sisters and cousins are mighty."

For a moment, Eminel's confidence faltered. She shouldn't have let them start. It would be hard to resist any offer; yet she could not accept, not if she wanted to keep her freedom. She could make no promises to Binaj, nor to any other matriclan. It wasn't out of the question that she would choose one or more husbands for mercenary reasons, eventually, but it was too early to do so. She'd just come out of a cocoon, perhaps no longer a caterpillar, but the youngest of butterflies, not yet ready to unfurl her wings.

Unsure how to react, Eminel instead let her eyes drift back to the crowd, searching for somewhere to fix her gaze. The riot of color and sound threatened to unbalance her. She looked for calm and, at last, found it: the young woman who stood motionless by the far door, her eyes cool on Eminel's. Beyda. Yes, that had been her: dressed both colorlessly and modestly, in a long gray tunic that covered her arms to the wrists and her legs to the calves. A belt of the same fabric accentuated her waist between the swell of generous hips and an equally generous bosom. Her hairstyle tonight was unusual, loose to her shoulders in a spray of wild curls. In her sturdy hands she bore a writing pad, a reed pen, and a small bottle of ink for dipping. She was a muted sparrow in a sea of cardinals.

Eminel grinned, then raised a hand and beckoned to her.

Slowly Beyda came. When she arrived, she didn't bow, and with her hands engaged with her writing tools, neither did she reach out.

"Did you have need of me?" the scribe asked.

"Always," said Eminel wryly, but had little else to say. She was too conscious of the men, who made her too wary to relax, but she was too intrigued to send them away. She needed Beyda, but here in public, among so many glamorous courtiers, it was like they were both other people entirely.

It felt like the men were drawing even nearer, though as the crowd in the audience chamber grew larger, perhaps there was simply less room. Xerio was still so close to her, and Alisher now drew his dancing fingers up her arm in a way that drove shivers all across her flesh. Even knowing they were trying to seduce her, here in plain sight of nearly the entire court, didn't make them even a whit less seductive.

Beyda's eyes narrowed. "Perhaps, if there's an offer of marriage on the table, I should write that down. Your names, please?"

Eminel needed a minute to think, but the power of her bodily feelings choked out thought like ivy choking a slender tree. Eminel had grown up with a constant stream of simple, affectionate touches from those she loved, and she hadn't realized how much she'd missed that—during the years with Sessadon and especially since the sorcerer's death—until she felt Alisher's fingers on her skin. And these fingers, reaching out not with affection but seduction, ignited even more powerful sensations. The feelings kept threatening to overwhelm her. A word would stop them, the fingers on her skin, the breath on her neck. But she didn't say that word. She didn't want them to stop.

Responding to Beyda's question without turning to face her, Alisher whispered his own name against the bare flesh of Eminel's shoulder, his hot breath laced with promise.

Eminel felt a hard knot in her throat as she swallowed.

"And you, potential second husband?" Beyda asked.

"Xerio," answered the younger of the two men, daring to rest his cheek against the queen's neck, close to where the snake necklace lay. The warmth of his skin on hers made her feel weak in the knees. Eminel felt herself almost stumble. Did everyone see? Did they know?

"Very well," Beyda went on, calm and steady, with a consistency Eminel clung to. "I shall record that you are here, interacting with the queen."

Was it her imagination, thought Eminel, or was there a hint of sarcasm in the way Beyda said *interacting*?

The men were simply ignoring the scribe now, but she continued.

Planting her feet, seemingly entirely comfortable, Beyda said, "It is my business to record the doings of the queen. What is taking place here . . ." She trailed off a moment, then seemed to regain her composure. "What is taking place here is clearly of some import. So who will explain that import to me? Are these men here by the queen's invitation? Are their attentions unwanted? Is the truth somewhere in between? I must record the facts for posterity. It's what a scribe does."

Eminel noticed after a moment that while Xerio's hands had stilled—a shame, that—Alisher had begun kissing her neck as if no one else in the room mattered, the feathery brush of his lips against the tender skin above her neckline sending a long, rolling wave of a shiver through her body.

"Queen Eminel," said the scribe, addressing her directly, not a trace of shame or judgment in her gaze. "Yours is the truth I look to accept. Do you wish it recorded that you are entertaining suitors, or is there some other note I should make?"

As pleasurable as she found the feeling of Alisher's lips, Eminel latched on tight to the clarity she saw in Beyda's face. It made all the difference. With the scribe there to anchor her, Eminel would align her body and mind, do what she knew was right without resorting to magic to make it easier. Easier now would mean harder later.

She could do it, Eminel told herself. She could resist the nearly irresistible. She moved her shoulder in a small but purposeful shift away from Alisher, turning her head so she wouldn't see disappointment clouding his beautiful face. Then she said to Beyda, "I don't believe we need to enter this into the official record. Thank you for your attention, scribe."

"Of course. I am yours to command." Again, that hint of sarcasm.

"Actually, let us make a simple note," said Eminel, regaining her confidence. "Two of my subjects paid me a visit, during the celebration, to offer their support for my reign. I solemnly thanked them and they left."

She could not see Alisher's face behind her shoulder, but Xerio lifted his head to look at her with regret, plus a hint of something more complicated.

Eminel repeated, this time more firmly, "They left."

This time both men took the hint and went, though as Alisher ran his finger down the length of her bare arm as he stepped away, there was a part of her, possibly more than half, that didn't want him to go. But she held herself still and let the moment, and the men, pass.

Once they'd left her side, Eminel worked hard to take a deep breath without looking like she was taking one. Everyone's eyes were on her. It was important to seem like she didn't have a care in the world. She reminded herself that this was supposed to be a celebration. Still, she couldn't resist sending a signal. She raised her right hand deliberately and smoothed her hair with her palm so they could all see the Talish cuff, the lamplight catching its polished surface and making it glow.

She knew the motion had worked when they all, as if commanded, looked away.

She must remain completely aware, thought Eminel. Completely invulnerable. She tried to see the positive: at least, she thought, no one had tried to kill her. The rest of the celebration passed in a blur. Eminel didn't let any more potential husbands close enough to touch, though at least a dozen were presented. She stayed above it all. She kept moving.

She raised a shield around her mind just in case. It seemed an easier thing, a smaller thing, to guard her own mind instead of trying to detect what was in every other mind at the celebration. She drew life force from the cuff to feed her magic, focusing her mind and her energy partly by instinct and partly using methods she'd found in the books Beyda showed her. Perhaps because she was already worn out from the excitement, the enchantment began to drain her more quickly than she'd anticipated. She pressed her feet harder against the floor, hoping she wouldn't slump.

The spell held. Eminel took one breath and then another. She was protected, she was alive, but she was tired. She would head back to her rooms. Too tired to stay.

✦

Back in her rooms, nearly too exhausted to stand, Eminel sank onto the cushioned bench and stared at the Talish cuff. She dropped the spell as soon as she was alone, safe behind closed doors. But was it already too late? Had she used up too much of the stored life force, left herself defenseless? She wished she'd asked Beyda to accompany her. The Queensguard posted outside her door would turn any visitors away, but still. The skin underneath the cuff tingled, a prickling sensation that worried her, though she could not articulate exactly why.

Tomorrow she would venture outside the walls of Daybreak Palace, find some way to gather life force from something not human. Or she could draw just a little bit from her rivals, couldn't she? A tiny bit from a hundred women couldn't hurt each one too much. But she should try a bird or fox or something first. She couldn't afford to get it wrong. Maybe Beyda had a scroll with an enchantment that could help her figure it out. She'd ask tomorrow.

Then, suddenly, without sound, the door to her chamber opened.

The woman entering through the open door was of middle age, soft and rounded everywhere, shockingly comfortable-looking compared to the courtiers Eminel had just seen at the party. If she'd been there, Eminel hadn't noticed her. The visitor's robe was not artfully draped or brightly dyed, merely functional, and her hair was twisted into a simple knot at the nape of her neck. Eminel wasn't even sure she was Arcan.

Unsure what to say, Eminel began with, "Hello?"

"I honor you as the chosen of Velja, Queen Eminel," said the woman, bowing low, but not waiting for a response before she stood again.

"I directed my Queensguard not to allow visitors," Eminel replied, mustering enough energy to sound imperious. "Yet here you stand."

Beaming, the woman said in a gentle, calming voice, "We are so glad you're here. I came to offer my services and support."

"Again," said Eminel, "I wonder aloud how you gained entry."

The woman seemed unbothered. "I apologize for interrupting your rest. I won't stay long. But it's important that you know me. Now that the Drought of Girls has ended, I will be the most helpful woman you can imagine."

A bit impatiently, Eminel said, "Well, then, who are you?"

The woman's smile remained gentle, her voice soothing. "My name is Sobek. My matriclan is Perai; you won't have heard of it, I'm sure, as it no longer ranks high. But it did once, and will again, because of me. My responsibility in the palace is to manage the discovery, retrieval, and training of all-magic girls."

"Oh," said Eminel, and hoped the wave of emotion didn't show on her face. Her mother had been so afraid of what would happen if Eminel's all-magic were discovered that she had left her life behind and fled the country, stayed on the run for years until death itself had stopped her running. This woman, or someone like her, was responsible for that fear.

Sobek said, "It is true that my skills have not been needed these past few years."

"Almost fifteen."

"Yes, to discover new girls, almost fifteen," said Sobek, the faintest hint of irritation in her tone. "But, Queen Eminel, everything is different now. There will be new girls, and some of them will be all-magic. You'll need my help to manage them."

"Before I accept your help," Eminel said, "a question."

"Of course. Ask anything you like."

"During the whole drought, a decade and a half, there have been no new all-magic girls," she began.

There was no condescension in Sobek's tone as she confirmed, "Because there have been no girls at all, yes."

"What happened to the older ones?"

"Queen?" A shadow fluttered across Sobek's face.

"What happened to them?" Eminel pressed, her head clearing at last. "The ones who came here for training during my predecessor's time. At the time of the last Sun Rites only two remained, I was told. Then there was only Archis, and with her death, now there are none." Eminel tried not to sound guilty for making that last bit come to pass. "Did they go back to their home villages? Are there any still here?"

Sobek asked carefully, "You want to know if there are any rivals for your throne, Queen Eminel?"

"No," she said in frustration. "No. I just want to know what *happened* to them." What she really meant but could not ask was, *If I had been brought here, what would have happened to* me?

"That depends," Sobek said, meeting Eminel's eyes but still giving the impression of wanting to dodge the question. Her words were slower than before, more halting. "Over the years . . . some asked to be sent back to their villages, those without enough talent to train, and the others, well, over the years, things happened . . . there are none here, in any case, Queen. You have nothing to worry about."

Eminel had never had any confidence in someone who told her not to worry. She wasn't going to make an exception today.

Sobek was still talking. "Because we expect to hear news soon of all-magic girls, I need to know how you would like to handle things. And I would like to give you some advice."

"Advice?" repeated Eminel, just to give herself time to think.

"Yes," said the woman, then something about her manner changed. She stepped closer, put her hand on Eminel's shoulder. Eminel thought that should have annoyed her, but she didn't feel annoyed. Sobek's hand was firm but gentle, warm through the shoulder of Eminel's fine-woven gown. Something in her touch felt wonderful. And when the woman spoke again, her words sounded so logical, so right, Eminel couldn't believe she hadn't thought of this already.

"I think you'll want to keep as many of your predecessor's guidelines in place as possible," said Sobek, "and even increase your vigilance. Send a new array of Seekers to search for all-magic; I can help arrange for and train them. They'll alert the palace as soon as such girls are born. Then, if the girls don't report of their own volition—most do, of course—send someone to fetch them here immediately."

Eminel found herself nodding.

The woman's soothing voice then said, "Then, once we have enough candidates, well, the highest-ranking matriclans very much enjoy the entertainment of watching the girls go through the trials."

"Trials?" She was curious. Sobek explained things so well, Eminel had no doubt she could explain what these trials might be. Eminel thought about asking the question, but the thought curled up and faded away. For the moment, she only needed to listen. Sobek would tell her anything she needed to know.

"Yes, they're very necessary," Sobek intoned. "To test the girls and determine the extent of their powers. Publicly, in competition. It's really the best way to find out what they're capable of. Once we know, we have a much better sense of where they might fit into the court. After so many years without girls, it will be doubly important to reinstate the complete system. The sponsors—well, we can talk more about that when it's time."

"Yes," Eminel found herself saying.

Sobek went on, her voice still warm and welcoming. "And of course there's the matter of my recompense. Your predecessor rewarded me for sustaining the system, of course, but it will be so much more challenging to rebuild from nothing. You understand."

"Yes, of course, of course," Eminel murmured.

They talked a while longer and Eminel agreed to everything the woman said. The trials, the funds, the plans. All such good ideas.

After Sobek swept out of the room, Eminel felt a slight chill. Was that a draft, in these luxurious rooms? If it was, nothing to be done about it now. Tomorrow was soon enough to worry about any of these things. That burst of energy she felt while Sobek was here vanished along with Sobek. Now Eminel felt exhausted again. She had pushed herself to do too much and now she was paying the price.

Eminel rubbed the Talish cuff. If she focused all her awareness on it, she could feel the hum of life force within, but she didn't know how many more enchantments that force could power. And it did not, in this moment, make her feel more alive.

Turning her back to the door, Eminel walked the few steps to the bed and let herself fall, finally. She wanted to sleep for days. Still, as the darkness of sleep began to draw her down, Eminel worried. Tonight, what would she dream? The blue woman had visited her regularly in her dreams, calling for chaos. The queen's other dreams had been vivid too, dreams of her past, as alive and bright and absorbing as if it were her present. Eminel could not fully rest even in her sleep, unsure what the night would bring.

Despite the wonderful news of the day and the confidence of having secured a newfound ally, Eminel was not sure, just now, of anything.

✦ 10 ✦

FEAST

Ursu, Paxim
Heliane, Paulus

Holding her white hair back with one hand against her shoulder, bending as far as her stiff spine would let her bend, Heliane leaned over the platter of small cakes. Her nose almost touched the nearest. Dessert was a silly thing to focus on when there was so much else at stake, and yet. The banquet to celebrate the end of the Drought of Girls was not simply an evening meal; it was essential that she manage every moment, every player, to perfection. She should be preparing for that. But cakes were easier than politics. Cakes, she could see, smell, and touch. Cakes, she could taste.

Heliane plucked a dainty cake from the center of the arrangement with her free hand and took a small bite. Tender and sweet, yes. Some kind of nut in them, ground fine with figs, gently laced with honey. Beautifully made. These would please her guests, certainly.

And she wanted them pleased. She wanted them satiated, impressed, off their guard. They were the three most powerful women in Paxim after her, the highest-ranking members of the Senate and Assembly, and she had invited them here to impress upon them the inevitability of her son becoming king.

Five of them at table, a lucky number. She'd asked Ama, begging her pardon, to serve as wine bearer; though it was far outside Ama's usual responsibilities, the queen also wanted the bodyguard in the room, and stationing her at the entrance as a guard would send entirely the wrong message. This was a night for the most powerful women in Paxim to relax, to celebrate, to talk among themselves. The fact that Paulus would be present with them at the table would be message enough.

A young man of ten-and-five now, but still her boy, her precious boy. She wished she could have taught him nothing at all about the world. She wanted him to keep his dreamy, innocent charm. He loved hearing stories of great loves and great deeds. He believed that bravery and intelligence were rewarded. He believed the gods gave freely.

But his mother knew better. Just as the gods gave, they took away. The All-Mother couldn't be relied on to grant humankind even a crumb. Any rewards would come not by a divine hand, but by a woman's own hard work, smart dealings, and sheer cussedness. When Heliane had been a child, she too had believed the best. Faith had been stripped from her in the long years since.

Upon the unexpected death of her mother, Heliane had risen to become a queen of ten-and-two; she'd married on a whim at two-and-twenty. In the years after, the All-Mother had taken almost everything, almost everyone, from her. The first boy stillborn, then three more children lost, one by one—the older girl, the older boy, the younger girl—and at last her husband. She'd had no way of knowing how long she'd get to keep any of them. That was the cruelest part. Accidents and diseases had stolen the people dearest in the world to her, plucked and carried them off, like the long fingers of an expert thief. Paulus, that dreaming, curious boy, was the only one left. He would be a ruling king if it killed her. It likely would.

The ache in Heliane's back turned sharp, and she had to brace herself against the five-sided table, straightening up until she found the point where the pain began to subside. If she caught the ache early enough, it wouldn't become a spasm. She'd had these spells at irregular intervals since her near death at the hands of the sorcerer Sessadon at the Rites of the Bloody-Handed. She stared down at the detailed mosaic under her feet to distract her mind until she could be sure she hadn't pushed herself too far.

She'd never been fond of this mosaic, finding it too ostentatious, but her guests would be impressed. It had been the fashion a century ago, when this splendid palace was built, to represent the leavings of a feast on the floor of a room used for dining. Discarded nut shells, the bones of a small bird, fruit peelings and pits, all were depicted in the mosaic now below her feet. Fortunately or unfortunately, the artist had been enormously talented. Had Heliane not known that no meals had been eaten in this room for months, she might have leaned down to pick up the walnut shell near the heel of her left foot. But it was not a real shell. If she rubbed her fingers over it, she'd feel nothing but the smooth surface of tile.

Heliane had kept the feast modest by design, not too much for five people, nothing too showy. But each course would be the best of everything. This wasn't a meal, not really. It was a battle in a long campaign.

Intimidation in the guise of hospitable ease. That was what she needed. It was here in the heavy, precious knives, the plates polished to a gleam, the pale cloth that draped the table, just as soft as the robes she wore. In the lacquered duck and the peeled chestnuts and the rare oranges with flesh as red as blood. All crowned with those delicious cakes. If she stole another, could she rearrange the remainder to form a slightly different pattern, disguising her theft?

No, it wouldn't come out right. She would have to settle for a bite from the kitchens if she wanted anything else before they arrived. Nothing laid out on that spotless, waiting cloth was to be disturbed.

The table was perfect. Now all it needed was the guests.

When she'd spoken with them in the Senate and Assembly earlier that day, she could have told the three lawmakers she wished to invite them to her residence for an evening meal. But that wouldn't have made the point she wanted to make. Instead she'd waited two hours— just long enough for them to get through their gossip, head back to their homes, and begin to settle in for the evening—and then sent messengers to request their appearance at the palace.

They would all know the request was not really a request.

She was still the queen, even weakened, even though she knew they called her the Fading Queen. They'd called her that ever since she'd lost her husband and all but one of her children. Still, she had refused to fade for as long as she could, until she'd nearly died at the hands of the rogue sorcerer. Now the pain was chipping away at her. But she still had her mind, her wit. As long as she could keep the people's confidence, which she would do for as long as she could, there was reason to hope.

To know that one was dying was exquisitely painful, yes, but there was also a pleasure in it. It allowed one to let go of carrying too much. She no longer spent time worrying about the finer points of politics or her legacy. Let the Senate and the Assembly do what they would. Let other women agonize over the long-term effects of Paxim filling up with men the way that a hole in the ground, during a hard summer storm, fills up with rain. She couldn't prevent that world from coming to pass and she would never live in it. She had only two goals, interlinked: prepare her son for his reign, and live long enough to see that reign secured.

She heard the metallic clang of the gong ring down the hallway, rippling against the stones and tiles like water. Her first guest had arrived. Heliane didn't go down to greet her, nor would she meet the other two when they entered; she would wait here, patient and stately, for them all to come to her. Her back twinged again. She braced her hand against the table. No one would see her tremble.

This consul, this leader of the Assembly, this magistrate. Let them come to her as she had commanded them. Let them be reminded Heliane, only Heliane, was queen. And with them would sit the kingling, royal and anointed. Paulus would do his lineage proud. A kingling could be just as powerful as a queenling if the queen wished it so.

The future would sit at that table. The three of them could accept it or they could understand that someone else, someone of the queen's choosing and not their own, would have their seat.

"Queen! The All-Mother's blessings on you and yours!" It was Decima first, full of what seemed to be genuine good cheer. The consul was a tall woman with deep-set eyes under thin brows, a nimble face that wore every expression well, from a forbidding scowl to a childish pout. Now that face sported the warmest of smiles. Decima had worked with the queen for two decades, and while they didn't always agree, their relationship was marked by mutual respect. Heliane extended her arms and welcomed Decima in a hearty embrace. She would acknowledge the other two more formally, but she was glad Decima had arrived first so she could greet her as what she was: a friend.

"Hide these for later," Decima said, in a softer, coy voice, and laid a soft pouch in her palm.

Without looking, Heliane knew what was inside: dried pears candied with snowdrop honey and rosemary, her favorite delicacy in all the world. They were hard to come by, embarrassingly dear. It was too kind of Decima to secure them for her—the cost of snowdrop honey was outrageous—but though the queen always considered declining the gift, she never actually did.

"Don't you worry," Heliane said, tucking the pouch into a fold of her gown to conceal it from the other guests. "There's no chance I'll share."

A few minutes later both Juni and Stellari arrived, and with formal bows and handshakes, Heliane welcomed the younger women to the feast. Juni was tentative, surprising in a politician, though as the least powerful of the three she was likely intimidated by the company. She had never before been to the palace. Heliane caught Juni staring down at the ornate mosaic, distracted even before their formal greetings were complete. Stellari, on the other hand, was all smooth confidence. Her braids were impeccable, her robe draped just so. There was something about her impenetrability that Heliane didn't care for. Though perhaps, Heliane had to admit, she might just be jealous. The young woman was a star on the rise: capable, whip-smart, inspiring to her peers. All the things Heliane had once been plus all the things—young, lovely, full of possibility—she would never be again. What Fading Queen, if she were honest with herself, would claim never to envy those who shone bright?

"Ah, and here is our fifth guest," Heliane said to the other women, and did not bother to conceal her pleasure at what a striking figure her son cut in his bright white robe. His shoulder-length hair was bound neatly at the nape of his neck, which made him look older and more severe. She was pleased that he'd figured this out on his own, though she tried not to read too much into it. Maybe it had been Inbar's idea. The thoughtful *cosmete* had put the queen's hair up in a dramatic but simple series of waves earlier, leaving time to consult with Paulus as well.

"*Thenas.*" Paulus nodded to the three visitors, using the most formal, polite term to address a group of powerful women. This, his mother had coached him on.

They nodded back to him, not bowing as they did to the queen, but obviously considering their actions carefully, showing their respect.

Heliane reached out for her son's elbow and guided him gently forward to complete the introductions. "Kingling Paulus, may I introduce Decima of Gencer, our consul; Stellari of Calladocia, our magistrate; and Juni of Kamal, leader of the Assembly."

Paulus extended his hand smoothly to each, repeated each name, and acquitted himself well. But Heliane detected the slightest of tremors in him. He was indeed nervous. She hoped it would pass once they sat down. She also hoped that having Ama in the room would help calm him, but might the bodyguard distract him instead? Had Heliane miscalculated? She could arrange the dishes and the decor down to the gnat's eyelash, and had, but people could never be predicted with complete certainty, even by the world's best diplomat.

Once the seated guests turned their attention to their plates, Heliane turned hers to the women she had brought here to intimidate. The queen watched carefully to see exactly what they would reach for and when, filing away the information for later, all the while being sure not to give away how closely she was watching. The demands of her station were many. They were exhausting, but she would not give them up until she was good and ready.

"First things first," Heliane said, once they were all seated. "Let's raise a cup to the end of the Drought."

"To the end of the Drought," they all echoed, cups high.

"In some ways, everything going forward will be different," said the queen. "There is hope again. I know the public confidence will return, even soar. But in some ways our country has been irrevocably changed by the Drought. And not all of those changes are bad. Change is powerful. Change is how we grow."

The others nodded along. She watched them carefully for disagreement, but they were all on their best behavior. Only Juni failed to control herself, her eyes flicking over to Stellari's face for a reaction the magistrate didn't give, then settling her gaze on Paulus, whose attention seemed to be wholly focused on his cup of wine.

From there the conversation flowed easily, more or less, as a delicious flatbread was served, then the exquisite duck, which Stellari in particular complimented effusively.

"How are your children, Decima?" asked the queen.

"Well, thank you."

"Do you have children?" Paulus asked Juni.

She flushed and said, "No, not yet."

"Oh, that's too bad, they're such a joy," said Decima. "Isn't that right, Stellari?"

Smoothly, Stellari touched her napkin to her lips, and said, "Correct as usual, Consul."

Decima turned to Paulus. "Stellari has a child of, what is it now, seven years old?"

"Yes, almost eight."

"Though your husband continues to live so far away in Calladocia?"

Heliane was familiar with the rumors; she didn't like that Decima alluded to them at table, a place that should be above petty squabbles. If Stellari chose to keep her child with her in the capital instead of sending him home to be raised by his father, that was her choice. The rumors were a way of attempting to explain the unusual arrangement, but the only one who really knew Stellari's mind was Stellari.

With no obvious emotion, Stellari speared a delicate slice of duck, then raised her gaze to Decima. "My husband doesn't particularly enjoy the capital, and he's very dedicated to his mother. I think it's admirable. I work a great deal, as you know. I don't make for consistent company."

"You gave a stirring speech in the Senate the very day you gave birth, did you not?" said the queen, her voice mild. "Very dedicated."

"I did." The magistrate turned to Heliane and went on, her voice even but not warm. "The same day the Senate voted to allow men to stand for office in the Assembly. You voted without me."

"An unfortunate coincidence," said the queen.

Juni said, "No one chooses when the child comes," an empty platitude, and for just a heartbeat Heliane saw disdain in Stellari's eyes before the senator returned to her placid expression. Stellari lifted the delicate forkful of duck to her mouth and nibbled it, possibly to keep herself from speaking words she might regret.

The rest of the conversation was perfectly innocuous. Heliane was almost ready to consider the night a success. But then she noticed that Paulus had drained the last of his wine again.

Paulus gestured again to Ama, who filled his cup, her face as blank as any good servant's would be, showing no emotion at her host's intemperance. But the kingling had indulged too much already, that was clear to Heliane. She vibrated like a plucked string. A little wine was a good thing, and at events like this, someone usually had a little more than a little. Tonight, though, she'd have put her money on Juni. There was something undisciplined about the young head of the Assembly, a lack of rigor. But tonight Juni sipped at her wine judiciously, careful only to match Stellari sip for sip. Especially in front of Decima, who drank nothing fermented, it would show poorly if Paulus were to overindulge. Heliane couldn't risk calling attention to it. She would have to figure out how drunk her son was and how best to provide an exit at the right moment.

The moment came just as the honey cakes were served.

"Before we enjoy our last sweet bites, senators," the queen said, "will you join me for tea on the upper balcony? The view is exquisite. Or feel free to take a last cup of wine with you, should you choose. Ama, please?" She gestured at her own cup.

When Ama bent to pour her wine, Heliane whispered discreetly in her nearest ear, "Get him out of here. Please."

The young woman gave a bob of her head so minor it looked accidental, but Heliane was sure her message had been received. And as the women proceeded to the patio, Paulus murmured, "Good night to you, *thenas*," and melted away.

Not the resounding conclusion to the evening she'd hoped for, thought Heliane, but at least not an embarrassing one. Her son had made a good impression, and that was what she expected them all to remember. Heliane breathed an invisible sigh of relief before following her guests outside, her aching back forcing her head high.

✦

When Ama whispered in his ear, "Say good night to the *thenas* and come with me," Paulus had been almost too surprised to follow her lead. But follow he did, speaking the words as she'd told him, then trailing her out of the room. Once in the hall outside the banquet room, she looked one way down the hall, then the other, then back into his face, her own gaze all business.

"Where can we walk?" she asked. "We should have a walk."

Paulus was confused, his head a little slow from the wine. "We should?"

"Yes," Ama said, a bit insistently. "Let's go. You lead the way."

He thought of a place he wanted to show her. She was always in charge. Now she was letting him be in charge instead, and he liked the change. It was only after several minutes' walking in silence that he thought about how odd it was that she'd pulled him away from the banquet, and when the earth seemed to sway gently, he realized what had happened. He'd been nervous, and she'd been the one to pour his wine; he'd kept draining his cup partly to calm his nerves and partly so he'd have an excuse to call her back again. It wasn't her fault, it was his. He was tipsy. Possibly a little more than tipsy. Walking would help. He felt a fool, but the worst thing he could do was call attention to it. He was sober enough to know that much.

Once they were outside, he murmured to her, "You have me at a disadvantage."

"Do I?"

"You didn't have any wine. You should have a lot of wine. Then we'd be even."

"Don't be a fool, we'll never be even," murmured Ama, and though she didn't exactly sound upset, her tone wasn't light enough to be joking.

They walked through the varied shades of evening, from complete dark to the warm glow of a torch and then into the next patch of darkness again, for what seemed like a long time.

"Here," he said. "I bet you've never been to this stable."

"No. The others, yes, but not this one."

Then he was in the familiar spot, standing in front of Philomel's stall. In the lamplight her striking gold-white coat didn't gleam as brightly as it did during the day, as if lit from within, but her beauty and rarity were still obvious. He reached his hand out to touch the mare's soft nose.

"This is Philomel," he said. "Philomel, this is Ama. Make her feel welcome, won't you?"

The horse nickered softly.

"Hello, girl. You're a lovely thing." Ama's voice was tender, so warm that she almost sounded like a different person.

"Isn't she just," he said on an exhale.

"Philomel, you said? She's a beautiful animal."

"She used to have more spirit," he said. Did he sound wistful? "She was younger then. Of course, we all were."

"How old is she?"

"Older than I am. You too, I suspect."

"Is she yours?" Ama asked. "Why haven't I seen you ride her?"

"Because of Zofi," he said, and even all these years later, his throat narrowed.

For all the stories Ama hadn't heard in Paxim, it appeared she had heard this one. She did not ask who Zofi was, only reached out to stroke the horse's nose. Quietly, she said, "I'm sorry."

"Philomel was a gift from Sestia," he said, still looking only at the horse even as he spoke to Ama. It felt easier that way. "The nation, not the god, though I suppose from the god as well. At the Sun Rites one year, the High Xara gifted each of the other queens one of her finest horses. Especially in this color—you'll have to see her during the day, she's breathtaking in the sun, as if she were crafted from pure gold— this breed is particular to Sestia. The Sestians almost never part with these horses, you understand, so Philomel was a prize of great worth, and my mother took great pride in her. She gave Philomel her pick of the stallions, and from there, Philomel gave us a whole generation of her progeny. They're not as gold as she is, but they have beautiful coats, and oh, the speed. But because Philomel was so valuable, my mother wouldn't let her be ridden."

"But your sister rode her."

"Once. Philomel was not only precious, but high-spirited. Untamed. Impossible to control. But my mother's insistence that the horse not be ridden only increased Zofi's thirst to ride her. And you— you know the result."

Ama nodded somberly.

"Afterward, the stable master wanted the horse put down. Philomel had been injured, you know, in the accident. My mother said no. She was out of her mind with grief and she still said, 'No, there will be no more death today. There has been enough.'"

Ama murmured, "And she's been here ever since."

"My mother or the horse?" asked Paulus, coming back to himself, a little less dizzy from the wine, but now a little dizzier from Ama's nearness. She had readied herself in some unusual way for the banquet, he realized. He had been this close to her before, many times, while they sparred, but then she'd smelled like sweat and metal. Now the only smells on her were olive oil and her own skin, and he wasn't prepared for how that made him feel.

Ama smiled at his jest, generously, and turned her gaze on the horse. The bodyguard looked different in this light, less serious, warmer somehow.

Almost without thinking, Paulus took his hand off the horse's nose and placed it on Ama's arm, warm, steady.

They'd touched each other before, of course. She was always touching him to correct him, to show him how to grip his dagger, how to flip the loop at the top of his sword's sheath to draw it in one smooth motion. But he'd never put a hand on her in this way. He heard her sharp intake of breath and dropped his hand, fearing he'd made her uncomfortable. Then he heard her sigh faintly. There was no anger or discomfort in that sigh. He liked knowing she was reacting to him. Even if it had been a stupid thing to do, he didn't regret his impulsivity.

"You tensed up," he said. "When I touched you."

"And?" She kept her eyes on the horse.

"You're not afraid of me." It was a statement, not a question.

"No."

He chose his words carefully. "Then you feel some other way."

"It would seem so."

Did she mean that as encouragement? He didn't know what to say. It seemed unwise, even with this much wine in him, to just blurt out how intriguing he found her. Instead he said, trying to keep his tone level, "Have you ever tried to tame a wild animal?"

"We didn't have wild animals in the Bastion."

"Of course," he said. "How silly. I pictured you growing up in Scorpica, but of course you didn't. Not everyone who fights is a warrior, not anymore."

"Not anymore," she echoed softly. Then she seemed to shake off her moodiness and said, "Kingling, are you telling me you'll try to tame me? I'm afraid that's not likely."

"No, no," he said. "I just wanted to tell you a story."

"You always do," she said, but there was no reproof in her tone. Only something like—could it be—fondness?

He searched for the right words. "A truly wild animal will never get close enough for you to see it, let alone touch it. I used to watch a little red fox out my window. Sleek, beautiful little thing. My sister wanted to pet it, but every time she reached for it, she'd just chase it away. I learned to be content with watching it from a distance. That was the most I could hope for."

"All animals are wild," replied Ama easily, seeming to shrug him off. "Domestication is a myth. No one's a better example of that than Philomel here. Bred to bear a rider, and then one day—"

Paulus held up his hand, closing his eyes briefly. It didn't take Ama long to recognize her mistake.

"I'm sorry," she rushed to say, and then her hand was on his arm, and he couldn't deny the warmth that surged across his skin under her fingertips. "I don't always—sometimes I just say what comes to mind."

"No," he said. "Don't apologize. I brought you here, didn't I? I'm not unaware of her history. But I've come to terms with it. I had years to."

"How does a person do it?" she asked. "Accept the unacceptable?"

"You just do, I suppose."

Ama looked away, looked back. "You, I mean. How did *you* do it?"

He shrugged. "I was so young when Zo died. I remember being sad, of course, but not the details. It's just still there, the loss, always. A gong is struck, it makes a sound, and the vibration goes on for so, so long. You go forward as best you can. And I make sense of the world the best way I know how. A lot of times, I use stories, actually."

"Do tell."

Her interest seemed genuine, and he wanted to keep her attention, so he quickly went on. "Every time I meet someone, or have a new experience, I try to find some parallel in stories. When Zofi died, I thought of Philomel as the legendary winged horse Golagal, who they say bore the first queen of Paxim, Roksana, through the sky so she could be by the side of her ailing daughter."

"Did the ailing daughter recover?"

"Well . . . no," said Paulus haltingly. It wasn't the question he suspected she'd ask. "She died, but Roksana was there with her, to ease her passage, to hold her hand."

Ama's whole body seemed to shiver, which surprised him. Her gaze settled back on the horse's nose. "Oh. Your Paximite stories don't always have a happy ending, then."

"No. But it helped me to think of Philomel as a holy, magical horse, something from a story. But it's not just the big things. When I was in the Bastion, there was one night—did you ever go to the tunnels they called Warrenward?"

"Warrenward!" she exclaimed, her attention back on him. Then she lifted a brow. "Didn't you leave the Bastion when you were ten-and-two? A little young for Warrenward, I'd say."

"I didn't know that. I liked this girl . . . I thought she liked me, too." He would've been embarrassed to tell anyone else the story, but here in the quiet stable with Ama, it just seemed like the right thing to say. "She said if I'd follow her down to Warrenward, she'd kiss me, and I thought it sounded like a good idea."

"Let me guess. She had something else in mind."

"Wanted to play a trick on the foreign kingling, I guess. So we go down into these dark tunnels, all twists and turns. I can barely see. She has a small torch, and she's holding my hand to lead me. I'm so nervous, my heart's pounding, and we just keep walking deeper under the earth. Then we get to a little blind alley—you know how those tunnels just end, and that's where people . . ." He trailed off, uncertain now that he was too far in to stop.

She saved him by completing the sentence in a whisper. ". . . get close."

"Yes. That. So I think that's what's about to happen. We're together in this little space, and she tells me to close my eyes, and then . . . when I open them, she's gone."

"And what does this have to do with your stories?"

"I'm getting to that. So picture me, ten-and-two, lost and wandering, for Panic's sake, scared out of my mind. Endless dark. Circling tunnels. I call out for help a couple of times, but not too loud, because I'm also scared of what might answer. So mostly I wander in silence."

The look on Ama's face shifted. Paulus couldn't tell exactly what she was thinking, but he guessed perhaps her expression was disbelief. He hurried to tell the rest of the story.

"So in some of the stories, when new spirits go to the Underlands and they don't know where to go, the Child leads them. Across the bone bridge, right, you know? And here I am, so lost, wandering in a place that might as well be the Underlands. I might as well be a shade. Then out of nowhere, someone's hand slides into my hand. Another kid, like me, I think, because the hand's the same size as my hand. And I feel better immediately, almost like magic. There's no light or anything, this person doesn't have a torch. Just a hand. And a voice. Because then I hear this whisper, and they say . . ."

"I know the way," whispered Ama.

"What?" stammered Paulus. He was still tipsy, but this was another level of dizziness, of confusion. "I mean, yes, that's what they said, and . . . wait. Have I told you this story before?"

"You didn't need to," Ama replied, and slid her hand into his.

Those hands—his, hers—were bigger than they had been three years before. But the size of those hands had matched then, heel to fingertip, and they still matched now. And Paulus knew.

Stunned, he said, "It was you. How was it you?"

"I used to lose myself there on purpose," Ama said in a voice of wonder. "I liked the mystery of it. There was never enough mystery in the Bastion. You knew your place, you knew your future, you knew everything. That wasn't for me. So when I was ten-and-two, I'd head down into Warrenward—not for the same reason the older kids were going there, you understand—and get myself lost in the dark purely so I could find my way out again."

"So you were the one who found me."

"It seems so," said Ama. "I didn't know it was you. If there'd been more light . . ."

Paulus completed her sentence. "Perhaps things would have been different."

Ama smiled her rare smile. "Perhaps."

He turned to her, face-to-face, putting his hands on both her shoulders. "Thank you. I didn't say it then, I was too surprised. You didn't even stay long enough for me to say my thanks. So I'm saying it now."

For once, possibly the first time, Ama would not meet his gaze. She looked down, backed away, letting his hands drop.

Perhaps he had misread the misty, fond look in her eyes? He began to frame the words of an apology in his head, but before he could get them together, she was speaking again.

"Well, I think you've sobered up enough to go to sleep," Ama said briskly. "Let's get you back to your rooms, and we'll have a cup of tea and sleep the rest of it off. Things will look different in the morning."

So with a last pat on Philomel's golden muzzle, he followed Ama back toward the palace. He knew she was right; some things would look different in the morning. But he was thinking of Ama herself differently now, with the night's revelations, and he was pretty sure a few hours' sleep wasn't going to change that.

She sent a servant for tea, the brew with the little yellow flowers that was always good for sleep, and stood over him while he drank a cup. She was right, he was starting to feel more levelheaded, at least in some ways. In others, he was still reeling.

And as she lay her bedroll in front of his door, preparing to guard him from the world, he let one word slip. "Wait."

Unhurried, unruffled, Ama turned to him. He could see her just well enough in the half-light from the lamp next to his bed to read the emotion in her eyes. It looked like curiosity.

"Sleep in the bed," he blurted. "This once."

There was a long pause before she asked, "Why?"

"To keep an eye on me. What if I get sick during the night?"

"Such an invitation!" she said, her tone light. "You want to get sick on me?"

"I don't. I won't," he said. "Just—just be near me. I can tell you a story, or you can tell me one. We can whisper to each other and then just drift off. Please."

Her expression was skeptical, but he searched her eyes with his, and what he saw there didn't look like resistance.

"Do I have to command you?" he asked, the tenderness in his voice balancing the imperious words, making them into something else altogether. "As your future king?"

A smirk showed on her face. "Do I have to knock you unconscious? As your bodyguard?"

"That won't be necessary."

"I could."

He half laughed, putting his hands up in mock surrender. "I know you could. But please. I'd . . . I'd really like your company."

It was a risk, one he would never have felt brave enough to undertake without the drink. Or was the drink a convenient excuse, not a reason? Was it really his romantic streak that, now that he knew they'd already met once in the dark half a world away, made him call out to her, pat the bed next to him, gaze at her in hope? It would make a story for the ages.

She lay down on the bed, and a tiny sigh escaped her mouth as she settled into it.

"As soft as it looks?"

"Softer," she said.

Suddenly Paulus couldn't look at her. She was too near. Too real. This same woman had touched all over his body to correct his form—his shoulders, his hands, his hips, even the lower part of his belly—and yet he felt like if they touched now, if his flesh merely brushed against hers, he might burst into flame.

He didn't reach out for her and she didn't reach out for him. Instead he began to tell her a story. Afterward she told him one. He turned off the lamp. Their voices twined in the dark, a reminder of the few words they'd exchanged several years before, neither of them knowing fate would bring them back together. He would never remember which of them fell asleep first, the musical words of the other still whispering in their ear.

In the morning he awoke first, his mouth open, and he hastened to wipe the liquid from his lips before she noticed. Then he checked to see if she'd seen him, and he had to smother a laugh.

Ama was completely unconscious, sprawled out across the bed, one arm over her head and the other wrapped across her stomach. One leg was extended, the other tucked under her, disappearing under the hem of her rumpled sleep shift. He would not have believed someone could sleep so soundly in such an awkward position, but by all signs, she was completely dead to the world.

He didn't want to wake her. He wasn't sure he even could. So he slipped out of the bed long enough to grab a book, then slipped back in. His head ached, probably from the wine, and he knew he wouldn't be able to fall asleep again. He was too aware of her. Instead he settled in to read, careful not to crowd her.

When she awoke sometime later, her eyelids rising slowly like the palace's iron gate, he grinned a wide grin.

"Good morning," he said.

"Mmm?"

"So drowsy, my god of vigilance?" he whispered, a little afraid to break the spell, but wanting to tease her gently, to enjoy the rare moment where she was more vulnerable than he.

She regarded him through one half-open eye. It was hard to tell whether her mouth turned up at one corner, but he thought perhaps she had a shade of last night's smile.

"A whole new you," he said, smiling down.

She grunted and began to roll away from him, and without a conscious thought, he reached to bring her back. His hand caught her on the waist, just above the swell of one hip, the warmth of her body radiating through her thin shift. As soon as he made contact, she froze, but she didn't move away.

He said, "Admit it. You like the bed."

She rolled back in his direction, looking at the ceiling and not at him, but still, keeping their bodies in contact. Her voice still a little groggy, she said, "I sleep soundly in this bed. Not sure that's good."

"You had beds in the Bastion, didn't you? Bunks, anyway."

"Not like this," she replied. "I assume yours was the same as mine."

"Well, I never slept in yours," he said, and then felt the embarrassment that probably should have come upon him the night before. His hand was still on her waist. He left it there. "I mean, I didn't have cause to compare. But every bunk in my dormitory looked the same."

"That makes sense." Ama seemed fully awake now, her voice merely conversational. "They're very dedicated to the idea of the same treatment for everyone. Even kinglings."

"You say 'kinglings' like there are so many of us."

"Over the years, there have been."

"You're not any older than I am," he said. "Don't pretend to mentor me."

She shifted position slightly to raise herself to her elbow, but didn't try to move her lower body away from his hand. "How old are you?"

"Doesn't everyone know?" he asked rhetorically. "Ten-and-five. Born the month the Drought began."

A new light came into her eyes, and he realized he knew the words she would say before she said them: "Me too."

"Fascinating." But what was fascinating him just then was not his age or hers, and they both knew it. It was his hand resting on her waist, her breath warm against his ear, the nearness of their bodies in the bed.

"Paulus," Ama said, holding his gaze. "It can't mean anything."

"Of course. Plenty of us the same age, just coincidence."

"That's not what I meant."

His heart pounded in his chest. He thought he caught her meaning, but he wasn't sure, and it was too risky to ask. He didn't want to hear the wrong answer. Honestly, he didn't want to talk at all.

So instead, he slid his hand down a handspan to her hip and gave a gentle, experimental tug to draw her closer.

She moved her body against his so smoothly, all in one fluid motion, it was as if she'd belonged there all along.

Paulus didn't know what to say. He could only say something wrong at this point. He waited, breath caught in his throat, heart hammering.

Ama's gaze drifted down to his lips, her own mouth opening slightly, so close he could both hear and feel her warm, sharp breath.

Then her lips were on his lips, the kiss soft and light, far more tentative than he would have expected, but even sweeter than he'd hoped.

This, he realized. This was what she'd been saying couldn't mean anything. But it wasn't the time to think about meaning. It wasn't the time to think at all.

Instead he gripped Ama's hipbone more tightly as he kissed her, kissed her harder as she curved her own hand around the back of his head and tightened her grip in his hair and he couldn't hold back a low, longing moan, kissed until their lips were swollen, kissed until he forgot there was ever a time when a world existed beyond this sensation, his mouth claiming hers, her mouth claiming his.

NEED AND ROT

Elsewhere in Ursu
Stellari

*H*ow dare the queen. How dare *she*, thought Stellari. Trotting out that young man, the kingling, as if it were a foregone conclusion that he would run the country. Giving him a place of honor at the table with the nation's most powerful women. As if he were their equal. As if he were anything at all.

After the banquet, Stellari let herself into the quiet house—she only kept day servants now, for privacy—and went immediately to her own wine cabinet, washing down the last of the queen's too-sweet wine with her preferred vintage, a drier, deeper red.

The aftertaste of wine in her mouth turned sour as she thought of the way Heliane had treated her. Abominable, reminding Stellari of that day they'd voted without her. And Decima, she never stopped needling Stellari about the child, about her husband in the country, as if there were something wrong with married people living apart. Of course the child had not been sired by Stellari's husband, but what difference did that make? All that mattered was that Aster had emerged from between Stellari's thighs. Though only Rahul had seen it happen, had been a desperate, frantic midwife, to hear him tell it. Stellari herself remembered nothing but pain and blood, darkness sweeping her away from the world, then waking, an unknown time later, to the disappointment of a sleeping boy-child in her arms.

Stellari had eaten little at the banquet, so as to appear above the concerns of the body. Now that she was in the privacy of her own home, her body's concerns had come roaring back. Eating was only one. After she devoured the last of the cured cheese and drained a second cup of the good wine, she set off to satisfy the next most urgent.

As far as anyone else in the city knew, Rahul was a nursemaid she'd hired to care for Aster, that was all, and he stayed in the house because the child might need help at any hour. No one knew how important to her Rahul was; that way no one could use him against her. She'd never introduced him to her fellow assemblywomen or senators, never brought him to social events, never let anyone know how she treasured him from the very beginning. But so much had changed between them. Ever since she'd bled for days after Aster's birth, wondering aloud if this meant she'd never have a daughter, and he'd replied, *It's all right, Aster is all we need*, things had never quite been the same. The gap between them grew over time, filling up with silences, missed opportunities, questions unasked and unanswered.

"Rahul?" she called quietly. He hated it when she returned late and woke up the child; yet she refused to roam the half-lit house, searching room by room, to find him. Let him come when she called. That was how it had always been, before. Before Aster.

"Rahul?" she called again, hoping her voice sounded sweet.

She saw welcome movement against the darkness, and then Rahul's figure resolved. He padded up the hall in her direction, wearing only the *psama* around his neck and a tawny knit waistcloth, loosely tied. He had never succumbed to the Paximite fashion for men to pluck or wax their chest hair, and she loved him like this, near-naked and vulnerable, both familiar and unfamiliar in countless ways. The mere sight shot a bolt of lightning from her throat to her belly and downward from there.

Rahul neared her, yawning, and she gestured to the empty couch steps away, clearly suggesting he seat himself there. She might or might not be able to get him to her room, so this would do. She was pleasantly surprised when he took to the couch at her bidding.

"What did the Fading Queen want, then?" he asked.

Stellari's body ached. She felt pent up, desperate. She reached for the knot of Rahul's waistcloth and had it open almost before the question was out of his mouth.

"It went that well?" he mumbled into her lips.

She said only, "Quiet."

Obligingly he repositioned himself on the couch so could she straddle his lap. As she sank down, she hiked her robe up so the backs of her thighs were bare against the tops of his. Quickly her own hands moved to untie and drop her more formal robes, too impatient to wait for his help. It took longer than undoing the waistcloth, but not by much.

Rahul's hands were in her hair, her lips on his, and she moved against him urgently. How long had it been? A week, two, three? He slept in the child's room and not hers, quick to rush if Aster called at any hour of the day or night. Stellari couldn't blame him entirely. She herself had stayed out late more than once, securing intelligence from other senators, befriending the useful. Rahul hadn't been her first priority—if she were honest, not even her second or third. Now, in this moment, she couldn't remember why anything else had felt important. She craved his closeness, the smell of him, his heat more intoxicating than the wine.

Rahul was speaking again. "But why did she summon you? Who else was there?"

Stellari didn't even spare the words to shush him again, only crushed his mouth with her own, moving her hand where their bodies met to give him something else to think about. He wanted to talk and she didn't. She was the one who emerged victorious, though really, neither of them had much cause to complain. Their mouths were too occupied to talk anyway. She shivered thinking of all the uses to which she wanted Rahul to put his.

"Ra-daaa," came a high, thin voice from elsewhere in the house, a long, drawn-out call.

Stellari felt Rahul tense instantly under her, his body instantly on alert. "I should . . ."

"Shh," Stellari said, redistributing her weight to keep him in place. "He might go back to sleep on his own. Just wait."

In the silence Rahul brushed one kiss against her neck, then another, and she laced her fingers into his hair to pull his mouth downward to her breast, arching in anticipation.

Another high-pitched call, this one a question, the invented name only Aster used. "Rada?"

She held Rahul down one more long moment, hoping against hope. The sensual warmth of his mouth near her skin vanished abruptly; she felt him holding his breath.

The child's voice, more urgently, repeated, "Rada!"

Without another word, Rahul shifted out from under Stellari, only using his hand on her hip to move her aside. She let her hand fall from his hair.

In the space of a few heartbeats she was naked and alone on the low couch, one foot tucked awkwardly underneath her, the other braced against the floor. She watched Rahul's retreating back with a mixture of disbelief and resignation. He bent to grab his waistcloth from the floor, tying it as he went to cover his nakedness.

Rahul was halfway down the hall when he mumbled something, which might have been, "Sorry," but it was too late by then. Stellari wasn't surprised, but she didn't enjoy being reminded. Anytime there was a choice, he would choose Aster.

She wanted to punch something, but the vases and statuary decorating the alcoves in the public hallway were far too valuable. She needed some other release. She swept her discarded robes from the floor and draped them over one arm, feeling sorry for herself. Then she turned back again to pour one more cup of wine. As the secondhand echo of Rahul's soothing, comforting voice drifted down the hallway, she carried the wine and her robes to her own room and kicked the door shut behind her.

Stellari had no one but Rahul to talk to, so who was she supposed to talk to about Rahul? She'd fought her way up from nothing to make this life for herself, and it had been enough, before the child. With the child, everything was different.

She thought about how close she'd come to not having the baby. Several years into the Drought of Girls, of course she had not wanted to bear a child, but neither was she entirely willing to abstain. She supposed women who preferred other women for their pleasures had a simpler time of it. Alas, she only wanted Rahul. They'd made a go of intermediate measures, but everyone knew that even if a man withdrew before achieving his pleasure and spilled his rain outside the *muoni*, if his rain were strong enough, a child could still result. It seemed that Rahul had extremely strong rain.

When she'd recognized the signs of a child growing within her, Stellari knew her options. She'd even procured the *pulegone* tea—easy to come by, with her connections—and brewed it for herself in the midnight kitchen. Second thoughts came upon her only as she stirred the tea, her spoon moving in circles that began wide and ended small.

The tea might do its work too well, might scour out her womb so no other child could take root there. She still had in her mind the picture of a little girl, with Stellari's proud nose and Rahul's piercing eyes, who could rise to rule Paxim after her. Perhaps Stellari would be the one to end the Drought—what a miracle that would be!—but if not, she'd have to bear a son to keep the way open for a future girl.

She believed the Drought would end. She had to believe it. Or what was all this for? Amassing power, arranging and manipulating and rising? Yes, she enjoyed power for its own sake, savoring every lick of it as proof that she was more than an unwanted, neglected girl so poor she'd once eaten the leather laces of a worn-out sandal. But the idea of a daughter to teach her ways, that had become a cornerstone of her vision for the future. Stellari's daughter would inherit all the wealth and status of the ruling family of Calladocia; imagine what a child with Stellari's intelligence could do, starting from such an elevated perch. There would be no limit.

So Stellari had poured out the *pulegone* tea in the farthest corner of the garden, dumping it on the roots of a scraggly *klilia* bush that would have died anyway, and set aside her misgivings. She continued the pregnancy, suffered the birth. She waited impatiently for the Drought of Girls to end, waited to claim her reward for her patience and forbearance. Waited for that longed-for daughter to become a possibility again. Now, eight years later, that reward, that daughter, seemed unspeakably far away.

Rahul and Aster seemed to belong only to each other, a unit unto themselves, leaving her no part of either. Perhaps because Rahul had been the one whose hands had ushered the child into the world, perhaps because Stellari insisted they pretend Rahul was only the nursemaid, perhaps for a dozen or a hundred other reasons, the distance between Rahul and Stellari grew, and closeness between Aster and Stellari never developed in the first place. Sometimes she got the oddest feeling that Rahul was keeping the child from her, but had she ever really made a request he could refuse? She saw Aster in passing, certainly heard him, even spoke with him once he developed speech, but she never called for him nor he for her. Rahul was only doing what she asked, what she wanted, at least in this instance.

Stellari pitched her robes to the floor for the next day's servant to deal with, settled on the bed, raised the cup of wine to her lips. She forced herself to focus. She must imagine the outcome she wanted. She put aside the half-filled cup of wine and closed her eyes, breathed in, and set her mind to the task: imagining what she wanted most.

Once upon a time she'd had nothing but her imagination, but there was no longer anything idle about wondering how far she could go. Stellari wanted all the power Paxim had to offer. All of it. But as she considered it, something became clear, as if the wind had blown clouds from the face of the bright, round moon. While she would hate to see a whelp like Paulus as the monarch of Paxim, her path to power would be clearer were he to take that seat. She could keep building resentment against him, keep stoking that fire, with those who opposed men's rule. So many others would take her side.

And she could encourage Decima to add more powers to the consul's role in anticipation of the boy's rise; if it smoothed the path for her son, the queen would support such an expansion. And then, once Stellari was consul—*inevitable*, she reminded herself a fellow senator had once said—she'd have the tools she needed, regardless of what the king did or didn't want. It would be hard in the interim stages, of course. Even though she saw its necessity, Stellari had no love for compromise.

But sometimes, compromise seemed the only choice, she thought. She gazed with a longing look at the closed door, though she could not see down the hall beyond.

Stellari of Calladocia might not know what to do within the walls of her own house, but in the weeks and months that followed, to strengthen her position in the halls of the Senate, she knew exactly what to do.

The magistrate was nimble, careful, subtle. Everything counted. How she presented herself, who she talked to, what she said. She dressed in humbler robes to chat with members of the Assembly, women like Juni of Kamal, those she hadn't associated with since her rise to the Senate. Over the long, hot summer, she cultivated them now as any intelligent gardener would tend her most precious crop.

Nor did she neglect a single senator, neither for her side nor against it. She worked hard to make it seem like she did not, in fact, have a side. Many of her new friends in the Assembly talked cheerfully about the open-mindedness of the government, how intelligent it was to give men a chance, especially now that there would be so many more of them. Shouldn't women and men be able to rule together in peace? Perhaps a few truly extraordinary men—mostly sons or husbands who had learned about intelligent governance by watching their mothers and wives—were capable of making their own contributions. Stellari stood listening until her face hurt from smiling at these absurdities. Her mind simply tucked away the information, adding it to her calculations, knowing the day would come when she'd need to factor it in. Information was never good or bad. It was simply information.

Once the Senate and Assembly came back into session in the fall, she attended Assembly sessions when she could, to both show her open-mindedness and gather more of that precious information. Everything became clear when she was watching Kint of Keterli—a strikingly handsome young man elected to represent a small district from the far west, on the Sestian border—give his first speech. She could barely stand to listen. Poor liquid-eyed Kint was halting, stammering, barely coherent. Yet she realized as she watched that she couldn't find it in herself to hate him. He'd clearly been forced onto a stage he wasn't ready for, trusted with a position he couldn't handle. Men had not put Kint of Keterli into power; men didn't have the vote. Who were the women, these traitors, willing to allow themselves to be represented—or worse, ruled—by men? What had driven them to make such a senseless choice?

The mothers of civilization had been right to keep the power for themselves. Those women had truly deserved to rule. They had wrested life from the deadly wilderness. They had tamed the wild land

and established communities where one person's life depended on the next, the purest form of trust. They built tribes and villages and clans. In every sense, they made life.

And many years later, when those communities grew too large and clashed too often, another set of visionary women brokered the Great Peace. They reorganized the land, establishing five queendoms, each on the right plot of land and peopled by the right women and men. Those women knew what it was to sacrifice. To strive. To make hard decisions and stick by them no matter the cost. Modern women were barely children in comparison, and men only infants.

As Kint droned on, his voice grew fainter and fainter to Stellari, until it was only like the buzz of a distant, drowsy honeybee. Worker bees and drones were nothing to the hive: they all danced and toiled and harvested in service of the queen.

The queen.

What, thought Stellari, had Queen Heliane done to earn her power? Been born to the right mother, that was all. That was the fatal flaw of monarchy and one that would never be righted, no matter who sat on the throne, as long as there were thrones to sit on. It was not the first time Stellari had thought it, but it was the first time she saw clearly what needed to be done.

Men were not the problem. Not even this experiment with representation, which she could only assume would go awry, when the Kints of the world, given space to run, would trip over their own clumsy feet and fall.

No. The rot began at the top; the only way to fix it was to start there. The queen. The consul. Both had to pay.

She only needed time to lay the groundwork, Stellari realized. It wouldn't do to rush. She'd take her time, choose carefully. She could be as patient as a mother bird sitting on an egg, fluffing out her feathers, settling onto a nest she had painstakingly constructed, twig by precious twig. Time was not important. Her path, her purpose, was clear.

✦ 12 ✦

VIPERS

Spring, the All-Mother's Year 517
Daybreak Palace
Eminel

The first time Eminel met with Sobek had been a disaster, though the queen hadn't recognized it at the time. She thought she simply agreed with Sobek because the older woman was so convincing, so obviously *right* about everything.

Luckily, the second time Eminel met with Sobek, two days after the party celebrating the end of the Drought, Beyda was present. That changed everything. The moment Sobek left the room, Beyda turned to Eminel, her expression stiff, teeth clenched.

"You know who that is?" Beyda asked, her voice cold.

"Sobek," Eminel said, as if that were all the answer needed.

Beyda stiffened even further, if that were possible. "It's my fault, really. I honestly thought she'd left the court, gone somewhere else in shame, probably back to Perai's ancestral lands. She hasn't participated in court life in years. That's why I didn't include her in the list of courtiers when we went over and over them. I'm so sorry."

"Sorry for what?" asked Eminel breezily. "She's delightful."

"She is delightful," admitted Beyda with clear reluctance. "But that's not all she is."

"What is she?"

"A mind magician. Her gift is in her voice. When she speaks, her power makes you want to believe her words."

Eminel thought back, knowledge dawning, and she felt a sudden knot in her throat. "So her offers of help with the all-magic girls, her demand for money, all that—I said yes, even if I didn't want to?"

"Not exactly. She made you want to. Think about it now, while she's not here. What did she say about the all-magic girls?"

"She said we'd bring them here. Run trials. And I agreed to it!" The more Eminel thought about it without Sobek present, the more she was aghast. "Beyda, we can't. We can't take them from their families, their homes, and—do you know anything about these trials that they used to run, to test the girls' skills? What they were like?"

Beyda's voice was grim when she said, "Enough to know that you're right. We can't."

Eminel began to pace, scuffing her feet against the rich carpets. "Her voice—her voice. Can I just use magic to silence her? Or I suppose I don't even need to use magic. There are other ways to keep her quiet. I can—"

"Stop!" Beyda interrupted sharply.

Eminel halted her pacing and looked at her friend.

Beyda reached out and took Eminel's hands. The scribe's fingers were strong and dry, slightly warm. In a warning voice, Beyda said, "Don't think like Mirriam. Think like Kruvesis. You know what I mean?"

Eminel nodded. The first queen of Arca, not the most recent, was the one to emulate. She'd almost gotten carried away. "You're right. You're right. And you probably have an answer to all this, so—what's the answer?"

"The power is in her voice," Beyda said firmly. "So if you correspond with her in writing, you won't be vulnerable."

"Right." Eminel considered how that would go. "But that won't work forever."

"No, it won't. You need a mind-shield against her. Have you shielded your mind before? Do you know how?"

Eminel had done it briefly at the celebration of the end of the Drought of Girls, but that had been a matter of minutes, and it had exhausted her; she'd shielded herself for a longer period only once. The memory flooded through her. Before the Rites of the Bloody-Handed, when she'd realized what Sessadon was, Eminel had shielded herself by instinct so the powerful sorcerer wouldn't find out. She'd done so without thinking consciously of life force or sand; she hadn't realized until much later that Sessadon's quartz heart had provided all Eminel had needed of both. Now she looked at her cuff and raised it high so Beyda would see. "But I don't know how much power it takes. What if I drain this? What if I don't have enough?"

Beyda seemed unruffled. "You can manage it, I promise you. For one thing, you can practice. For another, if you can't make a mind-shield yourself, you can find an ally to cast one for you."

Eminel's voice was small when she said, "I am not at all sure who my allies are."

Beyda considered this, then said, "Better to assume no one is, I suppose."

"Except for you?"

"Well," Beyda said dryly, "at least you know I have no secret magic to use against you."

"Do I know that for sure?" Eminel joked, trying to find her way back to better cheer. "Maybe I should dismiss you just in case. Can I do that? Dismiss my scribe?"

"You can," said Beyda, "but the Bastion will just assign you another. And who knows, she might be even worse than me."

"Probably right," said Eminel. "I'll take my chances with you."

"That seems best."

She squeezed Beyda's hands and released them.

Over the weeks that followed Daybreak Palace's first celebration during Queen Eminel's reign, the queen gradually lessened her self-imposed isolation, though she still spent the bulk of her time behind closed doors with Beyda. She met with Sobek, too, in order to keep the woman close, but never without the presence of a lanky, hollow-cheeked sorcerer named Iscla, whose talent at shielding minds was subtle and impenetrable. Iscla herself was not the most intelligent adviser, but Eminel knew that including her played well with the Volkan clan, and their support helped Eminel keep the ever-shifting currents of power within the palace in balance. When the pieces clicked into place, she found it satisfying. She preferred to manage her rivals and subjects at arm's length, but at least she was no longer afraid of managing them. Court had slid into a new equilibrium.

Until change came again, from an unexpected quarter.

Beyda was testing Eminel once again on the leaders, members, and ancestors of each matriclan when a rap came on Eminel's door.

"I wasn't expecting anyone," she said to Beyda, before calling, "Who is it?"

"Visitors for the queen," came a familiar voice from the stationed Queensguard. These days they were stationed in turns, two guards at a time to flank the door, now that Eminel knew she could defend herself if needed. Not that she had explained it that way to them.

"I am not accepting visitors," Eminel responded, aggrieved. It was the presumption as much as anything else that irritated her; why should she admit anyone who didn't explain herself first?

"We regret the interruption, Queen Eminel, but it is a matter of utmost importance," called another voice.

Eminel did not immediately recognize it, but Beyda whispered, "Nishti of Binaj. You should let her in."

"Very well. Only for a moment," Eminel grumbled in the Queensguard's direction, and the door swung open.

As the courtiers entered, one dressed in a striking shade of green and the other a warm chestnut, Beyda quickly stood and moved away from Eminel, her face solemn. Eminel understood the scribe was protecting her, having decided it was better for courtiers not to see Beyda and Eminel as friends, but Eminel still felt a pang at the loss. At least Beyda stayed in the room. The scribe's steady presence made Eminel feel less alone. Once Beyda took a seat on the floor, her plumed reed pen raised and her face solemn, Eminel gestured to the other women to begin.

"Queen," they said in unison, bowing low.

They hadn't formally introduced themselves, so she called them nothing at all, only bobbed her head to acknowledge their greeting. Careful to keep her voice neutral, Eminel said, "You have contradicted my orders and interrupted my work. I hope you have a very good reason."

"We do," said the more elegant woman, the one in the green, whose robe was slit at the shoulders to show bare skin, an unusual style for the court. There was no other decoration, not even embroidery around the calf-length hem. She herself, it seemed, was the decoration.

"Though our good reason is bad news," volunteered the other woman, whose garb was more functional. The chestnut-colored robe she wore had only a single line of embroidery around the neckline and hemline, yet Eminel could also tell the fabric itself was unusually finely woven, of very high quality. Fasiq would have loved to get her hands on that fabric for sale or trade, Eminel thought with a pang, and then tried her best to push the pang down and focus.

"Out with it, then."

"Our nation is under attack," said the less adorned woman, and cringed, as if she expected Eminel might strike her down just for saying so.

Eminel was shocked but forced herself to smother any true reaction. Instead she eyed them coolly. "And which of you is the councillor assigned to brief the queen on matters of war?"

They looked at each other with poorly concealed confusion. At length the taller woman, the elegant one, spoke. "That is not how the court works, Queen. Not for the past century, in any case. We take on the roles the queen assigns us, moment to moment, as she dictates. And you have assigned us no roles."

"Then why are you two here, among all those in Daybreak Palace?"

"We volunteered."

"No one else wanted to come?"

They looked at each other again. Again the more elegant one spoke. "They did, but our matriclans are acknowledged to be the most powerful. I am Nishti of Binaj, and this is Yasamin of Volkan."

"I can speak for myself," bristled Yasamin.

Nishti raised a brow, then gestured with an exaggerated motion for Yasamin to speak next.

Yasamin said, "In any case, Queen, it is important that you know what is happening, so you can make a decision about how to address it."

"Tell me what you know," Eminel commanded, and this seemed to please Yasamin.

"They strike from the far east," Yasamin began, smoothing down her sleeves, possibly out of nervousness. "The warriors, I mean. The Scorpicae."

Eminel felt a chill down her spine. She should have seen it coming. If she'd lingered in Tamura's mind for longer, back at the Rites of the Bloody-Handed, she probably would have. She knew the Scorpican queen's anger and impulsivity. It was easy to see, with the benefit of hindsight, how attacking Arca was the next logical step for a suffering nation's ambitious queen. Other queendoms could hunker down and weather the crisis, building their population back up once the Drought had ended—it wouldn't be easy, but it was at least possible. Scorpica would struggle. So they had done this instead.

"They attacked several towns in the far eastern desert," Yasamin went on. "Sometimes to pillage and destroy, sometimes to haul off goods and valuables. As far as we can tell, they don't plan to occupy the territory there—"

"Who would?" interjected Nishti with a nasty laugh.

Eminel saw the flash of annoyance in Yasamin's eyes. She almost dipped into Yasamin's mind to find the reason for it, but she couldn't risk draining the cuff. The other woman's reasons would come clear soon enough.

Gathering up her long sleeves, Nishti explained to the queen, "The farthest settlements in the east have very little communication with the palace. The majority are small and humble. Your predecessor never bothered herself with their maintenance."

"Other than to receive regular shipments of precious gems from Jesephia," Yasamin added.

"Gems?" Nishti's head turned with obvious surprise.

"It wasn't commonly known," said Yasamin, drawing the words out with what looked to Eminel like subtle but clear relish. "My matriclan suggested and executed the arrangement, these villages being our ancestral territory; I'm not surprised you were in the dark, Nishti."

The elegant Nishti bristled, but settled herself quickly, her mouth quirking up at the corner as she addressed Yasamin. "Everyone spends some time in the dark, don't they, when night comes? Don't you worry about what information I do or don't have. I'm certain there are many things you yourself don't know."

Eminel could hear the scratch of Beyda's pen, recording everything she thought necessary, her hand flying over the page, her head bent. The scribe could write in complete silence when she chose to; she was making sure the women were aware of her presence, of the importance of this moment.

"Such as? Now is the time to be honest. Here in front of our new monarch." Yasamin gestured toward Eminel, who was careful not to respond in any way. "Let her see that we have no secrets in Daybreak Palace."

Nishti laughed, a short sharp bark. "I won't lie to Queen Eminel. Better she should know the nest of vipers in which she finds herself. You won't catch me pretending that snakes are doves."

Though she needed to be careful not to take sides, Eminel also couldn't let her courtiers talk about her as if she weren't here. She reached up and stroked her blue snake necklace. She saw both of them receive the message.

The queen said, "I can tell for myself where doves and snakes are nesting; you may relieve yourself of the burden of pointing out which you think is which."

Nishti cleared her throat and resumed. "In any case, as best we can tell, the intent of the Scorpicae so far is to steal wealth and sow fear. Their raiding parties have been small, usually five or ten warriors, and none have been seen anywhere west of Hayk, hundreds of leagues from here."

"But we have enough scouts and messengers to tell us if that changes?"

"We do, my queen."

"Another report tomorrow, then, please. Beyda, note it?"

The scribe, her pen still scratching in that familiar pattern, spoke without looking up. "Noted."

Eminel said to the courtiers, "Tomorrow. Same time."

They exchanged uneasy glances. Yasamin was the one to form the question. "Which one of us?"

"Both of you. You seem to work well as a team."

Eminel almost laughed at how their shoulders tensed up in unison, both women obviously displeased but unwilling to say so. Certainly Nishti told the truth when she compared the courtiers to vipers; that didn't mean she wasn't a viper as well. These two, both angling for power on behalf of themselves and their matriclans, would keep each other in check.

Once they left, Eminel felt the fight go out of her immediately. She steadied herself on a nearby chair. Were the Scorpicae really attacking? The best warriors in the world, turning their swords against the Arcans?

Eminel realized she might lose this country, just when she was coming into her own in ruling it.

Then she heard Beyda's voice, low and steady, saying, "I think you handled that as well as anyone could."

Eminel turned. The young scribe's face was open, honest; if Beyda was mocking Eminel, she was hiding it well.

Eminel blurted suddenly, "What would you do, Beyda?"

"Do?"

"If you were me."

"I'm not," said Beyda, slowly climbing to her feet, tucking her reed pen away in its case, folding the cover over her writing pad.

Eminel waited for her to elaborate, but the other young woman simply stared back at her, as if she'd said all there was to say. When they stood near each other, Eminel remembered Beyda was much shorter than she; oddly, though the scribe spent much of her time seated on the floor, Eminel always thought of them as seeing eye to eye.

"All right." Eminel tried again. "I need advice. Please. I want yours."

"I'm only a scribe." Beyda shrugged. "And my superiors sent me to a nation that has treated its assigned scribes indifferently at best, and at worst, outright murdered them. So you might infer that I'm not even a very good one."

"I don't believe that."

"Neither do I, honestly," Beyda replied. "I just felt obligated to point it out. If the authorities in the Bastion treasure your wisdom, they don't pack you off to the Arcan court."

"Well. We are not in the Bastion."

For the first time in the conversation, Beyda smiled. "We most certainly are not."

Tired from the day, Eminel confessed, "You're the only one who treats me like a person. Not a threat, not a god, not a weakling, just— just like an ordinary woman."

"But you're not ordinary."

"I can't be an ordinary woman just because I'm a queen?"

"The last queen believed she was superior to all other women by divine right. So there's precedent."

"Just as you are not me," said Eminel, trying to gentle her tone into something teasing, something familiar, "I'm not the previous queen. And please, advise me. I don't want to beg, though I will if I have to."

Beyda smiled in response, though there was something not quite right about her smile, as if she had only read about the expression. Her version was something between a real grin and the way a threatened red fox would bare its teeth. She seemed to consider for a long moment, then said, "I'd send your most dangerous rivals east. Where the Scorpican attackers have been seen."

"For what purpose?"

"For what purpose does anyone ride out to meet an enemy?" asked Beyda neutrally. "To fight back."

"I'm not even sure the women I'd want to send have battle magic."

"Anything can be battle magic if you structure the battle correctly," said Beyda with surprising ease. "Within hours the entire court will be buzzing with the news of this threat. They'll expect you, as queen, to go out and wipe the Scorpican warriors off the map."

"I . . . don't think I can do that," said Beyda.

"I don't think you should. Since you asked my advice. My advice is, you send some of *them*—say a half dozen, whichever ones concern you most—on your behalf."

Eminel's fingers moved up to her snake necklace and she found herself stroking its glassy head with her thumb, an involuntary motion, but it seemed to help clarify her thoughts. "And either they win, which lessens the threat from outside—"

"Or they die trying," Beyda continued in affirmation, "which lessens the threat from within."

Eminel's smile was genuine. "Beyda of the Scribes, has anyone ever told you that you're a very intelligent young woman?"

"Yes. Not lately." Beyda's tone was matter-of-fact. "But observant people have noticed."

"Obviously no one's ever told you that you suffer from an excess of modesty."

"Because I don't," said Beyda. "Honestly, you're no fool yourself, Queen Eminel, but you do sometimes miss the obvious."

"I'll strive to be better," said Eminel. She was finally starting to get the hang of conversing with Beyda, who had no use for the flattery or insincerity that marked every other conversation Eminel had had in the Arcan court. Exactly what kept her needing Beyda's company day after day.

Beyda said, with a curt, approving nod, "Well, isn't that all any of us can do?"

◆

Out of the blackness rode the Rovers' wagon, Hermei in the driver's seat, bells that the wagon had never sported in life jangling on the oxen's traces.

The wagon pulled up short in front of Eminel, who stood on flat dirt. She was a fully grown woman, but she somehow wore one of her childhood dresses, dirty and torn. Draped over her shoulders was the rich blue cloth she and Jehenit had slept on in the temple of the Bandit God, that first night the Rovers had found them. Young Eminel had been only five years old, small, unknowing. Now she was a young woman, ten-and-five, and queen of a powerful nation, but did she know any more than she ever had? She was child and woman, queen and refugee, intellect and emotion.

The dream-Hermei hailed her, but his tone was suspicious. "Eminel," he said with concern. "What are you waiting for?"

"Is my mother with you?" she asked him. The question seemed urgent. She had to ask. Everything hung in the balance.

He didn't answer.

Then, from the back of the wagon, emerged the blue woman, and Eminel was struck dumb. The woman had no face. She didn't belong there, in the Rovers' wagon on a Paximite hillside. Yet the dream-Eminel was not surprised to see her. Eminel felt . . . what was that feeling? Was she glad?

The blue woman said something to Eminel but not in words. She spoke in sounds, in feelings, in pulses of energy. Without moving her arms, she gave a sense of motion; without lips, she conveyed a sense of longing to Eminel, a sense of urgency, a sense of power. As the indecipherable sound flooded through Eminel, she found herself weeping aloud.

Hermei climbed down from the wagon to wrap his arms around Eminel, saying, "It'll be okay."

But the dream-figure of the thief didn't smell like Hermei. He didn't smell like anything. His embrace provided no reassurance. She shoved him away so hard he fell to the ground.

"It'll never be okay," she hissed, to him and to herself. "Never, never, never."

Turning, Eminel leapt up to the wagon—the blue woman was there but somehow not in her way?—and put her hands on the curtains, ready to part them, terrified and hopeful at who she would find inside.

Then Eminel woke from the dream, gasping. She drew the air in, blew it out again, struggling to find her equilibrium. Air was somehow the key to breaking the spell.

Not a spell, she told herself. *No. It can't be a spell.*

The dream, in itself, was not terrifying. What terrified her was that she wasn't so sure it really was a dream. That blue woman, invading her memories, tempting her with power at every turn. That power still swelled inside Eminel, in every limb, far too real. She could *feel* it still.

In a way it was like the power that had swelled within her during the Sun Rites, just before she'd held Sessadon's attention long enough to allow Tamura to snap her neck. She didn't like remembering that moment; she didn't like thinking about Tamura, for one thing, whose warriors were now raiding and attacking and harrying the residents of Arca. But Eminel still wasn't ready to enlist other queendoms against Scorpica. Once she did, it would make this attack truly a war, and Eminel refused to be the queen who started a war. She could take care of it without outside help, she was sure. She just needed to figure out how.

Eminel rolled over in the darkness, opened her eyes, tried to take comfort in the outlines of familiar objects around her. Yet her palace rooms still felt strange and wrong. More than half a year here had not made her feel she belonged. The quartz cuff was locked tight and cool around her wrist, the blue snake necklace still heavy on her breastbone. She rose to a sitting position on the side of the bed, setting her bare feet down on the plush carpet. The woven patterns under her soles, at least, grounded her.

There was no logical reason to believe the dream came from Sessadon. The woman didn't resemble her, didn't speak her words, didn't act like the magician had in life. It was the feeling that disturbed Eminel. That particular unsettling joy, the exact same way she'd felt the first time Sessadon had taught her to wield all-magic. How Eminel had drawn on life force, drunk deep, and found it delicious. She didn't think that feeling could come from a good place. She also wasn't sure she could resist it.

Eminel pressed her toes into the carpet beneath her feet, stretched her back, pondered whether to lie down again. She doubted she could fall back to sleep, but it was the middle of the night, and her head swam with exhaustion. Here in the dark, shadows all around her, fingers still tingling from the memory of power, she let the question in.

What if the dreams came from Sessadon?

Yes, Eminel had seen the woman die with her own eyes. No, there was no way the ancient sorcerer who had both encouraged and betrayed Eminel could still be in the world. But this was not the only world. And she couldn't forget that Sessadon had once placed a vision in her mind that pushed her to leave the Rovers, moving Eminel like a *whishnuk* peg into a vulnerable position. Ripe to pluck.

What if the sorcerer was, somehow, manipulating her again?

Not every gift of all-magic was created equal. While women and girls with all-magic sometimes favored one or two elements in particular, Eminel was like Sessadon: equally talented across all six, earth and air, fire and water, body and mind. And in their years together, Sessadon had taught Eminel spell after spell, drawing on gifts of almost unlimited depth and breadth.

Sessadon's gifts had transcended limitations. Was it any wonder that Eminel considered, in moments like this, that they might transcend even the barrier between life and death?

Eminel pressed her toes against the carpet one more time and breathed out. Then she took her breath back in, lifted her legs, and lay her tired body down. She drew the blanket tight, hugged her shoulders with her own arms. Sleep. She had to sleep. Exhaustion would take her, she told herself, if she could just let go.

But as she lay in bed she could think of only one person, the only one she trusted in this whole gorgeous, rotten palace: the scribe. Every courtier from every matriclan had her own agenda, and not a single one of them, as best Eminel could tell, would pass up a chance to be queen in her place. So she needed someone who could not be queen. Who wasn't even from Arca. Who understood what it meant to be an outsider no matter where you went. And that was Beyda of the Scribes, in her rigid, truthful entirety.

Beyda, thought Eminel, drowsy, lost. *Would you have any answers for me?*

Then she was surrounded by black.

This time, as she dreamed, she willed herself to follow the same path from her last dream, to see the same sights. Hermei. The blue woman. The wagon. It all happened again, up to the tears. Then she saw herself parting the curtains of the Rovers' wagon, and saw herself stepping inside.

Then Eminel was in a stone hallway, torches casting just enough light to see by. As she stood and watched, the hallway swirled with people, all dressed in odd garments, tubes of fabric pinned at the shoulders with decorative pins and banded at the waist with broad belts. The garments themselves were pale and undyed, but the pins and belts sported a rainbow of colors.

Next to her stood a young girl, probably eight years of age, the shoulders of her garment bound with large circular buttons instead of pins. Her buttons were discs of horn, her garment unbelted.

"I'm late," said the girl. Then, increasingly agitated, "I'm late!"

"For what?" asked Eminel.

It wasn't clear whether the girl heard her or not, but the child began to hustle down the hall. Eminel followed.

They emerged into a room where row after row of children sat straight-backed on row after row of benches. Each held a slate tablet on their lap, a stub of chalk in one hand; each wore a garment with the same horn buttons at the shoulders. The girl from the hall made a worried noise low in her throat and took the last empty seat. Eminel stood; no one seemed to see her.

A woman in a long version of the pale garment belted with fabric the color of beech bark, her shoulders sporting sizable bronze pins in a hexagonal shape, handed a tablet to the child from the hall. Her voice was pitiless as she said, "Oh, Beyda. You'll never catch up."

Beyda? thought Eminel in the dream.

Tears streaming down her cheeks now, the young Beyda placed the tip of her chalk against the slate, but as soon as she'd done so, from somewhere in the room sounded a deep, echoing gong.

"Time," said the woman with the bronze pins, and as one, the other children in the room rose up and filed forward, each setting their slate in a neat stack. The stack grew and grew. Beyda scribbled frantically. *Oh, Beyda.* Eminel looked at her panicked little face and saw the familiar shape of the eyes, the mouth; yes, she could plausibly be an eight-year-old version of the scribe, which would make this . . . the Bastion?

Then the only ones left in the room were the woman and Beyda. Beyda was still scribbling madly, head down, as if the woman might not see her if she didn't look up. But the woman was walking toward her, step by step. *Beyda, Beyda.* It was all for naught. In one smooth, sharp motion, the woman snatched the slate from Beyda and snapped it over her knee, one jagged black half coming off in each of her hands.

And either the *crack* of the tablet or Eminel's own shocked gasp woke her up, because she came awake panting for air in the darkness.

"Shhh," came a voice from beside her. "It's all right."

Startled, Eminel almost swung the cuff forward, but stopped as soon as she caught sight of the familiar face. Familiar, but still unexpected, here in Eminel's bedchamber. "Beyda?"

"You were calling for me," Beyda told her. "So I came."

"Calling for you?" Eminel sat up. "You heard me through the tunnel? That doesn't seem possible."

Beyda solemnly touched a fingertip to the side of her forehead.

This was even more concerning. "I called you—in your thoughts?"

"It seems so." Beyda looked worried. "You said my name. You kept saying it."

"You heard me, and you came?"

"The door to the tunnel was open. It seemed wise to investigate. And you sounded very concerned."

"You were late for a test," Eminel told her. For some reason it seemed very important that she let Beyda know. "You were late and they didn't let you finish. And someone, maybe a teacher, broke your tablet?"

"Oh." Beyda's voice was soft, but in the dim light of the nighttime bedchamber, Eminel saw what looked like fear in her eyes.

Gently, Eminel asked, "Do you dream that sometimes?"

"Yes."

"Tonight? Was I in your dream?"

165

"I didn't see you," Beyda replied quietly. "But you must have been."

"Do you dream that often?"

"Sometimes," Beyda said. "But there are worse dreams."

"There are worse dreams. I'm sorry I was in your thoughts, in your dreams. I didn't mean to be."

"I accept your apology," Beyda said. "Do you think you'll be all right?"

Whether or not Beyda meant it that way, the question loomed too large for Eminel to answer. Acting on impulse, Eminel said, "It's late, and I'm . . . still scared. Would you stay?"

"If you wish."

"I wish," Eminel said.

Beyda climbed into the bed and, without being asked, wrapped both arms around Eminel.

Eminel almost wept with gratitude. She remembered the giant Fasiq holding her like this—how long ago now, how many years?—after her mother's death. That was the last time she felt truly comfortable, loved without question. Even though it was one of the worst days of her life, she still remembered that embrace fondly. Beyda's arms were smaller and softer, but her dedication to the embrace was the same. As if she were giving her whole self over. Holding nothing back.

When Eminel thought of Fasiq, she thought of the Shade, the love those two women had for each other, how bright it burned. They were comfortable with each other like this, she thought. Did one person fall in love with another because they felt that instinctual comfort? Was it love that led to comfort, or comfort that led to love?

Without considering it another moment, continuing to act on instinct in the shroud of midnight, Eminel brushed her lips over Beyda's cheek. It was warm, like the scribe's encircling arms. Beyda didn't move, neither toward her nor away, and Eminel thought perhaps the scribe hadn't even felt the touch, or registered it as meaningful. Blood rushed to her own cheeks. *No going back now,* she decided, and placed her mouth gently on Beyda's in a soft, steady kiss.

It was as steady as Eminel could make it, anyway; she had never put her lips on anyone else's, and it felt awkward, unnatural. Once her mouth pressed against Beyda's, she was aware of all the ways their lips didn't line up quite right. Then, after the initial press, she didn't know whether or not to breathe. Maybe she was doing it terribly wrong and that was why Beyda still wasn't moving, wasn't responding. Responding was definitely supposed to be part of it. Eminel knew that much.

Then Beyda did move, though not quite in the way Eminel expected. Her arms remained around Eminel, tight as ever. Only her mouth moved away.

In an even, almost apologetic tone, Beyda said, "I don't like that."

Eminel's face flushed with shame, and she moved her hands to cover it. "I'm so sorry. I don't know what—I—I'm so sorry."

Beyda still didn't leave her side. She kept one arm tight around Eminel and moved the other to gently nudge Eminel's hands downward so the queen's face was no longer hidden.

"You asked me to stay and I'll stay," Beyda said quietly. "You're very dear to me, Queen Eminel. But I don't desire you. I hope you're not offended."

"I'm not," Eminel said, and found she was actually, somehow, able to laugh.

"There are many kinds of physical affection," Beyda went on, seriously. "It is not uncommon to mistake one kind for another, especially in a time of crisis."

Eminel snuggled her head against Beyda's shoulder, nestling more deeply into the embrace. She felt even more comfortable now, more loved, than she had before. Like the giant, Beyda held her only to make her feel safe, to offer comfort. There was something glorious in that. Something right.

After a few long moments, Eminel asked, "Have you ever felt desire for someone?"

Beyda's response was quick, lacking any shyness or rebuke. "Is it important that you know?"

"No," said Eminel, closing her eyes. "I'm only curious."

Beyda said, "I'm not curious about desire. But I've wondered about love. What all the fuss is about. Do you know?"

"I'm not sure," said Eminel. "I saw two people fall in love once. It looked . . . nice."

"Looks can be deceiving. But if that's something you want for yourself, Queen, I certainly hope you find it."

"I don't know what I want," confessed Eminel. She could be her complete self with Beyda and no one else. That was truly rare. Possibly even rarer than the type of love she'd seen Fasiq and the Shade share, and that was rare indeed.

Maybe Beyda was right. She probably was. Eminel had simply mistaken one kind of affection for another: this was not the kissing kind, but something equally strong and deep. She was lucky she hadn't scared off Beyda with her error, but then, Beyda was not the type to scare easily. And thank goodness, in this court of untold snares.

She had one true friend, thought Eminel, and thank Velja for that. She would savor what she had.

The rest of the night, wrapped securely in Beyda's arms, she slept and did not dream.

✦

The next day, Eminel put her plan—the plan Beyda had suggested—into action. First, she sent Seekers. Her predecessors had sent Seekers paired with Bringers, but she didn't follow suit: these women struck out alone, with intent only to find, not to find and collect. They traveled in dark, hooded cloaks with no identifying insignia, hard to pick out of a typical Arcan crowd, easy to forget. Once a Seeker identified where the main encampment of Scorpicae was located, more powerful sorcerers would be sent in. That would take time, but it was the only way. Eminel didn't have enough powerful sorcerers to send them everywhere.

One thing she decided on her own, without asking Beyda, was to continue to keep the news of the Scorpican attack close. She wouldn't notify the other queendoms, and she forbade any others who knew to spread the word. It would be natural to reach out to Queen Heliane for help, as everyone knew the Paximites had spent the past few years training a strong army, but Eminel wouldn't take the risk. She couldn't put herself in debt to Paxim. As with choosing husbands, Eminel thought, it was far too early in her reign. Just as importantly, she worried that instead of allying with her against the Scorpicae, anyone she called might ally with the Scorpicae against her. After all, to them, Eminel was still a new queen, untested. If anyone knew the role she'd played in bringing down Sessadon, they would fear her power; but, irony of ironies, the only one who knew anything about that was Tamura. And if the Scorpican queen were at all afraid of Eminel, she certainly hadn't let it hold her back.

Fortune—or perhaps it was Velja—was on their side. Less than a month later, a Seeker named Adjoa reported back with the location of the main Scorpican encampment: a high-sided caldera known as Velja's Navel, on the border of Godsbones. It was a place of bad luck, Eminel knew, where no Arcan would want to go. But she would not be ruled by superstition. Perhaps the bad luck inherent in the black sand would settle not on the Arcan defenders, but on the Scorpican warriors who intruded there.

Even though the news came more quickly than she expected, Eminel was ready for it. She was ready to send her rivals to the front the same day she was informed where that front could be found.

As soon as the Seekers left Daybreak Palace, Eminel had begun, with Beyda's help, to comb through lists of the courtiers and their powers. They'd spent hours discussing and debating at length who could be trusted, who must be watched. The queen carefully selected one representative from each matriclan at court. Five of them she informed that they were being honored with the opportunity to show their strength against the enemy. The sixth was Iscla, the Volkan representative who had cast a mind-shield for her during conversations with Sobek; she would serve by remaining here.

The other five, at least outwardly, were eager to undertake the mission Eminel charged them with. If they had misgivings, they did not show them in front of their queen. Their powers were remarkable, and they leapt at the chance to demonstrate their usefulness. Parvan had a talent with fire, able to burn even the unburnable. The elegant Nishti, who alongside the more practical Yasamin had first brought Eminel the news of the Scorpicae attacks, turned out to be an earth magician who could raise golems, soldiers made of sand who moved and struck just like women but, unlike human women, didn't die. The other earth magician of the group, named Cyntar, had a similar but somehow more disturbing talent of causing dirt in the shape of hands to rise and grab at any feet passing; Eminel still got shivers remembering her demonstration. The oldest of those chosen, Sara, was a white-haired, thick-waisted woman in her sixth decade, who over time had honed her skill in manipulating the air so finely, she could make arrowheads of air: invisible, sharp, and true. And the fifth magician, Wodevi, was a body magician. Her slightest touch could break bone. Eminel did not ask for a demonstration of her skill, and though she privately wondered whether her newly formed corps would get close enough to an enemy for Wodevi's skill to be of use, she couldn't deny that she was more comfortable with Wodevi far than near.

The five assigned rivals left Daybreak Palace in the direction of the enemy-sheltering caldera with minimal fanfare; their send-off was private, their queen solemnly intoning how much their service was appreciated, pressing each of their hands between her own in turn and murmuring in her most sincere tones. But in truth Eminel didn't want the wider world knowing what she'd done.

And what had she done, in any case? She wouldn't even know until after the battle was fought whether it had been lost or won. Then and only then would she know whether this decision had been her best option, a terrible mistake, or perhaps a combination of the two.

✦ 13 ✦

DAUGHTERS

Weeks later
Velja's Navel, on the border of Arca and Godsbones
Tamura, Gretti

Hunkered down in their camp in the caldera, Tamura knew the Scorpican plan of attack would have to evolve, but she also knew she had no gift for strategy. She'd once imagined her force riding straight to the Arcan capital and taking it, triumphant—but that was an unrealistic dream. While much of the magic they'd seen in the far eastern desert of Arca was a disappointment, she'd be a fool to expect the same meager weakness at Daybreak Palace.

And while the realization had been belated, she realized she knew the power of the new queen of Arca's magic firsthand. Once her bands of raiders spread throughout the east of Arca, she'd heard the new queen's name whispered by victims and recruits, invoked in anger or prayer or futile last gasp. *Eminel. Eminel. Eminel.* Though the girl had never said her own name out loud at the Rites of the Bloody-Handed,

171

their minds had touched in a way more intimate than Tamura could express. Each one carried the other's name in her bones now.

Countless times, the Scorpican queen had turned over that fateful day in her mind, and the more she considered it, the more she realized she hadn't come to the decision to snap Sessadon's neck on her own. Someone had been inside her mind, nudging her to do what she did. On that platform, while Tamura had certainly thought of placing her hands around Sessadon's throat and choking the life out of her, it had only been a thought. It could easily have passed and she could've done a thousand other things: seized a ceremonial blade, waited for someone else to act, even fled from danger as so many others had been fleeing. Some other force had been there with Tamura, another intelligence alongside her own, pushing her to make that thought real. And afterward—digging into the dead sorcerer's chest, pulling out the quartz heart? She never would have thought to do that, not on her own. It had to have been an instruction from that young woman who'd met Tamura's eyes, there on the dais while the carnage was unfolding. Tamura simply hadn't put the two together—that young woman bristling with power, the new queen who'd taken her throne that same day—until it was too late.

The Drought was finally over. So why did it feel like Tamura's place in the world was more precarious than ever? The only reason she didn't fear Gretti, whose uneasy alliance with her had turned to hate the moment Tamura had gone ahead with the war despite the end of the Drought, was that both of them knew Gretti wasn't physically strong enough to defeat her. But there were plenty of ambitious women in Tamura's army. Hate wasn't even a necessary ingredient. Any one of them might decide, drunk on hammerwine or victory or anger, to Challenge their queen.

Some days she even wondered if Azur would do it. Ever since the death of her friend Ysilef, she'd carried a seed of rebellion—no one else had ever questioned Tamura so directly and publicly. And Azur was stronger now. As the First Mother, her power as a symbol was undeniable. Another reason to keep her and the baby close, thought

Tamura. To stay in line, Azur would need to feel treasured. Adding her to the council had been a step in that direction.

But Tamura had doubts she could not confide in anyone, not Azur, not any of her lieutenants. Not the quiet armorer Golhabi, who kept herself to herself, nor the smith, Zalma, whose ready grin and deadly hammer were always at her queen's disposal. The truth of it was that Tamura missed Gretti like a limb. The fact that the woman was still physically present, unchanged in every way except her curdled hatred of Tamura, made the ache all the more unbearable.

The problem wasn't that the Scorpicae couldn't win. It was that over time, if both they and their enemy lost combatants every time their forces met, the Scorpicae would run out first. The raiding strategy had worked so far, but she couldn't expect that luck to last. If they met a serious challenge, five or ten or even twenty Scorpicae could be wiped out in a matter of minutes. Over time, they'd lose dozens, then hundreds. There would be no coming back from that.

Tamura would have to increase the recruiting parties. They'd built much of their current force from the daughters of other queendoms, but at the moment, soldiers were still scarcer than supplies. Still, she had to believe that Scorpica could offer a home and a purpose to girls and women who were desperate for one. From what they'd seen in Arca's eastern reaches, there were plenty of desperate Arcan girls and women. Plenty of women in Paxim, too, must be discontented with the direction their nation was going—scouts had brought the news that Paximite men were being given more and more power, raising them above their historical station. That would never happen in Scorpica. What about Bastionites who chafed at their society's rigid strictures? Sestians who wanted more than a life spent farming, praying, burning bones, or chasing sheep in and out of meadows? Scorpica could welcome them all. All that was needed was to gather the discontented in. Give them a home. Celebrate and appreciate them. Make them warriors.

Tamura needed to put this effort in someone's hands besides her own—she needed to focus on the raids—but she had no councillors she could fully trust. And, for the love of the Scorpion, she knew who would be perfectly suited to the task. She knew who she needed was the one person who was the least likely to do her any kind of favor ever again. She needed Gretti dha Rhodarya.

She imagined Gretti standing there beside her. What would Gretti say, what insight would she offer? She imagined the conversation, hearing the words in her head, Gretti's admonishing tone.

Yes, recruitment must continue, the imagined Gretti said inside Tamura's mind. *But can't we think further ahead? What do we need for the future?*

The next generation, answered Tamura. *Baby girls.*

Yes. Like Madazur. And, hmm, how can we get them?

Pleasures, of course. But we can't exactly ride into these villages with legs spread and watch the men line up to offer their rain.

I don't doubt we could, said the imagined Gretti, with a bitter laugh that Tamura realized almost as soon as she heard it that the real Gretti would never give. The real Gretti was far too circumspect, not so unkind. Tamura thought harder about what Gretti would really say. *Here is not the place for it. But isn't it early summer? Won't the rites be starting soon?*

A genius, thought Tamura. Even only imagined in her mind, Gretti was a genius.

The Sun Rites took place only once every five years, but in the four years between, Moon Rites were held in the Holy City of Sestia. No sacrifices, less ritual, but the goal was the same: to honor the god Sestia, the Holy One, by celebrating pleasures with true abandon. In past years, before relations between the queendoms began to break down during the Drought, the Scorpicae had always sent a healthy contingent. Midsummer was already approaching; the first Moon Rites after the Drought would happen before the moon turned full again. Certainly the celebration this year, with the veil of darkness lifted, was sure to be wild.

Perhaps no men at the rites would seek out pleasures with Scorpican women, but that was no matter—they didn't have to know the women were Scorpican. There were plenty of Paximite women who wore their hair short, thought Tamura with excitement. Raiding parties could easily pillage enough tunics and leggings to costume one or two dozen warriors as pilgrims to the shrine of the Thrift God. Perhaps twenty-five, a lucky number. Instructed correctly, they could pass as women who had never lifted a sword. Women who would fling themselves into pleasure as if it were only celebration, not an act of creation, not an investment in a future army that would take time to grow.

Eternal Scorpion, Tamura thought to herself, sprinkling the last of the lily wine onto the smoldering coals of the fire. *All I do is for your glory. For you the blood, for you the beloved blade, for you the victory. Let your warriors multiply like the seeds of the sunflower. All this I wish in your name.*

She would gather the young women together, a lucky twenty-five, yes. There were three former followers of the God of Thrift who had pledged themselves to the Scorpion, and they could teach the young Scorpicae how to look and act, perhaps even point out where the right garb could be stolen. Then, once the young women were ready, she would send them forth to the rites with great ceremony. The raids and recruiting parties could continue uninterrupted, because there would be plenty of warriors left to carry those out, especially if she was careful to continue keeping the patterns unpredictable. She would put those journeying to the rites under Azur's leadership, because of course Azur had to be one of those who went. She alone had proven herself capable of bearing a girl after the Drought. If she could repeat the miracle, what a coup it would be both for her and her nation.

And it would keep Azur out of harm's way. Tamura knew how bloodthirsty this daughter was, had always known. This mission would kill several birds with one stone. And the Scorpion alone knew how many birds would have to die, figuratively speaking, for Scorpica as a nation to emerge victorious.

✦

It was strange how much quieter the camp felt without the youngest women, even though only two dozen had gone, and thousands more remained. But Gretti felt the difference in the camp, in the way the warriors carried themselves. There was another kind of hope now, more than just the fierce focus of war, but the stirrings of another future.

Gretti, for her part, was busy caring for Madazur, nurturing her with goat milk, rocking her to sleep. Azur had been one of the young women Tamura sent to the rites, and she needed to travel unencumbered. Sending a contingent to the rites made all the sense in the world; Gretti had in fact thought of it herself, though she didn't tell Tamura, still torn between her loyalty to the country and fury at the woman who had taken all the work they'd done together and twisted it for her own purpose.

But Tamura, either alone or with help from another adviser, had figured it out. Every young Scorpican should try her best to water the seeds within as soon as possible; Madazur needed sister warriors to ride at her side. She would almost certainly rise to be queen of Scorpica one day. The secret, thought Gretti grimly, would be getting Scorpica to last long enough for that day to come. And Gretti's punishment for turning her back on Tamura was that she was not sent to the rites, would not be indulging in pleasures, would not come back to the camp with a future warrior growing like a sapling inside her. In her quiet moments Gretti had been thinking more about motherhood, turning the idea over in her mind, wondering whether it was a path she wanted to take. But without the opportunity, it mattered little what she wanted. For now, she would care for the most precious child Scorpica had seen in a generation, and that would do.

Three weeks after the party of young warriors in disguise had left to trek across Paxim to Sestia to try their luck at the Moon Rites, back at the caldera, a day of promise dawned bright and clear. Tamura had sent five raiding parties, a lucky number, out to strike five villages. When the first returned, not only did they bring the five warriors who had left that morning, but two of the warriors rode double: they had brought back two additional women as well.

Were they prisoners? What had happened? Gretti always contrived to be nearby when raiders returned, with or without Madazur in her arms. Today the armorer Golhabi had consented to let the baby nap next to her, and Gretti had only herself to care for, a situation that made her somewhat uncomfortable. She knew how to care for others; she knew what they needed. She found her own needs somewhat of a mystery.

As soon as the new arrivals dismounted, the Arcan women both dropped to their knees in front of Tamura, touching their heads to the black earth. Their pendants of sand dragged on the ground. Any Arcan who wished to do magic either needed to stand on sand or carry sand, and Gretti knew that these pendants, called *psamas*, meant these women could do magic at any time. She hoped Tamura was thinking along the same lines.

"Queen Tamura," said Nikhit, her voice proud, "these women wish to join our cause."

"Rise," Tamura said to the two women, her voice carrying, "so that I may examine you."

The elder of the two was probably close to Tamura's age, thought Gretti. She had sharp, knowing eyes and a smear of the caldera's black earth on her forehead. The other was perhaps ten years younger, narrow in the hips, with an open, friendly face.

"I am Jenday," said the younger one. "I wish to join your fight."

The other locked her gaze on Tamura's face and said, "I am Lembi. I want to be Scorpican."

"Very well," said Tamura, a smile crooking the corner of her mouth. "We are always flattered by such interest. Would you like to tell me about your magic? Is it something we can turn to our use?"

Jenday looked down and said, "I'm afraid my gift is a modest one. But I can start a small fire without the help of kindling, and you may find that helpful here and there. And I'm a hard worker and a fast learner. If you give me a weapon, I will learn to use it. I am ready to dedicate myself to the Scorpican cause."

"And you, Lembi?"

The older woman shrugged lightly. "I have the gift of finding the truth. And you cannot trust Jenday."

Gretti realized that Lembi had been edging away from Jenday, preparing for this revelation, from the moment they'd risen. Now Jenday was closer to Nikhit, and as soon as Jenday's eyes went wide at the revelation, Tamura nodded to Nikhit, who stepped forward and restrained Jenday's arms in a hug that looked almost gentle. But Gretti knew Nikhit, had watched her train and even sparred with her, and she knew it wasn't.

Tamura said, "I will restrain her to be safe, but tell me, Lembi, how can I trust you? Perhaps you're the one with deception in your heart, and this is your plan to deflect suspicion."

"I will take any oath you choose, my queen," said Lembi, turning her palms upward. "And I can prove my gift."

Tamura said, "Very well. Prove it."

Lembi pointed to Nikhit, ignoring Jenday's furious glare. "Have this one ask you a question."

"Any question?"

"Any question."

They exchanged looks. Nikhit, still restraining Jenday, asked Tamura in a skeptical voice, "What was the first animal you hunted and killed?"

Gretti observed as Tamura looked back and forth between Jenday and Lembi, watching emotions play across both strangers' faces. Gretti saw the queen mark it when Lembi's hand went up to the *psama* around her neck, two fingers and a thumb resting lightly on the pendant's surface.

Then, her gaze moving up to Lembi's face, Tamura answered Nikhit's question for all to hear. "A coney."

Without hesitation, Lembi said loudly, "A lie."

Tamura cocked her head. "Interesting you should say so. If that was not the true answer, do you know what is?"

"No," Lembi said, without apology. "I see whether what you've spoken is truth or lie. My power is a mind power, but not that kind."

"Very well. It was a red fox," Tamura said.

"Still a lie." Lembi's tone was still factual, not pleased, not annoyed.

"Wolf?"

"No."

"I think perhaps it was a squirrel," said Tamura.

Lembi shook her head, just a little. "'Think' and 'perhaps' can cloud a lie. If you want my proof, give me facts."

"It was a squirrel." This time Tamura said it firmly, an assertion.

"Yes. It was," said Lembi.

"I see," said Tamura, her voice even, but she could not keep the grin from her face. Recognition had dawned.

Gretti, for her part, knew what Tamura was thinking as surely as if the queen had spoken aloud. Tamura had seen right away to what purpose she could put Lembi and her gift.

The next part, Gretti was afraid to watch, because both Arcans had claimed to be speaking truth. If one had proved herself right, the other was not just suspect, but a confirmed liar.

"So," Tamura said to Jenday, "we return to you and your willingness to, how did you put it, join our fight?"

But the answer was clear to anyone paying attention. Tamura didn't even really need to ask Jenday a question and have Lembi reveal it to be a lie. Everything she needed—everything any Scorpican needed—was in the way Jenday's formerly friendly face was twisted

179

in an angry rictus, clear fury aimed in Lembi's direction. After that, the questioning was just a formality.

Tamura put a knife into Lembi's hand and said, almost conversationally, "Lembi, have you killed before?"

The Arcan's eyes did not widen. "Only animals, Queen Tamura."

"Ah, you need not call me Queen. As a matter of fact, many Scorpicae who were first born in other lands call me Mother."

Gretti saw her moment and took it. Stepping forward, she said, "Well, Queen Tamura, this one is not your daughter yet."

Tamura raised an eyebrow as if in amusement, though her jaw remained tight. "Ah! You have an idea, I see, Gretti dha Rhodarya. Please, share."

"You have many daughters," Gretti said, projecting calm, choosing her words with care. "Perhaps our newest warriors might be welcomed as the daughters of others in the tribe."

A flicker of annoyance crossed the queen's face, but her attention was wholly on Gretti now, not on Lembi, who held the knife with uncertainty, nor on Jenday, who seemed unable to look away from it.

Finally Tamura said to Gretti, "I suppose the idea has merit. Did you want to take Lembi as your own daughter, Gretti?"

"I think there is a more urgent matter, my queen," said Gretti, taking one more step forward, inserting herself into the action. "And that is letting this attempted spy go."

"Let her go?" laughed Tamura. "You can't possibly argue for mercy."

"No, not mercy," Gretti said, trying to keep the irritation from her voice. "Strategy. We want her to sing her story far and wide. To tell everyone that the Scorpicae are welcoming daughters. And that only those true of heart and clear of purpose can join us."

Tamura said, "I still think we should kill her. Lembi?"

Lembi looked back and forth between the two women's faces, clearly overwhelmed. She said nothing. Her grip on the knife Tamura had given her seemed to loosen.

Jenday's eyes were wide pools. She was terrified.

Gretti addressed Tamura, looking past everyone else, focusing only on the queen. "If you want more Scorpicae to join our ranks, more sisters, more daughters, you let this one go. She'll tell the story. Won't you, Jenday?"

"Yes . . . yes."

Tamura was looking at Gretti, not Jenday, when she said, "I'll let her go. Only if you agree to supervise the addition of new Scorpicae to our ranks. I want them all tested to make sure their intent is pure."

"I think the only one you need for that test is Lembi."

"Yes, but that's not all we need. She'll perform the honesty test. But you'll find a place for those who pass. You'll decide who becomes whose daughter. You'll find out how they can be useful to us, arrange the training, find them homes, give them weapons. Do you agree to this?" Then and only then she let her gaze linger on Jenday, and after she did, the next thing she focused on was the dagger in Lembi's hand.

"I'll do it," answered Gretti without hesitation. She understood the unspoken message behind Tamura's words: agreement or sacrifice, nothing in between. "If you send Jenday on her way unharmed, I will begin immediately."

"Very well." Tamura gestured, and Jenday was released so suddenly she sprawled in the dirt.

"Go," Gretti whispered to her. "Tell the tale, just as I said you would. Let the discontented women and girls of Arca know that the Scorpicae will welcome them with open arms."

They watched her go until she was gone from sight.

"Well, then!" Tamura's voice was bright, almost unseemly, as she addressed Gretti. "And your new position begins. Whose daughter shall Lembi be?"

Gretti knew it was a test. She couldn't give the newest daughter to Tamura, and she couldn't take her for herself. It took her a moment to come up with an answer.

"Kneel, Lembi," she said, and the young woman obeyed immediately. Then Gretti beckoned to Nikhit, who reacted with surprise, but came as she was bid. Gretti placed the warrior's hand on the Arcan's bent head.

"Rise, Lembi dha Nikhit," Gretti intoned solemnly, and Tamura gave a sharp nod, indicating she'd chosen well. The other warriors circled around to welcome the new recruit, slapping her on the back and showing her how to fashion a loop in her belt to hold her new dagger, but Gretti hung back.

There was something in Tamura's eyes she couldn't read. Triumph? That was what it seemed to resemble most closely. Fine, let the queen feel she had won the day.

There were many battles yet to fight, Gretti thought, and not all of them on foreign soil. Just as important were the battles within.

And those, she intended to win. Gretti's eyes were on a far-off horizon.

◆

Several days later, as the sun set on the Scorpican camp, Tamura was restless.

Perhaps other Scorpicae were becoming accustomed to this black bowl in the earth, perched on the border between the red dirt of Godsbones and the golden sands of Arca, but Tamura grew more impatient every day. She missed Scorpica. The woods, green and welcoming. The cool mountain air of her native land. Whichever way she looked—east to the red dirt, west to the gold sand, or right down at the black earth under her feet—her eyes ached with the hostility of it all. She'd begun to hate the sun.

Of course, there wasn't much to love about the darkness, either. The caldera itself was barren, nothing growing in its ground, but beyond the lip of the bowl, from the wild east, one could still hear the unseen creatures of Godsbones calling. Tonight was no exception. Tamura shifted closer to the fire.

She had headed a raiding party earlier in the day, and despite a close call, her raid had been a success. As she waited for Khinar to return with the other warriors who had gone out, she prayed that the Scorpion had extended her favor to the other raiding party.

As it turned out, she had not.

Two hours after dark, Tamura picked a bit of fat out of her teeth and pitched it into the fire, where it made a popping noise and threw off a few sparks. The spoils of her party had included several braces of already cleaned and dressed coneys, and they'd feasted on the meat, knowing it wouldn't keep. They'd divided the total in half and devoured only the first half so far, keeping the other half against the second party's return. But now that group was hours overdue, and Tamura had sent the other warriors to rest, staying up alone to stand watch. As she did, she'd dipped into the supply set aside for the second party, just once. Coney tended to toughen as it cooled, and the cooks who had prepared it tonight had not left much juice in the meat. For this and many other reasons, she missed the warriors she'd sent to Sestia with Azur. She wondered how her daughter's mission was faring.

On some level, despite how vigilantly they'd prepared for this war, she had to admit—only to herself—that they were unprepared. They had read the maps closely, but there was information that did not show on maps. There was nowhere to keep an army in eastern Arca. The desert was too hot during the day, the water too hard to come by. At least Gretti, before she had abandoned Tamura's cause, had selected the caldera as the place to house their warriors.

Gretti had also been correct that resistance to their attacks would be weak. Tamura had feared the power of magicians to harm her precious warriors, but so far, the death of Dree in Jesephia had been their worst loss by far. It was as Gretti had predicted: though the women of Arca were powerful, those powers were meant for guiding, helping, growing. Bending those powers to the purpose of destruction was possible, but as yet, the Scorpicae hadn't seen it done.

Then Tamura heard something, a series of scratching noises, close enough to startle her. She heard breath before she saw movement, and she was on her feet with her sword in hand.

"Who is it?"

There was no answer but the sight of a figure in motion, drawing closer, and its way of moving caught her attention. It was too deliberate, the way each foot came up and back down to earth again, and when the figure entered the firelight, she saw the reason.

The figure was not a warrior. It was not even a person. It was some kind of woman-shaped figure made of sand, its face without eyes or mouth, and it came straight for her.

Its silence was unnerving, and Tamura sprang up to meet it with silence of her own, thrusting her dagger in that same motion, plunging it deep into the sand being's throat.

The sand being reached for that dagger in its throat, withdrew it, and stabbed back at Tamura.

The Scorpican queen dodged her own blade easily, but her blood ran cold; what was this thing, and how had it gotten past the guards? All too quickly she realized the answer. There had been no outcry. Tamura dodged another weak blow from the sand soldier and lashed out with one foot to kick the dagger out of its hand. She kicked the hand clean off along with the dagger, but even as she watched, the hand re-formed, and the sand soldier was advancing on her again.

"Hee-yai!" she yelled, the command to gather, and then the night lit up with fire until it was as almost bright as day.

At first it was nearly impossible for Tamura to track what was going on. Every warrior in the camp had risen to fight, but hands were erupting from the earth to grab at their feet.

Sometimes those hands detached and dropped to the black dirt, dissolving again and then rising in a different place, but sometimes they anchored a warrior to the ground, and it was too difficult to watch what happened once a warrior was fixed in place with no escape.

Letting the sand soldier grab her dagger from her, Tamura took advantage of the thing's momentary distraction to draw her sword and swung hard, cleaving its sand head from its sand neck. This seemed to slow it down, though the body still raised its hands to come for her.

Tamura took a moment to look at her surroundings. A moment was all it took to understand what was happening.

Five robed figures stood on the lip of the caldera, stretched out in a ragged chain, their arms and fingers dancing in different patterns. Five Arcan magicians. Of course it was five. The guards were dead, that much seemed obvious, and now the rest of the warriors fought for their lives.

Tamura said a quick prayer of thanks to the Scorpion that the young women were gone, that Azur was not here. Madazur, though, where was she? With Gretti, likely. Tamura couldn't spare the time to search. She was in the thick of battle. The best thing the queen could do for her granddaughter now, for the future of their whole nation, was make sure to win.

Then the flames began, bursting outward from scattered places. Small bits of magic exploded here and there. At first it seemed like utter chaos, but eventually, Tamura found a pattern in it, and in that pattern, she found a keen hope.

Individually, the Arcan attackers were fierce and dangerous, but they were not working together. They didn't even glance at each other. And any enemy scattered could be defeated.

Tamura focused on the closest magician, the only one of the five who had descended from the lip of the caldera, who was reaching out to touch warriors and dealing death with every touch. Even as Tamura watched, though the warrior under the magician's hand was crumpling to the ground, another warrior behind the magician lined up her sword and ran the magician clear through, the point of the sword emerging from her belly. The magician swayed on her feet and collapsed, the warrior drawing her sword out as she fell. From this distance Tamura could not hear, but she could see the warrior's lips moving, and knew she was offering a blessing to the Scorpion. *The fight is done.*

But around them, the rest of the fight was raging.

Another mage high on the lip of the caldera, so far her features were merely a smear under her cowl, appeared to be drawing a bow, though her hands were empty. Tamura turned to smother a fledgling fire next to her with her cloak, and when she'd put the flame out, turned back to refocus her eyes on the magician. The magician made the motion of drawing a bow again and her gaze met Tamura's; too late, Tamura realized she'd made herself a target.

The magician released the invisible bowstring.

Tamura bent to pick up the cloak she'd used to smother the fire and whipped it through the air in front of her face, its deep folds clustered, and she felt the unmistakable *thwack* of an arrow's impact. The fabric tore. Yet when she shook the cloak out, there was no sign of an arrow. It was as if the cloak had been shot with air alone, but air that could kill.

Tamura dove into her nearby tent and retrieved her own bow. Around her the sea of bodies swirled. Any number of fallen warriors was too many, but she couldn't save them all. She did the one thing she knew she could. Keeping her eyes trained on the magician, she notched an arrow to the bowstring, let go, and put that arrow through the magician's throat.

The chaos began to quiet. Hands of black earth still reached up from the ground, but she heard a shout of victory from not too far off—had that been Nikhit? Perhaps the smith, Zalma?—and suddenly every hand froze in unison, whether or not it gripped a warrior, and none moved again.

After that, with the enemy dissipated, the Scorpicae quickly gathered themselves and surveyed the damage. Tents and cook fires were quickly put to rights, but it took much longer to sort through the fallen and separate the wounded from the dead. Tamura herself didn't lay hands on any of the fallen. She barked commands and expected them to be followed. If she had been weary before the attack, she was now exhausted to her bones, an unfamiliar trill of fear bubbling under her skin.

She turned her attention to the fallen enemy. Four robed bodies lay at Tamura's feet, but there was no fifth. Whether the fifth magician had been vaporized, had disappeared herself, or had merely managed to run away in the madness of the battle, Tamura didn't know. But it didn't matter.

The enemy had been beaten back, defeated. And yet. Tamura and her army had counted on this caldera to keep them safe from the enemy, and it had failed. If the fifth magician had escaped with her life, she could tell anyone and everyone where to find the encamped warriors. And even if she hadn't, someone had sent these magicians here. Someone— maybe even Queen Eminel—knew where the Scorpicae were, and the bad luck rumored to attend Arcans who set foot in the Navel hadn't been enough to deter them. Someone could just send more magicians. The next time the Arcans came, they would come in greater numbers, and chances were, they would be ready to truly fight.

The Scorpicae could no longer stay in Velja's Navel. They would have to pack up and leave, to scurry like rats. There was no other safe place in Arca; they would have to retreat into the only place they knew no one would follow, back into the wild, desolate, dangerous land of Godsbones.

Perhaps, Tamura admitted to herself, that was why this victory felt so much like defeat.

✦ 14 ✦

THE GODS' WEDDING

Midsummer, the All-Mother's Year 517
Ursu, Paxim
Heliane, Ama

Three moons after her banquet celebrating the end of the Drought of Girls, Heliane woke in the morning, stared toward the ceiling high above her, and worried that she might lack the strength to rise from her bed.

Not every day started this way, but too many did. On days like this, a gray sky overhead and a dull ache throughout her whole body as if she were being gripped in a giant's fist, Heliane wished she felt only the pain that threatened to tear her apart when the mad sorcerer Sessadon had flung her from the sky. Her broken back, fused by a healer in haste after the rites, had been with her since that day, and she'd grown accustomed to it. But this new ache had no clear explanation, striking her with a far deeper fear. The wasting disease that killed her husband had come from nowhere, with no clear cause, no trigger, no cure. And it had started—if she remembered correctly, and how could she forget?—with Cyrus's strength fading. *The strangest thing, Heli. I feel so weak.*

So every day, she adjusted her strategies to keep her weakness secret. When important events required her presence, she took care to be seated before they began. She rose later in the day and retired earlier in the evening, saving her energy. She'd always preferred to dine lightly in the company of others, but she was so good at moving her food around on her plate that only one person knew she went most meals without eating a bite. That person was the servant boy who whisked her plate away. She doubted he'd ever mentioned it to the cooks, for fear of getting cuffed for bearing bad news.

Heliane had her ways of managing. She knew they would not work forever. But even on days like these, the bad days, she always had one question to consider: Was today the day she would give up?

No, she decided. Today was not that day.

Instead she forced herself to rise—slowly, with great care—and called out for someone to fetch Inbar, her *cosmete*.

The servants brought her morning tea, a bitter greenish-black concoction she drank unsweetened, which she could feel scouring her throat and waking her from toes to fingertips. As she sipped the tea, she nibbled on her favorite delicacy, the only taste she could tolerate on days like this. Decima had sent another pouch of the fragrant candied pears when Heliane hinted that her supply was running low. She wouldn't give up on living, she told herself, as long as the All-Mother still allowed her to savor this taste: the perfect sweetness of the dried fruit cut by the bitter undercurrent in the snowdrop honey, the sharp, herbal note of the rosemary. Perhaps she should have the cook bake a few into a milk pudding; perhaps she'd be able to keep that down. But for now, she sank her teeth in, glad she could find enough pleasure to cut through the pain.

Thus fortified, even as she noted with dismay that she'd lost the feeling in her toes again, she managed to sit upright in her styling chair. Inbar appeared with her usual creams and combs, brushes and pins.

The familiar touch of her nimble fingers against Heliane's scalp drew a contented sigh from the tired queen's throat. When Inbar had first begun to style her hair, so many years before, it had been ink-black, and now it was cloud-white. There was no one else the queen trusted with her hair on important days. She had decided that this would be an important day. The queen would appear in public, unannounced. Quash the rumors of her weakness, which were too close to the truth to let stand.

"What style today, Queen?" asked Inbar. Even her trusted servant's voice sounded not quite right to Heliane. Then again, it was very possible the fault lay not in Inbar's voice but in the queen's ears.

Heliane answered her simply. "Down, please."

Inbar seemed confused, almost offended, by the answer. "Down? No braids at all? What is your plan for the day?"

Heliane let a flash of irritation show. "My plan, Inbar, is to wear my hair down."

"But are you—are you going out of the palace?"

Crossly, Heliane said, "What difference does it make? You make my hairstyles, not my travel plans."

Inbar was silent for a long moment, her fingertips stilling atop the queen's head. Part of Heliane wanted to push against the *cosmete*'s fingers like a cat, hungry for touch; another part of her wanted to unsettle the woman, remind her it was not her place to question. Heliane remained unmoving.

Then Inbar said quietly, in a voice the servants and Queensguard in the hall wouldn't be able to hear, "I only wondered. I worry about your health. You don't seem well."

"I'm well enough," Heliane snapped. "Now if you don't want to comb out my hair, I can find someone else to do it. I'm well enough for that, too."

"I'm sorry, Queen." The servant woman bobbed her head, her manner contrite. "I had assumed you'd want braids, which was wrong of me. I need a moment to fetch a different salve. If you'll allow me."

The queen nodded, granting her permission for Inbar to leave the room, resisting the urge to blurt an apology. She shouldn't have been so harsh. The weakness had her on edge. And a lot was riding on today. Most of Paxim's senators were still back in their home districts, doing their best to make the next generation, but they would hear through the grapevine what Heliane did and did not do. It was for them, among other reasons, that she would make today's trip.

Once Inbar returned, she dabbed a fragrant salve onto the queen's scalp and began guiding it through with a special boar-bristle brush. If the *cosmete* seemed unusually quiet, she at least lavished the care upon Heliane that she was used to. Heliane breathed an involuntary sigh as soon as she felt the weight of the familiar brush, the reassuring scratch of the bristles passing over her scalp in long, slow strokes. She closed her eyes and breathed slowly. She couldn't afford to succumb to relaxation completely, but she let herself savor a few moments of peace.

"All done, Queen. It does look beautiful," the *cosmete* said.

"Thank you," murmured Heliane without opening her eyes. She knew Inbar had been thorough. No doubt the queen's hair was a gleaming white curtain bright as starlight. "Would you send in the *belmetes* and *gemete*?"

"Of course," Inbar answered, and was gone.

When the other servants came in, Heliane sent one to fetch her gold circlet with the ruby eye, reserved for ceremonial occasions, and set it gently on the crown of her head. She chose her deepest purple robe and stood stock-still while two more servants wrapped it carefully around her inert body, directing a third to belt it with an unusual saffron-dyed sash. There. Now she felt particularly festive.

Heliane sent word for Paulus to join her—he would bring Ama—and dispatched Delph to ready the Queensguard. While she was alone, Heliane mixed another strong tea with her own two hands, away from prying eyes. The taste was even more bitter, the color cloudy, but it would give her the energy she needed to push herself forward through the next few hours. Her eyes would be bright, her smile wide. And she was ready to be seen now. When her companions arrived, they would go into the city together to celebrate the feast day of the Gods' Wedding.

While nearly every major or minor god in the pantheon had been born to another god, few of those gods bothered with the institution of marriage, or so the stories went. On cynical days, Heliane wondered whether the stories of divine weddings had simply been removed from the record, since marriages differed so much between queendoms. Paxim's marriages were the most official, requiring a negotiated contract between the parties involved. The most famous was the marriage contract of Senator Gabrin and her two-fold spouse Juro, which had stretched to an astonishing ninety-eight pages. Sestia had only walking marriages, the Bastion and Scorpica no marriages at all, and in Arca, proper marriage was seen as a joining of a woman with two men. For gods to marry would mean aligning with one of those models, excluding the others. If there had once been stories of divine marriages, they'd been allowed to fade from the collective memory.

But one wedding was a tale still told, so rare it was simply called the Gods' Wedding: the marriage of Victory and Wealth.

The idea had taken root in Heliane's mind when the assemblywoman from Hayk had presented herself at the palace yet again, pleading her case, asking that the queen please consider honoring her city this year by attending the festival of the Bandit God. The festival had been disrupted several years before by some kind of terrorist attack, still unsolved, and attendance had been sparse ever since. The assemblywoman felt that a royal visit would encourage the crowds to come again. In her younger years Heliane would have happily gone, but Hayk was several days' ride, and she couldn't possibly muster the strength for such a trip. But she could make an appearance here in her own city and quell the rumors of her weakness, at least for a while.

"Mother!" Paulus greeted her, snapping her out of her reverie, and she rose, arms outstretched, to return his greeting. Ama lingered in the doorway, watching, as was her way. Both Paulus and Ama were dressed festively, the kingling's tunic embroidered from neck to waist with a riot of palm-sized flowers every color of the rainbow, the bodyguard wearing a marigold knee-length draped skirt instead of her customary leggings.

"Shall we go?" asked Heliane. "I'm eager to see the celebration."

It all felt so normal, at least for a while. The three of them strode down the hall to meet their carriage at the side entrance, Paulus chattering merrily about a half-dozen different variations of the story of the Gods' Wedding that he'd read in his books. When he said excitedly, "And in that version of the story, they knelt on a bed of narcissus, while all the other versions agree it was almond-flower!" Heliane caught a hint of a smile on Ama's face.

That was the reason that, as the Queensguard arrayed themselves around the carriage to ride on its outer boards, Heliane turned to Ama and said, "Ride inside with us, won't you?"

The young woman's face showed no emotion as she murmured, "Yes, Queen Heliane," and moved into position to follow Heliane and Paulus inside. But when all three were in the carriage, Heliane seated on one bench, Paulus on the other, the bodyguard paused where she stood, eyes downcast. It was obvious to Heliane that Ama's place was next to Paulus, so why did she hesitate? Why did Paulus's hand twitch upward as if he'd begun to reach out for her, but then thought better of it?

Heliane took pity on Ama and patted the seat next to her. "Sit with me, Ama," she said. "You can keep an eye on your charge well enough from here."

They arrived without incident at the city square. It was festooned with decorations, a pole fluttering with brightly colored ribbons marking the center of the square. Heliane halted for a moment when she noticed that ten fleet-footed young boys wove the ribbons in and out—had it not been for the Drought, an equal number of boys and girls would have been dancing—but she forced herself to carry on.

As soon as the carriage brought her to the edge of the square, she was confident she'd made the right decision. Beauty as far as the eye could see. Every building along the square was draped in garlands of flowers; the people themselves wore elegant gowns, flattering tunics, cloaks woven in the brightest colors known to woman. The sunlight was thin and yet, looking upon the scene, Heliane still felt warmth radiating into her. Yes, a good decision. The joy of the festival day was infectious.

"Lead us out, Paulus," she told her son, and he nodded his agreement. Ama followed him, this time without hesitation. The two of them held the doors open while the queen descended.

Heliane alit from the carriage and her Queensguard disappeared into the crowd around her, slipping carefully in among the civilians so the guards could monitor the situation without calling attention to their presence. She'd commanded them to do this, though Delph had of course resisted, preferring to block her monarch's body physically with her own. But walking among the crowd and being seen was the point of this whole exercise. If she were going to push herself to the limit and beyond, Heliane would make it count.

"Queen," Ama said quietly, so only she could hear, "do you wish that I walk with Paulus or do as your Queensguard has done?"

"Watch with them, but watch close," Heliane answered. Almost before she'd finished speaking, the bodyguard melted away into the crowd.

Heliane reached out to tuck her arm through Paulus's. From the angle of his body, she could tell he was trying to follow Ama with his eyes without making it obvious he was trying. The queen wanted to chuckle, though she didn't. For all her exhaustion, her mind seemed to be working as well as ever today—the tea must be helping—and a certain picture was beginning to come clear.

Heliane and Paulus strolled along through the square, the queen working hard to look like she wasn't resting her weight on him, and the crowd gave them space. Excited whispers followed them: festivalgoers had noted the queen's presence. Word was spreading.

"Are you sure this is a good idea?" Paulus asked, keeping his tone light, but she knew his concern was real.

"The best," answered Heliane, and she almost meant it.

They'd wandered into a line of booths featuring games of chance, and a booth keeper in a bright red cap held out a ball to Paulus. "Try your luck, Kingling?"

Paulus took the ball, testing its weight in his hand, his face thoughtful. Heliane saw her chance and plucked the ball from his hand, laughing.

"Hey!" Paulus protested, but not sincerely.

"What's yours is mine, what's mine is yours," answered Heliane. Freeing her other arm from his, she aimed the ball at the stack of wooden blocks at the back of the booth and let fly. Her ball struck true and the blocks came tumbling down.

The whole crowd around them whooped with joy, Heliane's and Paulus's delighted shouts drowned out by the sheer volume of other spectators.

Reaching one arm across the counter to the booth keeper in the red cap, Paulus took delivery of the prize, a flower-crown of enormous lilies the bright yellow of the summer sun. "A new crown for you, Mother," he joked, and polite laughter rippled around them.

Paulus had raised the flower-crown in both hands, ready to lower it over Heliane's golden circlet, when the crowd jostled and shifted, coming too close, and someone in a hooded cloak bumped into her from the side.

The cloaked figure knocked Heliane off-balance, and the queen felt herself falling. She let herself fall. She landed a bit harder than she'd hoped, the breath fleeing her chest, but there was no pain.

The queen and the person in the cloak both lay on the ground for just a moment, the sound of the crowd around them turning from delight to terror. In that moment, the hooded figure whispered into the queen's ear, soft words no one else could hear.

The Queensguard was almost upon them—Heliane recognized their shouts—but the figure rolled toward the game booth and under its front counter, which did not reach all the way to the ground, and sprinted away.

Heliane opened her mouth, readying herself to shout that she was all right, but no sound came.

She hadn't been afraid to come here. She hadn't been afraid when she fell, or when the figure whispered. But now that she was trying to speak, trying to rise, and could do neither, now she was afraid.

A figure dropped to its knees next to her, a face appearing less than a handspan from hers. Short curls, keen eyes, a faint scar on the cheek. Ama.

Ama examined the queen closely, seeming satisfied with what she saw. Sharp, confident, she whispered, "We have you."

Then Heliane felt the young woman's hand cradle the back of her neck, raising the queen's mouth to the bodyguard's ear. Gratitude filled her. This close, she would only need to whisper.

"Get us home," Heliane said, or hoped she said.

The quick-thinking young woman pulled Heliane to her feet with no apparent effort, then laced Heliane's arm through her own and gestured for Paulus to take her other arm. He stepped up quickly, shifting the flower-crown he still held to his other hand, and Heliane was supported on both sides in an instant.

Ama said a few low words in haste to Paulus, and he raised his head, cleared his throat. Heliane couldn't turn to catch his expression, but when he spoke, his voice betrayed no fear, no anxiety.

"All is well!" he called out. "May the blessings of the All-Mother, and the good fortune of Victory and Wealth, come to you this festival day!" He raised the bright yellow flower-crown high, waving to the crowd in every direction, and they applauded him. Then, unsure where to put the wreath, he plopped it onto his own head at a rakish angle.

Then they were in motion. From somewhere toward the center of the square, music began playing, a merry tune of horns and strings.

The queen, her son, and his bodyguard, arm in arm, pretended to stroll casually toward the barrels of wine at the far side of the square. In fact, Ama and Paulus were holding up nearly the entire weight of the queen, whose legs had gone to jelly.

Heliane wondered if they would steer her straight to the carriage, which would be a mistake. It would be too obvious if she left too soon. Relief flooded through her when Ama indicated a barrel and asked, "Would you like to sit for a moment, Queen, to enjoy the music?" Heliane found she could incline her head, and before she knew it, she was seated.

As the musicians played louder and faster, dancers began to swirl through the open space of the square. Eyes turned toward them, not her, and she was grateful. Ama and Paulus carried on chattering merrily, addressing their comments to Heliane more than each other, keeping up the pretense. She let herself fade, let her mind swim. She could rest. She had to. No one needed to know that the sky felt like it was pressing down on her. Once, when Scorpicae had still made up her Queensguard, one of them had given her a taste of the strong drink called hammerwine; she felt, in this moment, like she'd drained a jug of the stuff. She tilted her head, pretended to follow the conversation, though their voices only buzzed like bees.

Then a few words reached her from the milling crowd behind them, a snatch of conversation.

A poisonous whisper, all too clear. "You see how he crowns himself already?"

A different voice responding, more measured. "Oh, don't be so quick to judge. I doubt he means anything by it."

"Doesn't matter what he *means*." Sneering, unconvinced.

Heliane hoped Paulus hadn't heard. She would've done something about it, if she could do anything at all.

Two more songs, a few more minutes of rest, and Heliane heard Ama's voice whispering right next to her ear. "Queen, we go now. You need only walk a few steps. Are you ready?"

She nodded, and they went.

Once the carriage door was shut safely behind them, Heliane let herself fall sideways, stretching out across the seat, her head on Paulus's lap. She closed her eyes.

The next thing she knew, she heard the voices of angry women arguing from outside the carriage. Time had passed, she was sure, but how much?

"I can take her," Ama was saying, not yelling, but her voice was sharper than Heliane had ever heard it.

"You protect the kingling, not the queen," Delph shot back. "You forget your place. Leave her to us."

"I won't leave her."

"Follow us, then, but hands off, you understand?"

Ama's response was mumbled, and then Paulus said something soothing, and then strong arms swept Heliane up. At least her protectors had waited to argue until they were back at the palace. No one would have to know. And she was safe now.

She could truly rest.

Some time later—she had no idea how long—Heliane opened her eyes. A dimmed lamp cast light and shadow on her surroundings, which she recognized as her own bedchamber, thank the All-Mother. The next thing she saw was Ama and Paulus, sitting next to each other on a bench nearby. Their faces were grave with concern, their heads almost touching. As she watched, Paulus squeezed his eyes shut, turned toward Ama, rested his forehead where her shoulder met her neck. They hadn't yet noticed Heliane's open eyes. No one else was in the room. The suspicion she'd had upon leaving for the festival slid into place, solidified.

She turned her face away from them as if she hadn't been watching, then let a sigh escape. At the faint sound, she heard them scramble.

"Mother," exhaled Paulus, a sigh of relief.

Heliane turned back—how wonderful it felt, such a simple motion—and looked at him with affection. His lovely brow was tight with worry. Ama was already standing toward the foot of the bed, as if she hadn't just been at Paulus's side, and Heliane could see the relief on her face, too.

"Are you all right?" Paulus asked.

She wasn't, but she didn't want to say so. She didn't even want to think it.

"I will be," the queen lied.

Paulus said, "What can we bring you? There's water here, and wine, and those pears you love . . . I can bring the healer . . ."

"Nothing now," she interrupted. "And no one. I only want to rest. You should too."

Her son shook his head, reaching for her hand. She let him grip her fingers for a moment, then withdrew them gently.

"I insist. You can go."

For a long moment neither Paulus nor Ama moved. They glanced toward each other, furtive looks that made no clear connection, then returned their gazes to the queen's face, both of their expressions heavy with concern.

So the queen said to them, again, "Go." This time, they went.

Her body was still exhausted, and she hadn't lied that she only wanted rest, but now her mind was wakeful. It dipped and swooped like a bird in flight.

She probably shouldn't have gone out into the world, but it couldn't be undone now. Besides, she'd gained valuable information. The spy who'd jostled her at the festival had whispered important intelligence in her ear.

The Scorpicae are coming.

There had been other words too, hushed and hurried, but those were the most important. She'd heard from this same source that bands of Scorpican warriors had been raiding Arcan villages for months now, though the queen of Arca had kept the shocking news quiet. The fact that Heliane had heard this only from her private spy and nothing at all from her minister of war, Faruzeh, also spoke volumes. She would have to carefully choose how to manage the minister. But on that front, the time was not yet right.

The spy had told her so much so quickly. The Scorpicae had been driven from Arca by a powerful force. They were surging north through Godsbones, where no one would follow. Yet where could they possibly be headed? Not crawling home with their tails between their legs. No, the Scorpicae would not give up so easily, not when their queen had gambled everything.

Knowing what she knew, Heliane had no choice. In the morning, as soon as she was stronger, there were three things that couldn't wait.

Three things to solidify their future. An edict, for the nation. A letter, to a fellow queen. And tea, a special tea, for Ama.

Was Ama in love with Paulus? Or he with her? Perhaps. They were so attuned to each other, their bodies almost thrumming with tension when they touched. Heliane knew the signs. A desire like this, pulsing in her veins, had driven Heliane to marry Cyrus only months after they'd met. She wondered if history would repeat itself: she with her king, the kingling with this Bastion-born, army-trained girl. Similar but so different.

Ama and Paulus felt something for each other, maybe love, certainly longing. Clearly, they hadn't admitted it to one another, and possibly not even to themselves. There was too much tension. At some point, that tightly pulled thread would break.

A good diplomat could read people's thoughts on their faces, in the way they held their bodies, and Heliane was the best.

Yes. She knew exactly what to do about Ama.

◆

Ama restrained herself as long as she could, walking down the hallway behind Paulus as if she were truly only a bodyguard to him, but in the privacy of his bedchamber, she stopped pretending.

At every step, she'd let him set the pace. She'd always waited for Paulus to invite her into the bed, ever since that first night after the banquet when he'd asked her, so irresistibly, to stay. The kingling and his bodyguard would kiss to exhaustion, reluctantly parting for the night, him in the bed, her in her bedroll by the door. It seemed to Ama the right—perhaps the only—thing to do in the circumstances, her carefully measured way of keeping things from going too far.

But tonight, he needed comfort, it was clear. She saw it in the angle at which he held himself, the tension of his curled fingers, the way he strode across the threshold as she held the door open for him to pass. Ama wouldn't wait for him to ask.

So as soon as the door closed behind them, she reached for his hand and held it. He raised his eyes to hers, an unspoken question simmering there. She told him, "It'll be all right."

He responded, "You can't know that."

"True," she admitted. "It's a hope. A prayer."

Paulus looked down at their entwined fingers. After a long moment, he said in a hushed, fervent tone, "It'll be all right."

"And you," she said, squeezing his hand. "Will you be?"

His eyes met hers. "If you're here."

That was all it took. Ama released his hand. Then, without being invited, she climbed into Paulus's soft, rumpled bed.

His eyes stayed on hers as he circled the far side of the bed and lowered himself next to her. She saw the longing in his gaze, but uncertainty still swept in.

"If you want," she said, "we can just sleep."

"No," he answered, and kissed her.

Though she had not been invited, it soon became clear she was welcome. As soon as her mouth was on his, the tip of her tongue running lightly along the seam of his lips, Paulus eagerly turned the devouring mutual. He put one hand to the nape of her neck and the other to the small of her back, bringing her closer. Their bodies pressed together, shoulders to hips, as they'd done so many times before.

But Ama had broken her own rule twice in mere minutes—once to hold his hand, once to climb into his bed—and as if watching herself from a distance, as if she had no control over what was happening, she felt herself breaking it a third time, without apology.

Feeling bold, Ama canted her hips back and let her hand snake downward. Her fingers started at Paulus's knee and drew up, up, up his thigh, until she cupped the hard signal between his legs, standing at attention.

"Ama," he said against her mouth, half whisper, half gasp.

"Yes," she responded, not a question, feeling the vibration pass back and forth between them, rattling their bones.

Then all he said was an echo of that same word, *yes*, and she felt his hand moving just as boldly as hers had. The marigold skirt she'd worn for the festival only reached her knees, and the soft fall of cloth was easily brushed aside. In barely a few heartbeats of exploration, Paulus's searching fingertip moved between her legs to find and stroke the wet slit there, a moment that seemed to shock both of them equally. She couldn't help inhaling sharply, an abrupt high note on an *ahh* escaping her lips. For a moment, his hand stilled. His face rested on the side of her neck, his breath tickling her skin.

"Ama?" A question, this time.

"It's all right. It's good, I mean. Very good. Just that no one's ever . . . ," she said, trailing off, suddenly shy.

"Should I stop?" he asked, but his voice was so soft, it was clear how much he feared her answer.

She rocked her hips into his hand then, not knowing exactly what to do, but letting her body lead the way. She felt him smile into her neck. His stroking finger started again, teasing her in irregular bursts at first, then settling into a rhythm. In moments she was so slick that his finger lost the track and slipped off, and she shocked herself by growling, grabbing his hand to return it to the right spot, holding her hand over his wrist to keep it there. He chuckled low in his throat but didn't stop stroking as he resumed a regular pattern. She shifted, sighing, into his touch.

"Ama, I—" he whispered, and she feared he would pull back, pull away, but then he went on, "I've never done this. I don't want to do it wrong."

All at once, everything felt too serious. There was a reason she'd held herself back. Her attachment to him had grown stronger by the day, and if they let themselves have this, where could it possibly lead? But she reassured herself that this was just pleasure, not affection, just two bodies doing what bodies naturally wanted to do. This was one night. This was comfort, distraction. They had made each other no promises.

"You won't," she whispered instead, and took both his hands by the wrists. She ached as she eased out of reach of his delicious, teasing finger, but she wanted to give pleasure as well as take it. She couldn't do that with her head so addled. Instead, she took control.

Ama pinned Paulus's wrists above his head, easing her body onto his, sitting astride his thighs. She stretched out to lay her body over his, still holding his wrists back, and kissed him deeply. His mouth rose to meet hers, exploring, and she could not mistake his hunger.

And though neither of them knew exactly what they were doing, it turned out that they knew enough to fit one part into another, and before long, she'd taken him inside her in a startlingly new, utterly intoxicating kind of embrace.

They started and stopped, sometimes gasping, sometimes whispering and laughing, until she rose and fell in a regular rhythm that he raised his hips to meet, and the urgency rose, and the laughter fell away in the face of something far more serious, more insistent, almost holy.

Then they were rocking and panting together, their breath matching, and Ama could feel a pulse inside her—how strange, how wonderful— that she'd heard was a signal the man was about to spend his rain. She wasn't so giddy from pleasure that she didn't know this was the last possible moment to do the right thing for both of them.

"*Giddabak*," she whispered in his ear, her voice urgent.

It was Paximite slang, which she'd never have known if not for her fellow soldiers, and it did the trick.

One more deep, satisfying thrust and then he withdrew as she'd asked, pressing his hips down onto the mattress as she lifted her body free of his. He moaned and rolled sideways, thrusting a final time into his own hand, spilling his rain to water the bedsheets instead of her seed. The long, low groan working its way up from his throat was so breathtaking she was struck with an almost irresistible impulse to latch her teeth into that same throat. She wanted to feel and taste every last moment of his pleasure. She didn't give in to the impulse to bite him, but she did press her lips against his neck, feeling the warmth there as the groan spent itself out.

When it was done, she felt the pulse in his throat hammering away like he'd just finished one of their most grueling sparring matches.

"What are you smiling at?" Paulus asked, his voice a little hoarse.

Ama hadn't known she was smiling. But she answered his question honestly. "I was thinking it was just like we'd finished a training session. I suppose, in a way, we did."

"Ah, but with an important difference," he said, rolling onto his other side to face her. Then she felt his fingertip nudge between her legs again, and though she would not have believed she could grow even wetter there, apparently it was possible.

The words barely whistled out of her as his finger drew slow, small circles. "What's that?"

"You . . . aren't finished yet," he said.

She wasn't sure how to answer that; he was right that she hadn't achieved her full pleasure, but she didn't want to rush him, and besides, how did this all work? She was still a little stunned that they'd done what they'd done. All these new sensations, the feeling that he now knew her in a way no one else did, whether or not their physical intimacy had emotional meaning.

As it turned out, he didn't need an answer. When she felt him shifting position, she thought he might be getting up to clean himself. She knew he couldn't possibly be ready to repeat what they'd just done. But then she felt him settling his body between her legs, his fingers gently guiding her knees apart, and he edged lower on the bed. She couldn't quite grasp what he was doing, his body retreating even farther, his head bending lower and lower. She only realized his intent when she felt his broad, wet tongue repeat the pattern he'd been stroking earlier with his finger, finding the precious nub between her legs and licking it firmly, sweetly, insistently.

"Sweet Panic," she panted.

She felt him chuckling again, and even the chuckle was a revelation, a miracle of vibration against her tender nerve endings. With every lick she could feel tension building in her, an almost unbearable ache. She was close already to flying apart, so close. Did he know? Could he tell, from there?

"I thought you'd never done this!" she gasped, an accusation, only partly joking, though not entirely caring if she'd caught him in a lie. Truth did not seem the most important thing in the world just now, not in the face of this exquisite ache.

He lifted his head long enough to say, "I haven't."

"Then how could you—how do you know what to do?"

His laugh was genuine, and he tossed his head, and she loved the way his curly hair cascaded all around his eager face. She felt a pang in her heart that she would not let herself consider too closely. His eyes twinkled.

"I read it in a book," Paulus said, and after that his lips and tongue were too busy, for some time, to speak words.

✦ 15 ✦

EVERY SIGH

In the days following the Gods' Wedding
Ama, Stellari

What happened the night after the festival was unprecedented; so, too, was the insistent rap on the chamber door the next morning. The intrusion immediately shook Ama awake, despite the comfortable bed, despite the way Paulus's arm lay pleasantly heavy over her body as he slept.

She eased herself out from under his arm without waking him, a feat in itself, and pulled on her shift. Before she opened the door, she looked around wildly and yanked her bedroll into position at her feet. No one could know she'd slept the night in the kingling's bed; she swore to herself that next time she'd be more careful. Then she marveled at how quickly she assumed there'd be a next time. How much she wanted there to be. She ran both palms over her short hair and opened the door a crack to see who stood outside.

It was Delph, with a message for Ama.

When Ama was called into the queen's presence, it felt strange to be without Paulus, even for a few minutes. They hadn't been apart since that moment in the library when they'd first been introduced. But the member of the Queensguard who'd come for her, the intimidating one named Delph, made it clear that while Ama was with the queen, Delph herself would take charge of the kingling. Ama had no choice but to obey the summons. A few weeks before, she would've been thrilled to move independently from him, even for a few minutes; now she missed him the moment he left her sight.

Ama shook her head at herself. She'd let herself kiss him that first morning, sleepy-eyed and warm in his bed, thinking it meant nothing. But the next night they'd found their way to each other again, and the night after, and every night since. And then after last night, when they'd both surrendered to mutual pleasure for the very first time? Could it be a coincidence that the queen was calling for her now? But it had to be. The queen couldn't possibly know, Ama told herself. Heliane had been barely conscious the night before; how could she have learned what no one outside Paulus's rooms had witnessed? She couldn't.

Could she?

Ama arrived at the door of the queen's private chamber, and another member of the Queensguard opened it for her without Ama saying a word. In all the months since she'd come to the palace, she'd never been alone with the queen. Now here she was, in the queen's bedchamber for the second time in mere hours.

"Ama," said the queen, lying in the bed in the same position she'd been when Ama and Paulus had left her the night before. It reminded Ama how little time had passed, even though yesterday now felt like weeks, even months, before. Last night had been momentous.

Ama had never figured out what to do when Heliane addressed her. She didn't care to bow, as she wasn't truly a Paximite, but she did honor the woman, who was, after all, her employer. So she just said, "Yes?" and gave the woman her complete attention.

The queen had a gray cast to her golden skin, but her voice was steady. "When you return to Paulus, he'll ask you what we talked about. You'll tell him I thanked you for your help yesterday. Understand?"

"Yes, Queen Heliane."

"You can even tell him I praised myself for choosing you. He loves to confirm his secret belief that I think too much of myself. He'll enjoy that."

A bad feeling started at the base of Ama's throat and then spread up into her face and down across her shoulders at the same time, the warmth of her fear reaching her chest, her heart, her gut.

"So I take it," Ama said carefully, "that isn't actually what we'll talk about."

"It's part," said the queen. "I did make an excellent choice. I see how devoted you are to him. It seems you think of little else."

Ama had to tread carefully. "When would I have time?"

"True enough," Heliane went on. "You have always taken seriously my edict not to be out of his company. It'll be even more important now. This morning I take action to secure my son's future as a ruling king. Certain people won't like that. You need to be more diligent than ever before."

Was that why the queen had called her, simply to warn of a possible assassination attempt? Not that that wasn't serious. It was Ama's responsibility to keep Paulus safe, and she couldn't bear the thought of something happening to him, today even more than yesterday.

And it wasn't only her heart that ached when she thought of Paulus. A flash came into her mind of his curly head buried between her legs, a sight glimpsed through eyelashes lowered in pleasure, just hours before. The tense feeling in her chest moved downward and shifted into another type of feeling entirely. She could feel blood rushing to her cheeks, ashamed she'd let this inappropriate thought intrude. The queen of Paxim was speaking, for Panic's sake. Ama had to pull herself together.

"Not that I think they will try within the palace," the queen said, "but one never knows. And soon he will need to travel outside the palace walls. Into the Assembly. The Senate. You'll walk beside him on every stroll, ride next to him in every carriage. You must always be on your guard."

"Yes."

"What I mean is—you must protect him at all costs, Ama. You hear me? All costs."

"Yes," Ama said again, but this time her voice was softer, because she heard the meaning behind the queen's words. Heliane might as well have said it aloud. *His life is more important to me than yours. So if you have to die to protect him, do.*

"And Ama," Heliane said. "I have one more precaution for you."

Then she beckoned Ama closer. Ama bent over her, bringing her ear down to the older woman's lips, so Heliane needed only whisper. Ama looked down and saw that the queen's fingers lingered near the knife at her belt, and for a moment, she was struck with a powerful fear that the queen meant to cut her throat for what she'd dared.

But the queen's hand stilled, and she spoke quiet words, telling Ama to fetch what she needed from a certain drawer in a small chest against the far wall.

Ama opened the drawer. The only object within was a small cloth sack, slightly larger than her own closed fist. She evaluated it as she carried it back toward the bed. The contents were lighter than wood or metal, with no sharp edges. Dried leaves of some kind? Ama raised the sack toward her nose and sniffed. A plant, clearly, with notes of mint, and something like carrot, but several other herbs she could not identify. Children in the Bastion who showed an aptitude for herbcraft were trained in professions that required it. Plants had never been an interest of Ama's.

With the queen's unrelenting eyes on her, Ama ventured a guess at the contents. "A tea?"

"Yes."

"You said it was a precaution," Ama said carefully.

"Yes. A precaution. For you," said the queen. "Drink a cup every morning when you wake. A scant spoonful in a cup of water, either hot or cold. It will help you avoid . . . consequences that can follow particular activities. Do you understand me now, Ama?"

All at once Ama understood, and heat rose again to her cheeks.

Heliane knew. Of course Heliane knew. Ama and Paulus had hidden nothing. His mother was fully aware of their entanglement, of their intimacy. The tea was to prevent Ama from bearing a child sired by Paulus. She was fine for now, the queen was saying, but not forever.

That was no crisis, Ama told herself. Hadn't she told herself, even during their pleasures, that there was no meaning to their actions? She had never been promised forever and she would not weep to see it go.

It sounded like a lie inside her head, but it was a lie she insisted on telling.

When the queen dismissed her, Ama returned to Paulus's rooms, Delph gazing curiously at her before leaving and shutting the door behind her, the two of them alone once again. When Ama saw Paulus gazing sleepy-eyed at her from the mussed bed, she felt an unfamiliar squeeze in her heart. It had nothing to do with the things he'd done to her body the night before, nor what she'd done to his. It was the man himself, the one whose eyes shone with warmth at the mere sight of her.

In the months that followed, Ama could not shake the thought of the queen's unspoken message, even as she felt herself falling more and more in love with Paulus, her heart twining around his like two strands of ivy climbing the same wall.

Ama heard the queen's unspoken message over and over again as she brewed and drank her cup of tea every morning, just as she'd been told to do. She heard it as she sparred with Paulus in the mornings to hone his short-sword technique. As she lay with her head in his lap during those long afternoons in the library, him reading aloud to her from his favorite books of stories. Every night as he beckoned her to his bed, teased and pleasured her, and every night as she left that bed, despite his entreaties, to sleep across his doorway and replay every kiss, every stroke, every sigh in the silent dark.

For now, but not forever.

✦

Summer always transformed Ursu, and no summer more than the summer of the All-Mother's Year 517, thought Stellari. When the Senate was out of session, it seemed to empty half the city; the aftereffects of the end of the Drought of Girls had emptied the other half. The market that day was half the size it had been two months before, with only male vendors hawking their olive oil or duck eggs or honey. The marriage of Victory and Wealth the night before, it seemed, had kept the women of Paxim up late. Of course hundreds, perhaps thousands, had also gone off to the Moon Rites in Sestia. While there were more than enough men in Ursu ready to share pleasures and provide rain to water a woman's seed, Stellari could see why a woman would want to gather her water farther from home. She'd even considered it herself, as lonely as she was, even with Rahul still there in the house with her. He seemed determined to be no more than the nursemaid she told people he was. Only on the rarest occasions did he come to her, slipping into bed alongside her in silence, and she was always too grateful, too eager, to risk breaking the spell by asking him his reasons. She welcomed him, clutched and sighed and shattered, and afterward he never stayed.

There was another option, of course, and she tired of being reminded of it. The letters from her husband's mother had become both more frequent and unpleasantly imperious, insisting that Stellari travel back to Calladocia now that the Drought of Girls was over. Before, Panagiota's correspondence had always been polite, even a bit simpering, but now she took on a scolding tone. All the other senators, insisted the dowager, had traveled home to share pleasures with their husbands in service of bearing the next generation of Paximites. She implied that Stellari was shirking her duties by staying away. The dowager was almost certainly right, of course, but that didn't make her presumption less offensive. Letters, of course, could be ignored, and Stellari fully intended to ignore this one. She had too much to attend to in Ursu to risk travel all the way to Calladocia and back.

She couldn't leave the capital, and yet she felt trapped there, nothing being quite what she wanted it to be. She'd started spending more and more time in her garden, even though she hated gardening. The house felt too small. She was starting to understand Faruzeh's obsession with her garden, the calming pathways, the satisfaction of creating a profusion of color and fragrance from nothing but seeds, rich dirt, and time.

So when Faruzeh sent word that they should meet, two nights after the celebration of the Gods' Wedding, Stellari left her back gate unlocked and waited for the war minister under a young almond tree. It would be another year before the tree bore fruit. But during the day its spreading branches and long, delicate leaves provided intermittent shade, and on nights like this, she could smell its lovely fragrance on the breeze.

It was important that she and Faruzeh not be seen together aside from official Senate briefings, and usually Faruzeh was more circumspect, but when she had important information to share, the war minister lacked the patience for spycraft. And at least in the garden, Stellari wouldn't have to worry about Aster or Rahul, who would keep each other occupied in their world of two without leaving the house to interrupt.

Faruzeh got right to the point.

"Scorpicae," she said, "are attacking Arca. Raiding parties, no rhyme or reason, mostly in the east."

"Did a messenger come from Queen Eminel?" asked Stellari, instantly on her guard, hungry for every detail. She would forgive Faruzeh the lack of stealth when such incredible information was hers for the taking.

"No!" said Faruzeh, clearly more loudly than she meant to. At the sound of her own voice she started, then looked around, and when she spoke again, she whispered. "That's the most striking thing. We have no official communication from the Arcans. As best we can tell, they have told no one."

"They're keeping another queendom's attack on their own soil *secret*?"

"It appears so."

"And do we have any idea why?" asked Stellari. She immediately had a long list of suspicions, of course, but she wanted to know Faruzeh's.

The war minister scratched her shoulder with a long finger. She could never be still. "Perhaps they want to deal with the invaders in their own way. Perhaps they're afraid other queendoms will join the attack. But it seems odd they haven't asked us to ally with them, though we must assume the invaders are in the wrong."

"We must assume that, yes," Stellari agreed, more to mark time than anything else. "The Arcans hardly could have invited them in. Are we sure? Our spies? That the Scorpicae are on the attack?"

"They have killed and pillaged."

"But not occupied?"

"Not that we know of."

Stellari said, "And does the queen know?"

"Not yet. You are the first."

"Who else knows?"

Faruzeh said, "Only my spies. And they report to me, not the queen."

A prickle of excitement ran up the back of Stellari's neck at the very idea of having information that Heliane, in all her smugness, lacked.

"We'll keep it to ourselves for now," she said. "Unless you disagree."

"No, I agree. We'll watch and wait."

"And keep an eye on our own border."

"Yes. We've stationed two units there already."

A bit of flattery was in order, and Stellari was happy to provide it. "I knew you'd already have the right course of action underway. We'll talk more soon."

Stellari was still pondering what it might mean, all the ways an attack could be turned to her advantage, but first things first. No need for Faruzeh to linger. Stellari asked her to discreetly leave by the same gate she'd come in, which the war minister was happy enough to do. Next time, thought Stellari, they would have to meet elsewhere. Mistakes could never be entirely avoided, but she wasn't in the habit of making the same one twice.

And a good thing, too, because the minute she reentered the house, Stellari heard a knock on her front door. The day servants having departed hours earlier, she answered it herself. She peered out to see Inbar standing there. *What now?*

Stellari squared her shoulders, took in a deep breath, and opened the door to Inbar as if she hadn't a care in the world.

The queen's *cosmete* paused on the threshold, dressed in a drab tunic and leggings to help her blend in, a tan hood partially obscuring her face. Her movements were nervous, flitting, like a bird's. Even if she'd been a stranger, Stellari would have known the woman was trying to hide something. She could only hope that the people Inbar had encountered along her route were not as observant.

"Come in," Stellari said with a gesture of impatience.

Inbar's gaze darted over Stellari's shoulder into the home's interior. She took in the fine tapestries, the elegant lamps, the pleasant, drifting scent of myrrh that Stellari used as fragrance in her home. Something stern flickered across her face. Then she entered.

Inbar was one of the queen's most senior women, a fixture around the palace, who had been trusted to style Heliane's hair ever since she was a queenling. She'd also been a spy for Stellari since shortly after the debacle with the men in the Assembly. Inbar wasn't involved in every conversation the queen had, but she was sharp-eyed, observant, and forgettable. Best of all, she didn't realize she was a spy.

But coming here unannounced, looking like this? Stellari knew whatever she had to say was serious.

"Yes?"

"Your charms aren't working," Inbar said bluntly. "She could have died."

Stellari resisted the urge to slap the woman for taking that tone with her. But this was why the queen trusted Inbar, Stellari reminded herself. The *cosmete* was bold enough to say what she thought. "Is that so? Tell me what you think happened."

"She went to that festival, the Gods' Wedding. I knew it was a bad idea, but she didn't listen to me. Do you think a sorcerer planted the idea in her mind? Lured her out?"

"I can't be certain," Stellari said, trying to make her voice soothing. "Tell me more."

"I was worried for her. Out there. I gave her an extra application of the salve. You told me it would protect her, and it didn't. Someone knocked her to the ground. She came back collapsed. Weaker than I've seen her in years."

Inbar wasn't a stupid woman, but her mind ran on a narrow path: everyone was good or bad, everything right or wrong. To her, Arca was dangerous. Because she believed the queen needed protection from Arcan plots but was too proud to use magic against magic, she'd been the perfect tool. Even if Inbar was discovered, the poison could not be traced back to Stellari. The *cosmete* couldn't be forced to confess to any wrongdoing when she had no idea she was doing anything wrong.

"Weaker how?"

Inbar's eyes narrowed, but she went on. "Stayed in bed all day and night, not eating, not drinking. The second day she only nibbled on those candied pears the consul brings her."

Stellari had had her suspicions when the queen left the festival early, but the woman had covered her tracks well. The magistrate hadn't heard as much as a whisper about the queen's ill health. One assemblywoman Stellari had spoken with yesterday had even remarked on how well the queen had looked at the Gods' Wedding. At the time Stellari had been irritated; now she was intrigued.

"You were right to be concerned," she said to Inbar. "The queen is lucky to have your vigilance. It sounds like the Arcans did try to strike her at the festival. But she's strong. And with the salve's help, she's fighting the enchantment off."

The change in Inbar was remarkable. Weight seemed to slide from her shoulders. She needed an explanation, and Stellari had one. It was, thought Stellari, almost too easy.

"Has she called for a healer?" Stellari asked.

"No, she refused one. The only visitor she's had from outside is the consul."

"Oh, the consul, of course," said Stellari smoothly, her heart beating faster. "Bringing the pears, I suppose."

"Yes."

"Still," she let herself muse aloud. "That doesn't seem an urgent errand."

"She had papers with her," volunteered Inbar. "But the queen said she would sign them some other day."

"Oh, she did?" Behind her back, Stellari squeezed one hand into a tight fist, nails digging into her palm. She'd felt so pleased with herself only a moment before. Now she could see her whole plan was on the verge of falling to pieces.

Inbar said, "Are the papers important?"

Stellari kept her tone level. "Only the queen's safety matters. She must be protected at all costs. But perhaps our methods need to change."

So close but so far. In her whispered conversations with Decima, Stellari had pretended to want Paulus on the throne, pretended she believed people would be more accepting if a trusted consul like Decima were at his side. Heliane herself had been helped in her early days by a strong consul who served as regent, Stellari had reminded her. The proclamation Heliane hadn't signed would put a great deal more power, including the regency, into the consul's hands. Stellari's revenge would be hollow if the queen's death came at the wrong time.

Inbar said, "More of the salve? Stronger protection? I can try—"

"No," Stellari said, digging her nails into her palms harder to squeeze down her panic. "A different protection altogether. To confound the Arcans' magic. The salve you've been using, bury it, all right? Somewhere far from the palace. That will keep any sorcerer who was involved in the festival attack from following a trail of magic to you."

The *cosmete*'s eyes widened. Then she set her jaw. "Yes. And what should I use instead?"

"Let me find it for you." Stellari reached into a cabinet for a jar she could give Inbar, an unguent roughly the same texture as the last one, but harmless. Without new poison in her blood, over time, Heliane would begin to recover. And once she signed the proclamation, Stellari would put the final phase of her plan into action. She pressed the jar into Inbar's outstretched palm. "Here."

Inbar peered at the small jar. "Does it work the same way?"

"You apply it the same way, but in smaller doses," improvised Stellari. "To make it last. This one reverses magic. So anyone who tries to enchant the queen will find herself enchanted—and the criminal will be exposed. You'll have to be even more vigilant. Watch not just the queen but those around her. Can you do that?"

The *cosmete* curled her fingers around the jar, nodding. "I will."

"Thank you. Queen Heliane is lucky to have you. Now, be careful not to be seen."

Inbar melted away, moving with purpose, as she made her way back into the street. She'd arrived a mess and left confident. Stellari only wished she could work such a transformation on herself.

The house felt too close after the *cosmete* left. Stellari found herself back in the garden, pacing up one long path and down another, circling the young almond tree she'd stood under with Faruzeh only an hour before. There was so much to think about. She needed time to puzzle out her next steps, turn the facts over and over in her head.

First, she needed more information on girls who might have a claim to the throne. Her straightest path to power still involved Paulus becoming king, but she didn't have to let him stay that way. She was aware of the girls who had presented themselves or been presented at the palace, all the ones the queen had refused to see, but she needed to dig deeper. Who had not yet come out of the woodwork? Who was afraid they would expose secrets and lies by coming forward? These were the names she needed.

What would be best was a girl with some connection to the queen's family, born in Stellari's own district. Perhaps her husband's mother could assist. It could be a bargaining chip; if Panagiota could locate a likely heir from the queen's line, Stellari would promise a journey back to Calladocia, even a certain number of attempts at conceiving an heir of her own. Mothers and sons, she thought. She'd foreseen so much, but she hadn't realized she'd ever come to a place in her life when mothers and sons mattered so much to her.

As Stellari paced the paths of the night garden, possibilities bloomed in her mind like grapevines. They budded and ranged and she smiled to see them growing, stretching toward the sky. She knew that one day, one of these branches, the very vines she now tended, would bear not just imagined but real fruit.

16

NORTH

On the march through Godsbones
Gretti

Gretti marched northward over the strange red earth of Godsbones with the baby Madazur strapped to her chest, her chin bobbing above the thin, undyed linen blanket that kept the infant's downy head shaded from the burning sun. Now that Madazur was old enough to lift her own head, the baby preferred to ride facing forward, those wide brown eyes soaking up movement and light and shadow all around. If the child could talk, Gretti wondered what she would say, looking out across this strange and barren landscape. But the only home Madazur had ever known was the hollow caldera: bright sun, black earth. Perhaps she didn't find Godsbones strange at all.

But Gretti felt the strangeness of it at every step. On the southward march to Arca months ago, while the Drought of Girls still raged, she'd focused on nothing but their mission. So many of them had thought they were bound for victory. They'd imagined they would quickly crush the Arcans' spirit and be paid off handsomely to march back home, spoils and bribes and tribute weighing down their wagons on the return. That had not happened. Now red dirt caked their feet and calves again, and with their gazed fixed on the red horizon, it was easy to imagine creatures of Godsbones lurking behind every leaning rock tower, ready to spring. Gretti realized they hadn't seen a single pony in Godsbones besides the ones they'd brought with them. Possibly the wild ponies simply couldn't find grass to sustain their herds this far south, but it was too easy to read their absence in other ways. As avoidance. Punishment. Desertion.

Behind Gretti marched the newest recruits, a handful of the three dozen women who had been born Arcan but, in mere months, had become Scorpican to the bone. With Lembi to test their devotion, none of the new soldiers showed any signs of regret that they had turned their backs on the land of their birth. And Gretti could see the logic of it, though she wasn't sure these women were driven by logic. Some of them had arrived proud and fiery-eyed, like Lembi, but others, like the thin-limbed Oora and Markiset, had barely crawled into camp, starved-looking and hoarse with thirst. Any fool could see they'd been desperate. The far east of Arca was so dry, so hopeless; the foreign warriors had thundered in with promises and radiant health. To the strangers they vanquished, the Scorpicae offered pure, confident strength. They had a unified spirit, and even if that spirit was destructive, it offered something more than slow starvation. Who wouldn't want to be part of that, if they could?

Would the Scorpicae find as many recruits from Paxim—or perhaps even more? The most treasured ideal in Paxim was that of diplomacy. There must be hundreds—thousands—of women without a diplomatic bone in their bodies. And while Paxim's more ferocious women might be glad recruits to the country's army, Gretti thought the opposite could just as easily be true: that the fiercest, most aggressive women among the Paximites might rather fight against the men of their country than alongside them. Azur was unusual in her lust for blood, thought Gretti, but she was surely not unique in all the world. They warred for the souls of nations, but every woman who fought on any side was an individual, and individuals were far harder to predict.

Addressing the hasty council meeting held after the small force of magicians had driven them from the caldera, Tamura had tried to make a virtue of necessity. "Our new base will lie near Paxim so that when we're ready to attack, we can rip through their lands with decisive force," she'd said. "Paxim is closer to home. They have more resources by far, and most poorly guarded. Half their army is men, I've heard; foolish and weak, compared to our strength. They've trained with swords and bows, but not long. We grew up with weapons in our hands. We'll drive them before us until they give us riches and concessions. We will wring them dry. North to the future!"

"North to the future!" the Scorpicae around Tamura had echoed, and if anyone noticed that Gretti's lips didn't move with the rest, they kept it to themselves.

The baby made soft sounds, barely audible above the clanking of the marching warriors. Gretti planted a kiss on the curls of her dark hair, which hadn't grown enough yet to need cutting. The time would come. What would the world look like by the time that happened? Would more girls be born by then, and to whom?

Gretti palmed the baby's skull, humming a soothing tune deep in her throat. If she got the tone just right, the vibrations in the bones of her chest passed into the bones of the child, soothing them both. While she tried, she thought of the baby's mother, wondered whether Azur's trip to the rites would improve or further sour her. Gretti had not missed the First Mother. Azur was quieter than Tamura, yes, and hadn't yet proven herself as vicious as their queen; but Gretti feared that underneath Azur's tempered exterior, she might be even more calculating and heartless than Tamura. Gretti had helped raise Azur to the council because their nation needed strong voices besides

Tamura's, but as she walked north, she wondered, not for the first time, whether Azur's voice might do more harm than good.

It wasn't Azur's lack of interest in her child that worried Gretti. No girls had been born in so long, today's warriors had exactly one example of loving motherhood—Tamura's love of her adopted daughters—which was, of necessity, quite different from loving a single infant. That was why Gretti insisted that newly adopted warriors enter as daughters of other Scorpicae. They needed to reward and build new family structures within the broader tribe. And she had seen the future, not in an Arcan way, but a very practical, real one: it would take time for other Scorpicae to be born. In the meantime, Gretti couldn't stand having Tamura and Azur be the only mothers any of them knew.

As she matched new Scorpicae with the women they would learn to call mother, Gretti had not yet chosen a daughter for herself. She assigned the girls and young women to Nikhit, and Lu, and others. Even the smith, Zalma, now had a daughter who followed her through camp with a heavy, flat-faced hammer slung over her shoulder, an exact scaled-down replica of her new mother's. Gretti herself would recognize the daughter she wanted when she saw her. She wasn't sure when that day would come, but she believed in it. Her examination of every new recruit began with hope. If it didn't end that way, at least hope might be born anew the next morning.

No, it was not Azur's sometime indifference toward Madazur that worried Gretti. *A child without* tishis *is a warrior without weapons*, went the saying. Gretti herself was a willing *tishi* to any and every girl in the Scorpican camp; even the most vigilant mother could benefit from help in raising her child, and there was no nobility in pretending otherwise. What worried Gretti was that Azur seemed to be so deliberate, so calculating, about when she claimed the child and when she didn't. Azur was happy enough to accept accolades as the First Mother, and to wear the child at council as if Madazur's tiny body lent credence to Azur's every point; but let the child be inconvenient, and

Azur was thrilled to pass her off. Gretti had seen hundreds of mothers hand hundreds of children to *tishis* who would care for them in the women's absence, and she had never seen a mother look as indifferent as Azur had when she handed Madazur to Gretti before leaving for the rites. The First Mother might as well have been handing over an empty breadbasket. Yet half a moment later, when Tamura asked if Azur would miss her child, Azur somehow instantly called tears to her eyes. A woman who could switch her maternal affection on and off like a lamplight was capable, thought Gretti wearily, of absolutely anything.

She wasn't sure how they would know when they'd arrived at their destination, but one day, a cry went up and someone called a halt. Gretti stayed with the new recruits, patting the baby's head, and waited for orders. They came soon enough. The Scorpicae had found their new camp.

Their new base in Godsbones was not as comfortable as the caldera, but it would certainly do. Gretti would have approved the choice, had she been asked: they'd found a clutch of caves tucked away in the red hills facing a winding river. The caves were deep enough to shelter in, but not so deep that they held the cold and damp. The hill was high enough to prevent a mounted assault from behind the caves, but not so steep on either side that it couldn't be quickly scaled by defenders seeking the higher ground.

On the side facing the river, water over time had worn away the approach until all that was left was a natural bridge, so narrow and high the women on foot rearranged themselves to go single file, and the ox-drawn carts had to go the long way around. Other than one ancient cave-dwelling hermit who was quickly shooed away with a few mild threats, nothing impeded the Scorpicae from taking possession immediately. They had water, security, safety. It looked very much like an invitation.

So the Scorpicae, from their queen to their newest infant warrior, settled into their new camp with a sense of satisfaction. They were close enough to Paxim to strike its tempting targets, and deep enough in Godsbones to hide their numbers. Their raids continued. Recruiting continued. And if the Scorpion's warriors didn't exactly love spending their days and nights in the haunted red land of Godsbones, howls and hisses of unknown origin drifting into their camp from every direction in the inky night, this compromise certainly beat giving up the war entirely.

17

SUMMONING

Daybreak Palace, Arca
Eminel, Colena

When the messenger rapped on Eminel's chamber door, two weeks after she'd sent her rivals to fight the Scorpicae face to face, her first feeling was relief. Beyda had cornered Eminel's last three *whishnuk* pegs in a particularly clever trap, and the queen was tapping her finger against her lip as she waited for inspiration to come. Instead of inspiration, there came the knock, and Eminel was happy to call the messenger in.

Except that when the messenger said in a rushed voice, "Queen Eminel, we honor you as the chosen of Velja, and also I come to tell you that your presence has been requested by Parvan of Ishta," Eminel wished she could escape to the haven of the minute before, when *whishnuk* pegs had been her most serious concern.

Had Parvan returned alone, though Eminel had sent five sorcerers to beard the Scorpicae in their den? Or had they all returned and Parvan was simply their spokeswoman? Perhaps the truth was somewhere in the middle. Eminel became conscious of the long moments passing. Instead of asking the questions she had, nervous under the messenger's scrutiny, she only said, "Very well. I will receive her here."

The messenger shifted from foot to foot.

Eminel asked, with a feeling of foreboding, "What is it?"

"She says she will only meet with you in your audience chamber with representatives from every matriclan at court present."

"And why is that?"

"I'm sorry, my queen, I should have thought to ask. The fault is mine. She only gave her request and her condition."

Eminel glanced over at Beyda, but the scribe didn't immediately offer her thoughts in front of the messenger. A reasonable caution. Eminel decided this was a situation where a small, judicious application of magic would head off the need for greater. She'd been replenishing the cuff with life force from animals in the area, using an incantation Beyda had found in a scroll so old its edges turned to powder on her fingertips. Eminel had started with small animals—a finch, a shrew—and then built her ambition and skill. Last week she'd taken down an entire pack of sand-foxes that had been harrying the local livestock. She could spare enough of their life force for this purpose, she was sure.

Tapping her fingers subtly in the folds of her robe as specified by the incantation, Eminel dipped lightly into the messenger's head. Had Parvan returned alone? Unfortunately, the messenger was not at all sure. She had seen only Parvan, who had seized the messenger's arm and squeezed as she made her request—a request that to Eminel, watching images unspool inside the messenger's head, looked more like a demand.

Eminel knew what her response needed to be. Avoidance was out of the question. "Very well," she told the messenger. "I will see her in an hour."

"Perhaps two hours would be better, Queen?" came Beyda's voice. It was phrased as a gentle suggestion, but Eminel saw the wisdom of it. Keep everyone waiting. It would also give her time to dress in something more befitting her station, to appear as queenly as possible in a situation that was sure to test her royal mettle.

Two hours later, in the absolutely packed audience chamber, Eminel looked out over the sea of eager, tense faces and wished that she had denied Parvan's request.

Eminel had dressed in a robe the color of bone, paler than her skin, embroidered enough to fit her station but not particularly showy or fine. The neckline of the robe crossed low on her chest in a deep V, framing the blue snake necklace, with elegant golden threads swirling and repeating a snakelike pattern. Only her position above the crowd made her stand out; otherwise her bone-colored shape would have been lost in the sea of dyed blues, pomegranate reds, greens as bright as cedar leaves fanned out in full sun. She was a peahen in a sea of peacocks.

The only other woman in the room dressed in a drab color was the returning courtier, Parvan. She wore what she'd gone to war in. The rust-colored splotches across her tunic and leggings were, Eminel knew immediately, not rust. Parvan's leg was also singed up the side, the fabric partially blackened. She'd gone to war with her hair in a long plait, but it now ended in uneven edges above her shoulders. It appeared the plait had been burned off. Parvan's gift was fire, Eminel knew; had the magician been injured by her own magic or the work of others?

Tradition dictated that the queen speak first, though Eminel could not be sure Parvan would stick to tradition, so she hurried to make her first statement.

"Welcome, brave Parvan. We are pleased to see you here, though sorry you return alone. We join with you in mourning those who did not return." It was a guess, but an educated one.

Parvan inclined her head. Then she raised it and brushed back the hair that had been obscuring one side of her face. Soft inhalations sounded from the audience nearest her right side. The eye on that side was gone, or could be assumed to be gone, given the patch of fabric that obscured the area.

Eminel tried her hardest to appear unmoved. "Do not keep us in suspense. Did you drive the enemy from our lands?"

"Yes," said Parvan, with no joy.

On the back foot now, mystified by the courtier's reticence, Eminel said, "Congratulations! Your victory will be celebrated."

The watching courtiers applauded, but there was something missing. A quick scan of their faces showed watchfulness, not delight. They were applauding because they knew the queen wanted them to, not because they themselves wanted to, and every nerve in Eminel's body was screaming at her, *Danger, danger*.

So she addressed Parvan once more. "Perhaps you can tell us of the feats of bravery, your own and those perpetrated by others, that drove back the enemy."

The woman's remaining eye narrowed. "Bravery? I'm afraid there wasn't much of that. Mostly we fought and died, some loudly, some in silence. There was no chance to be brave in the face of that onslaught. We were overmatched, utterly."

Eminel had no idea how to respond. She didn't have the luxury of thinking about it for more than a heartbeat. So she chose the response she thought the court would find most familiar, therefore reassuring.

Staring down her nose at Parvan, she said, "I certainly hope you at least took our enemies down, screaming and dying as our own precious Arcans screamed and died. Did you?"

"We did our best."

"In the name of Velja, then, what did your *best* do?"

"I couldn't keep track of them all," Parvan said, her tone aggressive. "I was trying too hard to stay alive. Velja didn't give us this magic for battle. We never should have gone. You never should have sent us."

"You think Velja wanted us to roll over and die? Give our country over to the warriors? Fool! It should have been a rout! You should have wiped them from the earth! And you're not even sure how many you took down? Of a group of women with no magic at all, a group that might as well have been armed with belts and scarves?"

Eminel was hoping to terrify Parvan into submission—certainly the onlookers seemed to be impressed by the tirade—but while the other woman's body sagged, her eye still blazed.

The fire magician nearly spat her words. "We made a good showing, considering you sent us into a death trap."

"I see now I had too much confidence in you," answered Eminel, matching Parvan's anger. "You were weak, and you failed."

Parvan bristled. "I set their camp ablaze. Sara nearly killed their queen—"

"But didn't," Eminel interrupted, her voice sharp.

"No. But she took out half a dozen, at least. Wodevi got close enough to snap three necks."

"Let me see," said Eminel, striding to close the space between them and putting her palm on Parvan's forehead. Eminel didn't need to touch her to read her mind, but she needed everyone to *see*.

Parvan twitched but didn't step away. Eminel dove into her mind and saw the battlefield, saw the doomed magicians running and casting and shouting. She made a noise of disgust and shoved Parvan's head away, a little harder than she'd meant to, as she removed her hand.

Parvan said, "We did our best."

Turning her back, Eminel walked back to her throne and seated herself before replying. "Had you worked together, your best would have been enough."

"Easy to say."

"Just as easy to know. I won't take the blame for your lack of discipline."

"There is nothing like facing an enemy. Nothing."

"I have faced an enemy," Eminel reminded her, rising to stand and brandish a finger down at Parvan, her pretended anger becoming real.

"The most talented sorcerer the world has ever seen. And I won. None of us would be here if I hadn't."

"I won too! I mean, *we* did! We drove the Scorpicae out of Velja's Navel, sent them running into the wastes of Godsbones." Parvan sounded petulant, not triumphant.

"And four of you died doing it," Eminel said dryly. "Are they enjoying the victory?"

Eminel knew everyone was watching raptly, eager to see the women tear each other apart, with very little regard for who came out on top. Parvan had demanded that this meeting take place in front of an audience, and she was getting what she wanted. Was it just the dressing-down of Eminel that she wanted others to witness? Or was there something more? Eminel thought for a moment and flicked the fingers of her left hand in a quick pattern to shield her body, flinching internally at the need to further drain the cuff, but knowing she wouldn't have a chance to replenish the life force within it if her own life were snuffed out.

"The failure was yours," hissed Parvan. "I am covered in the blood of your supporters."

"You should be covered in the blood of our enemies." Eminel felt ill, disgusted. "Yet I am the one you question. Will you take no responsibility? Admit no fault?"

"I don't have to answer to you," said Parvan, her voice louder than ever. "I no longer recognize you as Arca's rightful queen."

An *ooooh* of surprise wended its way throughout the audience chamber, from matriclan to matriclan. Friction had become insubordination. This, then, was what Parvan had been working up to. Now Eminel understood.

It took everything she had not to look to Beyda for advice, but the queen could not be seen as weak, not here, not today. Insubordination could easily become insurrection. She must choke it out before it grew. "Parvan of Ishta! I will be merciful. You have undergone a trauma, I understand that. Despite your failures on the battlefield, you did your best to complete the mission I gave you. And though you failed to protect your comrades, you returned to report your failures instead of fleeing like a coward. So I will allow you one chance to retract your treasonous words. One. Apologize or regret." But she saw on Parvan's face that it wasn't enough.

Parvan spat, "I will not apologize, Eminel of . . . do you even know your matriclan? You're the one who will regret."

Eminel let the silence stand. Should she choose to play her hand, she had dozens of ways to destroy an enemy. If the cuff was too drained for the revenge she chose, perhaps it was time to draw life force from her enemies, gathered only steps away. She could drain Parvan, to start. Sessadon had taught Eminel so many things. How to infiltrate minds. How to force bodies to bend or break. How to destroy people, quickly or slowly, by nearly any method: fire or water, earth or air. How easy it would be to wipe Parvan, and anyone else who challenged her, right off the face of the earth.

Eminel caught herself then, and remembered her dreams. *Chaos.* If that word came from Sessadon, no, Eminel could not follow the edict. She had to strive for the opposite—or be lost. There had to be a way forward.

At length she said to Parvan, still biting, "I regret nothing but your foolishness."

"Visionaries are often mistaken for fools," said Parvan. "And my vision is clear. I see that you are not truly a queen of Arca."

"Am I not?" half laughed Eminel, stroking the blue snake at her neck. "The snake necklace says otherwise. I was chosen. I say you are the one who is no Arcan."

"Of course I am Arcan! I was born here, raised here, learned here."

Eminel raised her voice, bit off her words. "And now you will leave here. I send you into exile."

"Exile?" Parvan shrieked. "I defended this nation when you couldn't."

"I defended this nation by sending you, and you failed me. Your exile begins now. Go."

231

Someone scurried forward. Another member of Parvan's matriclan, one who had stayed behind. "Don't exile her, please," said the woman, falling to her knees. "Show mercy. She bled for this nation. A little mercy, please, great queen."

Eminel ached. As much as she wanted to show mercy, she knew what would happen if she did. Once she appeared vulnerable, the matriclans would descend upon her like vultures on a carcass. And like a carcass, she realized, they would pick her bones clean.

"My mercy means you will have the day and night to say your goodbyes, Parvan," she said, softening her tone only a little. "I want you gone by tomorrow's sunrise."

Eminel looked around the assembled crowd, their robes still bright as jewels, but something entirely different now in their faces. Some of their mouths were set in stony lines, others gaping open. It felt as natural as anything for Eminel to call to mind the incantation she'd used to drain life force from the pack of foxes. She twisted it in the fingers of her right hand and spread it out over the room like a net, draining just a touch of life force from every woman in the court. She felt their energy rushing into her cuff like tadpoles swimming up her veins, thrilling her. She found it harder than she'd thought it would be to stop, but just letting her eyes alight on Beyda's face, seeing the cloud of confusion passing over the scribe's features, that was enough to push Eminel in the right direction. The cuff gave a faint glow and then subsided. The queen let her hand fall to her side.

"We will mourn our dead," she said to the crowd, letting her words ring out over their heads, a proclamation. "And enjoy the knowledge that the nest of Scorpican invaders has been stomped out. Then we will make plans to revenge the fallen, and to hunt any warriors who might attempt to remain in our lands."

Eminel considered turning on her heel and retreating to her chambers, but was it important to make one more show of power? It couldn't hurt, she decided. Not all her power was magic.

"Go," she said in a booming voice above the silence, extending a hand out in what could pass for either command or benediction. Dozens of magicians obeyed her order. Some backed away, bowing. Some turned and shuffled away in haste. Only a few courtiers dared to meet her eyes, and those who did saw no warmth, no forgiveness there. All they saw was a resolute monarch, the blue snake glimmering against her skin, her garment the very color of the sand that powered their nation's magic. She was like Daybreak Palace incarnate, they would whisper to each other that night and into the next day. She showed herself a queen.

What she showed them was a monarch without regrets. The version she wanted them to see. That night they would not see the heartsick, regretful Eminel weeping in her quarters, soaking the sand-colored robe with tears.

It was only after the court began to file out of the audience room that one of her councillors took her aside to whisper. A familiar figure, one she did not love as much as she loved Beyda, but an important one to listen to, under the right conditions. Eminel flicked her eyes over to where Iscla stood, nodded to her, and relaxed into the comfortable feeling of the mind-shield, the impenetrable magic that protected her from Sobek's magic and any like it.

"Five new girls," Sobek said.

"All-magic?"

"So they say. May I have them brought in?"

"You may send a messenger to their mothers. Ask that they join us for a short time. If they do not choose to come," said Eminel, "we won't force them."

Sobek looked at her, and Eminel did not have to read her mind to know exactly what she was thinking.

"I think it's very important that we bring them in." Sobek's voice was gentle and warm, that soft, murmuring tone she had when she was using her magic to convince. "I have your permission to do what's necessary to accomplish that goal, don't I?"

Perhaps she would have convinced a lesser magician, but not the magician Eminel was now.

"I have given my orders," said Eminel, keeping her own voice pleasant but neutral. "They will be invited to the palace. They will not be forced."

Clearly displeased but resigned, Sobek said, "Very well, Queen Eminel."

"Thank you," Eminel replied with sincere gratitude.

"One more matter to address. An important message came while you were in audience," said Sobek.

She'd forgotten that Sobek didn't attend matriclan gatherings. Her matriclan had gained power since the end of the Drought but still didn't rank among the highest six, and Sobek was still the only Perai in Daybreak Palace. "A message? From?"

"Let us speak of it in private," said Sobek, and the intensity of the woman's gaze made Eminel want to dive into her mind and find the secret without waiting for Sobek to share. But that was not necessary, not yet. When words could do, words should do.

Instead Eminel beckoned to Beyda to follow her—she wanted the scribe present for anything important, and this seemed like it might qualify—and they both walked a step behind Sobek in the direction of her private chambers.

But Eminel couldn't wait. As soon as the three were alone, she pushed to know more. "And so? This message?"

"From one of your fellow queens," said Sobek.

Beyda and Eminel exchanged looks of concern, curiosity.

Eminel said to Sobek, "Very well. I'm listening."

❖

"I can't go back in time," complained Eminel to Beyda, frowning down at the *whishnuk* board. The queen had played sloppily, with uncharacteristic haste, and her pegs were now clustered at two of the five star-points, far from where she wanted them to be.

Beyda, always even-tempered, replied, "If you could, I doubt you'd waste that power on a game of *whishnuk*."

"Never try to predict me, Beyda. I might take you by surprise one day."

"You might," Beyda allowed, but she didn't sound convinced.

Eminel scrutinized the board in silence. It was Beyda's move, and Beyda never hurried. She didn't have a natural talent for the game, that much was clear, but she was also never rattled by her opponent's game play. The game favored a Bastionite temper. Eminel wondered what had driven someone to gift it to an Arcan queen.

Finally Beyda selected a jade-green peg likely carved of real jade, hopped it two squares forward, and usurped one of Eminel's favorite pegs, an amber piece inlaid with gold.

"Fig-face," Eminel cursed, more vehemently than she'd meant to.

The scribe observed her friend carefully, cocking her head in that way she had, and said, "If you're not enjoying the game, we don't have to play."

Eminel pinched her forehead between her finger and thumb and rubbed her temples. "I'm sorry. I'm distracted."

Beyda nodded, as if that went without saying.

"If I *could* go back in time," Eminel said, keeping her eyes on the board, "you know what I'd do?"

"Do you want me to guess? I'm not sure. Does it have to do with the message from the queen?"

"Yes and no. I want to answer her. I want to help. But I can't risk it right now. Too much going on here."

"Agreed."

"But I wish I'd never sent those five to the front. And I worry about what Parvan has planned. She wanted me shamed in front of the entire court, that's why she insisted on meeting me only with them all present, but I doubt her plan stops with shame. I worry she intends something more dangerous."

Beyda considered the idea. "She very well might," she agreed.

Eminel said carefully, "While I'm always grateful for your honesty, Beyda, what I'm looking for right now is reassurance." She'd learned, with Beyda, to ask for what she wanted.

"I'm not good at providing that. Perhaps you should ask Sobek?"

"And Sobek, too!" Eminel said, finally giving up pretending she was interested in the board. "I think she knows I can resist her. If I keep disregarding her advice, no matter how politely, she's going to want answers."

"You don't have to give them to her just because she wants them."

"But there are so many ways she can use her power. Even if I'm protected from her directly, can't she just talk someone else into doing what she wants? There are too many ways she can be a threat."

"If you're really afraid of her, you could send her away," Beyda said, still calm and collected. "This court is only custom, not law. You aren't required to keep a single woman in Daybreak Palace if you don't want to. Or, if you want to be a real Arcan queen about it, you could put her in the Fingernail."

"Wait, what? The prison?"

"And when you came here you'd never even heard of it. See how you've grown?"

"I still don't know much." The truth was, she'd read up on the magicians sent to the Fingernail. Their stories were in the same books she'd studied to learn about the Arcan court; nearly all of them, in fact, were former courtiers. Beyda had not tested her on the details of their lives, and she'd done her best to forget them. She would only let her mind ponder the logistics. "How do you keep magicians locked up?"

"Carefully," answered Beyda dryly.

"Was that a joke? Did you just tell a joke?"

Beyda said, "I made an observation."

"A humorous observation," pushed Eminel.

"If you like, I can note it in the record." This time, a bit of a smile.

"I think things are not yet dire enough to place my enemies in prison, let alone people I'm not sure are my enemies," Eminel said, trying to make light of it, but the very concept concerned her. The queen before her had imprisoned powerful magicians in the Fingernail to waste away. There could be a dozen, two dozen, three dozen Sessadons lying in wait, for all Eminel knew.

She did not sleep well that night, to say the least.

Eminel dreamed herself traveling backward through her life. First she was at the Rites of the Bloody-Handed, watching herself command Tamura with a force she hadn't known she possessed. Then she was watching Sessadon kill Queen Mirri from inside Mirri's mind, hearing the queen's puzzlement at Eminel's blame for the death of her mother, who had in fact been killed by Sessadon, not Mirri. Then she was training with Sessadon, learning from her, her face worshipful and adoring in a way that now made Eminel sick to her stomach. How had she ever been so naive, so trusting? She'd been a fool, and everything terrible that was happening now would not have happened if she'd only had the good sense to see through Sessadon's lies.

But the dream kept flowing backward, the fabric of time unraveling. Eminel was younger still, perched in front of a tavern's hearth with Hermei as he'd explained all-magic to her, what it meant, what she was. Then time spun back once more. A few months earlier, the slumbering Eminel caught sight of the face of Jehenit, alive again and beaming, and while dream-Eminel fussed about being forced to stay in the wagon yet again while the Rovers stole what was needed to survive, sleep-Eminel's tears slid down her cheeks and soaked her pallet. Ungrateful girl. Unknowing girl. The journey into her past showed her only her own flaws. So many mistakes, over the years. So many errors she could never take back.

The younger she got in the dream, the less she blamed herself for these mistakes and the more she simply felt her heart ache for the naive young girl who had no idea what she was, what she could do. The girl who brushed the coin-shaped mark on her mother's wrist with her thumb, enjoying its slick surface, not knowing it was a symbol of her mother's sacrifice. The girl who delved into her neighbor's mind and brought Jorja's secrets into the open air, forcing Jehenit to decide whether to stay in her homeland or run for her life. Their lives. Even younger, only a handful of years, reading the mind of a girl with wings and flicking bruises onto the winged girl, trying to heal her, getting it wrong, wrong, wrong.

Then the dream grew sharper, more intense, and Eminel saw the moment of her birth. Jehenit had never told her the story. How could Eminel dream what she'd never known? The tears flowed harder and her breath caught in her throat as she recognized her mother, younger than Eminel had ever seen her, crouched on the ground of a stranger's house, seized by racking pain, clutching the hand of a sick woman whose eyes were wide as the sky. Then the baby—her!—crowned and slid forth, slick with fluid, and then there was a flash of blue so bright it woke the real Eminel, the sleeping Eminel, with a gasp.

Before she saw anything else in her chamber, Eminel could only see the aftereffects of the surge of energy she, as a baby, had brought into the world, which turned everything bright blue for a moment. Then she saw only a fiery orange-red as her eyes tried to adjust back to reality, but it was impossible to tell what was and wasn't reality anymore. She was awake, but the dream did not, in that first moment, let her go. The image of that flash pulsed in her. *Blue. Blue. Blue.*

She awoke to Beyda sitting on the edge of her bed, one hand stroking Eminel's sweat-soaked hair and the other mopping away her salty tears. Her body burned hot all over except for an oddly cold sensation where the blue snake necklace lay against her skin.

"It happened again," she said.

Beyda replied, "I expect it will keep happening until something changes. The question is, what will you change?"

"I need answers," Eminel said. "I need certainty."

"I am not sure there is certainty in this world."

"Again," Eminel said, "we find reassurance is not your strength."

Beyda gave a small, wordless shrug.

Eminel thought about the queens before her, the years before her, hundreds of years. How a person who had lived through more than a century might have wisdom and insight to share. Then, looking at Beyda, Eminel said the thing she did not want to say. "I think maybe you were right about the Fingernail."

"What about it? Do you want to put Sobek there?"

"No. Definitely not. But I think—we might want to reach out."

"For what purpose?"

"Advice, I suppose. I need to know who my real allies are. Inside Arca and beyond it."

Beyda said nothing.

At length, Eminel felt she needed to break the silence. "Why imprison these sorcerers? Don't the villages take care of their own justice?"

"They do," said Beyda, "but at least as the official stories tell it—you know I traffic in official stories—Queen Viyan instituted the prison for the safety of Arca. She was afraid that the villages' attempts to capture and punish powerful sorcery could go awry."

"What do you think?"

"It's a plausible explanation. Sorcerers with the right kind of magic can evade capture and turn magic back on those who try to punish them. I could share stories that would stand your hair on end."

"Please don't," Eminel said, trying to make it sound like a jest.

"Understood. But in another way, it seems obvious that Queen Viyan wanted to keep an eye on these sorcerers, and maybe find a way of using their powers for her own ends."

"Power-hungry. Like all Arcan queens."

Beyda shrugged. "Not all."

"Most."

"Probably most. But personally, I've only known two. As far as I know, only fifty percent of Arca's queens have been reprehensible, half-mad individuals who ran this queendom entirely through fear."

"The other one you know barely runs the country at all," Eminel mumbled.

"Not at all. The other one I know is very smart and capable. And powerful, even if she isn't entirely sure how to put that power to use."

"And while she may not be as unhinged as the previous queen," Eminel said—it was easier to speak of herself as if she were a stranger—"she's being driven close to half-mad by these nightly dreams."

"Which is why I think taking action is a good idea. Action might help."

"It might hurt."

"It might. But we can do one thing from the privacy of this very room." Beyda turned to the racks Eminel had ordered installed to keep some of the most interesting incantations at her fingertips. Beyda considered, withdrew the scroll she wanted, and unrolled it on the low table in front of Eminel. "If you think you can manage the spell, we can scry to the Fingernail right now."

But Eminel was already lost in the incantation, already mumbling the words under her breath before she lost her nerve. She looked down the page and gestured first tentatively, then with more confidence, realizing these words and motions were all familiar, just in a new combination. She forged a connection across miles. She called on mind magic and air magic to send images and thoughts racing through that connection.

She thought of chaos, how it resolved into order and then dissipated back to chaos again, and how this was as it should be, and she would let this connection dissolve as soon as she was done with it; she just had to build it in the first place. Then she reached out, and waited.

Beyda said quietly, "How do we know if it worked?"

A face resolved in the air, looming a few handspans in front of Eminel, and a dry, hoarse voice shouted, "Velja's lower beard!"

Eminel would have laughed if she weren't so shocked; as it was, her mouth seized up somewhere between a smile and an O of surprise, and she closed her eyes so she could brace herself before opening them again.

"Didn't expect a visitor," said the voice. "I see you wear the snake. So you're a queen of Arca."

"Yes," said Eminel, then opened her eyes. As soon as she did, she wished she would have kept them shut.

The old woman in front of her looked like a corpse. The skin of her face mostly covered her skull, but not quite, and patches of bone shone through here and there. Her eyes had gone entirely white, as had the remaining patches of thin, threadlike hair atop her head. The horror of her face sat atop a thin, corded neck. The rest of her was shrouded by a buff-colored, sack-like garment for which Eminel was grateful. She didn't want to see whatever remained of the rest of the woman.

"You're dead," said Eminel, unable to stop herself.

"Ha! If only. I've tried to die a few times," said the white-haired sorcerer, her eyes glinting like polished bone. "Eresh won't take me, lazy cow."

"Your death doesn't interest us," interrupted Beyda, her voice more confident than usual. "We've called upon you for information."

Eminel was grateful for her friend's intervention. She forced her eyes to stay open, even though the wasted-away apparition made her want to retch. If Beyda could do the talking, Eminel could bear to listen.

The sorcerer's white eyes turned to Beyda, clearly taking her measure, unhurried. "And why should I help you?"

"Don't worry," Beyda responded, her tone nonchalant. "We don't really have need of you. I'm just curious to hear what you know. If anything."

"Don't try that with me, child," growled the sorcerer. "If you didn't believe in my power, you'd hardly have gone to all this trouble."

"It was no trouble. Don't you know who this is?" The scribe gestured at Eminel. "I suppose they don't tell you everything—or maybe anything—in that hellhole. But this is Eminel, Well of All-Magic, Master of Sand, and Destroyer of Fear. When you last walked the world, who was queen of Arca? Mirriam, Well of All-Magic, Master of Sand, and Destroyer?"

At Mirriam's name the sorcerer spat, and though nothing came out, her opinion was clear.

Eminel realized she remembered more than she wanted to of the magicians in the Fingernail, particularly those who Mirriam had imprisoned. If this sorcerer was who Eminel thought she might be, either by luck or because her story was foremost in Eminel's mind, she might be genuinely helpful. If she could be convinced to talk.

Beyda seemed to be gaining confidence. Did she, too, realize who they were talking to?

"So you know of Mirriam's power. If the old queen was that powerful, how powerful do you think this queen needed to be in order to defeat her?"

Eminel marveled at how Beyda was able to be so deceitful without telling a single lie. She hadn't known the young woman had it in her. It was a skill Eminel might need as queen; now she knew who she could learn from.

"How do I know it's not a trick?" said the sorcerer. "That you aren't some minor courtier doing Mirriam's dirty work?"

Beyda and Eminel exchanged a look. Eminel could speak directly into the scribe's mind if she wanted to, but it seemed disrespectful to do without asking, and they hadn't discussed it first. Eminel hoped Beyda would read in her look that she didn't have a good answer for this.

Beyda said, "The answers you could give us—if you choose to—

242

have nothing to do with Mirriam's power. The queen will tell you what she seeks." She turned to Eminel with a nod.

Eminel said, "I need to know who my allies are. And"—she made a split-second decision, forcing herself to meet the woman's white, blank eyes—"I wish to know how you would interpret my dreams."

"Well!" The desiccated sorcerer smiled, and it was terrifying. The teeth remaining in her head, not many, were yellowed and dark as kernels of seed corn. "You know of my specialty, then."

"Of course," Eminel said. She'd been guessing, but the answer confirmed her guess. "You're a mind magician."

"If whoever built the Bastion was a stonecutter, then very well, call me a magician," said the ancient sorcerer.

Eminel looked at Beyda; Beyda squared her shoulders and nodded. There was only one former courtier this could be. Eminel leaped into the fray, finding that her voice grew stronger, sharper. "You are the famed mind magician Nuray, of the Zahr matriclan. You were a powerful ally of Queen Mirriam in her earliest days. Your specialty within mind magic was dreams, and you would plant powerful, destructive nightmares in the minds of the queen's enemies. A mere taste of your power caused self-doubt and distraction. When you chose, you could drive women and men insane in the space of a single night. The morning after you planted a dream in the mind of the queen's chief rival, Lenov, she reported unbidden to the queen's audience chamber, prostrated herself at the queen's feet in front of an audience of dozens, and bashed her forehead into a marble footstool over and over until she broke all the way through her own skull. It was a brutal way to die."

"It sent a message."

"The message was received. You were good at what you did. But you were so powerful, gaining strength as you aged, that the queen grew concerned you might turn against her. You were her most powerful ally, and she turned against you. Now you rot in the Fingernail, refusing to die."

"I still maintain that you are likely a fool," said Nuray, her tone measured and appreciative, "but I admit that you have probably, at least once, read a book. And yet you reach out to me, as if I can't hurt you."

"You can't," interrupted Beyda matter-of-factly. "The counterspells of the cells in the Fingernail are permanently worked into the stone of the building and the very island itself. You still have your power, yes, but the stone that surrounds you makes it impossible for you to use it. Besides, there is not a speck of sand within a hundred leagues of the Fingernail. Even if you could overcome the counterspells and draw life force, the lack of sand would keep you powerless. You're only a danger if you get out, and in your particular case, the door of your cell was welded shut five decades ago."

"But if I get out," said Nuray, "what a danger I could be. Are you going to let me out if I help you?"

Beyda turned to Eminel in horror, wondering if that was in fact what her friend would promise, but Eminel only shrugged lightly. "As we have said, we only want to know what you know, if anything. There is no harm done here if you tell us nothing. But I rather think you're starved for company. How long has it been since you've seen another person?"

Nuray's bony shoulders twitched under her shapeless garment. "What does it matter anymore?"

"So I think you'll talk to us because you want to talk to us. Because it amuses you. Because you're glad that I know your story. And because you have literally nothing else to do."

"Fine," said the ancient sorcerer, raising her chin to one shoulder in an almost flirtatious motion. Eminel saw, for a fleeting glimpse, what the sorcerer might have looked like in her youth: elegant, angular, a cool demeanor on the outside and blazing fire within. Then the glimpse was gone and only the husk of the woman remained. It made Eminel's heart hurt. Death would have been a far kinder outcome for Nuray. Which was why it made perfect sense that Mirriam didn't let her die. The wasted-away mouth said, "Tell me your dreams."

Eminel began, haltingly, to describe what she'd dreamed, the most memorable and mystical things she could remember, all the way back to that first dream in the carriage on the way back from the Sun Rites. The blue woman who urged chaos. The Rovers, inverted. The story of her own life sliding backward through time, until it ended in her own blue-fire-wreathed birth. Without being told to leave Sessadon out of the story, she did so instinctively. She was surprised to find the story still, in most ways, made sense. There was no need to explain Sessadon to this stranger. If Nuray suggested that a strong sorcerer might be responsible for the dreams, well, then she would know to be afraid.

The blankness of Nuray's white eyes and the wasted shape of her cheeks made it hard to read the expression on the sorcerer's face. Was she amused? Appalled? Bored almost to tears?

Eminel could keep silent no longer. "Well? What do you think?"

Nuray made a motion with her mouth that would have been smacking her lips if she'd had lips. "Ah, queen. Are you concerned that this woman sheathed in blue who tells you to embrace chaos might be a powerful magician?"

Sickness rose in Eminel's stomach, dread that everything she'd feared about the dreams was true. If it was, she needed to know for sure. She forced herself to answer. "Yes."

"Then you are exactly the fool I took you for. Skull stuffed with cobwebs and hay. And you come asking me about allies."

"Yes," snapped Eminel, "that's exactly what I asked. And you told me nothing."

"Allies! You fool, you have the greatest ally any woman ever could. The only one you need."

Eminel wanted to look to Beyda, but forced herself to keep her eyes on Nuray. She had started this. She needed to see it through.

"You think your dream-figure is a magician," said Nuray. "Have you considered that she might, instead, be a god?"

Eminel struggled to keep her expression neutral, but she knew, even as she tried her best, that she was failing. She was too stunned to hide her shock.

The old sorcerer chortled. "I see you haven't. Who raised you, anyway, a herd of grass grazers?"

Eminel rose awkwardly, wanting to flee, even though the person she wanted to flee from wasn't physically present. "My upbringing is none of your concern."

"Didn't mean anything by it." The old sorcerer waved a desiccated hand. "Just that any Arcan child knows of Velja through stories. She introduced herself in dreams to some of her favorites, like Meskhanye. I always loved that story. Yet it seems obvious you do not know it, nor does your non-Arcan friend. Bastionite, is she? Well, are you?"

Beyda responded without answering the question. "Whatever the stories may or may not be, that isn't relevant. Is that what you think is happening? You think Velja herself is speaking to Queen Eminel?"

The old sorcerer laughed, a dry, rasping sound like corn husks ripping. "Only Velja knows, but I wouldn't want to be in your shoes. Like any ally, she can turn on you. And gods don't like it if you don't recognize them when they come calling."

Beyda and Eminel sat wordless.

Then Nuray laughed again, more cruelly this time, and Eminel again saw a flash of what the woman must have been like years ago, and this time, she did not like it. A woman who could cause another woman to beat her own head against stone until she cracked it open was barely worthy of being called human. Too much power was a terrible thing. It had destroyed Queen Mirriam's mind and wreaked the same havoc on Sessadon's. In the end, both women had valued power more than anything else in the world: more than life, more than justice, more than family.

Was this what would happen to her, thought Eminel, if she ruled too long? Or, once they fought the Scorpican threat, would power-hungry members of the court kill her before she could live long enough to go out of her mind? Was it only a choice between destroying and being destroyed?

"Don't worry," she said to Nuray, "you haven't helped us at all."

And Eminel closed her fist, severing the link. The hovering white-eyed face was gone in an instant, and all Eminel could see in front of her was the far wall of her chamber, the curtains hanging still as stone in the airless room.

Beyda was the first to speak. "A god. Did I understand that correctly? Is that the explanation for your dreams?"

Eminel said, "That's what the ancient magician thinks, anyway. It makes sense. The blue woman in my dreams says 'chaos' because she *is* Chaos."

"Do you believe in her?" asked Beyda, matter-of-fact as usual.

After careful consideration, Eminel said, "I'm starting to."

"And what are you going to do about it?"

Eminel didn't answer right away. She saw the beginning of a plan. It might take her down a dark road, but she could keep herself from getting swept away with ambition, couldn't she? She knew now what she didn't want. She didn't want to end up like the ancient sorcerer Nuray, only ever thinking of damaging her enemies, letting go of everything that mattered in life until she was a husk, unable to die.

Beyda prompted, "Eminel?"

Eminel answered slowly, "I don't think you'll like it."

"My feelings aren't that relevant," Beyda said. "Tell me. Was it something she said?"

"Not exactly. But I realized, I could be looking at this all wrong. I've been trying to manage the court."

"Yes."

"But what if there were no court?" Eminel asked.

Beyda blinked. "What?"

"It was something you told me, actually. You said the only reason there's a court here is because the queen says so."

"I did, yes," said Beyda, but the look on her face clearly indicated she wasn't following.

Eminel said, "I sent women who didn't want to work together to accomplish a common goal, and it backfired. What if I used their self-interest instead?"

"In what way?"

"You, I'll tell," said Eminel, becoming serious, her resolve hardening into certainty. "Them, I'll show."

✦

The summoned courtiers were terrified to come, but they came. The summons from their queen named a time for them to appear at the long-neglected arena where the trials of all-magic girls had once taken place. A few struggled to be optimistic—perhaps they'd be only spectators—but in the absence of reassuring details, dread bloomed. They only knew Eminel demanded their presence. And any hope that they'd be watching from the stands evaporated as they approached. Eminel stood alone in the queen's grandstand, waiting as those she'd summoned massed on the field itself beneath her feet.

Was the entire court here, breath held at their queen's behest? It looked like it. Those who counted the faces around them might have realized that a few key members were missing, but they were too nervous to be sure. Many remembered the last day Mirrida had issued such a summons: she'd announced her discovery of a conspiracy against her and slain conspirator after conspirator before their eyes. Eminel hadn't seemed as bloodthirsty, having slain no one since Archis, exiling Parvan when she could just as easily have killed her, but no one knew the queen well enough to assume the best.

They milled and whispered in the center of the field. Above them was the queen in her grandstand and rows of empty seats around her; at the opposite end of the field, the gates to the arena stood wide open, the spires of Daybreak Palace just visible in the distance. It looked like a toy castle from here, a child's plaything, perfect in miniature.

"I will not thank you for obeying my summons," Eminel began, voice ringing out. "We all know you had no choice. But I will assure you, what I do here today in the name of Arca will protect our nation's future."

The courtiers reassured by this promise were few.

"Part," she said, and moved her hands apart as if clearing a table.

Scrambling, the courtiers moved quickly—the crowd was too large to run—and hoped they'd correctly interpreted her command. When they stood in two bunches at the far sides of the field, leaving its broad, flat center unoccupied, she seemed satisfied.

Queen Eminel raised her hands and magic poured forth, seemingly an effortless flow, raising color in the sand where no one stood. First the outlines of irregular shapes appeared, thick borders slithering into view like snakes. Then came the tanned, gentle slopes of desert hills seen from above, dotted with blue circles and lines representing precious water.

The earth magician Colena of the Binaj matriclan, though her specialty was plants and not sand, was one of the first to recognize what the queen had done. As soon as Colena saw a familiar shape blush into existence on the far side of the outline, a ragged-edged province pressing its southern coast against the Mockingwater, she knew.

Before them lay a massive map of Arca.

And it felt almost as if the queen must be reading her mind when she called out, "Women and men of Binaj!"

Colena turned her face toward the queen's. Even this far away, Queen Eminel's expression seemed clear. She didn't look angry or vengeful, but she expected total obedience. Colena saw no reason not to comply.

"Binaj!" the queen repeated, and raised an indicating finger. "To your home."

From their scattered places in the crowds on either side of the map, the women and men of Binaj began to walk. Colena was hesitant at first to set foot on the map lest she blur its lines, but after three steps she realized it would take far more than footsteps to stir the queen's magic. When she arrived at the right place on the map, clustered with the other members of her matriclan within the shape of their ancestral lands, she felt a moment's relief. Then the relief blossomed into something more complicated.

A familiar face was missing, Colena realized. She knew every member of the Binaj matriclan at court, of course, but the one she knew and loved best was not here: her sweet-tempered daughter, Dellica.

"Merve, to your home!" called the queen's voice from on high. The present members of the Merve matriclan obeyed. Dozens of footsteps shuffled across the field from every direction, headed for the far eastern border of the map, where a glimmering shape represented the famed glass castle of Bryk.

Long minutes unfurled as the queen continued to move her courtiers by command. *Jale, to your home. Ishta, to your home.* With every clan named, Colena's tension grew. She didn't know the members of the other matriclans at court as well as her own, but she thought she saw a pattern in who was absent from the field, and it flooded her with unease.

When every person present stood where Eminel had sent them, bunched together in their matriclans like baby birds in their mother's feathered nest, the queen raised her Talish cuff in the air.

Everyone gasped a simultaneous gasp. It wasn't surprise, Colena realized; the breath was being taken from them, siphoned out. Her limbs began to feel weak. Even if she'd wanted to explain to those nearby what was happening, she couldn't. The enchantment drawing out her life force left her, and everyone around her, unable to speak. She thought she saw the beginnings of a shadow at the edges of her vision.

The queen's Talish cuff glowed blue, faintly at first, then with more and more intensity, until it gleamed like a small blue sun.

Spreading her fingers wide, Queen Eminel let them go all at once. Feeling rushed back into their numb limbs, air into their struggling lungs. Then she curled her fingers back into a fist and thrust it over their heads toward the open gates at the far end of the field, in the direction of Daybreak Palace.

The blue glow from the Talish cuff expanded, sparking, shooting forward from the queen's fist like a sheet of light. Some courtiers ducked on instinct, but the light wasn't aimed their way. It flowed across the sky overhead like a fast river through narrow banks, and it hit Daybreak Palace with a roar.

Colena couldn't help the scream that loosed itself from her aching throat. Was it possible the queen was burning the palace to the ground right in front of them? And if her daughter wasn't here, was she inside? Colena had never harmed a single living thing in more than five decades on the earth, but if the queen hurt her daughter, she would rip the woman apart with her bare hands.

But as Colena and the others watched, the blue gleam did not consume the palace. Instead it spread across the palace facade into a solid, shimmering blue wall. The wall of light reached from the golden sand all the way up to the palace's tallest spire. They could still see the palace through it, but there was not a seam, not a stone, that was not separated from them by the glowing blue wall their queen had made.

"Daybreak Palace is sealed," called Eminel.

The whispers around her became a roar like the Mockingwater's waves breaking on the western shore.

"We don't know where the Scorpicae will strike next," called Eminel. "But all that will save us is working together."

Colena didn't understand. Why this show, why this map, why this magic? Her own magic was powerful in its particular way—the year she came to court, she'd doubled the yield of the palace's nearby vineyards, securing honor for Binaj—but she couldn't do battle with the queen. If Queen Eminel said the palace was sealed, it was sealed. What did that have to do with working together? The words were out before she realized what consequences might result from saying them. Her voice was loud, sharp. "Queen, where in the name of Velja is my daughter?"

Eminel looked down toward Colena, picking her out of the crowd almost instantly. Perhaps she'd been expecting the question. She looked almost pleased. "Your daughter is safe," she said, directly to Colena, not unkindly.

Then the queen lifted her head and addressed the entire crowd, still huddled in their own smaller groups by matriclan, feet on the map where she'd aimed them. "This is Colena of Binaj. Her daughter, Dellica, loves growing things. Right now Dellica is in Daybreak Palace singing lullabies to a potted lemon tree. I swear by this necklace, and my rule it represents, she is safe."

Colena felt both sick and relieved; she doubted the queen would bother to swear if she were lying. There was something else afoot, and it might be cruel, but it would at least be honest.

"And Bonmei, too," Eminel went on, turning toward another matriclan. "Safe in the palace. I'm sure those of you from Merve recall her well. Barely ten-and-six, strong as an ox. Her water magic growing more powerful every day."

"Why Bonmei?" shouted someone from Merve, the voice high-pitched with strain and worry.

Eminel explained with an air of patience. "Bonmei is the youngest daughter of the Merve matriclan. Just like Dellica is the youngest of Binaj. The youngest daughter of each matriclan you represent—in fact, every young woman of the court under twenty years of age—rests safely in the palace, tended by servants in comfort, protected by my magic. They will remain here, safe from harm, until you return."

No one asked the question that was plain on every face: *Return from where?*

"Where you stand," said Eminel, indicating the map spreading beneath their feet, "you will go. You will travel home to your matriclan's ancestral lands. And you will defend those lands. Whatever it takes. If the Scorpicae come to you, you will cast them out. And you will stay there until I call you back."

A voice came again from Merve, possibly the same one, accusatory. "You can't force us to fight! What if our magic isn't strong enough?"

Eminel waved the hand with the Talish cuff dismissively, its blue glow leaving a faint streak in the air. "Magic is only one tool. You are women of power and influence. You may use any gifts at your disposal, not just your magic, to arm and train the residents of your territories to fight and expel our enemies."

"And then we can come back?"

"Then you come back. When I call you. And then you reunite with the future of your matriclan, your dearest daughters, who I promise you are completely safe within those walls."

A different voice off to Colena's left spoke out. "But what if the Scorpicae attack here?"

Eminel said, "My magic protects the palace and your daughters inside. This defense will endure."

In that moment Colena hated Queen Eminel more than she'd ever hated a person, hated her for forcing this course of action, hated her for tearing mother from daughter and endangering the high-ranking line of her matriclan. But though she hated Eminel, she understood her. And she would do as she was bid. Everyone here would. Already, feet were moving, shifting off the map and heading toward the open gates.

Given a choice, the high-ranking women of the Arcan court would never choose to travel so far across the hostile sands, to mingle with the villagers and townspeople they had left behind for the life of glamour they'd been leading in Daybreak Palace. They wouldn't choose to wear themselves out on the rough, long roads, yield to countless questions, work hard to organize groups of people who had never been organized in an undertaking like this. They'd never choose to become a military against their will, devoting themselves to preparing for an attack that might never come.

Which was exactly why, thought Colena, Queen Eminel hadn't given them a choice.

✦ 18 ✦

INTERSECTIONS

Late summer, the All-Mother's Year 517
On the road near Ursu, Paxim
Azur, Paulus, Heliane

Only three things in this world had ever brought Azur joy. First, the friendship of Ysilef, long dead but still mourned. Second, ending a life. Third, the pleasure of body meeting body, skin soft and yielding under her teeth, flesh hot against her tongue. During the Moon Rites of the All-Mother's Year 517, Azur flung herself with abandon into the third of the three, and the only problem with the satisfaction it gave her was how quickly that satisfaction faded away.

She'd enjoyed herself almost as much as she had at the Sun Rites that had planted Madazur, her body just as responsive as it had been back then, giving and receiving pleasures with a wild generosity everyone seemed to appreciate. She lost track of the number of times her body had bucked with delicious abandon under someone else's hips or hand or tongue; she extracted rain after rain from man after man with the steady persistence of a boneburner stoking a sacred fire.

But on the long ride back toward the Scorpican camp, only a day removed from those pleasures, all she had were memories. And perhaps, if the Scorpion smiled on her, a belly set to swell. That outcome would be unknown for a few months yet, long after she was back in the company of the full complement of Scorpicae on the far side of the world. In her bedroll at night she set her fingers to the task of satisfaction, fresh memories of what she'd done in the Holy City flickering in her mind, but it wasn't the same, and it wasn't enough. It was never enough.

Azur didn't know every single one of the young women who she led on this mission to the rites, but of course, all of them knew her. They knew she was the First Mother. Knew that she alone in their generation had proven she could bear a girl child. Some deferred to her to an embarrassing degree and others openly resented her leadership, but none of them contested that of all the women on this ride, she was in charge.

So it was strange when another pony drew alongside hers, the head of another warrior bobbing into Azur's line of sight. For the entire ride so far, both to and from the Holy City, the First Mother had ridden alone at the front of the column. Azur didn't turn her head, but she could still see the other warrior easily out of the corner of her eye, and she knew it was only a matter of time until the woman made what she wanted clear.

"You probably don't remember me," called the sleek young woman, who wore a cowl of rust-colored fabric draped over her hair and neck. The angle at which her sharp-nosed face poked out of the covering made her resemble a particularly alert and potentially troublesome fox.

Azur eyed her coolly as they rode side by side. "No," she answered in a flat tone. "I don't."

The fox-faced warrior seemed unperturbed. "You and I walked countless leagues together as children, after we were plucked from the countries of our birth and delivered north to become Scorpican warriors. We were transformed. I was once called Vira. When I became a daughter of Tamura, I chose the name Riva for my own."

"Clever," said Azur without feeling. Riva was absolutely correct that Azur did not remember her. From that time in her life, she only remembered Ysilef. *Mokh*, she missed Ysilef. Why could she never stop missing Ysilef, no matter how many years her friend had been dead and gone?

From the edge of her vision Azur could see that Riva was matching her pony's stride to that of Azur's mount, with no sign of impatience. Riva simply waited.

Seeing no way out but through, Azur asked, "So what do you want, Riva?"

"I think we have an opportunity."

Azur chose not to question the *we*, but she noted it. She gestured for Riva to go on.

Riva continued. "After we were trained, but before Tamura recalled warriors to Scorpica, I was assigned here to Paxim. My task was to protect a trading post not far from Ursu. The post needed more security than most. The arriving goods were unusually valuable."

Azur could easily predict what Riva wanted to say, at least in part, so she said it herself. "Because it was close to the capital."

Riva nodded. "And the palace."

"Yes," she said with a trace of irritation, "I understand."

"But you may not understand that the trading post in question is just over that ridge. Less than an hour's ride." Riva pointed with satisfaction at the horizon.

Following the angle of the other warrior's outstretched finger, Azur could just make out a smudge, one she would never have identified as a settlement, let alone a trading post of value.

It wouldn't do to seem too eager, so she didn't respond right away, but Azur's mind raced. On one hand, they should proceed directly back to the Scorpican camp with no detours. They'd been sent to grow the next generation of warriors; that was their only mission. Azur should be eager to rush back to the camp where Tamura ruled. A council seat and all the influence that it promised waited for her.

But on the other hand, she remembered how she'd felt there, trapped and sidelined by her role as the First Mother. Azur felt more like herself on this journey, closer to the woman she had once been, and she remembered having been a formidable warrior. Slaying enemies had always brought her almost as much joy as the pursuit of pleasures. Here on the open plain, the milk that had once swelled her breasts a faint memory, it was easier to remember who she'd been before Madazur. Her body was alive now, awakened. She had tasted so much. She was hungry for more.

So perhaps, before she returned to her previous position under Tamura's thumb, Azur might take down an enemy or two?

Anticipating Azur's potential objection, Riva spoke quietly, with a self-satisfied air. "I, for one, was never told not to attack anyone. Our mother told us to be safe. To be fruitful. To never give away that we are Scorpicae. But she never said not to notch an arrow onto a bowstring. She never said not to draw our swords."

"Not all of us even have swords," Azur said carefully, "in our costumes as peaceful weaklings. Some of us have nothing more than knives."

"We may not have the magic of Arcans," Riva said, and her voice took on a confiding air. "But if we descend upon that trading post, in the right numbers and the right location, our kind of magic will turn knives into swords and bows. Use one to obtain the other."

Azur found herself nodding in approval.

Riva went on, "Luxury goods for the palace pass through this post, but I wouldn't risk these women for silver cuffs and snowdrop honey. Troops that train at the palace need weapons. Those weapons arrive here. And it's all kept hushed. Even when there was an assigned force of Scorpicae, we were only a handful. A larger protective force would attract too much attention."

A plan began to form in Azur's mind. The more she turned it over and examined it, the more she liked it. And the more irresistible it became.

"I assume," she said to Riva, "you've thought about how to approach the other warriors? Do you suggest we promise riches, or separate those most likely to follow us from those who will resist before we make the offer?"

Riva grinned then, her smile transforming her from fox to wolf. She hadn't missed the crucial word repeated in Azur's response. *We.*

"I've considered the options," Riva said, gazing out over the plain, settling her reins across her pony's back as if they were merely out for a stroll through home country. "Some will refuse to follow because they're too afraid to risk the future warriors they might bear. We should praise those who abstain for that reason and send them on their way. Those who would follow us will follow us, and the others can go *mokh* themselves. If they don't share in the fighting, they won't share in the glory. That will be punishment enough."

The smear on the horizon was growing more distinct by the moment. Such a tempting target. So conveniently placed, only a short detour off their path. As if the All-Mother herself had dropped it there as a favor to Azur and to the Scorpion.

Azur pressed her bottom lip against her top teeth to let out the low whistle of command, and when she raised her fist, all two dozen members of the party drew their ponies to a halt. She extended a finger and described a swift loop in the air, and the warriors turned the heads of their ponies inward to form a ring. Then they waited in silence to hear what the First Mother would say.

"I wish to bring Tamura a gift," she said.

On Riva's other side, another of Tamura's daughters, this one a round-hipped, doe-eyed warrior named Zibiah, raised her soft voice just loud enough to be heard. "The gifts we bring our mother dwell inside our bodies."

"We all wish so, but there is no way to know for sure. We may or may not bear children, and they may or may not be warriors. We hope, of course. But I want to bring her something certain."

Zibiah looked unsure. "What did you have in mind?"

Azur tilted her head at the far-off settlement, then at Riva. "Riva?"

Confidently, Riva raised her chin. "The trading post on the horizon, three leagues south of the capital, is rich with some of Paxim's greatest treasure."

The petite, sun-bronzed warrior Orlaithe interrupted. "Rich or not, it's not our mission to attack. We aren't to draw attention to ourselves. Weren't you listening to the queen?"

Azur wheeled her pony for effect, her hooves pawing the air, then brought her back to earth right next to Orlaithe in a cloud of dust. No one moved, including Orlaithe, though Azur could see her strain.

Leaning toward her, but speaking loud enough for all to hear, Azur hissed, "I hang on every word our queen says. She is my mother, don't forget."

Orlaithe looked like she wanted to object that Azur was not the only one of Tamura's daughters present, glancing from face to face, but held her tongue.

"Believe me when I say I listened. She didn't tell us to crawl through this nation on our bellies. She said to travel in disguise." Azur gestured down at her torn, plain clothing. "We are ragged like pious Thrift-worshipping Paximites, not proud and clean like Scorpicae. They will call us bandits."

"It's a good plan," called out Zibiah, with more confidence than Azur had ever heard from her. Clearly, she'd been convinced.

"I disagree," snapped Orlaithe. "We can't put our bodies in harm's way. If we carry future warriors, we cannot be risked. I will not participate."

Azur knew this was a key moment. But she and Riva had prepared for it. Azur shrugged without losing her faint smile. "Very well, Orlaithe, I respect your choice. You may continue back toward Godsbones, and we will catch up once we've burned this place to the ground. If we don't find you along the way, we'll see you at the camp. May the Scorpion bless your path."

Azur used her knees to nudge her pony and deliberately turned her back on Orlaithe, as if the warrior were no longer worthy of her attention. Then she smiled at the others, and gestured toward the horizon. "You may all choose. Who curls up like a pangolin and crawls away with that one, and who rides to glory with me?"

The group separated into two quickly, with no further discussion. In the end, about half of them fell into line behind Azur and Riva. Azur would have liked more, but she would not show her disappointment. She would get to ride and pillage and slay. The rest was unimportant. She could feel hot blood already coursing through her, pulsing in her wrists, behind her navel, at her throat.

She addressed her warriors in a stern, terse voice of command. "Stealthy in, quickly out, do as much damage as we can. Are you with me? Will you ride in the name of the Scorpion?"

Emotions roiled across the faces of the young warriors. Some were plainly eager, others uncertain, emotions flickering across their features like the play of light on a wind-whipped sea. But after they glanced toward each other and then back at her, they spoke as one. "Yes, First Mother."

Azur could not keep the hungry grin from her face as she pointed toward the trading post on the horizon, now recognizable as a collection of buildings, and called out, sharp and quick, "We ride."

❖

The ride toward Hosios was hard enough, the path narrow enough, that there were long stretches when Paulus couldn't talk to Ama. She was right ahead of him, he riding golden Philomel, she on one of the mare's copper-colored offspring, so close and yet so far.

They needed this day together, Paulus especially. He sometimes felt like he couldn't breathe in the palace, knowing so many pairs of eyes tracked his every move. Heliane had seemed to regain some of her health lately, a fact for which he thanked the All-Mother daily. But in so many ways, the damage had already been done. Insidious whispers that certain senators had grown concerned about the future had reached even Paulus's protected ears, and if he had heard them, he doubted there was a citizen of Ursu who hadn't. If the gossips were talking about Heliane, he knew, they were talking about him. Evaluating. And yes, everywhere and always, watching.

But not today. The two of them had escaped, if only for a few hours. Today only Ama would look at him, and he shivered with anticipation of what he might see in her eyes. The way she looked directly at him, that hawk's gaze, used to unnerve him. Now it warmed his blood, made his heart race.

Still, her gaze at the moment lived only in his imagination. She wouldn't be able to look directly at him until the path widened and they could ride side by side. For now, he was alone with his thoughts. Paulus thought of his future, and he thought of Ama, and it was natural that once he'd considered the two things separately, he thought about both together.

The kingling hated the constant, speculative whispers that swirled around him of late, but they'd prepared him in a way he hadn't been prepared before. In the past weeks he hadn't just come to terms with the idea that he might one day be king. He'd actually begun to look forward to it.

The aftermath of the Drought of Girls was so unforeseen, there was no code for it in the laws of Paxim; they had simply never imagined that the queen would not only have no daughters, but no cousins, no nieces. Since the end of the Drought, countless women had presented their daughters at the front gate of the palace, claiming a connection to the queen. But Heliane wouldn't see them. If someone tried to tell her their names, she'd clap her hands over her ears like a toddler. She wouldn't support the ascension of any girl in the queendom no matter her blood, and her word was final. Heliane would acknowledge only her son. Him.

To further this, his mother had signed a paper that officially gave the regency to the consul, which comforted him. He'd known Decima all his life, and he trusted her. That wasn't why Heliane had done it, he knew—she wanted to shore up support for him, show the doubters that he would have the counsel of a wise woman to lean on—but it still made him feel better. Heliane herself had leaned on the advice of the previous consul when she'd been made queen so young; but to formalize the arrangement, that made everything feel real.

So Paulus would be king, the first ruling king of Paxim, and he would need wise women to surround him. Decima was a start. He fixed his gaze on Ama's retreating back and wished they were already at Hosios. He'd selected a destination that was a few leagues from the palace because he wanted hours of escape, but now he felt frustrated, wanting more time not just near Ama but fully with her.

As if she'd heard his internal cry for her attention, she looked back over her shoulder and shot him a smile. Even before he had time to answer her smile with his own, her expression shifted and she called out, "Don't grip her reins so high, you'll panic her," and turned back to the trail ahead.

In some ways, Paulus realized, nothing he did was good enough for Ama. He'd noticed it first on the training field. Perhaps because she was such a naturally good fighter she had no patience for his learning, or perhaps she held him to an impossibly high standard. It would've been better, he thought, if she'd shouted at him, but she never did. She only acted disappointed. Very few things struck him more deeply than Ama's disappointment. He suspected she knew that and playacted in order to motivate him. But his sword cuts were never sharp enough, his staff swings never brisk enough, dagger jabs never stealthy enough. She always wanted him to do more, be more. The upside of that was that he knew she truly believed him capable. That was what kept him going through all the mistakes, the failures, the striving. She'd never push him so hard to attain something she believed he couldn't do.

But as he followed her along the winding path, her horse and his horse picking their way along with dainty hooves, Paulus asked himself the hardest question: Could he do more without her than with her? Would she, knowingly or unknowingly, hold him back? Paulus would be the ruler, not Ama. He supposed that if they married—when had that entered his mind as a possibility?—she would have the title of queen. A man who married a Paximite queen had the title of king, so it seemed the reverse would be true, but perhaps that was a foolish assumption. He felt certain Ama wouldn't insist on marriage in any case. She wouldn't want to be mistaken for a ruling queen. If he had met a less power-hungry person in his life than Ama, he couldn't imagine who it would be.

He wished he didn't need to think of these concerns, but now that he was certain to be king, he needed to predict and accommodate them. He couldn't live his life in his mother's shadow, and he refused to live it in his lover's shadow either. It made him think of the story of Rudaba and Lansper. Perhaps he'd tell it to Ama when they got to their destination. The true hero of the story of Rudaba and Lansper was not Lansper, who had cleverly followed a trail, but Rudaba, who had been clever enough to lay it down for him to find. Paulus needed to be as clever as Rudaba, as dedicated as Roksana, as fierce as Alev, as steadfast as the nameless gardening king whose rare plant had saved his wife, Theodora, from certain death. Paulus had never found a model in the stories he could fully emulate, but if he chose the right elements from each of the heroes he admired, he could make his own story. If he followed the right examples, made the right choices, his would be a tale that future queenlings and kinglings were told before their royal bedtime.

And all at once, his anger at Ama's exactitude drained away. When he thought of a baby in his arms, one with Ama's flint-hard gaze and her ferocious spirit, he could imagine nothing better in the world.

He would be king. He would marry Ama if she wanted marriage, but he would love her and rule with her at his side no matter what, if she would have him. They would bear the next generation of girls to rule Paxim, future queens and queens' mothers, and that was how order would be rightfully restored.

The path widened and Ama slowed her mount until they rode side by side.

"Why are you smiling?" she asked, but he hadn't even realized he was.

"I thought of a story I want to tell you," he said.

"What kind of story?"

"A love story," he said, and didn't think about how it sounded until the words were out of his mouth.

But she didn't look unsettled or wary, only welcoming. "We've got time."

"Lansper was a talented weaver," began Paulus, confident in the words he'd known even before he could read them for himself, memorized through repetition at story time. "He made fine robes and sashes for the royalty of Queen Clio's court, including the queen's youngest daughter, Rudaba, with whom he shared a secret love."

"Secret love!" interjected Ama. "Even better."

He widened his smile and went on. "When Rudaba was kidnapped by a rogue Arcan sorcerer, Lansper searched the countryside high and low. He saw nothing and nothing and nothing, until, waist-high on a nearby bush, he spotted a flutter of bright red."

"A flutter?"

"Be patient," he told her. "When he got closer, he realized that it was a tuft of thread, bright as a berry. He followed the path beyond. Before long, he caught sight of another spot of color. As he found another and another, he realized his love was leaving him a trail. She was unraveling the crimson cloak he'd woven for her, thread by thread."

"Clever queenling," Ama said.

"They were both clever. He tracked their progress all day and all night, until they came to rest. When the thieving sorcerer tucked Rudaba into the branches of a high tree to sleep, Lansper wove a rope strong enough for her to climb to the ground, and Rudaba escaped. In thanks for returning her daughter, Queen Clio allowed the two to marry, and instead of choosing to live in the palace, they moved to the countryside, where Lansper wove soft blankets in which they rocked their children to sleep."

"Blankets," repeated Ama.

He smiled broadly. "That's my favorite part. I always imagined those children, swaddled up in the richest, softest fabrics, not knowing or caring about palace life, just secure in the knowledge that they were loved."

Ama said, "Ah, we're almost there. Race you!" And she spurred her horse forward, leaving him no choice but to race after her or fall behind. Brushing off his disappointment that she hadn't seemed to enjoy the story after all, he chose to race, and followed her up the rising incline to a beautiful high hill where they could see far into the distance. She reined in her horse at the hilltop, dismounted, and gazed out over the view with a sigh.

He wanted to ask her if she found the sight worth the ride, but it would crush him if she said no, so he saved his words. He dismounted, tied up both their horses, and neared her. Alone at last. His heart beat a little faster for it.

"Your mother would be appalled that we've ridden so far," Ama said as she spread a blanket on the grass in the shade of a leafy, broad-branched chestnut tree.

"I'd rather not think about my mother right now, thank you," he said. When Ama seated herself on the blanket, he settled his body as near hers as he could, nuzzling the side of her neck and brushing his lips up over her ear, to her forehead, her nose, then catching her mouth in a long, slow kiss.

She pushed him away playfully. "Food first," she said.

He made her laugh by eating quickly, ripping off a hunk of bread and stuffing it in his mouth, mumbling, "Let's get this out of the way then" in syllables almost too muffled to make out. But they settled down, eating and drinking, peering out toward Hosios in the distance, complimenting the view, enjoying each other's company.

The moment he sensed she was ready, though, he was quick to propose another type of satisfaction. He looked at the tree that shaded them. It gave him an idea.

"Stand up," he said huskily.

Her eyebrows went up at the note of command in his voice—she didn't generally respond to commands—but with an indulgent smile, she stood and looked down at him.

Paulus rose. He set his fingers against her waist and walked her backward until the tree stopped them, her back against its trunk. He felt her body tense under his fingers. He knew every inch of her so well by now. Her thoughts weren't hard to read.

"Relax," said Paulus. "You're doing everything you're supposed to do. You're right here with me. That's the oath the queen swore you to, right?"

"Right," sighed Ama. "You aren't leaving my sight."

"But," he said, running his hands along the sides of her body, pressing her gently against the trunk of the tree. "What if I asked you to close your eyes?"

"Meaning?"

"Would I be leaving your sight then?" His smile was mischievous.

"I believe we can obey the spirit of the law and not the letter," she said, answering his smile with her own, twining her fingers through his hair.

Paulus lowered his body, keeping his hands on the sides of her waist, his knees hitting the ground near her planted feet.

Ama looked down at him with that searching gaze. "Then again, danger can come from anywhere. Perhaps I should keep my eyes open."

Paulus kept his eyes on hers as he hooked his fingers into the waistband of her leggings and began to tug them down, exposing her hipbones first, then her whole lower half down to her knees. Her tawny thighs looked pale against the deep brown bark of the tree. If he hadn't been hard already, the mere smell of her would have done it, that faint whiff of musk in the open air.

Then he said, "Perhaps you should."

He looked up at her as he finished stripping off the leggings, helping her balance on one foot at a time as she stepped out of the bunched fabric. He looked up at her as he gently nudged her feet apart, making sure she was grounded on the bare earth with her bare feet, stable. He looked up at her until the last possible moment, brown eyes fixed on brown eyes, even as he used his thumbs to spread aside her most intimate folds, right up until he pressed his tongue to the hard knot between her legs in a firm, slow lick. She groaned, the sound working its way up from deep in her throat, and her eyes rolled up into her head, breaking the gaze.

He chuckled, knowing the vibration of his bones would pass into hers, another stimulus, another sensation.

"Steady yourself," he whispered, and saw her splayed fingers grip the bark on either side of her hips as she pushed her back harder against the tree. Then he closed his eyes and went to work.

Paulus kept up the pressure between her legs with his lips and tongue, slipping one finger and then two inside her to increase her pleasure. He heard her moan from high above. He felt one of her hands let go of the tree to sink fingers into his hair, to press him even harder against her, and he rewarded her eagerness with even longer, firmer licks, feeling her lover's knot swollen and slippery against his tongue.

But after another minute or two he felt something change. The hand on the back of his head released his hair, paused stiffly, slid around to the front. Her fingers cupped his chin. He paused at the touch. When he did, she guided his head back, away from her, and sank down to the grass beside him.

"Did you hear that?" she said quietly.

"Hear what? No."

"I can't focus," she said. "I thought I heard something."

He gestured. "Well, there is a whole wide world out there, with nothing between it and us."

She smiled, a bit sheepishly. "Too hard for me to turn off my vigilance, I'm sorry. If I can't focus, I can't, well, you know."

"I know," he said, thinking about sliding his hand between her legs again to test the theory, but if she said she wasn't interested, it was time to stop.

She gave him a lingering kiss, wiped his chin with her thumb. "When we get back to the palace, can we . . . ?"

"Pick up where we left off? Yes."

"Excellent," she said, kissing him again, and then breaking away to reach for her discarded leggings.

As soon as she had them on, she stretched her arms up, turning to look out over the horizon. The next thing he knew they were both on the ground again.

The last of his excitement quickly fading, he said, "What in Panic's name?"

"Shhhh," she hushed him with a finger to his lips. Then she used the same finger to point down the hill. "There."

Small figures growing larger, approaching the town at a rapid clip.

"Just a party heading to the trading post?"

"Raiders," she said. "Not traders. Bandits, I think. Armed."

He tried to poke his head up for a better view, but she pulled him back down, the front of his tunic bunched in her fist.

"They can't see us," she said quietly, "but we'll need to ride the long way around to avoid them. And get back to the palace as fast as we can."

Ama crawled on her hands and knees away from the lip of the hill, reaching back to grab the blanket they'd knelt on, and rose to her feet only once the angle of the hill blocked anyone from seeing them. She tossed the jars and cloth wrappings left over from their picnic into a knapsack held low to the ground, her brow drawn in worry.

As they mounted their horses, Paulus decided he could risk speaking, and he asked her, "Why do we have to go back to the palace? We can fight."

"Too late," she snapped. "They'll take what they want and be gone. We can't get involved." She clucked her tongue softly and steered her horse off the path, not the way they'd come, which would have exposed their position.

He kicked Philomel's sides and pulled up next to Ama. "But we could help. Warn them. Save them."

"Don't be a fool. You're too precious to risk. We're heading home."

Something in her tone irritated him. Who was she to say what they would or wouldn't do? He was the future king, by the All-Mother's fist. He could make choices too.

So Paulus said, "No, we're not," and turned his horse, finding the path again and taking it at a run, riding straight down to where the bandits, or whatever they were, were about to attack Hosios.

He was riding too hard to hear whether Ama cursed as she turned, but in moments he heard her mount's hoofbeats behind his. He knew she wouldn't shout; shouting would alert the enemy to her presence. She would have no choice but to follow him into battle.

Then they heard the first scream, a battle cry of "*Kii-yah!*" from one of the attackers, and an answering scream from the first Paximite at the trading post to see them coming, wordless, high and long.

"Scorpicae," breathed Ama, disbelieving, and when he looked at her he saw the truth in her eyes. This was not an overconfident group of bandits raiding a post to carry off some odds and ends. This was something else entirely.

By the time they arrived, the population at the trading post was already fighting for their lives. The raiders—or a group of them, at least—fought from horseback, blowing darts and swinging daggers into the crowd. He and Ama had the advantage of surprise if they didn't squander it; but they had no bows and arrows, only her sword and his dagger, so any fighting would be hand-to-hand.

He tried to remember everything Ama had taught him about battle in the space of a blink. *Sometimes your own plan goes out the window,* she'd said. *Then you figure out what their plan is, and wreck it.*

A roar of fire started up. The grain, it had to be. So they were destroying, not just raiding, and that changed the calculus. The warriors wanted to do as much damage as possible, and he would have to find a way to stop them. Fire would be disastrous, so he had to deal with that first. But as he rode toward the smoke, he saw the residents had already set up a brigade of water pots; then he saw a ragged woman, probably the saboteur, sprinting out of the haze. He readied himself to intercept her. Before he could, a woman dressed like a merchant emerged from the smoke and smashed a clay vessel on the saboteur's head. As the dazed warrior staggered, the merchant followed up with a knife to the gut. The merchant's eyes caught Paulus's and he nodded in acknowledgment, wanting to do more, but she didn't seem to expect anything beyond that. Then he heard a sharp whistle.

Some kind of order from the Scorpican commander, it must have been, because he saw more of the raiders jumping from their ponies, leaving one behind to guide the ponies away from the fray. From the ponies' wild eyes and stomping hooves, he wondered if they feared fire; if so, his horse probably would too, and it would be smart to steer Philomel away.

Ama was still behind him, and as he dismounted, Ama rode her own mount in front of him to cut him off. Without time to think, he took a chance and dove under her horse, then sprinted toward the battle. He heard her anguished, angry cry behind him but didn't slow. She didn't understand how important it was for him to prove himself. She would appreciate it only after they secured the victory.

He heard Ama drop from her horse and run after him, but he was already behind a Scorpican who was kicking over a series of olive oil jars one by one. Without hesitation he drew his dagger and stabbed the Scorpican in the side, shocked at how easily the sharp blade slipped into her flesh.

But the Scorpican, even as she bellowed her pain, turned and slashed at him with the dagger in her own hand. He jumped back instinctively. She missed by no more than a finger's breadth. Then Ama was there, with a low kick that took the warrior's feet out from under her and a quick flash of her own blade that opened the warrior's throat.

Ama turned to him, her face furious, but did not have time to speak even a word before more warriors were upon them.

The battle raged. Ama fought her way to Paulus's side, but the tide of battle parted them again when a Scorpican, clearly identifying Ama as the bigger threat, leapt in between the two.

It was impossible to tell the age of this one, her head wrapped in a reddish-brown scarf pulled forward above her forehead so it hung down like a cowl. The fabric shaded her eyes, so he could not see whether they burned like the eyes of the creatures in *The Tale of Alev and Vela*.

Paulus could only turn inward. There he found the heart of a hero. And he charged, letting loose a battle cry.

It felt good, for a moment. Then another enemy was on him and she fought every bit as fiercely as Ama did in their sparring, which was not good, since he knew that Ama could beat him.

But the villagers were in the fight now, everyone brawling with spirit and fire. A piece of rotten fruit caught the Scorpican in the shoulder, and she turned with anger in her eyes toward a boy at the edge of the crowd. The child had clearly thrown the fruit, and there was a terrified delight on his face as he realized the warrior, large and dangerous, now had him in her sights.

Paulus lunged.

The Scorpican grunted as the dagger caught her in the side; then she tipped over, fell to earth. He wasn't sure if the wound had been fatal, but he didn't have time to think about it; the next enemy was upon him, having abandoned a two-on-one fight against Ama, and then his short blade was clanging against her larger one, as he backed and backed and backed away.

This enemy backed him toward an alleyway, and suddenly, he could see it all more clearly. To her, he was retreating into a confined space, making a mistake. But there was no mistake here. This was where the fire had raged earlier, mostly smothered but still smoking, and this was where the warrior had kicked over the jars of olive oil, and it was only a matter of time until the smoking embers and the flammable oil met. Then everything would change. The fires would leap. The warrior would fall. And Paulus would feel exactly like that hero from the storybook he'd grown up on, the girl who razed the field of poisoned grain, and like her, he would rise from the ashes not only alive but victorious. The blaze of glory was his. Victory was his. No one could deny him. And above all, he couldn't wait to share his joy with Ama.

He didn't realize the fight was over until silence had settled around him, odd and alien. He thought there was something wrong. But instead, finally, things were right.

Ama was glaring at him with the fire of a thousand suns.

"Did they run?" he asked, feeling both stupid and brilliant at once, somehow.

"Yes," she said. "They ran."

For a moment he thought she looked more like a Scorpican than the actual Scorpicae had, a born warrior with fighting in her blood. He blinked and she was his own Ama again, fierce but familiar. There was no sight he would rather see in this world or any other.

"I did it," he said in a voice of pride and wonder.

Her response had none of his joy. "You fool."

"But we won!"

She only repeated, "You fool, you thrice-damned fool," and turned away too quickly for him to say anything more.

With the residents of the trading post thronging around, mourning their losses but celebrating how they'd run off the raiders, Ama turned her attention away from Paulus toward the throng. She told them she was an army captain traveling to a new assignment, a plausible enough lie; no one asked who Paulus was, and she volunteered nothing, didn't even look in his direction. He knew she was only doing what was wise. It was still infuriating.

In closing, Ama loudly congratulated the merchant who had killed a warrior single-handedly, and told her to keep the interlopers' mounts as redress for the wrongs they'd caused. He noted that she did not describe the attackers as Scorpicae, only raiders, and told them this particular band of raiders were not known to strike in the same place twice; Paulus had no idea whether this was true.

When she appeared, leading both their horses, and held out his mount's reins for him to grab, he tried again, "Ama," but she shook her head.

The whole ride home, what felt like endless hours in the saddle, he simply followed Ama. Her pace was brisk but he didn't complain. The trip was silent, and the sooner it ended the better. Even her retreating back seemed to radiate anger somehow.

When they rode into the capital, she still hadn't spoken. She slowed her horse enough for him to pull up alongside her, but she didn't look in his direction. When she turned south instead of north, he finally had a reason to speak.

"Aren't we headed to the palace?"

"No," she said tersely, and did not explain.

He thought he knew what she had in mind, and when she drew up in front of a stately, narrow house not far from the Senate, his suspicions were confirmed. They both dismounted, both tied their horses. She walked more slowly now, drew herself up, and he could tell that she was thinking about how they'd look to an audience. That was probably the only reason she let him walk alongside her instead of forcing him to trail behind.

Faruzeh of Ursu reclined on her patio, feet up, her fingers plucking figs from a bowl next to her. Instead of the forbidding, high-collared robe of her station, the only garment Paulus had ever seen her in, she wore a knee-length tunic, soft and worn. Her legs were bare. She looked like any Paximite woman of leisure. She lifted her eyes toward her visitors, but looked at Ama with only mild curiosity. It was when she recognized Paulus that she sat upright, hand going to her lap, figs forgotten.

"Kingling!" she exclaimed, her eyes taking in the blood on his scabbard, the dust of the road coating his garments. "Were you attacked?"

"In a manner of speaking," he said. "A raiding party of Scorpicae attacked the trading post at Hosios. We were there."

"We?"

Ama looked to Paulus, uncharacteristically. He realized she was positioning him to be the strong one, the leader. He appreciated it more than he could say.

To Faruzeh, he said, "I was there with my bodyguard. We made the decision to intervene."

Fully upright now, the minister leaned toward Paulus, her elbows on her knees and her fingers tented against each other. She ignored Ama completely, all her attention on Paulus.

"How many, would you say?" she asked.

He answered, "A dozen, perhaps, or a *pentagi*. Fewer than twenty."

"How many mounted?"

"All."

"How many got away?"

"Some," he said, and wished he knew. He could look to Ama for the answer—she probably had it ready on her lips—but couldn't risk looking weak.

"Did the ones who survived take the mounts of the dead with them?"

"No," he admitted. "We made a gift of them to the post."

The war minister made a sound with her tongue then, derisive, and settled her face into a scowl. "You should've brought the mounts back. We need more for our own troops. You can't fight a mounted enemy on foot."

"Of course you can," said Ama, a sharp edge to her tone. "It's just harder to win."

Now that Ama had Faruzeh's attention, the minister glared at her openly, raising her chin. "Has the kingling told you who I am?"

"I know who you are."

"Then you should know my responsibilities. It is on my shoulders, not yours, to win this war against the Scorpicae."

"Is it a war?" Ama asked. "Have they declared?"

"Declaration doesn't make a war. They have attacked. They have killed. You've seen them do it. Do you think they come to feed us sweet berries and oil our hair?"

Ama seemed to consider her response and then decide that no response at all was correct.

The minister went on, "You see the difference. You're responsible for the well-being of one person. I guard an entire nation."

Paulus interjected, "I am not just one person. I am your next king."

The minister fixed him with a glare, almost but not quite as fierce as the one she'd turned on Ama. "That is the plan, yes, Kingling. But plans have a way of changing."

"What do you mean by that?"

"Nothing, not a thing." She spread out her fingers in mock surrender, bobbed her head. "I simply mean that there is much unknown about the future. And now—this information is troubling, because it means the future could be even more bleak than we thought. Scorpicae, in Paxim!"

Ama said, "You'll want to inform the queen, I'm sure."

Then there was a long silence while Ama stared at the minister and the minister stared back. The silence stretched on so long that Paulus was tempted to break it himself. But he knew there was something more at play here, though he didn't quite understand what it was.

At long last, Faruzeh replied, "I will," and rose from her seat. She beckoned to a servant, who brought her high-collared outer robe. Drawing it on and fastening it was the work of only a moment.

Before the minister could move forward, however, Paulus raised his voice. "It is I who will inform the queen."

Neither woman seemed surprised, but neither disagreed with him either. At length Faruzeh said, "That is your right."

With the three of them traveling together, Paulus couldn't say anything private to Ama, and he assumed that was perfectly all right with her. Her anger had clearly not faded. He was beginning to wonder if it ever would.

He warred with himself. On one hand, he had drawn enemy blood, acquitted himself well in his first-ever battle. He and Ama had saved lives, and only because he'd chosen to take action; without his choice, who knows how many more residents of the post would have been lost? He was a hero. He wanted more of it. Was this how it would feel to be king? Why had he ever doubted he wanted that?

But would any of it be worth having without Ama? He thought about how she had yielded to him under that tree. Mere hours ago, but it felt like a lifetime. The taste of her, so sweet. The knowledge that he had pleased her, stoked her hunger for his touch. He couldn't imagine that he'd had those things for the last time in his life. He'd been right to join in battle—he was certain—but if he'd known she would turn away from him, possibly for good, he was not at all sure he would have done it.

Still, it was done, and as he preceded the two women into the palace, he felt strong. He wavered only when he saw how weak his mother still looked despite her recent recovery, how she'd faded. A stab of guilt hit him. How dare he risk himself when his death would destroy her? But he was here. He'd returned not just alive, but victorious. She would see, and she would be proud.

He was ready to tell her the story.

✦

Heliane held her face as still as she could, listened as calmly as she could, but when she heard how close her son had come to dying, it took all she had not to scream.

She covered it seamlessly. She'd had so many years of experience never showing how she felt, never saying what she meant. She was a diplomat. Diplomacy was more than getting people to do what you wanted, and it was more than manipulating their feelings; it was managing their very perception of the world.

So she managed Paulus's perception of how upset she was by quashing any outward sign of it, and she played everyone in the room like a different musical instrument to produce the tone and song she wanted. The trio of interlopers had interrupted a meeting with the agriculture, commerce, and finance ministers, and she'd let them do it, reading in an instant that whatever had brought this unlikely threesome together couldn't wait. No one would see anything but calm on her face. Not until she decided to let her true feelings show.

"And you," she asked Faruzeh, though she knew the answer, "were you there?"

"No, my queen." The war minister's eyes were downcast. "The kingling reported to me upon his return. He felt, I assume, that I should know."

"It was a good decision," said Heliane, nodding toward her son.

Ama stood just behind him, and though Heliane didn't look directly at her, the young woman figured prominently in her thoughts. If she had to guess, it was likely Ama and not Paulus who had made the political decision to follow protocol and report first to the war minister. Ama could be quite blunt, and she had little patience for formality, but she was savvy enough to know everyone's place, including her own. Paulus was emotional and headstrong. On that front, the day's events simply proved what Heliane already knew.

"We can marshal forces immediately," said Faruzeh, her voice sharper now. "Chase them down."

"But if they rode out immediately from Hosios, they'll be hours ahead of us already. Is that not what you said, Paulus?"

"Yes. They rode due east, but no one can say whether they continued in that direction. And we've already lost the time it took to ride here."

"We could still give chase," insisted Faruzeh.

Heliane raised her hand, waved it dismissively. "Let them take the message back to their people that we are to be feared. If we send anyone in that direction, let it be a scout. A spy. Not a single soldier."

"Queen?" Faruzeh lowered her brow.

Heliane felt suddenly tired, but showing that exhaustion was out of the question. Instead she made her voice louder, firmer, as she responded. "No forces are to be sent from their stations, Faruzeh. Not until we know more. Do I make myself clear?"

The minister's mouth was set in a hard line. Her lips barely parted when she said, "Very."

"Thank you for coming," said the queen, in a way that made it very clear it was time for the minister to leave.

"I await your further word," said Faruzeh, bowing only to the queen before she left. She didn't so much as glance at anyone else in the room, though most of them were just as important as she was in the palace hierarchy, deserving of full respect. Her eyes were on the queen and then the door, and then she was gone.

"Thank you all," the queen said, looking to the other ministers, and one by one, they made for the door. All except Ama, and when Paulus saw that Ama did not move, he too stayed.

When the last minister was gone and only the three of them remained in the room, Heliane let herself sit. The sound that came out of her was halfway between a sigh and a groan.

"Are you all right?" asked Paulus, rushing toward her side, but she held up a hand in his direction.

"We're not here to talk about me."

He nodded. "I'm sorry. I—"

His mother ignored him and pointed at Ama. Ama seemed to have been expecting it; her jaw was set and her eyes did not waver. "You let him fight? Against those numbers? Why did you take such a stupid risk?"

"It was my fault," interrupted Paulus.

Ama cut him such a glare that he fell silent and said no more.

"I take responsibility," Ama said, talking only to Heliane. "It was a risk, but a calculated one. In that setting with those numbers, with the residents fighting alongside us, I thought we could capably take down the enemy. In fact, we did."

"And?" said the queen frostily.

"And?" Ama echoed.

Her voice gaining force, the queen said, "It would be customary at this point to offer your resignation. As recompense for your error."

Partially cowed, Ama only admitted, "It would."

"And if you cannot be noble and offer to remove yourself from my employ—since you have failed in your one assigned task—I'm sure you would understand and accept if I chose to end that employment."

Paulus felt his heart drop and his body edge forward, his mouth opening to declare that he'd made it impossible for Ama to do her job, that it was all his fault, he would do anything as long as Heliane didn't send Ama away, please, please.

But Ama fixed her gaze on him again, and he needed no more than a moment to read what was in her eyes. It wasn't his place to rescue her. She would rescue herself if that was possible, and if it wasn't possible, she would accept the consequences. Unlike Paulus, she had very little. Honor was one of her only possessions. She would not part with it.

"I won't offer to leave," said Ama. "My failure was partial. Your son stands before you, whole and hale. He now has a story to tell about his bravery in battle, something no previous kingling has had to recommend him. If you tell the story right, it will sway more supporters to his side. Handled correctly, this day serves as proof that Paulus is ready to be the nation's first ruling king. He fought well, with the skill and bravery of a far more experienced soldier. I was proud to fight by his side. But if you tell the world he only engaged in battle because his bodyguard erred by letting him fight, it will inspire precisely no one."

The queen gazed at her evenly but gave no indication of whether she liked what she heard. Paulus knew, though. Ama was saying all the right things. Heliane didn't really want to dismiss Ama; Ama was letting her save face. He loved Ama even more in that moment than he'd thought possible.

"More importantly? The Scorpicae are here," continued Ama. "In your territory. The threat to your son has escalated. You need me more than ever."

"I have the right to dismiss you," the queen said flatly.

"Of course you do," said Ama, the challenge gone from her tone. "The choice is entirely yours. If you tell me to go, I will leave this room, leave this whole queendom, and never return."

Paulus couldn't breathe.

Ama continued, "But would sending me away make things better, or worse? I can and will do good here, I swear. I ask your forgiveness and your permission to remain. Do I have them?"

The queen cocked her head, giving a show of deliberation, but Paulus could tell her choice was already made. "Very well. You do."

"Thank you, Queen Heliane," said Ama, bobbing her head in deference and lowering one knee a few inches. On anyone else it would have looked graceless, but for Ama, it was as good as a bow.

After they left, Heliane wasted no time. She had reached out once to an unlikely ally, and though she'd received no response, she hadn't given up hope. Things were more dire here by the day. If anti-Arcan sentiment flared up fiercely enough, she wouldn't be able to halt what the Senate might set in motion. It was time to push for something more drastic. She might not win, but by the All-Mother, she would try.

✦

Ama and Paulus left the room together, as they had to, but neither spoke as they walked. Paulus waited until they were back in his rooms, the door closed behind them, to say the question he'd been dying to ask out loud.

"Did you mean it?" he asked. "What you said to my mother. Are you proud of me?"

She turned away without answering. He told himself he should never have asked the question. Heroes didn't beg their lovers for approval. Heroes knew they'd done the right thing. He needed the courage of his own convictions.

But he ached for her smile.

"Ama," he said. No reply.

Instead, she washed herself with the water and cloth from the basin left for him, wiping away dirt and crusted brick-red blood. Paulus watched and waited in silence. When it was his turn, he washed in the dirty water she'd left him so he wouldn't have to allow anyone else in the room. He would drink his tea of yellow flowers cold tonight for the same reason. His body ached in a way it never had before, one purple bruise welling on the back of his shoulder and another on the side of his knee, but he didn't make a sound. She hadn't, so he wouldn't. She was the warrior he wanted to be. After he'd scrubbed off the worst of the damage, he dressed himself in a long, soft sleeveless tunic for sleeping. He still watched Ama, still felt intensely aware of her every move. But she kept her own body, covered now, far from his, her face turned away.

As Paulus climbed into bed, turning the blankets down on what he'd come to think of as her side, Ama still didn't look at him, not even a glance. Finally he couldn't stay silent anymore. They had fought and won. He was both exhilarated and exhausted, his blood coursing in a way it never had before. Yet under that newness was the same current he'd been feeling for weeks. Everything in his body called to everything in hers.

"Ama. How long will you be angry with me?" he asked. He tried to make his voice gentle, to make it sound like an apology, not an accusation.

Still no answer.

"One night I could take," he said genially. "Well, perhaps not the whole night. Part of a night. An hour or so. Will you be mad at me for an hour?"

She lay her bedroll in front of the door. She focused exclusively on her task, as if he were nowhere nearby, as if he didn't exist at all.

He watched while she unbuckled her sword and set it on the left side of the roll, away from the door, but well within her reach; and while she shucked her leggings and tunic, baring herself completely as if it were nothing, and just as nonchalantly pulled on the hip-length tunic in which she sometimes slept. It was too warm for clothes at night, but he understood her message. She didn't need words to speak volumes.

"Okay, maybe two hours, then," he said, as if they were really conversing. "I'll give you that. I understand your anger. And I'm sorry, all right? I apologize. I shouldn't have ridden into the fray. It was foolish. I know I could have been killed. It would have wrecked my mother. I think it might have hurt you, too. I think you—I think you love me enough that you wouldn't want to see me die."

He couldn't see her face, but he thought he heard a sound from her, an emotion she was smothering, but whether it was derisive laughter or an emotional sob, he couldn't tell. So he forged ahead.

"Please talk to me, Ama," he said. "I'm so sorry."

Quietly, so softly he could barely make out the words, she said, "I can't."

She climbed into her bedroll. He turned toward the wall, attempting to settle himself, but could not even get his eyes to close. Sleep had never felt so far away.

An hour later, in almost complete darkness, he lit the lantern, rose from the bed, and stood next to her bedroll. Because she was turned away, he couldn't see if her eyes were open, but the way her back rose and fell didn't look to him like sleep.

"Ama."

She stilled.

"I can't sleep," he said. "I'm going to the library."

She sighed audibly and threw aside her woolen blanket. Standing, she extended her arm toward the door to indicate that he should proceed. She followed him through the hall, shadows flickering along the walls as they went. He noticed that her footfalls, unlike his, made no sound. Once they arrived, he settled himself on the soft cushions of his favorite seat and lit the lamp to read.

But for the first time, the words on the page in front of him meant nothing. He knew the story almost word for word already, every part of it—the heroism of Alev, the fidelity of Vela—but he couldn't make his eyes focus. All his attention was on Ama, and all she did was stand next to the door, staring up at the square of empty window, far too high for her to see anything but the stars.

"It isn't the same," he blurted, tossing the book down onto the cushions. "Without you. Leaning against me. With me. I need you, Ama."

At last she leveled her gaze at him. She was exhausted, he could see it now. They'd both cheated death, and he'd acted like the only thing that mattered were his feelings. All-Mother's *muoni*, he was a fool.

"I can't," she said, exactly as she had in his bedchamber.

He realized he'd changed only the location of their disagreement. So he pushed, less gently. "Why not? Tell me that, at least."

Her voice was stony. "You disobeyed."

He bristled at that, the words pouring out now. He didn't want to miss his chance to be heard. "Disobeyed? What am I, your child? Your subordinate? How are your words orders, Ama?"

"You are my *charge*," she said, and her tone shifted to something less like anger, more like anguish. "And yes, in a way, subordinate. I trained you. I have more experience than you. In a battle situation, only one of us can be in command."

He wanted to joke, *Why not me?* But he knew why not. He wasn't as good as she was, not yet.

"Ama," he said. "I'm sorry." He dropped the book and held out his hand to her, entirely unsure whether she'd take it, but she stepped forward and touched her fingers to his. She didn't let him draw her down next to him, but she kept her fingertips against his, warmth zinging between them.

"You didn't listen to me," she said, still angry, not really listening. "My entire reason for being here is to keep you safe. And I failed to do that. You wouldn't let me. You rode straight into danger, made it so I couldn't do anything to help you, to save you. Do you have any idea what that feels like?"

"That's the reason you came here," he said, trying to understand. "For the position of bodyguard. To keep me safe."

She nodded.

"But is it the only reason you stay?" He tugged on her fingertips again, and this time she sank onto the cushions beside him, the lamp not far from their clutched hands.

She was quiet, but the silence was different now. Not disapproving. Their shoulders pressed together, the thin fabric of her shift doing nothing to cloak her warmth. He knew why she stayed. They both knew.

He avoided her eyes in the low, flickering light and instead dropped his head, placing his lips against the warm flesh of her neck. Even though she'd washed, he felt like he could taste the afternoon sun on her, the same taste she'd had under that chestnut tree.

She still said nothing to him, not with words. But as he kissed his way up her neck, she turned her head on an exhaled breath and caught his mouth up with her own, a passionate kiss, full of intense hunger.

"I'm sorry," he mumbled into her lips.

"Shhh."

He pulled back just far enough to speak clearly. "I love you."

She didn't repeat the words back to him. She covered his mouth with hers again. But there was something unresolved, a tension, that he could feel in her body even as she embraced him. She seemed to be considering.

Finally, Ama turned her head, placing her cheek to his, not meeting his gaze.

"I can't lose you," she whispered into his shoulder.

He reached up to stroke her hair, to soothe her. He cupped the back of her head with his hand. "You won't," he promised.

"You can't know for sure."

He murmured into the curve of her ear. "I swear to you. By Panic. By the fist of the All-Mother. By my own right hand. By everything."

After that, wordless, they lost themselves to pleasure. It had never been quite like this, desperate and hasty, her body so rough against his it hurt them both, as if showing him how she felt required more force than she'd ever used before. Not force for harm, but force for strength. Clashing against him, wanting to swallow him whole. He was more than happy to be swallowed. When his book slipped off the cushions and thumped to the floor, neither of them even turned to notice.

They didn't stop to fully undress, only moving things aside to make contact between the parts that desired contact most earnestly. She hiked up her shift and straddled him as he yanked the neckline down to fit his fingers around her nipple, but the pleasure as she sheathed him inside her in one swift movement rendered him utterly helpless, and his hands dropped, fumbling. She cradled his face in both hands and kept it firmly fixed to hers, eyes closed, foreheads pressed together, skull bumping skull through the thin skin between.

"Never disobey me again," Ama said, panting as she rode him, her voice desperate.

With an equally mad desperation, Paulus promised in a hoarse whisper, "Never. Never."

ASCENSION

Ursu, Paxim
Autumn of the All-Mother's Year 517
Stellari

The *cosmete* had to replait Stellari's crown of braids three times. The servant kept rushing, and a skein of dark hair would slip from her grip.

"Sorry, *thena*," she said, voice trembling.

"Start again," answered Stellari, firm but not angry. She wanted to lash out, let the woman know how unacceptable this all was, but she knew from experience that would just slow her down further. On a day as important as today, Stellari had set aside time for contingencies, but even expert planning had its limits.

She was already impeccably garbed, but the crown could not be neglected. Her appearance in the Senate today would be the most important of her life. A sloppy crown of braids would be perceived by the other senators as a lack of care, not only inaccurate but unacceptable.

She reviewed and tested the plan as the servant pinned the finished braids on the sides of her head into spirals, then finally started on the forked central braid that would complete the intricate pattern. Where could Stellari make up time? What else might go wrong along the way?

Her mind continued to soar and twirl under the crown of braids once the *cosmete* finally finished it to her satisfaction.

Then Stellari was off, forcing herself to walk at a stately pace even though her heart pounded in her chest. She'd need to focus on one step at a time. Get to Faruzeh's, where the wagon would be waiting. Give the enforcers their instructions. Do what needed to be done.

As planned, when Stellari approached the wagon parked behind Faruzeh's garden, the war minister herself didn't appear. Her instructions had already been given. Stellari stepped up to the back of the closed wagon, rapped her knuckles in the signal pattern—three quick knocks, two slow—and the doors swung open to admit her. She rode in silence with four enforcers, two women and two men, to their destination.

The day servant who opened the door at Decima's house was a young man in flax, his dark hair smoothed into a neat queue at the back of his neck and bound with a row of small ties instead of braided. His eyes darted from face to face. Still, he kept his calm. "Please wait here while I inform the householder that she has visitors. Who shall I say is calling?"

"We don't wait," said the tallest enforcer, and pushed her way in. The other three followed. Stellari brought up the back. They'd discussed how this would go. She was never to be in the lead.

The young man staggered back, too surprised to react in time, and Stellari watched his eyes. He looked to the right, so she cleared her throat and signaled to the tallest enforcer, Yosh. Yosh went through the archway to the right and the rest followed.

Decima sat at table, the remains of a breakfast of fresh apple and sweet cheese—a clean-sliced core, a wedge of white rind—on the plate before her. The consul was dressed to appear in the Senate, just as

Stellari was, though her braids had not yet been pinned up in a crown. Instead they lay heavy on her shoulders, looking almost like a cascade of snakes. Decima sat with one hand curled in her lap, the other raising a clay cup to her lips. She looked tired, thought Stellari.

As she'd imagined how this stage of her plan would unfold, Stellari had expected outrage, fury, objections. But when four grim-faced enforcers stormed into Decima's dining room, followed by the magistrate, the consul didn't even rise. From her seat she looked up at the enforcers, who even in those first moments were moving to flank her. Gently, she set down her cup. Then she asked, "What are the charges?"

The chief enforcer, too, was taken by surprise. Stellari could see Yosh mentally running through the speech she'd prepared, skipping ahead to where Decima had decided to begin. "It's treason, *thena*."

"She's not a *thena* anymore," snapped Stellari. "She no longer deserves our respect."

Decima's gaze slid sideways, briefly appraising Stellari, then focused on the chief enforcer again. "Am I able to defend myself against this charge? Or would that be fruitless?"

"At some later time, there may be a trial," Yosh told her, voice stiff and formal. "Now we take you into custody for your own protection."

"Protection," scoffed Decima, and Stellari saw the first flash of fire in her eyes. But she still remained in her seat, one hand near the cup, as if she would resume her breakfast as soon as she'd finished this conversation.

"Once the news spreads that you've been poisoning the queen," said Yosh, "do you think you're safe here?"

"I imagine," Decima said dryly, "I won't be safe anywhere."

"Queen killers shouldn't be safe," hissed one of the other enforcers, the thick-necked man, his fingers bunched into a fist at his waist. "Even if they don't succeed. They should be punished."

Decima said, "Is there any evidence of this treason? This supposed poisoning?"

Yosh said, "This is not a conversation. This is an arrest. Ready yourself to come, or be taken."

Decima took a breath and let it out. Then she lifted the hand from her lap, and Stellari and the enforcers all saw what that hand held: the sharp knife Decima must have been using to cut the apple she'd just eaten. The blade was thumb-length, polished to a gleam. At the sight of it, the enforcers drew their own blades. Stellari backed away, toward the far end of the table, so she wouldn't be in their way.

"*Thena*," said Yosh to Decima, her tone a warning. Stellari resisted the urge to correct her again.

Now Decima's eyes went to Stellari's. "Your doing?"

Stellari said, "No. Yours."

Decima's gaze hardened even further. She lay the knife on the table with her fingers atop the olive-wood handle. The knife was slender, but it looked effective. To Stellari, she said, "You'll consign me to my fate and take the news to the Senate yourself, I imagine."

"Yes."

"With some evidence that what you say is true."

"Enough, yes."

"Very well." Decima slid the knife down the long table toward Stellari. One of the enforcers muttered something too soft to hear, but no one sheathed their weapons. The knife made a skittering sound as it slid across the wood and slowed, point still turning, in front of Stellari.

"If you're going to do it," Decima said, "have the courage to do it yourself."

Stellari thought about all the possible responses she could give. In the end, simplest was best.

"Very well," she answered, and picked up the knife.

◆

When Stellari entered the Senate, she noted the empty places, the gaps in the Senate's smile. No one in the room would be surprised at a few absences on what they thought would be a typical day of business. The fact that Stellari had arranged for each of these missing senators to be late or absent—a flagon of fortified wine sent anonymously to Isolde, a wheel on Malim's carriage loosened in the night—would occur to no one. But the vote would come out the way Stellari wanted it to. She had made sure the margin would be wide enough even if some of the senators she'd delayed somehow managed, against the odds, to make it in time. She had never forgotten, would never forget, what had happened when only one vote made the difference.

Her crown of braids and blue robe were unsullied from the morning's business, but she'd acquired one new thing, which she bore in the crook of her arm like an infant. A cloth sack, nondescript, but heavy. Heavier than Stellari would have guessed, before.

When Stellari strode to the front of the room, a few senators began to notice. When she reached into the rough-woven bag she carried and pulled out an object too small to make out, voices hushed. By the time she lay the object at the consul's stand and turned around to face the other senators, the room was silent.

"Caller," Stellari said. "Begin our day."

The caller shook her head, pointing to the empty consul's stand. "She is not here."

"She will not be," Stellari answered. "And I will explain. But we must start the day."

The crier shook her head again, as if to clear it. Then she swallowed hard and called out, "In the name of the All-Mother, the queen, and the peace of Paxim! Let the senators gather for the commencement of this session."

It was time for the ceremonial motion, a slap against the thigh, and Stellari slapped hers hard enough for the sound to echo. A sprinkle of other senators complied, but most didn't. They had noticed who was missing. Only those closest to the front, with good eyesight, could see what Stellari had set at Decima's empty place: the consul's battered silver ring, symbol of her office, with its dull sapphire eye.

Stellari chose not to wait. She faced the ranks of senators and called out, "I invoke the rule of Ostilia! Let the doors be shut."

Murmurs rippled. Ostilia was invoked only on matters of national security, when secrecy was required. As soon as the invocation was done, the doors to the outside were closed, and the senators searched each other's faces for reassurance. Stellari knew they wouldn't find it from each other; she needed to make sure they saw it in her.

"Fellow senators," she began, mixing a note of regret with her confidence so they would receive her words correctly, "this summer, we almost lost our queen. Those of you who were here saw it: Queen Heliane weakened, day by day. It was not simply the weakness that takes the aged and fading. The queen was poisoned."

Stellari paused briefly to let the murmurs begin. Then she continued. "It was only by the grace of the All-Mother that our blessed monarch's death was avoided. I was lucky enough to stumble upon the evidence of this plot. And it pains me to tell you that once I discovered the plot, I quickly discovered the culprit."

Stellari only needed to flick her gaze back toward the empty consul's seat. They all understood.

The resultant shouting was pleasant to her ears, of course, but she needed it to die down quickly so she could continue. She gestured for quiet, then closed her eyes for a moment as if in pain.

"How did this happen? I hear you asking," she said, though she'd planned her line long before any of them had spoken. "It seems Decima made a regular gift of a rare delicacy, candied pears with snowdrop honey, to our beloved queen. Every bite the queen enjoyed fed her poison. A few more doses, I'm told, would have killed her."

The best lies were almost true. Decima had, just as Stellari said, gifted the queen candied pears. They hadn't been poisoned, but the story made sense. Everyone would sing this tune. And the poison's true source, the salve applied by Inbar directly to Heliane's skin each time the *cosmete* styled the queen's hair, would never be suspected.

Senators continued to cry out. "Where is she? Let her stand trial for her crime!"

To silence them, Stellari reached for the nondescript bag under her arm, raised it high, and let its contents fall.

Dark braids tumbled onto the floor. They seemed to writhe and twine like snakes, though they were only dead things. Hair that would never grow again, severed from the scalp that grew it. Gasps of shock as the braids fell gave way, once they lay still, to silence.

This was going exactly as Stellari hoped, but she couldn't get complacent. It wasn't over yet.

"For her own protection," said Stellari, "the poisoner is being held. The war minister Faruzeh guarantees her safety until the time is right for a trial. In the meantime, we have an urgent matter to address."

No more pauses from here on out. She had the floor, and she had to hold it as if it were her very life.

"We have no consul. But we are in a crucial time. Scorpican warriors have already been seen in Paxim. In a national emergency, the magistrate is to serve in the consul's stead. This is the law. But I will not presume to step into the consul's role without your approval. The decision is yours, fellow senators. I put myself in your capable hands." There. She had done all she could. Now it was someone else's turn to speak.

And just as she hoped, the next voice that rang out in the Senate chamber belonged to the caller. "The magistrate, acting in the stead of the consul, has called the vote! Aye for Stellari to act as consul until the next election, nay to deny her the role. Let the counting of votes begin."

Stellari considered her performance over the next quarter hour some of the finest acting she'd ever done. She looked regretful, and worried, and apprehensive; she hid her delight, her anticipation, her joy.

The count was a formality. There had been times she was in the dark, times she was uncertain, times she'd been taken by surprise. This was none of those. Stellari knew with utter certainty how every woman in this body would vote. She could have listed off each one with her eyes shut. So when the final vote was called—they'd continued to count even after her victory was assured, to ensure that all votes were recorded—it was almost anticlimactic. All that had happened was exactly what she had known would happen.

Stellari was consul of Paxim. And she would have every power the role put into her hands, every power the Senate knew about and more.

To mark the occasion, Stellari would have liked an ovation, raucous shouts of joy. But a light smattering of applause and the complete absence of objections, for now, would certainly do.

Then she nodded to the caller to close the session, which she did, and strode toward the exit without looking back. Behind her, feet shuffled, hands grabbed. She didn't have to watch them to know what they were doing.

The senators near the front of the room, the highest in rank and seniority, were scrambling on the floor like animals, like children. The luckiest tucked their prizes into pockets within their robes, satisfied. The unlucky emerged empty-handed. But in the days to come, those who had claimed Decima's discarded braids would hand them to their *cosmetes*, who would weave them into the senators' own hair, creating higher, broader crowns.

Stellari had no need. She'd already taken everything from Decima she wanted.

◆

Two hours later, no one who saw Stellari in the privacy of her own chambers, her braids unbound, hair streaming down her bare back, would have recognized her as the woman who had addressed the Senate so gravely.

"And after the count," Stellari said, rising to her knees on the bed, "they said, 'We extend our thanks to Consul Stellari for her hard work in the cause of justice,' and I just nodded, with the right abashed look— you would have loved to be there."

She was warm-cheeked with victory and with drink. It would be hard to say which had made her more giddy. The goblet in her right hand danced merrily, and a little bit wildly, through the air.

Her plans had been thorough, and had even included sending Aster to stay overnight with another senator's son as company, killing two birds with one stone and leaving Rahul at loose ends. He'd been annoyed at first, of course. But once she'd explained that she couldn't retrieve the boy early without losing face, and she'd carefully chosen a household she knew Rahul himself trusted, he'd let himself be soothed. A cup of wine and careful, coy attention did a great deal to relax him.

And now, all night, he was all hers. She would savor her victory and she would savor him, and for a few hours their pleasure would be all that mattered in the world. No aftereffects of the Drought, no child down the hall, no elected men, no drum of pending war. Just wine and pleasure and triumph, at last.

And perhaps, finally, the watered seed of a daughter. They had coupled now and again since the end of the Drought, despite the tension between them, and she'd foregone precautions, but no seed had taken root. Pleasure was, of course, its own reward. But a daughter whose seed was planted tonight would surely be blessed with the power of her mother's victory. She'd be born with all the luck Stellari had been forced to make herself.

Stellari wrapped both hands around the wobbling goblet so she wouldn't spill, and took a long, long drink of wine.

Rahul said, "I didn't need to be there. Here is where I want to be," and reached for the curve of her naked hip.

Teasing, she twisted away from him, shaking her unbound hair, sending it spilling over one shoulder in loose, wild waves. With one hand, she raised the goblet to gesture again. "You can come to me whenever you want. We can be like this. Any day, any night."

"Stellari," he said, his eyes dark with longing and something else she couldn't identify. "We've both made bargains. We've both sold some of our present to buy our future."

She felt her fingers tightening on the goblet. "That present can include pleasure, can't it? Not just swift lust against the kitchen wall with your hand covering my mouth or mine covering yours."

He lifted the hand she spoke of, kissing her fingers, then nipping a fingertip with his teeth. "If I remember correctly, that lust against the kitchen wall left you mewling like a kitten, too weak to stand. Or was I mistaken?"

She shook her head. "Not mistaken. I just—the child is old enough now, he doesn't need you—"

He cut her off. "Aster does need me. More than you know."

"Why? What don't I know?"

Rahul ran his hand over his hair, exposing the white scar briefly, then said, "You've never wanted to know, have you?"

Stellari looked at him and readied herself to lie. But she could feel her triumph, her fierce joy, leaking away. She had to hold on.

"I only mean," she said, shifting toward him on her knees until her hips were tantalizingly close to his, "that tonight, we have hours. And a bed. And each other. And you don't need to cover my mouth with your hand because no one else is here to hear me scream your name."

His face softened a degree or two, and he raised his fingers to touch her lips. She thought he would kiss her, but instead, he leaned back on his heels and sighed.

She would not ask him why. She didn't want to know.

Into the silence, he said, "I'm sorry. I want this. I want you. But I also have to tell you, so let me tell you, and then we can put it out of our minds."

No escaping it, then. "Tell me."

He held up the *psama* he wore, pinching it between his fingers. "The source who brought me sand is . . . no longer able to do so. I need to journey to Arca myself. It's the only way."

What he said made no sense. The sand would only drain away if he were using it for magic, casting some enchantment. "Why would you need more?"

Looking at the *psama* and not her face, he said, "I just need to make the journey. Aster will come with me."

"You want to take my child to *Arca*? What if someone finds out? An enemy, either here or there? I'm the consul now!"

He wrapped his hands around her shoulders, stroking her upper arms. "I know you need to think of all the scenarios. All the worst things that could happen. But I need to do this. For our future."

"Ours? Or yours?" As soon as it was out of her mouth, she knew it was a mistake. They both had things they wanted, craved like air. She'd always maintained that they could both have them. To force a choice, that was madness.

But Rahul kept stroking her, soothing her, running one palm over her hip and cupping it lightly in the way he knew she liked. "Ours. Your power and mine. Look at today. How quickly you're rising. Consul Stellari."

He was right, she thought, and it was best to take the offering of peace. They had already wasted too much time.

"Consul," she echoed, with a sly smile.

Rahul shifted closer to her, pulling her by the hip, and she felt his hardness against her, tantalizing. He dropped his mouth to her neck and whispered softly just below her ear, "I've never pleasured a consul."

Stellari threw her head back and laughed. "I should hope not! Decima would have been rather a comedown."

"There's only you," he said, his voice still soft, his breath tickling the sensitive skin of her ear, her neck. "Only ever you."

She placed her fingers in a star shape on his chest and pushed him gently. He leaned back, a question in his eyes.

"Down," she said.

He raised a thick eyebrow. "You'll have to be more specific."

"Lay back," she whispered, pushing gently again, and he smiled as he obeyed. He stretched out his body across the sheets, cushioning his head on one bent arm, looking up at her. She loved to see him this way. Willing. Waiting.

She rearranged herself to straddle his upper thighs, not letting the center of her touch the center of him, not yet. They had time.

"To our future," she said, toasting him with the goblet and enjoying the bittersweet taste of the red wine on her lips, teeth, tongue.

"Shame I don't have a glass to raise," he murmured.

She leaned down over him and put her wet mouth to his, sighing as his lips opened under hers. She licked at the inside of his mouth with her wine-stained tongue, thorough and diligent, until she was sure he could taste what she tasted.

He slid a hand up her belly over her ribs until he reached her breast, exploring lazily, stroking the cool underside with the back of his hand, then crooking a finger to brush the peaked nipple. "You're right," he said.

"In so many ways."

"I mean that this—" He gestured with his free hand at the bed beneath them. "This is good. When it's just us. Worth waiting for."

"The best things are," she said, and shifted forward, just until she knew he could feel the wooly curls between her legs brushing against the base of his shaft. "So . . . don't go yet."

He groaned and slid the hand that had been toying with her breast up to cup the side of her head, fingers sliding into her unbound hair. His gaze caught hers, fierce and hungry.

"Stellari," he said seriously. "Good things will happen. We'll make them happen. Everything we deserve."

She pressed forward on him, then drew back, watching his reactions, savoring. Rahul's eyes were so dark, so liquid. Had she ever felt so seen by any other eyes? He was trying so hard to give her what she wanted. She should do the same for him. He stared up at her and she found herself telling him what she knew he most wanted to hear.

"One day, you'll walk into that monstrosity they call Daybreak Palace," she said in a husky, low voice, "as if you own it. Because you will. In through the front door, straight to the throne. You'll unlock the secret. Crack old wards like eggshells. Men will take up their rightful place as full magicians again. And yours will be the most powerful magic of all."

The longing on his face was almost painful to watch. No one even knew if Arcan men's "full" magic could be restored, because no one knew whether they'd had more than illusion magic in the first place. The old stories said they once had—their gifts had been the same as women's, until they were misused—but those were just stories. People believed what they wanted to believe. Stellari could no more dissuade him from his goal than she could clear the walls of the Bastion in a single leap.

But that face. That desperate, yearning face. Perhaps he wanted the restoration of men's magic more than he wanted her, after all. She consoled herself: in the end, if all went according to plan, it wouldn't matter. There would be no difference between who she was and what she offered. He couldn't live without either.

"Now," she said, dropping her voice to a purr, "show me what's worth waiting for."

As he pulled her down to him on the sheets, both laughing with delight as bare skin met bare skin, the goblet tumbled from her hand. It bounced harmlessly and rolled across the floor, spilling nothing.

She had already drunk it dry.

✦ 20 ✦

CONTROL

For two weeks, Ama thought of nothing but what had happened at Hosios. Why were the Scorpicae riding through Paxim in disguise, and what would have happened if Paulus had been one speck less lucky? She shivered to think it. Ama checked with Heliane for intelligence reports, and even though Ama had no official role in the security of the nation, Heliane shared. Every day there was nothing to report, they both breathed a little easier.

But Ama had another plan, one she kept to herself. If she had to choose between Paulus's safety and Paxim's—though she hoped she would never have to—it was no contest. She was hopelessly in love now, she saw it with open eyes; there was no separating her love from her duty. She counted herself lucky that for now, if she squinted, the two were exactly the same.

299

The truth was that she knew Paulus's victory at Hosios had gone entirely to his head. Something had to be done. She'd been careful not to give him an opening to talk about it, but she knew the day would come when he couldn't resist boasting. It was coincidence that that day came on the same day her plan began in earnest.

When Ama suggested that they spend the morning in the library for a change, Paulus shook his head. "No, let's head to the training field," he told her. "I want to focus on my footwork with the longsword, make sure my reach is effective farther out. Send those Scorpicae running scared next time they cross my path."

Telling herself not to respond too sharply, Ama focused on logistics. She said, "But I'll be on the training field all afternoon."

"And where will I be?"

"With me," she responded. "I think you'll enjoy it. What I'll be doing is for your benefit."

"Oh," he said. "Outside? That reminds me of Hosios too." He drew closer to her, skimming his fingertips lightly up the length of her arm, from wrist to shoulder.

Her mind was occupied with the plan, but her body responded anyway, gooseflesh rising under his touch. She tried to push the sensation away so she could make her point. "About Hosios. I know you're proud. And you should be. But that doesn't mean you're ready to charge into full-fledged battle."

The disappointment on his face was clear, and she knew she'd addressed it too directly, without enough nuance. Nuance was not among her gifts.

Paulus bristled but didn't withdraw his hand entirely. His words stayed playful, but his voice grew sharp. "And what puts that decision in your hands, dear one? I'm the hero of Hosios, after all. Not to mention, as you know, the future king."

"If I don't want you to go, you won't go," said Ama, trying her best to keep her tone light and teasing, but she doubted she'd fooled

Paulus. "Before you take the field, I have conditions."

For a moment, the silence between them was charged, and she was afraid he would pull away. She should have been gentler. She knew what he needed and she'd failed to give it to him.

But Paulus was surprisingly gracious, raising both hands in mock surrender. "Very well, my protector. I'll hear you out."

Ama breathed a sigh of relief on the inside, and to show him there were no hard feelings, she raised her eyes with a flirtatious tilt. "Protector's all I am?"

"I never said all," Paulus growled with a smile. "Would you like me to give a demonstration right here and now? What else you are to me?"

He stepped toward her, his gaze honest and lustful, and she danced a step away, but not too far to be easily reached. As he brought his face toward hers, she lifted her chin. His mouth landed on hers hungrily and she kissed back with an equal hunger, giving and taking, feasting on his warmth. Finally she broke the kiss off with a soft groan and laid her fingertips on his chest, where she felt his heartbeat.

"I see," she murmured. "Let's take this up later, then. But not too much later."

"Agreed."

They compromised on two hours in the library before any training, and both were careful to steer their conversation away from anything controversial. When they did take to the practice field, they set to work with heavy longswords, leaping up on the old tree trunk to test their footwork, an exercise that never failed to send one, then the other, tumbling to the ground in a cloud of dust. But they kept their footing more often than they lost it, becoming expert at keeping their balance even in the crunch. Ama noticed that Paulus fell less often than she did, which no doubt pleased him. She didn't remark on it, not wanting to sound condescending, but she was glad he'd performed well. It would put him in a better mood for this afternoon's events.

As they took a break for their midday meal, seated in the shade of the palace wall, Paulus raised his eyes to hers. She knew he was finally going to ask. "So what happens this afternoon?"

She met his eyes over a bite of soft cheese, chewing slowly before responding, "I have a plan."

"That doesn't surprise me," he said. "Go on."

"We can't have what happened at Hosios happening again."

He bristled a bit at that, but she put her hand on his arm. Gently, she said, "Let me finish."

"All right," he answered.

She met his gaze directly. "We were lucky."

"We were good."

"We were lucky and good," she admitted. "Next time, that might not be enough."

He looked away.

"Even heroes need help," she said. "Like Alev and Vela, right? Stronger together than apart."

He smiled at that. "You're already my Vela."

"A different story, then. When Theodora put down the rebellion. She doubled her Queensguard, then doubled it again, then kept doubling it until she had an army large enough to defeat those who would take her throne from her. She wouldn't have succeeded without those women."

He nodded solemnly. Had she found the right way to reach him?

"The next time you clash with the enemy," she told him, "you'll ride with an elite unit of Paximite soldiers. That way, no matter what enemies you face, you can bring home the victory like you did at Hosios."

She could practically see Paulus turning over the revelation in his mind. He didn't seem completely offended. That was, at this point, the most she'd hoped for.

Paulus said in a measured voice, "I see. And will you be part of this elite unit?"

"Of course I will, you fool," she said fondly. "What other fighter would I trust you with besides myself?"

"You don't think you have a rather inflated view of your own skill?" His voice was gentle, teasing, and she realized she'd won him over.

"Modesty is for people who aren't truly the best," she scoffed back.

"I see." He seemed to consider something, and then said, "Do you have a name in mind for this elite force yet?"

"No." Inspiration struck. She could give him a way to feel in control, so easily. "Would you like to name it?"

With no hesitation, he asked, "Can we call it the King's Elite?"

"Absolutely," she replied. "That's a great name. And it's almost time to meet them."

"You've chosen them already?"

"Not exactly. Shall we go?" She rose to her feet and gestured.

Paulus rose, followed her for a few steps, then hastened to walk next to her the rest of the way.

As they headed toward the open field, Ama said, "We have some promising candidates. I asked your mother's advice, which she was more than happy to give. And we had some trusted parties put the word out in the right places."

"They'll all be women, I suppose?"

She flicked his arm playfully. "Now, now. I only want the best people for the job. And we cast a wide net."

"Who did you catch?"

"Trainees from army camps. Members of the long-standing bandit patrols. Guards from the enforcement groups your mother put in place after the Scorpicae withdrew."

"Like the Queensguard?"

"Bah," Ama responded, allowing herself a brief scowl. "She won't let me have any of the Queensguard. Which, if I'm honest, is probably correct. We don't want her dying any more than we want you dying, do we?"

"I should hope you're more attached to me than you are to her."

"Rather attached. Do you believe it?" Her voice was husky.

There wasn't even a whisper of annoyance left in his voice as he told her, "I do."

They had arrived on the flat plain where the competitors waited. There were far more than she'd expected, more than a hundred. This would be fun.

She told Paulus, "Now, as you know, my standards are high. Few of these will be good enough. But if you want to find gold, you mine the whole mountain."

"How will you decide who's good enough?"

"I'll fight them, of course," said Ama, and charged forward. She'd ensured that the competitors were prepared, so as sudden as it looked to Paulus, it was carefully orchestrated. They knew who she was; she didn't need to know who they were, because in how they fought, they would show her.

"Ama!" shouted Paulus, but she was already in the fray, her blood seething with delight.

"All comers!" she shouted. Then she gave the order to fight all-out, the command Floriana had taught her what seemed like a lifetime ago. *"Golajha!"*

The first warrior to approach her was a woman bearing a longsword in both hands, but Ama could tell just by the way she held it that she was no expert. The woman had interlaced her fingers on the hilt; any serious resistance would bend her wrists and fingers back to the point of pain. A borrowed weapon? In any case, an amateur.

So Ama sidestepped toward the second comer, a clean-shaven man a few inches shorter than her, his hair cropped down to a mere fuzz on his scalp. There was something unusual in his stance, and she took only a moment to note it: one shoulder was much higher than the other, his upper back sharply hunched. His trunk, armored in leather, was thick like a barrel of wine. The tunic under his leather armor rose high on his neck and its hem danced low on his thick thighs, but his muscular arms were bare. Ama could tell right away he posed a more serious threat.

He raised his staff to meet Ama's with impressive speed, and the smack of wood on wood was satisfying. He grunted, and she heard the pleasure in the grunt, the clue that he, too, was satisfied to be joined in battle with an equal. She pulled back and spun her staff to poke at him, and he danced back with a smile.

"Just a moment, if you would," she said.

He nodded with a courtly, elegant formality, and stepped back to give her space. She saw his eyes flicking behind her, confirming what she suspected; the woman with the longsword had plucked up her courage to strike.

Instead of spinning to meet her new opponent, Ama braced her front foot where she stood and raised her free leg to deliver a sharp back kick, turning her head just enough to sight and take aim. Her heel landed exactly where she wanted: on the curled knuckles of the woman's interlaced fingers, jarring her into releasing her grip, knocking her weapon free onto the sand.

"Thank you for your time," she said curtly, and returned her full attention to the man with the muscular arms.

He raised his weapon and his eyebrows, almost flirtatiously, and their staffs clashed again, high and low and high. She tested his limits by repeatedly attacking his low-shouldered side, searching for weakness, but she found none. He had clearly trained to counter his deformity, and his weapon flashed just as nimbly from the right as from the left. Experimentally, Ama jabbed toward the leather at the base of his throat. He ducked instead of leaping back, keeping his eyes on hers to watch for an opening. When he rose, his staff nudged hers from much closer in, forcing her to spin back to regain the upper hand.

Then he said, in a warm tenor, "Two nearby on your right, two just behind on your left. I'll wait."

"Thank you." Ama didn't have time to say anything else; she could barely get out both words. There was work to do.

Two women came at her from the right, their attacks coordinated, and she spun to place one on each side. Because she was right-handed, she struck to her left for the element of surprise, coming down hard on the woman's ankle and then bringing the staff parallel to the ground to do the same with the second attacker. She struck hard enough on the first one but not the second. She couldn't lift the staff fast enough to parry the woman's sword coming at her exposed shoulder, so she dropped to the ground instead until it passed her, then popped back up to lash out with a kick directly to the woman's chest. Then she was up and both of her attackers were down, but more attackers were just beyond, and she didn't even have a moment to brace herself.

A spear jabbed at her and she knocked its point into the ground, spitting at her attacker for good measure. The woman came at her with bare hands and Ama kicked her between the legs. When she was down, the fourth one came: a man with a dagger who danced lightly on his toes, trying to egg her into making the first strike. Instead she matched his own dancing steps with hers, moving so the fallen attackers were in between the two of them, and his brow creased with displeasure at being denied his combat.

"Come on, then," Ama growled in a low voice.

The next attacker, too eager, shoved the man with the dagger out of the way, unwittingly helping Ama by knocking him to the ground. But there were still more coming. Ama thought about asking the man with the muscular arms for help; she could feel him watching her.

But it was Paulus who spoke. "Ama, do you need me?"

"I'm all right," she called quickly, worried that he might enter the fray anyway, and put another plan into action.

She backed against the nearest practice dummy to use it as a partial shield, and when the next attacker came at her with a scythe-like blade the length of his forearm, she spun behind the dummy so his blade sank into the dummy's bulk instead of hers.

Sand began to pour out and Ama grabbed a handful in her palm, blowing it into the eyes of anyone who got near enough. The man with the scythe took the brunt of it and howled. She gripped the wrist with the blade and twisted it, forcing him to let go with his blade still buried in the dummy, and she kicked him in the hip for good measure, knocking him to the ground and again blocking some of the attackers on the ground from rising.

It felt unseemly to enjoy fighting so much, but she relished every moment. None of these people would really try to kill her; she was of no use to them dead. The path to employment was not to kill her, only to beat her. She almost laughed at the thought. Of course they could not beat her. She would glory in watching them try.

"Thank you," she told the people on the ground. "You can go."

"And me?" came the voice from beside her.

"Hold!" Ama shouted to the remaining comers, stopping them as effectively as if they were puppets with cut strings. Then she turned to the man who'd fought well and waited patiently. "You. What's your name?"

"Nebez," the man said simply, wasting neither movement nor air.

"Nebez," echoed Ama. "I'm Ama. You fight in the Paximite army?"

He nodded. "Used to. The Swans."

She raised an eyebrow. The all-male unit known as the Swans was legendary, known to contain the best and most effective fighters in Paxim. It consisted almost entirely of pairs of male lovers, twenty-seven couples making up the main body of the force. They were united under the leadership of one single commander, for a total of a lucky fifty-five. The general who had first organized the unit believed that bonded pairs would fight hardest for each other, but the commander needed loyalty to the unit above all.

"And why are you no longer with them?" Ama asked.

Nebez looked away then, the first sign of any weakness she'd seen from him. His fingers twitched on the staff he still held as he seemed to search for words. At last, he said, "Ambition. Not mine."

Then the flirtatious smile was back on his face, the enthusiasm he'd shown during the fight returning. "I'll tell you the story someday, Ama."

Ama had seen and heard all she needed to. "Nebez, we'd be honored to have you join us." And she indicated with the tip of her staff that the man should approach Paulus, which he did, grinning widely.

Paulus held up a finger, *one*, and returned Nebez's grin, offering his hand for the shorter man to shake. Now Ama could truly turn all her attention to the fight. She felt lighter already.

The sand in the dummy had poured itself out. Ama had planned to grab another handful to hold in reserve, but she'd missed her chance. She readied herself for the next wave of attackers, who had been biding their time, eager for their turn to prove their worth.

"*Golajha!*" she shouted again, and they rushed her.

Ama fought hard, sweating and swearing, but it was only the sheer number of fighters that tested her, not their skill. She fought a quarter of an hour without pause, finding only two fighters in that time that she thought might be worthy. She was just beginning to despair when an approaching figure caught her eye.

Ama recognized right away that there was something different about the thin woman with two short swords. Even before the woman leapt, fast as lightning, Ama saw the tension in her limbs and her cool, steady stare. This woman didn't fight from anger. She fought because she was born to it. It had been a long time since Ama had seen such a natural fighter, and she knew there was only one place where woman warriors this instinctive were raised.

And only because she was watching the woman before she leapt was Ama able to intercept her. The woman's swords were both out, one swinging down from a height and the other cutting sharply in from the side. Both swords were angled perfectly to deal Ama a stunning blow, but not to kill her, and the artful execution of such a complex attack nearly made Ama fall to her knees in awe.

Instead, though, with a grin so wide it made the old wound on her cheekbone ache, Ama turned her staff to deflect the higher sword while she kicked the lower sword away, keeping both from hitting home.

"Well done," murmured Ama, curious what the woman's response would be.

But there was none, no change in the woman's manner. She was entirely focused. The fight was on.

Ama evaluated the thin woman in flashes because there was no time for anything else, their fight was so fast-paced, sharp, unpredictable. Her skin, tanned dark by sun, suggested a life of wandering. Her arms, lean. Her throat, marked by an old wound, certainly older than the one on Ama's cheekbone, possibly older than Ama herself. The woman favored one leg slightly, suggesting another old wound, but her speed was remarkable in any direction. Whatever the weakness, she'd had time to get used to it.

"What's your name, then?" asked Ama, pretending cheer, hoping to cover the fact she was starting to tire. The woman's right hand thrust downward and Ama barely moved her foot out of the way in time, the blade missing her toes but grazing her sandal; she turned, expecting a sword from the left, but instead she felt the right sword move again, its tip approaching her knee, so she had to execute a full spin and smack it away with her staff as she retreated.

The woman answered, in a rasp, "Don't have one."

Ama danced lightly, reversing the spin of her staff so it approached the crown of the woman's head from the top. But suddenly the woman was no longer in the weapon's path. The staff kicked up a small puff of sand, striking the spot where the woman used to be.

Ama said, "We will need something to call you." She brought the staff back up again quickly, grazing the side of the woman's leg before she parried it away.

"You've had enough?" The woman pushed Ama's staff down with her parrying sword, and Ama was not at all sure she could bring it back up again, though part of her burned to try. If they both fought as hard as they could, who would come out on top? She relished not knowing. Even Nebez, the former Swan, she knew she could beat in a one-on-

one fight given enough time and space; with this woman, she had no such certainty. Outside of Paulus's bed, she had not felt this good in months, possibly years.

Her choice was made. Ama moved away, pulling her staff out from under the woman's sword, then took one more deliberate step backward. She spun her staff and laid it on the ground between them, inclining her head in a sign of respect.

Ama said to the woman, "I will be honored to fight alongside you. How should I address you when I do?"

The rasping voice answered, "I have sometimes been called the Shade." Smiling for the first time, the Shade spun both swords in the air and sheathed them, bowing to Ama in a smooth motion.

"Pleased to meet you. My name is Ama."

Instantly, the Shade's eyes widened. Ama was standing close enough that she could hear the woman's sharp intake of breath.

"What is it?" Ama asked quietly.

The Shade glanced at the crowd around them, seeming to note that Ama was far from the only person regarding her with curiosity. Then she turned back, focusing her attention on Ama alone, and cocked her head. "An unusual name."

Ama pondered her response. "It is."

"I knew an Ama once," the woman said slowly in her husky rasp. "She was much younger. But brave, like you. Bold."

The realization was like a snap of lightning in pitch darkness.

Ama felt the air grow charged, so heavy and sharp it was hard to believe no one else felt it. But no one else understood this conversation. Only she and Vi—she stopped herself. Could this possibly be who Ama thought she might be?

"What happened to her? Your Ama?" Ama heard herself ask.

The woman who called herself the Shade looked at Ama for a long moment, brown eyes intent and—hopeful? "We parted ways," she said. "But she has never left my mind."

When the woman's thin fingers floated up to the scar at her throat, Ama was suddenly sure. Yes. It was Vish.

And as delighted as she'd been minutes earlier, free to fight her hardest, Ama's happiness grew almost beyond reckoning. Vish alone knew Ama's true history. Ama couldn't have asked for a better fighter to stand beside her, no matter the enemy, no matter the battle. Vish's appearance here and now, her talents as a warrior seemingly stronger than ever, seemed like a gift from the Scorpion Herself.

Hope bloomed in Ama's chest like a flower. She showed none of it on her face; she simply gazed at the other woman, arranging her features in a careful mask of approval, the same expression she would have shown if she were only impressed by the woman's fighting prowess.

"I look forward to fighting alongside you," she said, hoping Vish would understand the private meaning behind her public words. "Your skills are welcome. We defend against a hostile force of born warriors."

"Yes," came the echoing answer. "There are none who fight like the Scorpicae."

"Except," said Ama, "perhaps, us."

The answering glint in Vish's eye removed Ama's last shred of doubt that this woman was indeed her long-lost *tishi*, her mother's closest friend, the woman who had saved her from certain death at Tamura's hands by spiriting her away to the Orphan Tree.

With Paulus and dozens of others watching, Vish thrust her arm out, not in the Scorpican motion of trust, but the Paximite version, a steady handshake.

Ama took it, shook it firmly, and with her other hand made a furtive, small version of a long-ago sign, almost forgotten. She flicked the index finger of her free hand inward, then formed a fist and raised it, but only to her shoulder, so others would not see.

Good hunting.

Vish grinned at the sign, nodding, tightening the grip of her fingers in Ama's. "Yes. Perhaps us."

✦ 21 ✦

HOME AND HUNTING

The Scorpican camp, Godsbones
Tamura, Azur

Tamura had lost sleep wondering how she would manage to get word to the group of young warriors returning from the rites that the Scorpicae had abandoned the caldera camp at Velja's Navel, but in the end, coincidence did the work for her. She should have realized it would happen that way. With the number of raiding parties and recruiting missions they had crisscrossing the north of Arca and the south of Paxim, one of the parties was bound to cross Azur's path. While Azur's group had traveled in disguise, the recruiting parties were designed to be as visible as possible, though they knew how to disappear if they were spotted by the wrong people. When the young warriors returning from the rites rode their stolen Paximite horses across the narrow red stone bridge in triumph, hundreds of warriors streamed out to welcome them.

All around her, warriors shouted in joyous reunion, but Tamura felt no pleasure, not even relief. She picked up immediately on the signals others missed. The warrior queen knew exactly how many young women had gone on the mission to the rites and she could tell, with her very first glance, that two of them had not come back.

With her second glance, Tamura saw there was a schism between two groups of the returned, though it was not immediately apparent what they'd disagreed about. The first group was led by Orlaithe, then a second, led by Azur—improbably, not riding at the head of the entire troop—clearly separate, bonded in their own unit. Tamura was careful to give away nothing on her face, no appearance of disjoint with the celebration around her, but she watched, keen to discover the secret.

Careful examination of the second group, the one led by Azur, told the tale. Their horses were heavier-laden; they'd clearly hauled back valuable goods, almost certainly pillaged or stolen, that the first group hadn't.

And the women in Azur's group bore marks of violence here and there. They hadn't stolen, then, but fought for their prizes. Their clothes were clean and whole, but on exposed limbs Tamura caught sight of cuts, bruises. Ankles or wrists braced with tight wrappings. Clothing could be changed, and clearly had been, but not everything was so easily disguised. Tamura saw that her fox-faced daughter Riva rode uncharacteristically low on her mount, her body curled in on itself with her right arm tucked against her side, clearly protecting a wound. Bodies that had not yet had time to heal told the story. Had Tamura been less hardened by the years, she would have felt queasy when she realized what had obviously happened to the two that hadn't returned.

Then Tamura's eye was caught by motion from the direction of the caves: Gretti was bearing Madazur high in her arms, offering her to Azur, who was still on horseback. Azur reached her arms down for her daughter, the First Mother's shout of joy ringing out over the whole camp. The girl shrank back, perhaps frightened by the noise, possibly not even recognizing the woman who greeted her after months of absence. Tamura could tell by Gretti's face that she wasn't entirely saddened by this turn of events, and Tamura wasn't sure she herself regretted it either.

But then Azur leapt down from her horse, crying happy tears, still performing outsize joy. Once she'd nestled the child in her arms, exclaiming over and over what a strong, big warrior she'd become, Madazur nuzzled her face close against her mother's once-familiar skin. Warriors who had been watching the exchange let out a collective, relieved breath, and went back to their greetings and their celebration. Azur bore the girl on her hip as she walked from group to group, greeting them, a broad grin on her face.

Tamura held out as long as she could, but once the first wave of joy had died down into an atmosphere of calmer collegiality, she tapped Azur's elbow with her fingertips. When Tamura had her daughter's attention, she drew her toward the privacy of the queen's tent. Azur paused at the tent flap for a minute, switched Madazur to her other hip, and then dipped her head to come inside.

Without niceties, Tamura began.

"You attacked in Paxim?" she asked Azur. "Was I not clear on your charter?"

"Not entirely," said Azur, running her fingers along the center pole of the tent, swaying gently to keep the baby calm, not meeting Tamura's eyes.

Tamura had brought Azur into her private space for this conversation, knowing that if they clashed in front of the others, there would be no taking it back. She would be far better able to manage the situation if it was just the two of them, not the whole tribe, in attendance. Azur was still her daughter, after all. Tamura thought she'd be able to point out the younger woman's misstep, to bring a flush of shame to her face once she realized how she'd erred.

But perhaps it wouldn't be that easy, Tamura realized now. There'd been no regret in Azur's tone. "'Not entirely'? What does that mean?"

Azur still didn't meet her gaze. "You never said not to attack."

"I told you not to draw attention to yourselves," the queen said in a low voice. "You were told to blend in, to hide in plain sight. I sent you to the rites to serve the cause by bearing more warriors. That was your entire purpose."

"And that is exactly what we'll do, Scorpion willing."

"Yet on the way back a group of you risked your lives in battle, and you lost two of your number. Were you even going to tell me?"

"I know you by now, don't I?" Azur said with a deliberate, measured tone that had begun to sound insulting, as if she were talking to the baby on her hip and not the high-ranking woman who was both her mother and her queen. "I know you're not easily fooled, so no, I wouldn't have tried to hide the truth from you."

"And did you succeed?" Tamura asked, not sure the answer made a difference, but still needing to hear it. "At whatever you set out to do?"

"We made a beginning," Azur said defiantly. "I won't apologize for using my judgment."

"I taught you better," said Tamura.

"You didn't teach me," Azur replied. The child in her arms began to fuss. Azur lowered her voice to a whisper, but despite the lower volume, every word sparked with intensity. "I learned, but not at your hands. I learned in a skirmish in the north when my best friend died because we were overmatched and I couldn't save her. I learned when I was introduced to the pleasure of the body and the pleasure of snuffing out a light, neither of which you had any hand in. I learned when my daughter, a child born from my own body, the first warrior in a generation, tore her way out of me and lit the world afire. I have learned a great deal, Queen Tamura."

Tamura said nothing, but after a pause, Azur's face began to soften. This time she met the queen's gaze. "And I am grateful to you for nurturing me. For ensuring that I grew up with sister warriors, where I've always belonged." Seemingly unable to leave it at that, she added, "But you were not my teacher."

"Perhaps not. But I am your mother and your queen."

"Of course, you are both," Azur said, dipping her head, as if she had never even hinted otherwise. "Would you like me to kneel at your feet?"

"I would not. You know that."

"Then tell me what you do want."

Tamura wanted to reach out and shake Azur, grab her by the shoulders to make her see. But she knew that would only harden the young woman's resolve, and besides, the queen couldn't put her hands on Azur while the future of their nation rested in her arms.

Instead, the queen stepped forward, resting her own hand against the center pole of the tent, forcing Azur to step back. Tamura's posture was aggressive, but her words, when she spoke, were kind. "We're in this together, Azur dha Tamura. I want us to lead together."

Azur looked doubtful but not afraid. She held her ground. "And what does that mean?"

"I'm about to embark on a dangerous battle. Before I go, I'll name a successor to rule if I don't return. Do I need to be clearer?"

"You are clear." The cloud on Azur's brow dissipated, her expression reshaping into keen interest. She switched the baby to her other hip, joggling her gently, and the child made a noise of contentment.

"But no more of this," said Tamura, pointing at a bruise on Azur's foot, a deep, livid purple her sandal didn't cover, where she'd clearly been injured in the attack she'd instigated. "No more defiance."

"I understand. What is your plan?"

Tamura had told no one else, and for a moment, she was afraid to say the words aloud. But Azur was a member of the council, and if she were to be named Tamura's successor, it made sense that she should be the first to know. "No more small strikes. We change. We muster a major force, ride against one city, and throw our full force into taking it."

"Invasion," said Azur in a wondering tone.

"And occupation," said Tamura. "We take that city and keep it. Force them to ransom it back from us, or let us steal from them without repercussions, showing the world our superior strength, their weakness."

Azur smiled almost hungrily, her hand reaching up to cup the back of Madazur's head, squeezing before letting go. "Paxim won't be ready."

"No," said Tamura. "Not in the least."

"Invade and occupy," mused Azur. A new light came into her face. "I would rejoice to be part of that plan."

"You are part of the plan. You're essential." Tamura reached out to clasp Azur's right forearm.

There was no hesitation as the First Mother gripped her arm in return.

But then Tamura said, "I'll name you my official successor. And you'll remain here, safe."

Azur snatched her arm back as if Tamura's touch burned.

"You are the First Mother," Tamura said, her voice hushed, urgent. "We cannot lose you. Madazur cannot lose you."

"I wouldn't be lost."

"You can't be sure."

"I am," insisted Azur.

"This is not a discussion," said Tamura, finally snapping with the full force of her authority. "Or some braid-crowned Scorpion-accursed *negotiation*. You won't join this battle, Azur. If you attempt to do so, I'll assign warriors to hold you back. You lose face if you try. And you lose your position as successor. Am I clear?"

For a fraction of a moment, there was a wounded look in Azur's eyes. She covered it quickly with a burning anger, just as genuine. "Yes. I understand that I am no longer a warrior to you. Only a symbol. So I'll do as you say and stay here to be looked at, if that's all you want of me."

Without waiting for a response, Azur turned and left the tent, the child on her hip making an indeterminate noise that could have been a squeal of either fright or joy.

Tamura didn't follow them, nor did she stare out the tent flap where they'd gone. She'd said her piece. She was fairly confident Azur would fall in line. The First Mother would chafe against her queen's orders on the inside, might even complain to one or two trusted confidantes, but she wouldn't go into outright rebellion. It was much smarter for Azur to hang back. And whatever else she was, the First Mother was smart.

Tamura had to count on it. She had no other options.

✦

When the warriors marched out toward the place Tamura had chosen as their target—a city called Hayk—Azur stayed behind with the weak and unfit. She burned with unstoppable fury, which she didn't show. Some contrary part of her hoped that without her, the Scorpican force would be defeated. Other parts of her knew that was a futile, awful wish. But Tamura had shoved Azur to the side while praising how vital she was to the future, and the First Mother could hardly bear the paradox.

On the first day, Azur moped around the camp, avoiding conversations, interacting with others only in the most desultory fashion. She bounced the baby on her lap, finding her more interesting now that the child was more than a parasite, even found herself smiling back at Madazur when she smiled, but half an hour of that was enough. She handed the baby over to Riva, who was happy enough to practice caring for the daughter she hoped she was growing inside her. Alone again, Azur heard a rumor that a messenger had arrived asking for another handful of warriors, Azur not named among them, and that was the last straw. She had to take some sort of action, even if she couldn't join the invasion in progress. If she had to sit here and smile at a babbling infant for weeks on end, she would absolutely take leave of her senses.

And so, on the second day after hundreds of Scorpican warriors had marched westward out of Godsbones, Azur strode out of the caves with her head high. She wore a full quiver of arrows slung over her back, bore her bow in hand. If anyone disapproved or wondered where she was going, their faces didn't show it. A tall warrior named Olan was brushing out the ponies' coats and looked askance at Azur as she came to claim her pony and mounted up.

"Riding?" was all Olan said.

"Hunting."

"Where?"

"Not your business," replied Azur, "but nearby."

"In Godsbones? I don't believe Tamura would approve," said Olan, uncertain.

"Oh, is she here? I don't see her."

Olan turned her attention to a red-brown pony's coat. Angry, Azur decided she would press her point.

"I could use company," she said, trying to keep her voice light even as she addressed the other woman's back. "Why don't you ride out with me?"

Olan stiffened. "Me? I'm not much of a hunter."

"All the better. Great time to learn."

Olan turned and squinted up at Azur.

From her comfortable seat atop the pony, Azur felt it was time to throw her weight around. What good was it to be the First Mother and a member of the council if she couldn't take control when she wanted to? "You can ride double with me or bring your own mount. Which would you prefer?"

Olan considered for a long moment, and finally said, "I'll ride my own." It took only a moment for her to fetch her weapons, settle onto the back of a deep red pony with a wild mane, and fall into line behind Azur.

Azur tossed her head as she rode out, pleased. She was the leader here, and eventually, she would be the leader of the entire Scorpican nation. She would not be second-guessed.

She led Olan northward along the river, which forked an hour's ride from camp, and she took the less-traveled fork. The river there was wilder and narrower. There was a small pine forest along that branch, the thickest stand of trees she'd seen anywhere in Godsbones, sheltering foxes, wolves, and coneys. Even if this forest was still unmistakably Godsbones, with its stunted trees and unrelenting red dirt, she still found that the cool breeze and smell of pines here reminded her of Scorpica. But she had never hunted here. As Olan had pointed out, Tamura had never permitted it; even when they camped in Godsbones, hunters had dipped carefully into the woods of Paxim, and before that, the Arcan sands.

It felt good to hunt again. The bow in her hands felt natural. In the past year, her body had grown and spit out a girl, something new; but all the old things she'd loved were still there. As she thought of taking down an animal with an arrow through the throat, a thrill ran down her spine. She loved that feeling. She would reclaim it. No one could take it from her, not a squalling infant, not an overprotective queen.

Azur wondered if another warrior was growing inside her already. She'd thrown herself into pleasures with both joy and duty back in the Holy City, but at this remove, Azur found herself hoping that her seed hadn't been watered. A second daughter would solidify her position, but a son would be disastrous. Since she couldn't choose, she'd rather not take her chances.

"First Mother," whispered Olan from behind her, just loud enough to hear. "Over there?"

Azur followed the angle of Olan's pointing finger along the curve of the river and yes, she saw it too. A flash in the distance, a motion that was neither leaf nor branch. Pale fur, catching the sun.

Up to Azur's chin went the bowstring, her fingers curling and releasing in the space of a heartbeat. Thwack of the arrow. A howl cut short, then silence.

Down from her pony, dropping the reins with a muttered *ressi*, the command to stay, Azur hustled toward where she'd last seen the prey moving. Either Olan would follow behind her or she wouldn't, and Azur didn't particularly care. The tall warrior might have spotted movement first, but Azur had been the one to bring the animal, whatever it was, down. She hoped Olan wouldn't ask for credit. With a few more swift steps, Azur covered the remaining ground to the riverbank and came upon the still, bleeding body.

It was a white wolf, dead. She'd taken it down herself in a single shot.

Azur was almost incandescent with joy. It felt so right, so fulfilling. Finally she was herself again. She would be remembered forever as someone who brought life, but it was dealing death that made her heart swell. It felt so easy, so right, like this. If Olan were even a smidge more appealing, Azur would have kissed the other woman on the mouth, Azur's blood was running so hot and high, her joy irrepressible.

But when she turned to Olan, who had indeed followed her all the way to the riverbank, the tall warrior's face was drawn with shock, her expression dazed.

Seeing Azur's quizzical expression, Olan said, "It's . . . not right."

"What?" Azur almost laughed, still intoxicated from the thrill of bringing the wolf down single-handedly.

Olan only pointed down.

At first Azur didn't see what she meant. A white wolf was a rare catch, and Azur was already thinking about what came next. The meat wouldn't be tender, but probably worth hauling back to toss into the stewpot, adding flavor to an evening meal. The pelt, she would keep for herself. So white and fine and thick. She wanted to feel that fur against her back as someone pleasured her—it didn't really matter who, just any hands, any skin, any breath that was not her own.

Perhaps she could find someone to indulge with in secret, as she'd once done with Dree. Or once her sister warriors gave birth to more daughters, companions for Madazur, Azur could find her own sort of companion. Riva, for example, who was strong and smart. After the raid, had Azur felt a kind of spark between them? She didn't think she'd imagined it. Certainly she'd heard tell of previous leaders whose most important councillors had been their companions in body as well as in mind. Just because Queen Tamura never sought pleasures with other warriors didn't mean it couldn't be done.

"Azur?" said Olan hesitantly.

"What?" she snapped.

Olan's voice was so quiet, so hesitant, it was hard to hear. "You don't see?"

"It's a white wolf!" Azur threw up her hands. "Four legs, a belly, a back, a head—" And then she saw what Olan saw.

On the wolf's head, not just ears. Above the ears, horns the thickness of Azur's thumbs twisted into a sharp double curve like goat's horns, but the same pure white as the wolf's lush fur.

A *horned* white wolf.

Not possible, Azur told herself. Such things didn't exist. A horned white wolf was only a mythical animal from the stories, one of the fabled creatures the Scorpion had once slain to earn her immortality. No one alive had ever seen one in the flesh. They could not, thought Azur, be seeing it now.

Olan had begun to cry. "We shouldn't have done it. We'll be punished. We'll be—"

"Oh, shut up," Azur snapped. "Stop this 'we.' You had nothing to do with it."

But Olan was pacing, her emotions racking her body, edging toward panic. "We'll tell Tamura. She'll know what to do."

"You know who we'll tell? No one."

"We can't keep it a secret. The gods will know. Everyone will know."

"What gods?" scoffed Azur, gesturing around them. "Who do you see here? Oh look, the All-Mother is perched on the rocks to the north! What a miracle, since she's been gone for hundreds of years, but she just happened to be here for us!"

"Don't blaspheme," whispered Olan. "This is serious."

"This is *nothing*," barked Azur. "Not if we don't tell anyone. I skin the wolf, I bury the head, I bring back the pelt. Done."

"And when they ask questions?"

Azur fixed the tall warrior with a glare. "They won't!"

"If they do?"

She threw her hands up again, her anger rumbling within. "If anyone asks, I'll say I left it as an offering. Or I'll say a lion fought me for the meat and I let her have it. Or I'll say I slipped and it fell in the *mokhing* river. But why would they even ask? Who in the name of the Scorpion is going to say, 'Oh, you killed a white wolf? Did it by any chance have horns?' I'm not worried."

"I am," said Olan, wiping tears from both cheeks with a fast, two-handed swipe.

"And I don't care," said Azur with emphasis, kneeling next to the wolf's body. She turned her back on Olan. She unsheathed her dagger.

Pausing for a deep breath, Azur looked at the blood smeared on the red rocks. The bright sun pinned to the blue-white sky. The unmistakable horns that curled out of the wolf's head just above the ears—a jarring sight, unsettling. Odd, but supernatural? It couldn't be. Perhaps if Olan hadn't pushed her so hard, Azur would've felt more hesitant about skinning the wolf, but in the face of Olan's embarrassing panic, Azur had convinced herself there was nothing wrong here. This was just some sport wolf, some strange mutation, something that happened in every species, including humans. Just an aberration. It was time to claim her trophy.

Azur took one more long, deep breath and blew it out. Then, with a sure hand, she began to cut.

✦

Olan watched in horror as Azur slit the throat of the horned white wolf, the powerful creature she hadn't had the right to kill.

This couldn't happen. Azur had already done too much by taking the beast's life, but to carve her up, that was an even worse sacrilege.

Olan had tried reason. It wasn't enough. Someone had to stop Azur, and Olan was the only one here.

Staggering away as if to vomit, which she thought she might well do, Olan faced out toward the river. With closed eyes, she prayed for a sign, not even sure who she was praying to. When she opened her eyes again, she saw how the riverbank was littered with large, smooth stones. And a flat-edged, fist-sized stone of a different color—black instead of red—lay between her feet as if someone had laid it there at her request.

Only I can stop this.

Before Olan could talk herself out of it, she'd hefted the rock with both hands, transferred it to her right, and headed back toward Azur, the red gravel of Godsbones crunching under her feet.

Azur, crouching, was still sawing away at the corpse. Olan took two more steps forward, hovered over Azur where she crouched, and begun to swing the heavy black rock right at the back of the First Mother's bent head.

Quick as lightning, Azur rose and twisted, hands empty—she must have dropped her knife on purpose to have both free—and as the rock swung at the spot where her head used to be, Azur caught the stone easily in her cupped hands.

Stunned, scared, Olan let go.

Then Azur passed the fist-sized river stone into the palm of one hand, cupped the hand around the far side of the stone like the pocket of a slingshot, and without a pause, whipped her arm forward and upward, bringing the stone with enormous force against Olan's temple, caving in the side of Olan's head.

The force of the blow knocked Olan off her feet. Her body partly crumpled, partly flew, falling sideways. She landed hard in the red dirt, rolling until she came to a halt on her back, eyes staring up at the high, indifferent sun.

"Mokh," she heard Azur's voice say. Was there wonder in it? Fear? Regret? Olan couldn't tell. And she couldn't see Azur's face from where

she lay. There were no clouds in the sky but something was clouding her eyes, blurring her gaze, until she couldn't tell the difference between the blue sky and the yellow-white sun.

Even though Olan couldn't see Azur, she could still hear her, and the First Mother seemed to take an eternity to carve and skin the wolf. The stink of blood hung heavy in the air. Olan couldn't get a good breath in her lungs, but that felt all right. Slowly she realized her vision and hearing had both shifted. While the white haze of clouds still hung over her right eye, she'd lost the vision in her left eye completely. In much the same way, the sound of Azur at work drifted into Olan's right ear, sounding as if it were all happening leagues away.

And the pain. Such pain. There were no words for it.

Even if she could move, thought Olan, what could she do? When Azur had implicitly threatened her back at the camp, she'd been shaken, and she'd ridden out for the hunt with none of the precautions she'd usually take. She'd dropped her bow and arrow. She doubted she could reach the knife strapped to her thigh; the arm on the injured side of her body seemed to have joined company with her useless eye and ear. She'd brought no water, no jerky, no willow bark, no bedroll. If she'd simply said no to this hunt, if she hadn't tried to do the right thing, she'd be back in the camp, snug in her bedroll or enjoying a last swig of hammerwine from a shared skin before settling in for the night. She would have thought it an ordinary evening, not even knowing she'd escaped this fate. But she was here instead. Wishing it were otherwise, far too late.

At long last the terrible tearing apart of the wolf was done, and she heard Azur whistle for her mount. More grunting, arranging, preparing. Then, with awful slowness, Azur's feet crunched against the red gravel near Olan's head. Olan was surprised she could hear them with only one ear, especially this close to the rushing river, but there was nothing else for her body to do, she supposed. She was only waiting now. She didn't want to even think of what she was waiting for.

"Pity you got too close to the river," Azur was saying. "Pity you fell in."

And Olan felt her body shift in great jagged movements. She realized it was because Azur was moving her with her feet, kicking Olan with one foot and then the other. Then Olan rolled, felt nothing for a long moment but the air. Then came the shock of hitting the water. The current carried her away.

Hours later, Olan opened her eyes one last time. She'd washed up on a bank she wouldn't have recognized even if she could see clearly. Only the bone-white moon gave light. The water was cold now, numbing, and it was a blessing to be free of the pain.

The dark returned, closed in. Then there was only quiet and Olan's own panting, draining breath.

Then Olan thought she saw someone, for a moment. A dark, woman-shaped hole against the dark. But she couldn't be sure of anything. Only her own breath, coming slower, with great effort.

Light gone, mount gone, wolf gone, lives gone. Only Olan remained.

Her body lay beached, half in the cold water, half on the wet red dirt of the foreign riverbank. It was not comfortable, but Olan was beyond comfort. The sky was dark and the ground was cold and there was no sun, no warmth, no life to speak of, and no one left, anyway, to speak.

✦

To the Scorpicae in the riverside camp, the sunset seemed the same as any other since they'd arrived in Godsbones, red sun reaching for red sand, the light leaking away as if it ran, like water, for lower ground.

When the blue sky had darkened to black and all fires but one had been extinguished, the warriors lay their bedrolls down. Some stayed in the caves themselves, some in the shade of the cliffs that buckled and bent, green scrub providing shelter here and there for those who preferred it. Even though this area of Godsbones was newer to them than the caldera, the caves at their back made it feel like a safe haven, a secret land in which their enemies wouldn't dare to seek them, the next best thing to home.

They felt safe. But they were not safe.

In the dark beyond the circle where the firelight failed to reach lurked waiting creatures. Some of them, the Scorpicae would have recognized easily. Mountain lions, thick muscles rippling under their thin gold-white fur. The shaggy ponies the Scorpicae loved, nickering and flicking their tails whenever flies dared to cluster. Rats and foxes, red squirrels and bee-eaters. These animals were quarry the warriors knew well, the same creatures they would see on the slopes and in the woods of their own homeland. Warriors might see some of these animals and smile.

Other creatures would have seemed like imagination, nightmares, madness. A white wolf with horns on its head, its pale fur rust-colored from rolling in the dust, the red stains around its mouth a different shade of red, too bright, too sharp. A bull that at first looked like two bulls standing close together, and only from the right angle could one see that there was only one four-legged body, one tail, the single creature cleaving into two at the neck.

And they were too close, not to the warriors, but to each other. The creatures should have fought and tumbled. The fox should have snapped up the squirrels in its sharp jaws, the lion should've torn out the pony's throat. But instead they clustered close, one of the bull's heads close enough to brush a white wolf's shoulder. Their breath was a chorus and they shifted from foot to foot, their peace uneasy, restless.

Because among the animals was one figure that resembled a woman, but like the two-headed bull, she wasn't what she first appeared to be.

Her arms were barely thicker than bones, the line of her nose sharp, her eyes hooded. Her fingers were long, as if stretched too far, spindling out like a tree's narrowest branches. She only had the form of a woman until you looked closer. She was a shadow, a hole cut out of the darkness, an absence of color and spirit.

She was Eresh, god of the Underlands, moving as a shade on the surface of the earth in the one place that belonged to Her aboveground, and She did not like what She saw.

Godsbones belonged to Her and her creatures. She'd already been angry with the way these warriors trampled Her land on their way to do violence, showing no respect, no reverence. Then, this latest horror: a warrior not only killing one of her creatures, but murdering a fellow countrywoman to cover up the crime. Eresh's heart roared in anger. Of the three god-sisters, She had the fewest ways to express her displeasure aboveground, but She was no less aware of sacrilege. She only had a longer horizon to build her resentment and plot her revenge.

Eresh wasn't opposed to war on principle; carnage aboveground took from her sisters' citizenry and added to her own. By now She'd claimed innumerable souls, far more than either Sestia or Velja. If the Scorpicae had only marched through her lands, even though She bristled, She might have let it pass.

But not now. She was bound not to harm those who worshipped her sisters—the three had entered into an agreement around the time of what the worldly called the Great Peace—but these Scorpicae worshipped a half-human, not even divine. Eresh had entered into no agreement whatsoever with the immortal hero, a sort of demigod, called the Scorpion.

So Eresh had a favor to ask and a plan to begin. If the favor was granted, she could begin immediately. It was a simple plan, elegant in its simplicity. There were five gates between the Underlands and the world Above. All were closed, all guarded. But they were gates, not walls. Any gate could, under the right conditions, be opened.

She needed a sister. She needed a favor. She needed a shade, the right kind, with a wish unfulfilled. That was all. Once begun, the plan would curl outward like a vine, a flower.

And when that plan came to fruition, this mistreatment would not stand.

✦

Unseen by human eyes, the next morning, along with the sun, what had once been Olan rose.

There was no discernable moment when the shade entered the body. The dead woman lay there half-in and half-out of the river, limbs still, eyes open to the pale, cloudless sky. The tempting scent of blood had drawn a pair of vultures wheeling above. Not far off, a mountain lion drew nearer, ears perked. Then life, or something that looked a lot like it, was present. It was unlike a spark or smoke or anything else filling up a physical shell; no one watching would have detected the moment when the body went from just a body to something more.

She rose slowly, with care, giving no sign of haste. There was perhaps a touch of awkwardness to the way the body turned sideways to kneel, stiff, halting. Knees in the dirt, then the hands, one palm and then the other on the ground. Then the back stretching like a cat's after a long rest. Then, at last, she truly rose.

Both ears could hear. Both eyes could see. The side of the head that had been caved in, caked with blood, was healing itself. The blood that the river hadn't washed away began to vanish, the few last pebbles pushing out and falling to the ground, landing with the softest of sounds, unnoticed. In a few moments the whole right temple, uninjured, was clean and cool to the touch.

No one was there to see. They would not have known, anyway, what they were looking at. The body moved with Olan's limbs, saw with Olan's eyes, but it was not Olan.

She stood alone in an alien, inhospitable land. At the first sign of motion, the vultures changed their path, gazing down from a final wide arc, then wheeling away. The hungry mountain lion slunk off in silence, her exit as stealthy as her approach. No animals, no people, no company.

She didn't know what to think of this. She didn't know what to think at all. She hadn't known what to expect, but she'd been told to remember

329

everything, to be ready to make her report when she returned. She tried to force herself to remember these feelings as they happened, but it was so hard to hold on, the workings of her mind as ephemeral and wispy as smoke in a strong wind. Time was a loop and an ocean.

She had no idea how long she'd been dead. She hoped it hadn't been long. Once she saw her fellow Scorpicae, she would know. Was Tamura still queen? She could tell she'd risen in Godsbones; did that mean the Scorpicae were prosecuting the war from here, instead of the caldera? And most importantly, if it hadn't been long—was there any chance she might find Azur? She burned with the sun's fire to see her, smell her, touch her again.

The body that used to be Olan stared up at the open sky, tears coming to her unfamiliar eyes, and a sound halfway between wonder and anguish tore itself free, ragged and low, from her unfamiliar lips.

The body had a wrongness about it; it wasn't at all like hers had been. Her spirit didn't belong in this body. It didn't fit. Her own was broken, rotting—what had happened to it? she wondered. Still under all that earth? It didn't matter now. The meat of her brain was gone but her mind was here, her thoughts were here. She knew who she was, even inside this awkward, unfamiliar frame. She stretched its fingers, flexed its feet. Breathed in air through its mouth to fill its lungs. She would find a way.

There was no guidance for someone like her because there had never been someone like her. Should that give her comfort? As the day began to warm the air around her, she felt nothing but fear. Fear of the unknown because it was all unknown now, every moment, every motion. She had thought there would never be a feeling worse than realizing she was dead, but now she was no longer sure.

She was alive again, or something like it. Now she had a mission. She would prove that a shade could rise from the dead, could take form, could control a body so it walked and talked and moved among the living.

The god was waiting on her; Dree dared not fail.

22

A MESSENGER

Ursu, Paxim
Paulus, Ama

The two women's swords crossed. One woman howled and the other howled back. As he watched, Paulus was jarred by how fierce and angry they sounded, given that their furious howls frequently dissolved into laughter.

Ama was sparring with the Shade, yet again, even though the sun had sunk to touch the horizon. No matter how many new soldiers joined the King's Elite, Ama always seemed to want to fight with this one. She'd insisted on it tonight even though the usual time for sparring was long past, and Paulus had to remain nearby, no matter how bored he became. Briefly he fantasized about slipping away, just getting right up and striding around the corner into the palace. Then he thought about how angry Ama would be, and he felt a stew of tenderness and resentment, and lost any desire to move.

Earlier today he'd had his own sparring match in front of a specially invited crowd of Paximite nobles, part of a formal presentation of the King's Elite. His mother's idea, naturally, but Paulus hadn't hesitated. In the crowning exhibition match, Paulus had gone up against Nebez, and he'd been proud of himself for emerging victorious. Not just anyone could hold their own again a former Swan. The fight had been close throughout. Possibly Nebez had let Paulus win in the end. But the purpose hadn't been to determine the better fighter: it had been to impress the right people, and there, Paulus had accomplished much. The sight of his mother's proud smile would linger in his mind for weeks. He knew he'd cut a fine figure, triumphant in the helmet he'd had made for the occasion, polished to a shine with the long black horsetail affixed to the crown flaring and spinning with his every move. He countered Nebez's attacks and sprang his own like a series of well-laid traps, his armor gleaming, his sparring sword held high. That was the image he'd wanted to leave with his mother's subjects, his future followers, and he'd done it.

But the fight he watched now, this was more real. He was glad Ama and the Shade hadn't sparred as part of the exhibition. The difference between what he and Nebez had done and what these women did was too clear. He knew he should be glad that fighters this skilled were on his side; they were both clearly masters. Far better to fight with them than against them, that was the logical conclusion. But Paulus had never been a creature of logic. He wasn't starting now.

What Paulus didn't like, if he were to admit it, was the complete dedication of Ama's attention to someone who wasn't him. He didn't think that Ama had any kind of sexual attachment to the older woman. The Shade wasn't that kind of threat. But Paulus had the distinct impression that if Ama could have left him behind to be with the Shade—for a few hours, maybe a day, not forever—she would. There was something about this warrior she couldn't stay away from. She wouldn't tell Paulus what it was. That, above all else, worried the kingling. The secrecy. He and Ama had never had secrets from each other before, not since the night of the Gods' Wedding. Since that night they'd been closer to each other than to anyone else in the world.

The sun finally sank behind the horizon, night coming on. No one moved to light a torch. Paulus supposed he should have done so—the women were too busy with their match—but he did not, at this time, care to move.

The Shade heard something before either Ama or Paulus knew there was something to hear. Her head went up, her eyes alight. She blocked Ama's blow sloppily, and Ama whooped with joy first, not realizing. Then she looked to the horizon, where the Shade's gaze was fixed.

"Well, blind as a forest of cocks, I am," Ama muttered.

"A boy," the Shade said, and pointed far off. If Paulus squinted carefully, he realized, he could see a faint dark smear—a cloud of dust?— on the horizon.

After a few more moments they could all hear the sound of the horse's hooves approaching, and as the messenger boy neared, they waited in silence. He wore the bright red tunic of the royal messenger, a garment made to fit a girl. But of course there were no girls of this age, and boys like this dotted the countryside, ready to spread word of great things or terrors.

The boy finally drew up to the training ground and, in one smooth motion, slid from the back of his horse. He was small, certainly no more than ten years old, and so exhausted he could barely stand. Paulus's heart knotted up. He could tell from the boy's expression that his news wasn't good.

Without preamble, the boy spoke, clearly fatigued. "Scorpican warriors on the move."

Ama was the first to reply. "Where?"

"Coming to Hayk, they said." The child hunched over, hands on his bony knees, and took a slow breath. "Our scout heard. In the next few days. They will strike."

Paulus wanted to raise his eyes to Ama's, see what she thought of this revelation, but he fought the urge. He had to think of himself as a king now, a grand ruler who future generations would celebrate. The first ruling king's decisions had to be his own. So Paulus kept his attention firmly on the exhausted messenger, whose small back was rounded as he bent. When the boy saw him looking, though, he straightened up. *I will be the king he needs,* thought Paulus.

The kingling asked, "Striking at Hayk, that's what they said? You're sure?"

The boy nodded solemnly.

"Thank you," said Paulus, moving closer to lay his hand on the boy's shoulder. "You've been of great service. Stop by the kitchens and let them know I said to give you whatever you want. Can you make it there?"

The boy's nod was so brief it was more of a bob, and then he was gone, head no doubt filled with dreams of honey cakes and milk puddings, rewards for a job well done.

◆

Dismayed, Ama watched the boy disappear into the palace, the panting mount he'd left behind the only evidence he'd been there at all. Paulus gazed in her direction for a moment without speaking, brushing invisible dust off the thighs of his leggings, tapping his fingers once against the hilt of his dagger. Ama could tell by the light in his eyes exactly what he intended, and she felt a cold, brisk wash of fear.

"No," she blurted, "you can't."

Paulus answered immediately, "Can't what?"

"Go to intercept the Scorpicae yourself."

"Whyever not?" asked Paulus, a new barb in his voice. "I'd take the King's Elite with me. Isn't the whole point? For me to use their strength wherever I choose?"

He was right, of course, but it was too soon. She felt her heart seize. "I never said wherever. You didn't even ask how big the enemy force is, whether they're mounted or on foot, what weapons they carry. We need more scouts. Time to plan."

Paulus's hand was on his dagger again, an instinct she'd trained into him, his voice sharper yet. "Every minute we take to plan is a minute wasted, Ama. We can't spare them. The warriors will strike Hayk before we can get there."

"Yes, that's possible," she agreed reluctantly. "But better to take our time and win than to rush in too soon and lose."

"I won't sacrifice a town we can save."

"Do you know Hayk?" They both turned at the husky voice, so caught up in their quarrel they'd forgotten the Shade was even there.

From the way Paulus frowned at the woman's question, Ama knew his answer was no. She asked Vish, "Do you?"

"Yes. Very poorly situated for defense."

"Probably why they chose it," muttered Ama.

The older woman nodded. "Narrow valleys going in; dead easy to set up an ambush."

"So if we hurry, as I said, we could ambush them!" said Paulus.

Vish shook her head slowly, side to side, with clear regret. "Not if they're already there."

Ama's worry grew. She had to handle this just right. To Paulus, Ama said, "On unfriendly, unfamiliar terrain? We need to take our time."

"No. However challenging the fight, the people need to know I can serve as commander," he said, each word edged with iron. "They need to see me battle against all odds and win."

"And if you don't win?" Ama blurted, and immediately regretted it.

Paulus didn't respond right away. He seemed to realize he was clutching his dagger too tightly. He flexed his fingers, pulled them back in to make a fist, then let them dangle loosely at his side. Then he turned to Vish, saying in a toneless voice, "Leave us."

Vish did as he said, turning away without even meeting Ama's gaze. Ama knew her *tishi* needed to keep her distance to avoid revealing their connection. At the same time, the speed with which Vish turned her back left Ama feeling exposed, almost abandoned.

Once they were alone, Paulus moved a few steps to seat himself on the fallen tree trunk that they often trained on, the only place to sit besides the ground. He looked up at Ama, his gaze turned hard in the dim light of early evening. "You have so little faith in me?"

He needed reassurance, it was obvious. She lowered herself to sit next to him, careful to put herself close enough to touch if he wanted. "No, no. I believe in you absolutely. I will back your play at the right time. But this isn't the right time."

"It's the right time if you come with me. Fight at my side, Ama. Like we did at Hosios." His expression shifted back to fondness, and he reached out for her hands, which she hesitantly gave over. "The people should see us both in action. Stand alongside me now as you'll stand alongside me when I rule as king."

Ama looked down at their joined hands and thought of Queen Heliane, who trusted Ama only as a protector, not a partner, for this headstrong young man. If Ama were allowed to stay beside him when he became king, it would only ever be as a sword for hire, nothing more. Which was better, Ama had decided, than not being near him at all. Whatever it took, she would stay.

"You do . . . want to stand alongside me, don't you?" Paulus's voice was hesitant now, his question taking on a different meaning. She realized her silence had worried him.

"What you do as king is your business," Ama answered carefully. "I don't interfere with that. My only priority is to keep you safe. You'll stay inside the palace for now, and when the time is right . . ."

He withdrew his hands, then pulled away, rising to his feet. "No. You keep saying that. When the time is right. It's right *now*, Ama. Your protectiveness is absurd."

"Absurd?" she echoed.

He threw up his hands. "What was the point of that whole exercise where you fought all those comers? Was it just about your ego? Is the King's Elite really to ride out with me against the enemy? Or did you just amass an overgrown Kingsguard to trap me inside the palace, for the love of Panic?"

"Not to trap you!" She felt her voice getting too loud and brought it down, closer to her normal speaking voice, though she knew every word still thrummed with tension. "The King's Elite is exactly what I told you I meant it to be. To strike out with us as we move to engage the enemy in battle. When it's the right time to do so."

"Then why not now? Ride with me."

"The Elite's not ready."

"Some of them are. That one you just fought. And Nebez, right? Maybe Yesika? How many of the Elite could you take into battle if you had to?"

She considered the question carefully, though didn't want to give him any more fodder for his argument. She'd show him respect by being honest. "Ten."

"Plus you," he said. "You've always thought you're the best fighter there is; I can't imagine you wouldn't count yourself."

She ignored the barb and pressed on. "But against how many? Dozens? Hundreds? Ten elite soldiers and yes, plus me, that's eleven I trust. Just eleven. Against a trained enemy, a deadly enemy, without number."

Paulus's eyes narrowed to slits. "Eleven?"

She counted again, then nodded. "Eleven."

In a stiff, soft voice, he asked, "Oh. Not twelve?"

And too late, Ama saw the trap. Eleven fighters she trusted, including herself. That was what she'd told him. If she'd counted Paulus among that number, she would have said twelve, not eleven.

But he was not a fighter she trusted, not for something this important. She hadn't thought to count him. And now he knew it.

"Paulus, I—"

He turned his back on her and began walking before she could even complete the thought. She hastened to follow him, sheathing her sword as she went, staying a half step behind him even though she could have caught him easily.

He didn't stop until they got to his rooms, and once the door was shut behind them, he finally turned to her. The pain on his face took her breath away.

She had no words that would make this better. Maybe nothing would. But she tried the only thing that came to mind. She reached out for him.

Ama had reached out for Paulus in almost every way imaginable before this: respectfully and dismissively, with lust and with incomprehension, to correct him and to embrace him. They had been guard and guarded, kingling and subject, lover and loved. She was a new woman every time she reached; he was a new man every time he reacted to the reaching. Every time it was a new moment, and this time, it was a dizzyingly uncertain one.

Ama reached out to Paulus, her heart spilling over with love and regret and uncertainty, fearing he would pull away but knowing she would never forgive herself if she didn't try.

Instead of yanking his arm away Paulus did something arguably worse. He let her hand fall upon his arm, but that arm might as well have been stone. He gave nothing away under her touch. He looked at her, but only as he might regard a stranger, no emotion in his eyes. Underneath she suspected he was still smoldering; his anger could come striking out at any moment. But the fact that he could just completely turn everything off, that scared her. She was not a woman who scared easily.

Finally Paulus spoke. "Leave me."

She lifted her hand from his arm but didn't move her feet. She let a challenge show in her gaze, open and fierce.

His steady stare didn't change. He repeated, "Leave me."

For the first time, she defied him. "No."

"I don't want you here tonight."

"That isn't your choice."

"All-Mother's *muoni* it's not," he spat, the anger finally starting to sizzle out. "If the future king of Paxim tells you to do something, woman, you do it. And I'm telling you to leave."

"You didn't hire me," Ama said, standing her ground. "The queen did. To guard you. How am I supposed to guard you if I leave you?"

Paulus froze. Whether she had gotten through to him, she couldn't tell, but he finally broke off his steady gaze. He ran a hand through his curls, looked away, and let out a deep sigh. He walked to the side table and she thought he might call a servant to prepare them tea, but instead he poured himself a cup of rich, golden lily wine. After a long moment, he hooked two fingers over another cup and slid it forward on the table, almost to the edge. Then he filled it, the same as the first cup, and held it out to her.

When his gaze met hers again, his eyes were softer. There was something conciliatory, something promising, in his voice when he said, "All right. All right. We can sort this out tomorrow." He bent his head to drink.

Mimicking him almost automatically, she took a long drink of the wine, then swallowed, before she said, "Shouldn't we be planning?"

"Yes, we should," he agreed, his look far-off. "But we can't get there in time. As you said. It makes more sense to consider things carefully. The boy will spread the word. The war minister will hear, and my mother, and they will make a plan. They'll insist on taking the time, just like you did. Tomorrow morning we'll join them and take coordinated action."

She wasn't sure what had changed his mind so fast. Had her words sunk in? She took another drink of wine and agreed, "If you say so."

He tilted his cup back to empty the rest down his throat, then wiped his mouth with the back of his hand and set the cup down. "There's something else I want to do tonight."

She thought she knew what he meant, but as angry as he'd been before, she couldn't be sure. She remained still as he came close enough to run his fingertips down her arm to the elbow. When he tapped her wrist on that arm, she realized he was encouraging her to drink the rest of her wine. She was happy to oblige. The wine was sweet and thick. Warmth coursed through her.

Then Paulus took the cup gently from her fingers with his other hand, tracing the length of her arm in the other direction this time, up to the shoulder. He set her empty cup down on the table next to his. Then he reached out to guide her chin toward him, his eyes narrowing with intent, clearly hungry for her kiss.

When their lips met, Ama's anger didn't disappear, but it began to melt at the edges. In only a moment Paulus's tongue was in her mouth, his hand between her legs, cupping, exploring. She stumbled back half a step at the suddenness of it, her body's enthusiastic reaction to his. When the wash of pleasure came over her, there was no room for anything else.

Ama let herself become her body. She made the choice to hold nothing back: the low groan he coaxed from her throat, the hungry grip of her fingers slipping down the front of his leggings, their mingled sighs. Without a word they moved blindly toward the bed, clinging inelegantly, not willing to stop kissing even to open their eyes.

Despite its rushed beginning, once they fell to the bed, their pleasure-taking was leisurely, unhurried. Ama savored the luxury of long, slow waves of pleasure as Paulus took time to explore her body, even as well as she felt like he knew it already. This time he inspected every inch with hungry eyes, gentle fingers, insistent teeth and lips and tongue.

At last, he brought her to the brink of ecstasy buried in her to the hilt, grinding his hips against hers with his hands locking her hipbones against him, and when he whispered, *"Giddabak?"* she murmured, *"Stay, stay,"* and he shuddered hard as his rain came. She almost cried at the intimacy of it. She must be exhausted, or drunk, she decided, though she'd only had the one cup of wine. She was never so sentimental, even about Paulus.

After he'd had time to rest, he reached out for her, and teased her with his fingers until she, too, finally shuddered in pleasure, bucking and crying out, and he smothered her cries with his mouth on hers, chuckling afterward, lavishing kisses upon her forehead, cheeks, chin.

Both pleasured, both content, she was tempted to stay, but as different as their pleasure-taking had felt tonight, she knew the routine. She always left the bed to return to her own bedroll, always. She'd only slept next to him once, the night he'd asked her to, the night of the banquet, before they'd even kissed for the first time. As heavy as her arms and legs were, she forced herself to swing her legs over the side of the bed to the ground, to prepare to leave him. But then she felt him catch her wrist.

"Stay," he said. "Just tonight. Please."

Paulus sounded so earnest, so loving. She couldn't help but give in.

He folded her into his warm embrace, the bed's padding under them irresistibly soft. That was how she fell asleep, him still kissing her gently and lightly. As she slid into darkness, she wasn't sure if his lips were still moving over her skin or if she was just imagining those touches, feeling comforted, feeling loved.

When she awoke, much later, she wasn't sure where to start. Eyes still closed against the darkness, at first she remembered only pleasure, but then it all came flooding back, the messenger, their awful clash. He would have to see reason, she thought. She wouldn't rush to say she was sorry first, but neither would she shrink from it, if that was what was needed. He had to know how deeply she loved him. Most of all she wanted more days, weeks, years waking up with him beside her. His mother might not approve—even without *giddabak*, the tea Heliane had given her would prevent a child from taking root—but Paulus wanted her by his side today and forever. If that was the case, did anything else matter?

She was already beginning to smile as she rolled over toward him, opening her eyes. Then the smile died on her lips. She blinked once, twice. And she knew the truth immediately.

No, no, no.

She didn't try to talk herself into believing that he'd been kidnapped, that he was hiding, that she was reading these signs wrong and the empty-looking bed was a trick of the light, that he was just there under the smoothed-down cover, waiting for her.

He was gone. He had gone without her.

She found only the book of adventures lying where his head should be. She almost reached out to touch it but stopped herself. If she put her hands on it, she'd throw it across the room. If she started throwing things, she might never stop. She'd throw the bedding and the screen and the chests, the jug of wine and their empty cups and the table those cups sat on, all of it. She had to keep a lid on the confusion, the anger, the regret. She should never have closed her eyes. She should have known. She'd let Paulus outsmart her, and now she was not the only one who would pay the price.

Eleven fighters she trusted, she reminded herself, that was what she'd told him the night before. She wondered how many of them he had managed to take. The Shade would have rejected his offer and alerted Ama immediately: her fealty was obvious to all, even though they did not know Vish's true history, so Paulus would have known better than to ask.

But the men, ah, the men. She was willing to bet at least five had joined his foolhardy adventure. She wasn't sure whether Nebez would go, but certainly Yusuf and Baris, so eager for Paulus's approval. If five had joined him, that meant a mere half-dozen half-trained men against an unknown number of lifelong warriors. She hoped Paulus would be smarter than that. She hoped he would commandeer a number of troops from some post nearby to supplement what he had managed to steal of the King's Elite. If he thought to do so, he could easily add thirty, fifty, seventy troops to his number. Perhaps with Nebez's help he would draft the Swans, another fifty-five soldiers—the best in all of Paxim besides the Elite, worth twice that number due to their skill and training. That was, if the Swans would go, which she couldn't even guess, never having asked Nebez if he'd parted with them on good terms. Paulus might be rash, but he wasn't stupid. He'd try to get the best possible soldiers he could, if it could be done quickly. She hoped, despite her anger, that he could convince or command the Swans to join his wild mission. She wanted him to return to her. She would wish for anything that would make that possible.

No matter how many fighters Paulus had with him, though, the outlook was grim. Even if Tamura had only a fraction of her force with her, which seemed unlikely, Paulus and his fighters would be outmatched. And in a way it barely mattered. Even if the number of Paximite fighters matched the number of Scorpican warriors, it wouldn't be anything close to a fair fight.

Paulus's force lacked the element of surprise. They were riding into terrain that Vish had already warned them was perfectly suited to set up an ambush. And they did not, Ama told herself sadly, have her.

Quickly she dressed, then moved through the halls without obvious haste, not wanting anyone to ask her why she wasn't with Paulus. Everyone was used to seeing the two of them paired everywhere they went. It felt odd and wrong to move through the palace alone, as if she were half-naked, or suddenly missing a limb.

She had just one more chance, she decided. If she'd been the praying kind, she would have muttered prayers under her breath as she wound through the palace and out across the grounds. Instead she invoked the god that Paximites so often swore by, more apt than ever before. *Panic. Panic. Panic.*

Ama didn't bother with the main stables; there was only one horse fast enough to catch up with men who had several hours' lead. They would have taken enough of the regular mounts to transport however many of the King's Elite had jumped at the chance to accompany the kingling. Ama suspected they might have released the other horses, too, driven them off into the nearby fields beyond the fence to make it harder for anyone else from Ursu to follow. But those mounts didn't matter. Only Philomel did, and the golden Sestian mare had her own stable, kept separate from all the others. That was where Ama rushed.

But when Ama planted her feet on the echoing planks of the small stable, she saw exactly what she feared she'd see. Philomel's stall stood empty, her tack missing from the wall. The last green leaf of hope died on the vine.

The reality hit Ama then, cold and hard, unmistakable. If Paulus had gone to fight Tamura without her, she thought as she clutched the wall to keep from swaying, he was never coming back.

23

FALLING AND RISING

Approaching Hayk, Paxim
Tamura, Dree

All was in readiness. Tamura was unafraid as her small force passed through the narrow valley, clusters of trees on the hillside reminding her of the Scorpican wildlands she missed so much. The color was right, though the smell would never be the same. She had closed her eyes once to sniff the air, hoping to let it transport her back home, but the wrongness of the scent—too much birch, not enough pine—drew her immediately back. The shock of it was almost physical. Now she didn't close her eyes anymore.

Dozens of Scorpicae moved forward, steady and uncomplaining, through the day's gathering heat. They'd sent the ponies around the long way to Hayk with the rest of their force, given the pinched neck of this valley, the rough rock underfoot. The deep V of the valley blotted out any noise or shape from the world beyond. Here, besides the clank of Scorpican armor and the whisper of their sandals on the ground, all the women could hear was the call-and-response of merry birds hidden among those clusters of thick-trunked trees.

Tamura had forbidden conversation to keep everyone alert, but her mind was already fixed ahead, on Hayk. She didn't think much of her enemy's chances. Her spies had watched the Paximite army's training camps, and from their reports, the quality of the soldiers was wildly uneven. Whole swaths of their fighting force seemed to be no more than men and boys at play; there was one all-male army unit called the Swans that apparently was almost as good as an all-female unit, but they couldn't be everywhere at once. At last report these Swans had been stationed near the capital, where Tamura had no intention of going. If there was to be a reckoning with Queen Heliane, the Paximite queen was the one who would have to approach. In the meantime, Tamura would take Hayk and make it her own.

That meant taking and keeping it, and stripping it of the supplies that Tamura's army needed. Grain, swords, water barrels. A thirsty army might fight to the last breath but would be unable to find the one more breath beyond the last one that could decide a close, scrapping fight. None of the women walking today thirsted. They were ready in every way. So perhaps they would be ambushed along their route, but that did not concern their queen. She was confident in her nation's superiority. On a level field, all else equal, a column of Scorpicae could beat a challenge from a Paximite army twice their size.

Except this narrow valley was not a level field, and when two wedges of heavily armed Paximites suddenly appeared before and behind them, all else was not equal.

"Halt!" a voice called from ahead of them, and the army stood in their path. They had been waiting, still and silent, as the Scorpican column approached.

Eighty strong for certain. Women and men, well-armed and well-armored, with a man at their head whose magnificent helm glinted in the sunlight. Something was different about the warriors who stood immediately behind and beside him, as if they were a separate unit within the larger group. Men at the point of the arrow, though the rest of the wedge was mixed. The queen of the Scorpicae noted their positions, evaluated their strengths, sized them up, all within the first few seconds they lay within her sights.

Tamura raised her hand to halt the column behind her, and they drew close without needing to be told to, erasing the spaces between their bodies and raising shields as tight as shingles along both sides of their position.

"Tamura of Scorpica," called the Paximite leader, voice bouncing against the rocks until its echo buried itself in the thickly leaved branches of the trees lining the valley. "We demand you halt your attacks and present yourself for justice. If your troops swear to leave our land, we'll escort you to the capital to stand trial. Do you surrender?"

Tamura looked at the man, tilting her head, considering him for a long moment.

"Answer me!" he shouted. "Paxim demands your surrender."

She nodded to show she'd heard him, the amber scales of her helm bobbing, but said nothing. It would dignify the request to speak aloud. She raised her palm and lifted it high, turning it in one direction and then another like a paddle.

Even under his helm she could tell the man was grinning. The thick black horsetail atop the helm cascaded down, easy to see from a distance, but it would be a drawback close up. Any enemy worth her salt would seize it in close combat, putting her in an excellent position to take the man's head right off. It wasn't always a good thing, to be visible.

Grinning like a fool, he planted his feet. He indicated the rest of the group around him with a proud gesture, as if he'd produced them himself, by magic.

But he was human and so were they, Tamura told herself. She knew how to deal with humans.

Tamura lifted one finger and crooked it downward, and her archers in the trees let fly.

She wasn't a cruel woman, she told herself, but today she watched the Paximite soldiers' expressions swing from confidence to terror as the wave of arrows soared and crested over them, casting shadows as they came. When the arrows struck vulnerable places—eyes, throats—the screams were short. Sometimes they struck in arms or legs instead, anywhere not covered by armor, and then the screams went on longer, howls of pain rising and stretching out across the valley.

After the first wave of arrows there was a pause, but not because there had to be. Scorpican archers could have a second arrow on the string long before the first one landed. They paused because it was part of the plan.

Half the Scorpicae turned, well-trained, to face the half of the Paximite army that had attempted to cut them off from retreat. Little did the Paximites know Scorpicae did not retreat; they would have done better to put all their troops in one place. Not that it would have mattered as the arrows rained down from above. There were only a dozen Scorpican archers in the trees, but all twelve of the arrows in the first rain had found flesh. Now a second rain came, all focused on the soldiers of Paxim who stood in the westmost clump, and this time a few arrows bounced off armor but even more found soft targets: the ear of a woman who'd lost her helm, the hip of a man who was only mailed to the waist.

Tamura faced toward the east but her army on both fronts obeyed her call when she screamed, *"Kii-yah,"* the signal for the next phase of battle to begin.

As the archers found their new positions, the battle joined in earnest, footsoldiers of both armies rushing forward to make their stand. The air rang with staves and swords clashing, swinging, striking. Though the Paximites were more heavily armored, the Scorpicae moved more quickly. A bare thigh or upper arm mattered little if the opponent's sword couldn't reach far enough to strike where they were softest. Warriors did fall, but when they fell, most took two or even three of the enemy with them.

Through it all, Tamura kept her eyes on their leader, waiting. Leading her people didn't always mean standing at the front of a wedge in battle. She had plans, contingencies. The leader of the Paximites held back, so Tamura did too.

But when the man in the horsetail helm surged forward, sword drawn, it was Tamura who stepped up to meet him.

The grin had faltered as he watched his countrywomen and countrymen slain, replaced with a grim expression of resolve. His grip on his sword was sure. Tamura raised her shield to block his first swing, but he was clever; instead of swinging at her middle, he adjusted the swing mid-stroke and hit her on the side of the leg, clanging just at the top of her greaves and skidding the side of the metal blade against her knee. The wound stung. First blood was his.

Tamura ignored the pain, tossed away her shield so she could move more quickly, and dueled him in earnest.

He'd been well-trained, she'd give him that. For every jab he had a parry; for every thrust he knew just how far to dance away. She considered continuing the dance, just spinning and sidestepping, until she wore him down. He was a worthy enough fighter that she had to consider that option. But she knew she was more tired than he; she could feel the day's travel in her legs, and she was willing to bet he'd ridden and not walked at least some of the day. Despite her strength, she had limits, and they would slow her down just enough to give him an opening. She couldn't afford a mistake.

She could kill him immediately, of course; all she had to do was signal to the archers in the trees. They'd fire until fletched feathers stuck out all over his body like branches of the Orphan Tree. But she wanted to take him down herself. Whoever he was, he was obviously one of Paxim's best. She wanted to send a clear message that she, Tamura, wasn't afraid to fight, and when she fought, she fought to win.

The battle continued around them, her fellow Scorpicae fighting their own matches while protecting Tamura from further intrusions. She had time to make her decision. So she decided.

She shifted her feet, almost dancing backward, moving slowly toward her discarded shield. The Paximite with the horsetail helm watched her with eager eyes, seeing something that looked a great deal like a retreat. He was too smart to follow closely, but he followed.

Tamura got her toe under the shield, watching for his reaction. He was trying to predict her next move. He raised his sword, ready to swipe at her if she bent to retrieve the shield, which it looked like she was about to do.

She squatted an inch or two, hand still outstretched, wary but still watching him. He readied his sword.

Then she lowered herself another handspan, stretching the fingers of her right hand toward the shield's edge. She balanced, suspended. And as she leaned forward, appearing to put all her weight on her front foot, her opponent let loose a mighty swing.

As soon as his sword was singing through the air with all the force of his body behind it, too late to stop, Tamura paused. Then she lifted her front foot—the back still bore her weight, she had never shifted fully to reach—and flipped the shield toward him, where it crashed into his armored calves with a resounding clang.

The Paximite's sword continued through the air, meeting no resistance. Though he tried in vain to slow his swing, it was too late. His entire body twisted as the heavy sword swung past Tamura.

As he did, a handspan of bare skin was exposed between his mail shirt and the belt of his leggings. That was where Tamara jabbed her sword.

The point of her blade sank without resistance into the soft flesh of his side, thrusting through the meat of him until it tapped hard against his mail shirt from the inside.

The Paximite in the horsehair helm gasped and fell, impaled on the sword, dragging her toward the ground with him. As much as the weight of his falling body hurt her twisting wrist, she did not let go. The Paximite fell face-first on the ground. Tamura bent to one knee, keeping her hand on the hilt of the sword, feeling for movement. She counted beats in her head. *One. Two. Three. Four. Five.*

She checked for movement again. None came.

The fighting around them began to slow as the Scorpicae brought down more and more of their opponents, body after body hitting the ground and failing to rise again.

In the moment of relative quiet, she heard a name.

"Paulus," cried a short, barrel-chested man with a hunched back and one raised shoulder, just before Zalma's flat-faced hammer landed in the center of his back. The impact flung the Paximite soldier forward like a child's toy, dropping him, hard and sudden, to the ground. Like the man whose name he'd called, he did not rise again.

Paulus.

When Tamura realized who it was that she'd struck down, horror and joy twining within her forced out a high, strangled laugh. No wonder this Paximite had worn the decorated helm with the long black horsetail, clearly meant to demonstrate his importance. No wonder he had charged her with such confidence, such command. Her laugh was a cackle and a gasp of disbelief.

And he was certainly dead. She checked to be sure. She unbuckled the chin strap of the horsetail helm as gently as she would have stroked the cheek of her granddaughter Madazur. As she pulled off the helm, his last breath escaped with it, almost as if the pomp of it had been the only thing anchoring his soul to his body. The wound in his side gave one more gout of blood and then it only oozed. The heart was no longer pumping. The eyes were open, staring up past the overhanging green trees of the valley, gazing unseeing toward the narrow band of blue sky.

She had killed the kingling of Paxim without even meaning to. Before this, Tamura had slain first a queen and then a mad sorcerer who'd wanted to be queen of the entire world, one with a shield, one with her bare hands. Now she'd slain a future king. Well, not a future king anymore, she supposed. Not a future anything. His death would break the Fading Queen's fragile heart.

If she wasn't meant to wage war on Paxim, thought Tamura, the gods had a strange way of showing it. This was a sign, she realized. Push on. Harder. Stronger. Paxim would need a ruler; why not her?

The arrows continued to fall until every one of the Paximite soldiers lay silent and bloody on the ground, from the fiercely armored women who'd ridden at the back of the column to the man with the crooked shoulders who'd shouted Paulus's name. The valley that had smelled so green now stank of blood. Scorpican soldiers lay dead among the enemy, and Tamura paused long enough to command her warriors to evaluate whether any of the fallen Scorpicae were in fact alive. As for the soldiers from Paxim, she did not bother with an inspection. If they weren't dead now, they would be soon. Miles from home, arrows clean through them, the flapping wings of vultures already audible. That reek of blood, though. It reminded her there was one thing left to do.

Tamura raised her wet sword, the kingling's blood now so thick it dripped only slowly, reluctantly, onto the thirsty ground. She shook a few more drops from the blade, then raised the sword high overhead, letting loose a piercing whistle. Her troops turned at the sound, whoops of joy dying on their lips. They fell silent, waiting on her words.

"The Scorpion drinks the blood of the defeated," Tamura said. "The fight is done."

The Scorpicae cheered.

"And now, the city," she called, and pointed toward the other end of the narrow valley, toward Hayk.

After the ambush in which she slew the kingling, the battle for Hayk itself felt anticlimactic. The smaller Scorpican force reunited with the larger one, and they charged into the city just as planned. They commandeered houses, rounded up residents and herded them at sword point to new quarters, built barricades and assigned guards to protect the town from any attackers. Afterward, they commanded the villagers to cart off the dead, both from the valley outside the city and from the city itself, before the bodies could begin to stink. Tamura realized she didn't know how Paximites dealt with their dead—did they bury them, like Arcans, or burn them, like Sestians? She would find out, she realized, in the coming days.

Hayk defeated, victory whipping their spirits to a frenzy, her warriors sang out their joy.

Though the Drought of Girls had been an appalling disaster, Tamura was not above taking lessons from the sorcerer who had invented it: time can be both your worst enemy and your most powerful ally. Give a bad situation time to get worse and people will turn on each other. So let the news of Paulus's death roil the country. Let uncertainty mount. Let the infighting—because of course there would be infighting, all these braid-crowned senators at each other's throats—do half the work of destroying the country from within. And if Paxim weakened, so did the Five Queendoms.

Paxim was the crux of it all, the sole diplomat. If Paxim wasn't there to broker peace, there wouldn't be peace until the strongest nation desired it, and Scorpica was without question the strongest nation. Sestia was all religion and resources; the Scorpicae could ride across it and scoop up anything and everything they wanted while farmers and shepherds wept and the priests in their palace-temple prayed in vain. Arca, they'd already chosen to ignore. Now that she knew most of the magicians there lacked the skills of Sessadon and Mirrida, abandon them to their hostile, useless sands.

So that left only the Bastion standing between the current land of Scorpica and the rest of the world, and Scorpica could exist both above and below the Bastion. And if the Bastion didn't like it, well, they could be next. Tamura knew the stone walls of the Bastion would present a challenge, and indeed she had no idea how they could bring the Bastion to heel—but one day ago she would not have imagined slaying the kingling of Paxim at sword point in a shaded green valley.

If the gods wished for her victory, victory would come. And if they did not wish it, why did they keep giving Tamura everything she wanted before she even asked?

✦

Dree's second death was nothing like her first.

It was her own fault, dying in the first place. Dree had let that Arcan girl, the last of three gem-hunting sisters, get the better of her. That fateful morning, Dree had ridden toward the desert village of Jesephia with Azur foremost in her mind. It was time, thought Dree, to set aside her shyness and confess her feelings at last, *mokh* the consequences. She'd had no idea she'd die before she'd get the chance.

Even as the raid began, Dree was in her element. The villagers scattered before the invading Scorpicae like beetles. With satisfaction Dree watched the first sister die, then the second, and hadn't hesitated to dash after the third. She'd followed the fleeing magician underground, through the twisting tunnels, all the way to the wall of gems Dree sought, one of the most beautiful sights she'd seen in her whole life. She'd realized she'd been outsmarted only when the tunnel above her head began its collapse. Slow, then fast. Too late.

She'd had only that brief flash of awareness before the sand smothered her—had only a moment to think, *Oh, Azur, I should have told you*—and her first life ended.

In Dree's first few moments of death, she knew right away where she was. On the bridge to the Underlands. And she recognized the two faces nearest her, because they belonged to the two sisters she had seen die not long before her in Jesephia. But the third one, the one who had killed Dree, was not there.

Without words she asked the shades of the sisters—because she knew, with no doubt, they were all shades now—what had happened to their sister. They answered her, without words, that Gogo could breathe underground. No amount of earth could crush her; she would simply dig her way free, eventually. The chase had made sense, then. Too late to do Dree any good.

Then the sisters were gone and she was no longer on the bridge, she was in a vast and featureless room. The only other figure there, Dree had never seen before, but instantly recognized: Eresh, god of the Underlands.

"I know what you want," said the god without preamble.

What Dree wanted was Azur, but that was a who, not a what, so perhaps Eresh actually didn't know? But what the god said next settled any doubt.

Long fingers tapping against the arm of Her throne, Eresh said, "You want a second chance."

"Yes," answered the shade of Dree hungrily.

So the deal was settled. Eresh would send Dree up through a newly opened gate between worlds—She didn't mention how it had been opened, and Dree didn't ask—into a body Dree could use. In that body she was welcome to do whatever she liked, including finding Azur and declaring her love. And when that body died, whether it took hours or years, Dree's spirit would return to the bridge to the Underlands. Dree would tell Eresh all that she had learned. That was all the god asked, and Dree saw no reason not to seal the bargain with Her.

When Dree opened her eyes again she was alive again, Above.

Immediately she felt the difference; this body wasn't hers. There was much more of it, for one thing, arms uncomfortably long, the whole thing surprisingly heavy. Eresh hadn't told her how the body had been chosen. Dree only hoped its previous inhabitant had already been dead.

The new body didn't respond to commands as quickly as the old. In life she'd been a powerful warrior, fast as a fox in the night. Was this body frustratingly slow because the warrior who'd worn this body before had never been as talented as Dree, or would Dree be able to overcome the differences with time? Time might be something she didn't have.

As she came walking into the new Scorpican camp—easily found by the sounds of life ringing out over the lonely red dirt of Godsbones— she noticed a buzz of activity at the river's edge. She was just trying to decide whether to move toward the cluster of Scorpicae or away when a shape separated herself from the crowd, beckoning.

"Olan! There you are!" called a warrior who looked somewhat familiar, though Dree didn't know her name. "The column's waiting. Hurry."

Dree in the body of Olan opened her mouth to tell the other warrior that Olan wasn't her name, but somehow, she couldn't. She tried to open her lips, to speak the truth, but no words would come.

The other warrior made a grunt of disapproval. "I know you didn't want to join this battle. But that doesn't matter. An order's an order, isn't it?"

Dree managed to nod her body's head in assent. She was, after all, still a Scorpican. The blood running in these veins was still Scorpican blood. So Dree followed the other warrior, who slapped the hilt of a dagger into her hand and pointed toward a gap between two other warriors, clearly readying themselves to march. Dree in the body of Olan fell in line.

Only as they were already underway, at a distance, did Dree spot Azur, so striking even from afar that it stole Dree's breath from her borrowed body. How strange. How wonderful.

You want a second chance, Eresh had said, and oh, how Dree did. To confess. To unburden herself and see what came of it. To make it clear that what she felt for Azur was not only lust, not only hunger, but so much more.

But the moment was gone before she could act. Dree's—Olan's— column of warriors was already on the move, leaving camp, headed for an unknown battlefield. The First Mother stood by a cook fire with her baby girl in one arm, half-heartedly stirring a pot with the other, talking with one of the older warriors in a voice too soft to hear at this distance. With her disobedient new mouth, Dree couldn't call out to her, and this didn't seem an auspicious moment. She had come all this way for Azur, back from death itself. She would return to her once the battle was over. Dree would do her duty first.

She muttered a prayer inside her head, since the lips of her body would not obey her desire to speak it aloud—*Scorpion, watch over us as we ride into battle, may the glory be ours if You will so*—and they were off.

The battle itself, her smaller force joining up with the bulk of the Scorpican army at a village called Hayk, was like nothing Dree had ever seen in her first life. She'd raided, yes, scrapping and darting among far-flung desert villages, but this was a true battle. The Scorpicae were massed in a large force, making use of strategies she'd only practiced back on the training fields of Scorpica. It felt like a lifetime ago, Dree realized, because it was.

It was her own fault she had only this body, Olan's body, to fight with, but that didn't mean she couldn't make the best of it. Even if her too-long arms would not respond the way her old ones did, so ready and strong, she could still wield a weapon and cut the enemy down like dried reeds along a riverbank.

After the battle, as they settled into the town they'd won, warriors lay down their bedrolls in great circles inside the line the watch had established. Dree in the body of Olan pretended to comply, but inside, her shocked mind raced. Why were they not riding back to Godsbones immediately? In the Scorpion's name, they had defeated the enemy; why would they stay? No. Azur was in Godsbones. Dree, whichever body she wore, needed to be in Godsbones. She wouldn't stay here another minute.

Only she was so cold. Were the dead always cold like this? She stopped to swipe a thick cloak from the body of a dead enemy. There was a deep rip in the back, framed in dark red, that she didn't notice until she'd left the body behind. But all told, she'd do better with the cloak than without it, so she fastened the thick pin at the shoulder and enjoyed how its folds began to warm her arms immediately.

Not even the walk back to Godsbones deterred Dree. She would walk across the entire queendom, across all five queendoms, if she needed to. Then she would confess her feelings to Azur, press her lips against those lips, and swear to spend the rest of this second life making Azur as happy as she could.

When she approached the Scorpican camp at last, daybreak not yet touching the horizon, Dree in the body of Olan forced herself not to run. She slowed as much as she could, but her pace was still hurried and restless. The watch let her go by, recognizing a fellow warrior, and didn't hail her to talk. Things might have ended quite differently if they had.

Had she been seeking just any warrior, Dree would have been forced to walk between row after row of bedrolls in the caves. But she remembered that back in the caldera, the First Mother had been housed in a special tent marked with a triangular amber pennant. She would search first for that flag. And when she found it, Dree in the body of Olan, still wrapped in the warming Paximite cloak, slipped in through the tent flap and beheld, in wonder, the sleeping woman she had come all this way to find.

Azur lay on rumpled blankets, the shift she wore in sleep clinging everywhere, rucked up on one side all the way to her rounded hip. Dree had only ever clutched that hip one sweet afternoon in a rain-drenched cave, cupped it in her hungry palm, but she would never forget the feel of it. All reason vanished from her mind. She was here now. She would hold Azur again.

Dree lowered herself onto the blankets, settling next to Azur, not knowing what would come next. The baby must be in another tent; it was just the two of them here, alone. Dree reveled in Azur's smell, the exact musk she remembered from the cave, those stolen moments on that rainy day when she'd first fallen in love with Azur. And here they were again, reunited. Dree could not believe her luck.

She was with Azur at last, nestled against her. She lowered her hand onto the curve of Azur's hip, cupping it, and everything about the moment felt right.

Then she felt Azur start awake and turn, a quick, angry movement, and heard her whisper, "Who—what?"

Dree pressed harder with her hand than she meant to. She'd meant to push away from the former lover, who, it was now clear, didn't know her. How could Dree have forgotten the body she wore wasn't hers? She opened her mouth to explain, to apologize, but only a grunt came on stinking breath. Olan's body wouldn't obey. Panic rose in her like a tide.

"Enemy!" Azur gasped, her voice frightened at first, and then louder, angrier. "Enemy!"

Dree tried to push away from Azur but couldn't find leverage, and all around her flapped the Paximite cloak, hampering her even as it warmed. Error stacked on error, she realized. She shouldn't have done this; she didn't know what she should have done instead, but it didn't matter. None of the mistakes she'd made could be undone.

"No!" shouted Azur, and then there was a warmth under Dree's borrowed ribs, a warmth she had never felt before. She knew what it was, of course. Blood meeting air.

At her first death Dree remembered no blood; the collapsing mine had crushed the last breath out of her in the space between heartbeats. The end had come fast. This time she lingered.

This time Dree felt the blood gushing out of the fresh wound in her soft flesh, Olan's soft flesh. She saw the wet red knife in Azur's hand. Azur, the woman she'd loved from afar, killing her. The woman she'd longed for who didn't understand who Dree was, and perhaps, even during that first life, never had.

"It can't—you can't be . . . ," Azur said, wonder and terror in her voice. *"Olan?"*

Dree tried to shake the head, but the body that had only sometimes obeyed her was completely beyond her control now.

Then Dree's shade was on the bridge again, past all five gates of the underworld in a blink, this time alone.

No, not alone.

She was the only figure in the center of the bridge, but another figure was nearing her. A small one, smaller than a full-grown adult, at least she thought so from where she was. Blurred around its edges. She blinked what would have been her eyes if she'd had eyes. Then the figure resolved.

It was the Child.

"Come," said the Child, reaching out a small, delicate hand. The rounded features of its face were neither friendly nor unkind, but somehow its slender form conveyed a sense of welcome. "Let me show you where to go."

Yes, she was a shade once more, Dree realized. Free of the borrowed body she'd inhabited for her second, short life aboveground. Well and truly dead.

Dree had no body to clutch at in despair, no eyes to weep with, so she wept in the way only a shade could weep, overcome by longing, confusion, regret. She owed the god a report of what had happened Above, she knew. She should follow the Child. But there was no bottom to the well of Dree's sadness.

Why rush, for a god? What could time mean to Her? So Dree would cry a while longer, before the report, before the rest of it, whatever came after.

24

A DUTY

Ursu, Paxim
Nebez, Ama, Vishala

Nebez would never know the name of the woman who saved him after the bloody, disastrous battle of Hayk. The Scorpican warriors had waded through the wedge of King's Elite that had followed Paulus, such as it was, with so little difficulty it was laughable. Only none of his compatriots were left to laugh. When the Scorpicae had shouted with joy in the bloodied valley, declared that they were occupying the city, dispatched messengers to spread the word that Paximites who wished to join their army could find them here in Hayk, only silence answered their shouts. Bodies could not speak. Nebez had not been entirely sure he was still alive, and when he realized he was, he wasn't so sure he wanted to be.

Nebez had taken a fierce hammer blow in the battle's heat, and only two things kept him from certain death. The first was the buckled harness of thick leather he wore under his tunic to flatten his chest and keep his malformed shoulder blade from growing further out of alignment. He'd never intended it as defense, but it had absorbed and dispersed much of the strength of the blow, which might otherwise have snapped his spine. The second thing that saved his life was a stranger's vigilance. When the Paximites remaining in Hayk, which had quickly surrendered, had been ordered to cart off the dead, one of the women lifting his limp form had recognized that he was still breathing but did not give him away. This was the woman he would always be grateful to, and never be able to thank.

Once darkness fell and Nebez found himself, with some surprise, still breathing, the woman returned with a pack of food and drink and half carried, half dragged him to a cave on the town's outskirts.

"I can do no more," she said, her dark eyes darting, as if she would put herself at further risk by looking him in the face. "But perhaps the All-Mother will bless you. One never knows Her ways." Then she left him, walking backward and erasing their footprints in the dirt as she went.

In the following days, pain was Nebez's only companion. The deep, deep bruise purpled the visible parts of his torso from armpit to hipbone, darkening almost to black at the edges where the blood pooled. But Nebez was no stranger to pain. His misshapen back and shoulder, the twisting deformity that had complicated his birth and everything after, had been his lifelong companions. His ability to persist, like the layered leather binding that had redistributed the force of the hammer blow, was essential to his survival after Hayk. He had reshaped this body before, a body that others had once seen as a girl's but Nebez had always known belonged to a boy, then a man. His mother had gently but repeatedly asked whether he might see himself as both male and female, the kind of person Paximites called two-fold, but Nebez had never wavered. He was a man. Men in his situation in Arca could seek out magic, but he had to make do with frequent infusions of winter cherry and a rare strain of cohosh, which over time brought his appearance more in line with his reality. Even now a precious packet of dried herbs rested safely inside under his harness, next to his heart. His body hadn't always been a friend to him, but it was the only one he had, and it had kept him alive so far. As he watched a second day dawn from inside his haven, he was certain they would pull through this darkness together.

After he felt strong enough—three days after the battle? Four?—Nebez crept from the cave, watching carefully for enemies around every corner. For the first few leagues, he crawled. Once he estimated that the town's outer border lay two leagues behind him, he stood, his body protesting. He stretched to test his limits, feeling his way back to awareness of each muscle, each limb. Then he began the long, solitary walk back to Ursu. He might not make it, but he at least he wouldn't die in that occupied town, buried forever among dead friends and enemies. Even if he could reach the queen, he wouldn't be a welcome messenger. But he would not shirk his duty.

Two days into his journey, the All-Mother smiled on Nebez once more. He'd decided to follow the river, sacrificing a bit of speed for the certainty of knowing he wouldn't get lost along the way. One afternoon, as he crested a hill, he spotted a magnificent mare drinking at the water's edge. She was the unmistakable gold of a wheat field in sunlight. This could be no horse but Philomel, who Paulus had ridden mere days before, excited and confident, toward Hayk.

Nebez tried to make his voice sound as much like Paulus's as he could, though the effort made his eyes sting with unshed tears. The white-gold horse perked her ears up at the sound. Nebez murmured, cajoled, lightly beckoned; at last, wary but convinced, the horse let herself be caught and ridden. The two of them made their way back to Ursu.

Along the way Nebez came to terms with what he had to do. He absolutely did not want to be the bearer of this news, the worst he could possibly bring to the queen; yet without him, who would do the terrible work? He doubted anyone else had survived to bring back the tidings. Nebez had had the courage to leave Ursu with the kingling; he'd force himself to summon the courage to return without him.

When Nebez rode Philomel into Ursu, before he approached the palace, he stopped first at the small stable to return the horse to her stall. Once the bad news had broken, no one would think of her. As he curried the mare with long, soothing strokes, trying to ease his own soul along with hers, he could have sworn he heard a rustle in the hayloft. After a long silence he decided he must be paranoid, expecting at every turn the Scorpican enemies he'd left far behind. At long last he squared Philomel away in her stall with abundant hay and corn, and murmured his thanks one final time.

"I'm sorry for your loss," he said to her with a gentle hand on her mane, a way of practicing the condolences he would have to give over and over again.

When Nebez presented himself at the palace gate, face and hands clean but tunic still stained with someone else's blood, they knew right away to usher him into the queen's presence. He didn't feel ready when he saw her, but he would never feel ready. Not for this.

Heliane was gowned and adorned as regally as ever, long white hair plaited neatly behind her. But when he looked closer, he saw the deep shadows under her sleepless eyes. She rose all in a rush, no hesitation, and asked, "Well, soldier? Share your news."

"Queen . . . I . . ." He couldn't catch his breath.

The air itself was alive with fear. The words that came next, when they came, would change everything.

The queen's eyes raked him: the blood, his obvious exhaustion. "Alive or dead, fool?" she shouted. "Don't stand there dumb as a cock, anything else can wait! Is my son alive or dead?"

Nebez could put it off no longer. "I'm sorry," he whispered.

Heliane fell, and no one was close enough to catch her.

In the hubbub, Nebez looked around. He spotted an improbable figure behind him, recognized her instantly: Ama, who had chosen and trained him for the King's Elite, but hadn't ridden with them to Hayk because Paulus had insisted on leaving her behind. At the time, Nebez had followed Paulus blindly, believing his kingling knew right. But now Nebez wished he'd done anything else. How different things would have been if he'd insisted on telling Ama the kingling's plans. The kingling never would have faced Tamura; the Scorpican queen's blade would never have pierced Paulus through. Nebez saw it all clearly now, sick with regret.

As the chaos around the queen intensified and Nebez himself was ignored, Ama neared Nebez and spoke to him quickly, quietly. "How?" she asked.

Nebez answered her honestly. "In battle. Our ambush went wrong. The Scorpican queen slew him with her own sword."

The change that came over Ama's face was awful to see, and Nebez recognized in her his own regrets multiplied. Her only job was to protect Paulus and she had failed. She, too, would have given anything to go back in time. She, too, wished the impossible.

Now Ama was walking toward the fallen queen, who had revived enough to open her eyes. The queen murmured something to the attendants around her and they hauled her up to a sitting position, bracing her in place with their own bodies. Whether the queen had heard him explain who killed Paulus, Nebez didn't know. Heliane's eyes settled on the approaching young woman, and Nebez was taken aback at just how much hatred burned in the queen's gaze.

Ama only stared at the queen for a long moment and silently lowered her head.

Heliane whispered to her attendants again and they shifted, rising, as one creature; they bore her up so she could stand. The queen's voice was surprisingly strong when she said to Ama, "You. Get out."

In a quieter voice, calm as a cloudless sky, Ama said, "If you choose to kill me, I won't fight you."

The long moment of tension when neither woman moved seemed to stretch on into eternity, and Nebez knew he was not the only one holding his breath, worrying, waiting.

✦

The first blow was the queen's open hand, catching Ama across the cheek, hard upon the old injury that had been fresh when she first arrived at the palace. Ama barely had time to register the sting when another blow came, this one from a closed fist. Same hand, same side, higher up, knuckles against her temple.

Then the blows began to rain down hard, so fast upon each other there was no discerning one from the next.

Wringing herself free of the attendants who had been holding her up, staggering forward but not letting herself fall, the queen seemed to stay upright powered by pure rage. Ama could have moved away at any moment. Instead, she remained.

The queen's fists struck every part of Ama's face, eye sockets to ears, then ranged wider, punching her hard in the breast, the stomach, the throat. That made it hard to breathe. But did she deserve to breathe? Ama asked herself. She had let Paulus seduce her into a deep sleep and he had stubbornly escaped, fought, died. She'd failed in her mission. The physical pain of the queen's surprisingly persistent, sharp blows was no more than Ama deserved, and possibly far less.

The fists came, at last, to a halt. No one had stopped the queen; no one would dare. It appeared that she had stopped herself. After a few moments of hearing the queen's ragged breathing, Ama decided to try opening her eyes. The right one was fine, but the left came slowly, already swelling from where the queen's knuckles had struck. The expression on the queen's face was unreadable. There was anger, yes, but something else, too, and with her swimming vision Ama could not tell exactly what it was.

Then the queen planted her feet, panting. She swayed once, planted her feet again, and remained upright. A long moment passed. It seemed to Ama that the queen was either considering her next move or trying desperately to keep herself from pitching forward again.

Then Queen Heliane, eyes still blazing, reached down to her belt with steady fingers. In one unbroken motion, she drew her knife.

It took all Ama had not to move then. The queen really might kill her. Had Ama meant it, she asked herself, when she said she was willing to die? But living was the only way to guarantee that Tamura would pay.

But the decision wasn't Ama's, she decided. She placed it in the hands of her dead lover's mother, the queen of the nation, who had trusted Ama with her heart and her future and seen both dashed when Ama failed.

So Ama dropped her limp hands to her sides, fell to her knees on the throne room's gold-and-white mosaic. She didn't beg. She didn't even speak. But she hoped to break the spell, to bring the queen back to herself. To show her that she posed no threat. If Heliane wanted to kill her, at least let it be a murder, a merciless execution. Let everyone see. Ama wasn't sure the queen, as far gone as she was in her misery, had forgotten herself wholly enough to slay a woman on her knees.

And Heliane's first touch was surprisingly tender. She curled her fingers under Ama's chin, tilted her head gently to the right. Then she took the tip of her belt knife and cut in a sharp, controlled line, splitting the skin open along the scar on Ama's cheekbone. After the initial sting Ama barely felt the pain. Later, she knew from experience, it would throb day and night. Right now she only turned her eyes upward to the queen's, letting the blood streak down her cheek to stain her skin, her tunic, the floor.

"Leave us, then, as you came." The queen's voice was a harsh rasp, all daggers and thorns. "Ama of nowhere, you are banished from Paxim lifelong."

367

There was nothing faded about the queen of Paxim then. Every inch of her was alive, but with the bright, hot fire of pure anger. Ama knew the queen was close to collapse. Once the anger was gone, there would be nothing else to hold Heliane together.

Ama breathed in and out. She let her gaze fall to Heliane's feet. The thick, dark blood from her cheek dripped close to the queen's slippered toes, a few gold tiles away, but did not touch them.

"Get OUT!" howled the queen.

Ama rose, stumbling, and was gone.

She fled, heart still hammering, hand covering the cut on her face, back to Philomel's stall. That was how she had known of Nebez's return; ever since Paulus rode away in the night, Ama had hidden in the stable, uncertain of her future or her place in the world. As there were no horses in that stable anymore, no one was there to see. Only Vish knew she was there, and snuck food to her, though Ama barely spoke anything beyond a word of thanks. Now Philomel was back in her familiar stall and Ama stood with her forehead pressing into the side of the horse's golden neck, her tears flowing freely.

"I'll avenge him," she whispered, her fists in the horse's long, pale mane.

She didn't hear anyone enter, but she hadn't been attentive; the first thing she heard was a sharp intake of breath, and when she turned, there was Vish.

"Your face," Vish said first, stammering in her husky whisper.

"It's nothing," said Ama.

"Who?"

"The queen," Ama replied tersely.

"Why?'

"He's dead."

Vish's voice trembled with sympathy. "I'm so—"

Ama cut her off. "She was right to do so. I am exiled. I must leave Paxim."

"Or make it seem as if you've left."

Ama stroked the horse's neck, showing no reaction.

Vish went on, "I've wandered almost every inch of Paxim. Three leagues north of the city there's a stone cottage, abandoned, with two dogwood trees in the front yard, one tall and old, one short and young. That's where I'll go."

Ama kept her focus on the horse. She knew what Vish was asking, but she couldn't answer, not yet.

Vish said, "I'm going tonight. You've been exiled, and there's no King's Elite without a king. I can't fight for a country you don't fight for. You are my country."

Ama looked at her then, hand stilling on the horse's mane, eyes spilling over with tears. She couldn't speak the words out loud, but she couldn't do what Vish was asking. She couldn't hide. She knew what she needed to do, and her actions would speak for her.

But even as she moved for the door Vish was, somehow, even faster. Vish slung her back against the closed stable door and held her hand out in warning.

"No, Amankha. No."

Ama's true name touched her heart through her wave of fear and anger, but she shoved away the tender sentiment, her voice harsh as she said, "I didn't ask your permission, *tishi*." She softened her tone a little to add, "The only man who's ever mattered to me is dead. Tamura will pay."

"Wait. Think. What if you could save thousands? Tens of thousands? A nation?"

Ama said, "Scorpica, you mean? The nation of Scorpica is not my responsibility."

"Not if you die today, no."

"I don't intend to die."

"Neither did Paulus," snapped Vishala.

The reality hit Ama just a little harder than she was ready for, and her body sagged. Quickly the older woman's arms surrounded her. Ama didn't relax into the embrace, but she let herself be held, because she felt like a bone statue in the heat of a fire, ready to fly apart at any moment.

After a long silence, Ama said, "You can't tell me not to avenge him."

"I'm not."

Ama raised her head to look at Vish, still angry, but with a note of curiosity alongside the anger.

Vish said, "Think what happens. If you could even find the Scorpican army right now. If you could even locate Tamura."

"I know exactly where she is. She's in Hayk. They occupied it."

"The *Scorpicae*?"

Ama's glare was fire.

"So unlike them," said Vish. "Why?"

"I don't know their *plan*," said Ama, her voice strained. "I've heard the same rumors as everyone. They're recruiting. They're letting themselves be found. Showing their strength. But I don't have to defeat the entire Scorpican army. Just Tamura."

Vish's eyes were troubled. "If you could even get close enough to fight her. And if you could, against all odds, slay her. Do you know what would happen?"

"Yes," answered Ama flatly. "She would be dead."

"So would you. Her warriors would avenge her on the spot. You'd be just as dead as both Paulus and Tamura."

"Yes," said Ama. "I have no aspirations otherwise."

"Don't you want to take your rightful place?"

"My place was with him," she said, her voice breaking this time.

"It was," Vish agreed gently. "But no longer. And I know nothing dulls that pain, not even time. I am no less angry at Tamura today than I was the day she killed your mother."

"Then tell me what you mean."

"I think you know. Avenge Paulus. Avenge Khara. But do it the right way."

"If you tell me to spare her, I'll draw my sword on you."

Vish's eyes narrowed at that, but she continued. "Take your rightful place as the ruler of Scorpica. Stop Tamura and end this war."

"I intend to."

"But to take her place, you must be a Scorpican."

"Am I not?"

"Not to them, not yet. To them you would be Ama of Paxim, former bodyguard to the kingling Paulus, not Amankha dha Khara, born to the queen of Scorpica and her rightful heir."

Ama's eyes began to burn, remembering what Heliane had called her. *Ama of nowhere.* But her mind leapt forward as she finally understood what Vish meant. "But the Scorpicae recruit. They'll adopt women of any age and make them warriors. So—if I let them make a warrior of me, I'll be just as Scorpican as anyone."

"It won't be a quick undertaking," cautioned Vish. "You need to make friends. To Challenge her, you need a second. Someone who will speak for you. Risk their own life for yours."

The seriousness of the task was beginning to sink in. "Once that's done, I speak the words."

Vish nodded. "Once you've spoken the Words of Challenge and your second has spoken for you, the queen may choose the weapons, and she may also choose the time and place of the clash."

"But she must fight me to the death, once the Challenge has been issued, correct?"

"Correct."

"So I'll go, become a Scorpican again, and claim my right to Challenge the queen for her crown."

"If you choose."

"I choose."

"Then the only thing to decide," said Vish, her voice hesitant, "is when you're leaving."

"Now," said Ama, her jaw set, her fingers tangled again in Philomel's white-gold mane. "I'm leaving now."

✦

After months in which Paulus had been no farther away than the distance a few long strides could cross, thought Ama, now he was forever beyond her reach.

He was gone and she was—what? Who? The loss of Paulus, the loss of her position, cut through Ama like a blade. She had to focus on her new purpose. She'd find and join the Scorpicae. She'd have her vengeance and stop this senseless war. Paxim had never belonged to her, nor she to it, nor had she really ever felt at home in the Bastion. She hoped Scorpica would be different. She feared it wouldn't. Perhaps she'd never feel at home anywhere but the one place she could never rest again: in the warm, forgiving shelter of Paulus's embrace.

Under cover of night, she saddled Philomel, who pawed and snorted but did not attempt to do her any serious harm. Once out in the cool night air, Ama felt the prickle of tears at the corners of her eyes, but she wouldn't stop for tears. She wouldn't stop for anything now. As they rode away from the palace, when she heard no shouts of outrage or chase, she spurred the horse to a gallop. If she was to leave all this behind, best to do so quickly.

But only a few leagues on, exhaustion overtook Ama, a tiredness deep in her bones. She leaned forward against Philomel's golden neck, feeling the mane whip her face with stinging force, and tried to fit her body to the horse's as they headed for the horizon. Her thighs stung with the effort of staying on Philomel's back, an unaccustomed ache in her hips and knees. Her eyes wanted desperately to close.

When dawn came, it woke her still on the horse. Philomel had stopped to crop some grass alongside a river. It was a miracle Ama hadn't slid off in the night. Knotting her hands into the horse's reins, she supposed, had kept her from tumbling to the ground. Philomel snorted and moved forward again, following the river, ambling forward through daylight under an overcast sky.

At last, groggy and overwhelmed, Ama had to call a halt. It was too dangerous to continue; if she fell with her hands in the reins and Philomel didn't stop, the horse might either trample or drag Ama, and the risk was too great. She found a grove of green-leafed oaks to hide them both, far enough off the road not to draw suspicion, but close enough that they could resume their journey quickly when she was ready. She was so tired. There was an unsettled feeling in her stomach, too, and it didn't go away when she drank water from a skin. It was when Ama leaned against a trunk, letting Philomel's reins slip from her hand, that she realized the reason she was so uncomfortable, so exhausted, and she wept.

Normally so attuned to her body, she'd lost track of herself—in this and so many ways—after Paulus had ridden off to his death. It hadn't occurred to her to think about the thickening in her waist. In the days when Paulus had been with her, he'd loved to place his hands on that waist, and she knew exactly how his hands felt curving on either side of it. She hadn't let those memories linger now that he was gone. But here, under this tree, she took stock, and she could not deny the only conclusion.

Ama was tired. She was thickening. Everything ached, from her shoulders to her breasts to her thighs, and not just where the queen's blows had landed. Her feet hurt not because she was unused to travel, but because they'd swollen inside her boots. Considered all together, it didn't take a midwife to recognize the signs. In the cradle of her aching hips, Ama carried a child.

She'd been wrong about Heliane the whole time. That was why she wept.

When Heliane gave her the tea, she'd told Ama it would prevent pregnancy. That, Ama realized now, had been a lie. Heliane had done it so that Ama wouldn't take other precautions. The queen hadn't been trying to keep Ama from conceiving. She'd wanted her to conceive.

Queen Heliane had wanted a child for Paulus. And now, when it was too late, that child would come.

She would sleep first, she decided, but once she was rested, she'd return to the capital. As willing as she was to risk her own death to finally defeat Tamura, Paulus's child couldn't suffer the same fate.

The tears streaking down her cheeks felt like a cleansing. When the rain began, she welcomed it. Philomel lowered her head under the falling droplets but Ama raised hers, turning her wet face up toward the sky, laughing and crying and wishing for all the world that she could tell Paulus, somehow, what they'd done.

I'll keep her safe for you, she told him in her mind's eye, and then cried more because she had no idea if it would be a boy or a girl or both or neither, and in any case, it was far too late to matter.

The rain had thinned to a drizzle by the time Ama spotted the vague outline of Ursu on the horizon. She'd had time to make a plan as she rode. She couldn't go into the city, and certainly not to the palace. It was too soon to put herself in Heliane's hands. There was only one person she trusted, only one place to go.

Ama circled the city, turned northward, and estimated the distance as they moved through the dusk. It wasn't dusk anymore by the time she found it, thin starlight showing the way in the surrounding dark. A stone cottage, solid, but with an air of long neglect. Two dogwoods in the front yard, one tall and gnarled and ancient-looking, one a mere sapling nearby, its sparse branches thin as fingers.

Sitting astride Philomel, Ama stared at the trees, thinking this must be the place, but suddenly struck with fear that it might not be. Then the door swung open, and a figure emerged, carrying a lamp. In the lamplight Ama caught the profile of the one face in the living world she most wanted to see.

"*Tishi* Vish," Ama called, her voice trembling, "I have news."

Vish reached out her arms in welcome.

◆

Everything she'd fought for, thought Heliane, was gone.

A week since she'd heard the news of Paulus's death and the palace was never quiet, yet it felt like the Underlands itself. Everyone around her seemed like shades. Or perhaps she was the shade, Heliane thought. But if she were dead, she'd at least be with her family. Here aboveground she was profoundly alone.

She should reach out to Ama, to apologize, lift her sentence. What happened hadn't been the young woman's fault. Heliane had heard the truth from one source and then another, every account agreeing in this one particular. Paulus had snuck out in the middle of the night to keep Ama from stopping him. That had been his death sentence. That kind man Nebez had made everything clear to Heliane, then fled the scene in obvious discomfort, but Heliane had sent her people to find him and bring him back again. She rewarded him for his bravery by putting him in charge of the remaining elite force, the hand-chosen fighters Ama had been assembling to protect Paulus. Heliane could do the same, find that girl and bring her back, and she wanted to. Even that strange, severe young woman would be welcome company for Heliane. Right now the Fading Queen had no one. Decima had been arrested, discredited, and dismissed; Paulus had joined his siblings and father in the Underlands; and only Heliane remained to die. Well, if she had time remaining to her aboveground, she would make the most of it.

Heliane tapped her quill against the parchment and breathed as deeply as she could, though it triggered a dry rattle in her chest.

She would write a letter, but not to Ama, not yet. Another one first. What she had to write wouldn't fill the hollow where her heart had been, but it might be her nation's only hope. The dream of handing her queendom down to her son was dead. But she could take one action, a drastic one, to protect and preserve the queendom. Someone had to stop the Scorpicae. Heliane couldn't do it herself. So she had to ask the one woman in the world who could.

She'd swallow her pride and write again. This time, she'd send a special messenger instead of trusting the official channels. Swear the runner to secrecy and promise great rewards for the task. A young woman this time, not one of the palace's usual boys, someone she could order to put the letter directly into the hands of no one but Queen Eminel. If the Arcan queen did not respond this time, well, all would be lost. All the more reason to try.

Heliane dipped the ceremonial quill and began to write, each scratch against the page echoing within her own hollow-feeling bones.

25

PLANS

Weeks later
Near and in Ursu, Paxim
Eminel, Stellari

The Grove of Peace, not far outside of the walls of Ursu, was one of the most beautiful places Eminel had ever seen.

Eminel knew there was a sacred grove in Sestia where the queens ate cherries before each Sun Rites, but she had never been there. She supposed in a few years, when the Sun Rites came again, she'd see that one for herself. If the world hadn't ended in the meantime. She hated that she needed to admit that possibility, but she couldn't shake it, the idea that things they'd always taken for granted were, in this strange new world, up for grabs.

This grove was sacred in a different way from the Sestian grove where the cherries grew, but they both shared one rule: no weapons were allowed. Eminel supposed that was why she had been summoned here instead of the palace or elsewhere in Ursu. She bore no blade or staff as she approached the grove, yet it wasn't really possible for her to enter unarmed in the strictest sense. After all, Eminel herself was a weapon. She'd traveled all this way with no entourage, no guard; secrecy and enormous potential were all the protection she had and all she needed.

She was powerful enough to imagine nearly anything now—all that life force from the former court at Daybreak Palace carried in her cuff and humming softly in her veins—but she couldn't imagine choosing to do someone harm in this grove. The only sound was the gentle sigh of a breeze in the aspen trees, which flicked and fluttered, showing the leaves' white undersides. Even tense with expectation, knowing how much was at stake, Eminel felt the grove's calming influence. She flexed both hands to stretch her fingers, curled and uncurled her toes inside her boots. She took in a deep breath, savoring the fresh, clean air, and readied herself.

Two tall women, one slender like a reed and the other boulder-solid, flanked the entrance to the shaded grove formed by two gracefully bent aspens. Between the trunks was darkness, but somehow, it was a welcoming darkness. Eminel sensed no enchantment here. For better or for worse, her feelings were genuine. She didn't even fear the guards. Whether they feared her, she couldn't say without delving into their minds, and she had no intention of committing such a violation. She would assume the best until she had evidence otherwise.

"Welcome, foreign queen," said one.

The other said, "Our queen awaits you."

"Thank you," Eminel said. With one step she stood between the guards, and with the next, she was inside.

Had she not been told to expect the queen of Paxim, Eminel would've taken the woman in the grove for a shade. She seemed insubstantial, gray. Especially surrounded by the heartbreakingly lovely, vivid colors of the grove—lush greens so intense Eminel's eyes began to ache—the woman's figure was like a pale brushstroke, easily dismissed as an artist's error.

But the woman moved and turned toward Eminel, showing herself to be human. No shade, no brushstroke, showed pain so clearly in every feature on her face. The ache Eminel saw there took her breath away.

Eminel wanted to speak first, but she didn't know how to start. Thank Queen Heliane for her hospitality? Ask her, without preamble, what matter had been so urgent that she'd summoned another nation's queen? There were rumors that the Scorpicae had attacked a full-size city in Paxim, but the palace had confirmed nothing; Eminel could hardly criticize Heliane's secrecy when she herself had forbidden spreading the word of the Scorpican attacks within her own borders. Unsure where to start, Eminel didn't start at all. She soaked up the calm feeling of the grove, somehow both warm and cool, and waited.

"My son is dead," began the queen.

The stark nature of her statement felt like a fist against Eminel's heart. Now, thought Eminel, she knew the source of the woman's pain. She knew the bottomlessness of it. "I am so sor—"

Heliane's hand cut through the air. "No. I do not want condolences. If I wanted someone to feel sorry for me, I have thousands of those here."

"As you wish," said Eminel, bobbing her head, then lifting it. In a firmer voice, she said, "I won't tell you I understand. I'm sure no one does."

Heliane looked away. "One woman does. But I'm not ready to talk to her yet. Soon, perhaps. But not now."

Eminel didn't know how to react to that. Heliane's words did not seem meant for her, though there was no one else here to hear them. Rumors in Arca said that the queen of Paxim had been destroyed by her treatment at the hands of Sessadon, but she didn't look destroyed to Eminel. Weak in body, yes, but she must still be strong in spirit. Heliane wouldn't have humbled herself to ask for the help of a foreign queen otherwise. A weak woman, faced with such a loss, would simply have waited to die.

What had she done instead? Eminel realized the only way to know was to ask. Raising her eyes to the queen's grief-stricken face, she said,

"Then please. Tell me what you do want. I will try to help."

"Try will not be enough. But I think you are more than capable of doing what I need." As limp and exhausted as the Paximite queen's body appeared to be, her gaze was fire.

"Which is?" asked Eminel.

"To defeat the Scorpicae," explained Heliane. "As you did in Arca. We know where they are; we have lulled them into arrogance. Ride at the head of my army and wipe them out."

Eminel took a moment to absorb this. The plea for help made sense now. Even if she had not let word of the battle at Velja's Navel travel through official channels, the unofficial ones had clearly done their work. She understood why the Paximite queen wanted her for this task; whether Eminel could or should do it, that was another matter. Driving an enemy from your own homeland in self-defense was different from chasing them from someone else's. And of course Eminel hadn't been the one to drive the Scorpicae from Arca, but there seemed little point in drawing that distinction. Even if this wasn't Eminel's fight, she felt the pull of it, the idea of wreaking havoc for the best reason in the world: because, as counterintuitive as it seemed, sometimes violence was the only path to peace.

So Eminel asked the only question remaining. "Do you want them defeated, or do you want them destroyed?"

Heliane looked down. Without her fiery gaze, she looked overwhelmed, even as she spoke harsh, demanding words. "What I want is my son back. But there, I know you cannot help me. Unless . . ."

Eminel knew what the Paximite queen was asking, and shook her head in response. "My magic does not reach into the Underlands."

"I thought not," said Heliane, pretending lightness. "To answer your question, do what needs doing. Defeat them soundly enough that they will leave us."

"And if they won't leave?"

"Kill every last one of them on our soil."

It was the answer Eminel had expected, but she needed the queen to say it aloud. Heliane hadn't even hesitated. Eminel nodded gravely.

Heliane tilted her head, evaluating. "I believe your powers stretch almost beyond my reckoning. Is that a fair assessment?"

Eminel considered. It wouldn't have been true the previous year, early in her reign, but it was true now. She'd learned to use the Talish cuff, to store life force there, to draw it off as needed to power her magic. With Beyda's help, she'd also studied a dizzying array of enchantments from the records at Daybreak Palace, spells to create and destroy, capture and crush, magnify and starve. Each one could be beckoned to her fingertips with the barest whisper. And her confidence made a difference too. Eminel knew now, without a doubt, that she was the most powerful sorcerer in the known world, and not just that, she had the god Velja on her side. Yes, Heliane was correct. The Paximite queen could not begin to understand the magnitude of Eminel's all-magic. "Yes, it's fair."

"Then let me know what you need and I will provide it."

Eminel thought. "You said you know where their force can be found?"

"I do. They have occupied a city called Hayk."

An ache blossomed in Eminel's chest, taking her by surprise. She recognized the name. It was the last place she had been with the Rovers, the last happy day, during a festival of masks. She'd been stolen from them by a Seeker. What happened in Hayk had set her on the path to Sessadon. No other city in Paxim, or anywhere else, stood out so vividly in her memory.

The sorcerer couldn't fully hide her pained reaction, and Heliane's brow lowered. "What is it?"

"Nothing," Eminel lied, and got back to the matter at hand. "What else do I need to know? Should I coordinate with your minister of war?"

"I'm not sure," Heliane admitted. "I no longer trust her completely; I think she might have allegiances beyond my interests and the country's."

"Introduce me to her," offered Eminel. "I will find out what we need to know."

"She won't talk to you."

"She won't need to."

For the first time, understanding Eminel's meaning instantly, the Fading Queen smiled. "Words cannot express how grateful I am for your assistance, Queen Eminel."

Eminel nodded. "The Scorpicae ran amok in our lands for too long. We'll prevent the same thing from happening here. Together, we'll further the cause of peace."

"And I would like our nations to be friends. When this is over. When we can work together to rebuild the peace we once enjoyed."

They grasped each other's forearms, making the promise solemn. Eminel knew she could have asked the queen of Paxim for anything and Heliane would have given it. But the truth was, there was nothing the queen of Arca needed. The idea that their two nations would be friends, that was enough for now.

It only later occurred to Eminel that she should have thought about whether Velja would want her to make this pact. But by the time that occurred to her, she'd already sworn assistance. Already made a solemn vow to Heliane. Already readied herself, grim joy swelling in her heart, for the attack.

The use of the grove had been a precaution; now that they'd made their agreement, Eminel was escorted back to the Paximite palace—unlike Daybreak Palace, it didn't seem to have a name—in the company of the queen. On the way, she could see the woman's strength fading moment by moment, but Heliane was still able to tell her what she needed to know.

After considering it on the way, Heliane told Eminel it was not yet time to meet with Faruzeh. They would not officially tell the minister of war that the Arcan queen was here, because technically, the minister of war could forbid the Paximite queen from carrying out her plan.

Heliane needed less than a day to gather the elite force that would travel with Eminel to Hayk, both to protect and assist her. Everything was already in motion. Eminel found something comforting about the idea of being surrounded by strength that differed from her own. Not a magical nest of vipers, like the Arcan court, but a band of sisters and brothers, shoulder to shoulder, united against a common enemy. A force that marshaled all their skills, all their abilities, to drive that enemy back from whence they'd come.

"But one person I will introduce you to," said Heliane, "and then I must rest."

Eminel was growing concerned at how fatigued the queen looked. Even one corner of her mouth seemed to be drooping, and she slurred her words just a touch, in a way that alarmed Eminel. She wanted to reach out and put her hand on the queen's shoulder and send a surge of magical energy into her to restore her. But it would be wrong to do it without asking, and if she asked, she knew exactly what Heliane would say. So instead Eminel said, "I'll be more than happy to meet her."

"Him," corrected Heliane, and looked toward the doorway. With perfect timing, an outline emerged.

The man who approached was short, thick-chested and clearly strong, moving with efficiency instead of grace. He would have stood out among the delicate men of the Arcan court, thought Eminel, like a hawk among sparrows. When he inclined his head in the suggestion of a bow and then raised his gaze to hers again, she noted his hunched back and crooked shoulder, but what struck her most deeply were his eyes.

"Queen Eminel," said Heliane, "may I present Nebez, the commander of our elite force. He will stand beside you to spearhead the attack on occupied Hayk."

There was something Eminel found instantly trustworthy in Nebez's gaze. It took her a moment to place. Nothing else about the two men was similar, but those eyes—the shape of them, the sun lines at the corners, the warm intensity—reminded her of Hermei's.

"I'm honored, Queen Eminel," he said, his voice sweeter and higher than she would have expected. She'd thought he would be gruff.

Eminel wasn't sure what she was supposed to say in response, but she was rescued from the need to respond by Heliane.

The Paximite queen said, "Please, use the room as long as you need it. Call for food and drink or anything else you might need. When you tire, Queen Eminel, the servants will show you to your bedchamber."

Eminel wanted to convey her gratitude to the other queen, but Heliane was gone before she could. Probably better that way. For now, she had what she needed.

"Shall we plan our victory, Nebez?" she asked conversationally, and was rewarded with a wide grin. His eyes looked even more like Hermei's when he smiled.

The two sat side by side and talked for hours. She told him of her magic, of bringing storms and fire and wonders; he told her of the King's Elite and the Swans, the two strongest military units in Paxim, both almost incandescent with power, both placed by the queen under his command. An hour in, they called for slates and chalk to draw and redraw the battlefield. Two hours, strong tea. Four hours, more chalk, more tea, and cheese and bread to fortify themselves.

Shortly before dawn, the queen of Arca sent specific instructions to the kitchen on how to sweeten warmed goat's milk with exactly the right amount of honey. As Eminel and Nebez sipped it, readying themselves to snatch a couple of hours of sleep before they rode out against the enemy, they finalized their plan.

◆

It wasn't that Stellari hadn't seen this coming. Of course she had. She'd known it was possible from that first letter, or even before. It was just that there had been so much else to do.

Before installing herself as consul, she'd prepared fastidiously for the role, but it was still almost more than she could handle. The amount of work to be done, the sheer bureaucracy of it, left little time for her own behind-the-scenes machinations. She was still tracking every potential heir to the throne who presented herself at the palace, though the queen turned every last one of them away. Each of their claims took time to investigate, time Stellari could ill spare. And if she didn't know all the factions, all the possibilities, her regency would crumble before it even got off the ground. The edict she'd been so careful to craft in the event of the queen's death hadn't anticipated Paulus's death before the queen's, an oversight she still castigated herself for. The edict was better than nothing but it wasn't enough. These days, nothing felt like it was ever enough.

And that was how she'd gotten into the situation before her now. The possibility had been in the back of her mind, but it had stayed in the back; worrying was unproductive, so she hadn't wasted time on it. But a letter would have made the difference, she told herself. She could and should have spent the precious minutes to draft a letter.

Because now, her letters unanswered, the formidable matron Panagiota of Calladocia herself stood in the doorway of Stellari's house in the capital, and next to her stood her son Evander, Stellari's husband, who Stellari was now seeing in the flesh for the third time in their lives.

"Panagiota! Evander!" Stellari greeted them with pretended enthusiasm, just in case anyone was close enough to see.

As if what Stellari had said were an actual invitation, Panagiota moved forward to come inside, her embroidered tunic grazing the floor. It was the fashion for the wealthy in the outlying districts to wear their tunics so long their hems touched the ground; they could afford servants to launder and repair such things. It was an ostentatious habit, thought Stellari, though she knew that if she'd bothered to visit Calladocia, she would without question have had several tunics made in the style.

Stellari heard a noise behind her and turned, assuming it would be the servant who should have been there to open the door for their uninvited guests. But instead she spotted the small, sharp face of Aster, who knew he wasn't supposed to appear before guests unless requested. Stellari opened her mouth to castigate him and then closed it again as motion on the floor caught her eye.

A small red ball rolled across the floor in her direction, finally coming to a halt against the side of her bare foot. Aster had clearly been chasing the ball, and just as she considered whether she should bend to pick it up, she saw the larger shape of Rahul appear in the doorway behind the child, saying in a disapproving voice, "Aster, you know you shouldn't . . ."

When he saw the visitors, he fell silent.

Both the man and the child looked at the two strangers. Aster's face showed confusion, curiosity. Rahul's face showed nothing at all.

"My grandson, I see," said Panagiota, though she didn't bother to make it sound convincing.

"*Thena,*" breathed Stellari in a warning tone. Of course everyone in the room knew the child hadn't been sired by Evander, but Panagiota didn't know that Rahul knew, never having seen him before, not knowing where he fit in Stellari's household.

The matron of Calladocia was a smart, conniving woman whose power outstripped that of anyone else in her home district. But she was a power player for the country, not the city. Here she wasn't smarter than everyone else. To stay in Ursu, thought Stellari, Panagiota would need to adjust her strategy. Then Stellari shivered at the thought of her husband's mother lingering here for any length of time. To cover her reaction, she bent and picked up the red ball, twirling it idly between her fingers as she straightened up again.

Evander, for his part, said nothing as he stared at the boy. What emotion was that in his eyes? Stellari couldn't tell, and she didn't have time to focus on it right now.

Of the five in the room, Rahul was the first one to find words. "Excuse me, esteemed ones, please pardon our interruption. We are on our way to play in the garden." His voice was calm, almost cheerful. It was exactly what an actual nursemaid would have said, and how he would have sounded when he said it. He took several steps forward and plucked the red ball from Stellari's hand, managing not to even brush her skin as he did so, then gestured to Aster. Without a word, the child followed Rahul and the two disappeared down the long hall. After a few moments they all heard the door to the back garden open and close, the squeak of its hinges the only sound in the silent room.

Finally the house servant appeared, stammering an apology, and Panagiota waved the back of her hand at the young man dismissively, demanding wine and tea. To his credit, he looked at Stellari for confirmation, and with a nod of the consul's head, he dashed off to bring refreshments.

Stellari fell into the familiar routine of hospitality, offering her husband and Panagiota the finest, most comfortable seats, letting them natter on about the length of the journey, all their shared relatives at home, how pleased they were to find her looking so well. Evander rarely even caught Stellari's eye, but she would rather look at him than Panagiota, so she had the chance to examine him thoroughly. She was surprised to find that five years of absence had been kind to him, given him time to develop. He'd always been delicate, not exactly to her taste, but there was something in his modest, long-lashed gaze that she now found intriguing. She watched his long fingers plucking at his own floor-length tunic, almost as if worrying the strings of a harp. There was a grace in those fingers she hadn't seen before. She began to wonder how they would feel against her skin. Perhaps, Stellari thought, this unwelcome visit could be turned into something more welcome.

After she'd become consul, she and Rahul had managed to steal time more frequently for pleasures, often hasty, occasionally more luxurious, but her body showed no signs of the seed of a daughter taking root within. She'd begun to wonder if the birth of Aster had wrecked something within her. Or perhaps Rahul, already having the son he'd wanted, might be taking some precaution of his own. It would be worth trying pleasures with another man to see if her seed were more welcoming to his rain. And here was a man with whom pleasures were not just permitted, but encouraged. If pursuing pregnancy with her husband made Rahul jealous, all the better. She could endanger a fair number of birds with that one well-chosen stone.

But that first night, there was no chance to turn things to her advantage. As soon as they'd finished the refreshments, Panagiota complained that the journey had been so long and with the sun soon setting, it was time for the servant, if he was capable, to show them where they'd stay. The servant showed Panagiota to the room for guests, then took Evander's luggage to the bedchamber where Stellari slept, then left for his own home. At some point Rahul and Aster had slipped back into the house, and Stellari heard the murmurs of their low voices in the kitchen, but she stayed away, not trusting herself to keep her distance from Rahul. She had spent years building up a wall so that no one would know what he meant to her. With nosy Panagiota in the house, all that work could be swiftly undone.

So as night fell, long-fingered Evander was already in her bed, but Stellari chose not to rush there. She'd just poured herself a glass of the good red wine, not the one she'd served the guests, when she heard a knock at the back door, from the garden. And she knew with a sinking heart just who had the audacity to approach from that direction without sending word first. Another unannounced guest, then. It was becoming an unwelcome trend.

As Stellari opened the back door onto the garden, Faruzeh's brow was a storm cloud. Without preliminaries, she spat out her words. "She and I have disagreed."

"The queen?"

Faruzeh glared at her with a surprisingly condescending look, given the situation. Stellari had wanted to have Faruzeh in place when she rose to power, but how bad had this disagreement been? If Faruzeh was no longer war minister, did Stellari have to humor her anymore? Better to keep her options open.

Stellari covered her discomfort with a half laugh and said, "Tell me more."

Faruzeh glanced at the house behind Stellari, and Stellari immediately caught her meaning. Stellari stepped out into the garden and closed the door behind her. She gestured for Faruzeh to begin walking farther from the house, where they would not be overheard.

Deep in the garden, between the fledgling almond tree and a bank of waist-high *klilia* bushes, Stellari fixed her gaze on the war minister's face and waited.

Glaring down at the white flowers shining in the darkness, Faruzeh told Stellari, "We had a difference of opinion."

"So you said. Go on."

Faruzeh sighed dramatically. "As I told you, we've been skirmishing around Hayk just enough to seem engaged, but sent no troops to mount a serious attack."

"Of course, of course. I still think that was the right approach."

"And I thought the queen agreed. She pretended that she did. But apparently she was just biding her time."

An ache bloomed in Stellari's belly. It reminded her of the beginnings of birthing pains, back when her labor with Aster had begun on the floor of the Senate, that formless squeeze deep within. And worse, her helplessness against that squeeze. As little as she wanted to hear the answer, she had to ask the question. "Out with it, then. For what purpose?"

"Heliane begged help from the Arcan queen."

The profanity Stellari let drop would have blistered lesser ears. Gathering herself immediately after, she said, "And did she share with you her intent in making that decision?"

"She did not," said Faruzeh. "But I imagine she asked for help because she wanted help. The rest, I can imagine. If the raiding Scorpicae have moved north into our country, it follows that they were driven out of Arca. And if Queen Eminel was successful in defeating them there, she is our best hope to quickly, decisively defeat them here."

Stellari considered a moment. She had many things she wanted to say. She knew better than to say them.

Instead, she told Faruzeh, "Best for you not to linger. I have guests. But you need to do the thing you least want to do. Crawl back to her on your belly and apologize."

"What?" Faruzeh's expression was unambiguous.

"If you're war minister when I rise to power, I can keep you there. But if you're out of position, I cannot raise you. The hours, even minutes, will be critical. You *must* be where we agreed."

"But she rots this nation from the inside!"

"And that will be dealt with. I swear to you. Swallow your pride for now, and I promise you a better reward in the future. Do you trust me?"

It wasn't that Stellari knew for sure Faruzeh trusted her. She didn't expect a truthful answer, only an expedient one. And in this position, at this moment, only a fool would say no. Faruzeh wasn't a fool. Grudgingly, the war minister said, "Yes."

"Good. Very well. I'll contact you as soon as it's safe. Go."

The woman went, and Stellari was alone with her thoughts in the darkened garden, even if her heart felt like it was racing too fast to allow her to think.

At first, it seemed like disaster. The queen of Arca, here in Paxim? In league with Heliane?

But the more Stellari thought about it, running scenarios through her head as she plucked a *klilia* flower apart petal by petal, the happier it made her. If it became known—and she'd ensure it became known—that the Arcan queen had been invited into the very cradle of the Paximite civilization, people would be angry. Even if it was the right decision. Even if Queen Eminel did succeed in turning the tide and driving the invaders away. The truth hardly mattered. It only mattered what people thought. What they feared. And an ally who was strong enough to defeat one's enemy was strong enough to defeat anyone— what would save Paxim itself from that savage strength, if Arca's loyalties were to turn?

All Stellari had to do was call into question those loyalties. Invoke the fear and resentment that had built up over the past fifteen years, tap the current of anger she'd been stoking that entire time. The populace itself would do the rest.

The consul went back into the house, returned to her cup of wine. She looked at the stairs that led up to the second floor, where her husband's mother was quartered, then down the long hall toward the back of the house where Aster and Rahul slept, and finally toward the door of her own bedroom, where Evander waited.

Then she drained half the cup in one swallow, opened the front door, and lit the green lantern facing the street to signal for a messenger.

She couldn't send a message directly where it needed to go; it would be a circuitous route, sending a note to someone to send a note to someone else until finally her message reached the palace. The thread would take half the night to unspool. But it worked in her favor to remain where she was. Once she handed off the first message, she went back inside her house and sat down. The doors around her were closed, the night quiet. She sipped her wine lightly, slowly, as she waited.

She thought of the families she had befriended, all the women who felt their girls had a claim to the throne and found only Stellari offered them a willing ear. There was the baby whose blood connection to the queen was nearer, her mother arguing a stronger claim, and the woman of twenty whose connection was not as near, her claim not as strong, but with impressive charisma and ability. Stellari hadn't yet decided which one to back. The choice would be moot until it became very, very important indeed. Tonight's action would drive that urgency.

At last there was a knock on the door, a skittering like pebbles from the light touch of nervous knuckles. Stellari answered it, finger to her lips to signal for quiet, and Inbar, her face drawn with worry, stepped inside.

Many times in the past few years, Stellari had second-guessed using Inbar as her spy, but she'd never second-guessed her decision to lie to the woman from the very beginning. Inbar would never confess that Stellari had given her a poison; she had no idea that poison was what Stellari had given her.

And what she didn't know she was about to do would be the last thing Stellari ever needed from her.

"I don't think it's strong enough," Inbar began, without introduction.

Stellari was curious to find out what Inbar knew. "Why wouldn't it be?"

"The Arcan queen herself is in our midst! Whose magic is more powerful? Do I put the queen at risk of detection by continuing to use your charm?"

Well, then. Clearly Inbar knew about the arrival of Queen Eminel, and if the *cosmete* knew, probably everyone did. Stellari placed a heavy hand on the woman's shoulder, pretending to reassure her but happily fanning the flames of her concern. "You are right to be worried. This is why I reached out."

"Ah," Inbar breathed. "I knew you'd know what to do. The Arcans can never be trusted. It was one of them behind the Drought of Girls. Who knows what other mischief they have planned?"

Stellari was thrilled to hear Inbar parrot back the lines Stellari herself had been spreading for years. It was easy enough to make people believe a thing. Everyone was eager to place blame; designating a target for their blame was almost a kindness. Turning against a common enemy kept them from turning against each other.

"No matter how strong their enchantments are, I promise you, they are not as strong as our will. Turn your back now, and close your eyes. I will fetch what you need."

While the *cosmete*'s eyes were closed, the consul rattled cabinet doors and struck the shelves, pretending the salve had been hidden deeply away. In truth it was easily reached, on an open shelf too high for the child. Things were safer higher up.

When she had the stoppered jar of salve in her hand, Stellari reached out for the servant's hands and curled her fingers protectively around it. She pressed almost hard enough to hurt.

"Here, Inbar," said Stellari. "Only you and I know how much the queen needs our protection. Only you can ensure her safety. Will you?"

Inbar nodded solemnly.

"This salve is stronger. It needs to be. The Arcans' dangerous magic is so close to her now. Do not let this salve touch your own skin, only the queen's. We can't risk confusing the charm. If you touch it, you may take some of the protection for yourself."

"I would never—only the queen matters."

Stellari squeezed Inbar's folded hands around the squat clay jar. "Because of you, she will be safe. Paxim won't be overrun. We will stand strong. Do you accept the burden?"

"I accept."

Still cupping the servant's hands in her hands, Stellari bent to kiss Inbar's knuckles, then met the *cosmete*'s eyes, just for a moment, with an intense gaze. And then, for once, she told Inbar the absolute truth. "What you do will make all the difference."

26

THE SECOND BATTLE

The tenth month of the All-Mother's Year 517
The occupied city of Hayk
Eminel, Tamura

When Eminel approached the Paximite city of Hayk for the first time in five years, she felt she was wearing every single nerve on the outside.

The last time she'd come to Hayk, she'd been hollowed out over the death of her mother, but at least she'd been surrounded by friends. The Rovers. If only she could have stayed with them. What she wouldn't give to be riding in the back of that wagon right now, the inside of which she'd known by heart, every crack and crevice, the way the light peeked mischievously through one side of the curtain on long, late summer afternoons.

But what had happened here in Hayk had brought those carefree days to an end. The Seeker had found her and stolen her away, intending to deliver her to Daybreak Palace. If that woman had completed her mission, the young Eminel—helpless, ignorant of her true capabilities—would have been taken into the trials that Sobek spoke of. Sobek had never explained the details of the trials, but Eminel had gleaned enough from the memories of older magicians at court, and what she learned horrified her. Girl set against girl, many of them maimed or even killed in spectacular ways, and those who survived often sent to figures of authority who drained their life force like milk from a goat's teat. Only the rarest, the most powerful and highborn, like Archis, survived to truly contend for the throne. And even Archis had lost out in the end. No, if the Seeker sent by Mirriam had succeeded in dragging Eminel back to Arca, if she had not fallen under Sessadon's spell as a child, she would not have had a better life. She might not have had much more life at all.

This time she'd ridden most of the way in a troop wagon, Nebez by her side, until they disembarked a league outside the city for their final, deliberate march. From this vantage, parts of the city looked just as she remembered. Two buildings of creamy white stone marked the western edge of the settlement, a tall triangle and a squat box, the latter forming one side of the town square where she'd once danced in a gilded mask until the world erupted in fire. And this road was the same, its width and shape familiar, the deep, crooked ruts Hermei had told her came from one heavy wagon swerving to avoid an accident and then years of wagons afterward pressing that same rut deeper into the earth, not knowing why, only knowing it was there to be followed.

But the last time, the approach to Hayk had not smelled of rot, the gentle wind carrying an unmistakable note of decomposition. Last time there had not been four or five columns of faint smoke rising throughout the city, leaving Eminel to wonder whether they'd been set by the occupying Scorpican force or the Paximite citizens searching for a way to fight back. Last time the grass on both sides of the road had not seemed to glint and gleam with scattered bits of polished metal. Eminel poked curiously at one piece and took it up in her hand before she realized it was a fragment of broken armor, razor-sharp along one jagged edge and crusted with something the color of rust that wasn't rust. She dropped it back into the grass, trying not to think of what had happened to the rest of the armor or the person who'd worn it, whichever side she'd fought for.

The sound of constantly clinking metal, an army on the move behind her, knocked her out of her reverie. Hayk itself wasn't the only thing that was different. Eminel was a queen now, powerful and magical, and behind her were arrayed hundreds of Paximite soldiers, women and men ready to fight and die for their country. They were not her people and Paxim was not her country, thought Eminel, except that—was it, in a way? Here she had spent the sweetest years of her childhood. Here she had learned to read and write, hide and hunt, laugh and love. The Rovers had been her family. To honor that family, she would fight. With the help of Nebez, and the commanders who served under him, she would clinch the victory.

That surge of confidence kept her moving forward, light and powerful, until the moment she first saw the Scorpican forces moving toward them from between the buildings of the occupied city, and she quailed.

Because there she saw Queen Tamura. Unmistakably their leader, her head encased in a magnificent golden helm that clung tight to her scalp, Tamura didn't stand at the front of her force the way Eminel did, but unlike Eminel, she wasn't cloaked in magic that shielded her from bodily harm. The sight of the warrior queen was a fist to Eminel's heart. That familiar face with its sharp glare, the mind Eminel remembering invading all too well to accomplish her own goal, the hands Tamura had used to kill Sessadon and dig the quartz heart from her chest. All those things were against Eminel now instead of with her. The thought froze her in her tracks, her feet stilling on the high side of the unevenly worn road.

"We are ready," Nebez said. "Will you lead or follow?"

Eminel had only a moment to decide.

She answered him, "Lead."

When the Scorpicae raised their weapons, Eminel thought she was ready. A victory here was a victory not just for Paxim, but for future peace across the Five Queendoms. It felt wrong, but she had to deal death, if she wanted to keep the hope of peace alive.

Perhaps there was still uncertainty within her. Perhaps that was why, when she raised her hands and reached for her power to buffet the Scorpicae troops and weaken them for the first Paximite strike, Eminel failed.

✦

At the moment her troops marched out under a blue-gray sky to defend Hayk from the Paximites, Tamura thought nothing could stop them. There was no army she feared. The forces that Paxim had sent to try to recapture the city so far had been more like raiding parties, more nuisance than threat. At least half the time, no one on either side died in these skirmishes, noisy and unserious. Tamura herself always fought to win, but she suspected some of her fellow warriors had begun fighting to survive first and win second. Still, the Paximite forces rarely stood still long enough to put themselves in a position to be killed even by the most focused warriors, firing from afar with arrows and running off, lobbing oil-filled jars of clay with lit wicks that exploded upon impact, harrying rather than engaging. Tamura, even without a genius for strategy, had a strong suspicion that she knew their plan. At some point, when they thought the Scorpicae had been lulled into overconfidence, Paxim would send a larger force.

This, today, was that force.

The Scorpicae were vastly outnumbered, she saw that instantly. She also registered the separate forces, the mixed group of women and men at the front, then several troops of only men arranged behind, all with weapons drawn. Those Swans she'd heard so much about, most likely. But larger numbers wouldn't necessarily give the Paximites the edge they needed to win. Not when they were taking on an entrenched, superior force like hers. The size of the Paximite fighting force and its composition did not in the least worry Tamura.

She only began to worry when she saw who stood at their head: a woman in the simple dark cloak of an Arcan, its length swirling around her. In the shadow of her throat where the hood was thrown back, eagle eyes could see blue glass glinting. Tamura didn't need to see this magician's face clearly to know who she was.

Quickly, Tamura raised her hand to call a halt. The ponies slowed, then stopped, behind her. Behind them the foot soldiers stopped as well. The largest force they'd ever concentrated in one place, warrior women born in Scorpica or adopted into its fold, was ready to defend Hayk with all they had—and Tamura hesitated. For her, the field of battle had been entirely changed by the presence of one enemy.

The young queen of Arca raised her arms.

Tamura looked to the sky, listened for something, but there was only silence. Hundreds breathing. The sound of coming violence that had not yet come.

She would wait no longer. Perhaps the sorcerer queen would not change the course of battle after all. Tamura felt her confidence returning. She felt her blood heat.

"Kii-yah!" Tamura cried, raising her sword, and sent the first wedge of mounted warriors screaming straight for enemy lines.

The Paximites had a moment to bring up their shields and hunker down against the oncoming onslaught—Tamura thought she heard a man's voice shouting, "Brace! Hold!"—and then the two forces ran headlong into one another, the sound of metal on metal like a great, jagged roar.

Quickly the line between the enemy forces broke, some ponies surging past the first row of shields and into the ranks of soldiers, others stopped short with their riders stabbing downward into the crowd, one and then two horses screaming, rearing up, sword hilts protruding from their bloodied throats. Tamura herself rode forward, unable to stay back when she saw her warriors fighting for their lives. Her sisters, her daughters. She wheeled her mount and charged ahead to where Nikhit had tumbled from her wounded pony. Tamura brought her mount alongside Nikhit and thrust out a hand to haul her up from the ground, carry her back to safety so she could ready herself to attack again.

But it was not Nikhit's arm that reached up to Tamura's, and instead of yanking her comrade upward, the queen found herself being yanked down by an enemy.

Tamura hit the ground hard on her right side, curling up by instinct, and her enemy's sword passed so close to her ear she heard it whistle.

Then she heard another blade singing, a cry of pain, and saw that Nikhit had stabbed the offending Paximite through her neck from right to left. The Paximite's sword fell from her limp hand, clattering on the ground next to Tamura and waking her from her stupor. She had to get up. On the ground, she could be speared or slashed by any one of a hundred hands, stomped by the ponies of her own army. She had to stop acting like she was invincible. She needed to get back to safety, or Azur would be queen of the Scorpicae before the day was out.

Tamura leapt to her feet, drawing her sword as she did so, and got her bearings, noting that Nikhit had grabbed the reins of Tamura's pony. No, thought Tamura, she was not invincible, but neither was she any ordinary warrior. So before she ran for safety, she set her sights on the nearest Paximite, a woman in leather armor swinging a club tipped with spikes. Tamura kept herself still while she waited for the woman with the spiked club to run at her, and at the last moment, Tamura dove into a sideways roll that brought her right back up to her feet on her opponent's left side.

By the time the Paximite raised her club to strike again, Tamura's sword had already connected with the woman's hip, cutting through her tunic and then everything beneath like a knife through butter. The tip barely snagged on the bone underneath the flesh.

G. R. MACALLISTER

The woman shrieked and folded, and for good measure, Tamura took aim as soon as her throat was still. Afterward, it was clearly a permanent stillness.

"The battle is done," murmured Tamura, and wiped her blade clean on the dead woman's long tunic before she ran for her pony.

But the battle for Hayk, truly, had just begun.

✦

In desperation, Eminel tried pulling energy to her fingertips as Sessadon had taught her, trying to summon a storm as she'd once done in an attempt to kill the previous queen of Arca. More than anything, Eminel remembered the *taste* of that feeling, how the currents in the air swirled at her command, how that air grew heavy until she'd swear she felt it pressing against her skin.

But this time, the air didn't move, the water didn't come. Her hands in the air had no effect. The battle had joined around her already, her delay costing them precious moments, but Nebez was lightning-quick to command the troops forward when he saw her failure. Blood from both forces was already staining Hayk's uneven roadway.

Think, she told herself, shaking her head until her brain felt like it was rattling inside her skull. What power did she have? What power could she use? Everything depended on her and her inert, raised hands. Her future, Arca's, Paxim's, everyone's. She was the most powerful all-magic sorcerer in the world. Failure was not an option.

Then fear rose in her, giant and looming, and she remembered two times when she'd felt fear like this. One, when she'd destroyed the Seeker without even meaning to, with her first instinctual eruption of magic. The other, when she'd faced down Sessadon at the Rites of the Bloody-Handed, the time she'd felt a surge of power like polished wood, power that was not hers, filling her up from the inside.

Now she realized, for the first time, whose power it had been.

"Velja!" she shouted aloud. Then she prayed under her breath, as she had at the rites, not realizing at the time the power of the invocation, just murmuring something she'd heard her mother say. Now she used the prayer for what it was meant. Now she summoned Velja's power.

"Velja, be with me."

This time she felt the power surge within her, the almost unbearable potential she knew she bore. She looked ahead to the troops protecting her, those who'd surged forward when she faltered. Then Eminel ran for the enemy, finding the line between the Scorpicae and the Paximite armies, not a clean line, but as clean as she could make it in the moment.

In the center of the rutted road, she threw herself to her knees and splayed both hands flat on the uneven dirt, facing toward the Scorpicae, toward Hayk. She closed her eyes. Seeing was nothing in the face of knowing.

Without incantations, without hand motions, working solely on instinct with the power of the god behind her, Eminel emptied her mind and her being and flooded the space left behind with one sharp, resounding word.

Destroy.

The blast required a tremendous amount of life force. Eminel stripped it from her opponents without mercy, immobilizing them, then sent a blue surge of energy through the ground.

Destroy.

An unearthly boom sounded, the earth shaking, then there was one long, eerie moment of silence before the screaming began.

Eminel opened her eyes to see what she had wrought. Blue fire danced across the landscape, beautiful and terrible, dancing up the warriors' armor and weapons and across their skin. In some places the warriors' clothes and hair were on fire, helms melting, swords warped; in others, the very ground itself seemed to burn. One mounted warrior, bold, rode forward through a column of flame. Her pony immediately bucked her off and the warrior, her garments on fire, arced through the

401

air like a comet. If Eminel had been able to smother the fire, she would have saved the pony. But she tried to manipulate water to soak it or air to smother it, and neither obeyed her commands. She had unleashed wild, destructive magic, and there was no changing its path.

Her hands still flat on the ground, Eminel hung her head for a moment, feeling the surge of power that had filled her now subsiding in a whoosh, leaving her hollow. Every shred of enchantment drained away. She heard as well as felt the power leave her, making a sound like harsh wind. Then she heard another sound drawing near—hoofbeats—and she raised her palms upward by instinct, not knowing if she was trying to fend off a blow or signal her surrender, only knowing she needed to move. The magic had protected her before. But now the magic was gone.

Instantly there was a searing pain at her left wrist, just above the Talish cuff, and she glimpsed a gleaming sword's edge, wielded by a figure in gold. She snatched both arms back and wrapped them around herself. Velja's power was gone but could she still reach for her own? She did, muttering an incantation that settled an invisible shield over her like a dome, and not a moment too soon; the pony's hooves struck a space above her body and made a sharp sound against it, as if against wood or glass.

The sorcerer had done what she could, weakened the enemy with a tremendous lash of force, and the soldiers of Paxim would need to take it from here. Eminel had channeled all her power and everything Velja had lent her besides. All she could do now was save herself, hunching under the barrier she'd built, trusting the Paximite army to bring the victory home.

At first the barrier seemed to hold. But before long, the pain in her wrist roared up at her, numbness giving way to the stunning, sharp pain of a thousand needles. So much pain. Too much pain. Eminel had never felt anything like this and wasn't sure she could take it. The barrier began to vibrate, then fade.

In the many books of Daybreak Palace, in an attempt to understand her mother, Eminel had delved deep into what it meant to have healing magic. Healers could displace pain, taking it from someone else's body into their own or moving it from their own body to someone else's. Eminel herself had never tried it. But the need was urgent now. Eminel shoved the pain out of her body, too hurried and half-mad with agony to wonder where it might land. She wanted only relief. In the moment, nothing else mattered.

✦

Tamura had neutralized the magician, the most important thing to do, and for a moment, she let herself savor the satisfaction. She hadn't killed Queen Eminel as she intended, but the woman was hunched and hiding inside some kind of protective spell, curled in on herself like a pangolin. Tamura was sure that the Arcan queen would not have the strength to interfere in the battle any longer, not after what the sword had done. Perhaps that would be enough.

But when Tamura turned to look back at her army, she saw the havoc Eminel's magic had wrought and knew the Scorpicae could not win this battle. Everywhere, her warriors were staggering, suffering. Many already lay motionless. That would have been enough to give her pause, but she heard a war cry rumbling in men's throats, and she saw the all-male troops stampeding toward the remaining Scorpican troops, ready to give everything.

Still, doomed or not, Tamura would not yield. She pressed forward. She howled. She slashed and swept. She smashed the pommel of her sword against skulls and wielded the sharp sides of the blade to hack at arms, legs, bellies. No matter how many she fought, more kept coming, and the realization that she could not win the day made her want to cut her own throat to overcome the terrible sensation of waiting to see which of these enemy soldiers would be the one to bring her down.

But no, thought Tamura. She would not defeat herself; if she were to be defeated, someone else would have to earn the right.

So from atop her mount she swept her sword through the gathered enemy, sometimes hitting her targets, sometimes missing, but never slowing down. She saw her warriors vying valiantly, and many succeeding, but so many had been weakened by the sorcerer, and the enemy's force was so strong. The Scorpicae couldn't hold out forever.

The only honorable thing would be to stay and fight to the death. If she couldn't succeed in this life, Tamura could at least do her best to earn her place in the battlefield beyond.

She found herself pushed back to where the magician hunched on the ground, looking small and vulnerable, but even as Tamura watched, arrows and swords failed to penetrate the magician's charmed circle. Something would have to be done about that, but not now, Tamura thought.

She was breathing in the moment between attacks when pain came upon her like she'd never known.

It began at her wrist and roared upward like fire, stealing her breath, and at the same moment she felt her pony shudder—was she feeling the same thing?—and the pony's howl was disturbingly human as she rose up on her back legs in desperation, rearing, trying to escape the inescapable.

Tamura was thrown.

All she remembered after that was soaring backward through the air, shock flooding through her at her own weightlessness; she did not even remember landing, striking the earth head first.

Tamura did not wake up until much later, battle already lost, along with the hours after. She woke up surrounded by warriors who'd been driven from the battlefield, those who'd chosen not to fight to the death but instead to take their queen with them in retreat. She woke up with an arresting pain in her head that warped the world and blotted it out. She woke up in *mokhing* Godsbones.

She wished she'd never woken up at all.

✦

Hunched under her magical shield, eyes squeezed tight shut, Eminel missed the moment when the battle noise around her shifted. She'd drawn a great deal of life force from the enemy ranks to do her magic, but as their ranks thinned, she was drawing more and more of her own. At some point she'd need to let the shield down. When she did, she'd let the pain back in.

Her numb left hand, she remembered, which someone in gold had struck with her sword. Tamura, it must have been, she realized. Would Eminel have enough magic to heal it? How much would it take?

Then Eminel looked down and laughed.

The hand was not numb. The hand was gone. Tamura's sword had cleaved it from her body.

Eminel laughed again. She had been so overcome by the pain, the pain itself had become her focus, and she hadn't even known she was maimed. Imagine that, she thought. How strange magic was. How deeply it changed everything.

Eminel was too tired to move, too tired to decide anything. Too tired to look for her hand, which was probably buried under someone else's body at this point, a disgusting trophy any enemy soldier who'd survived was welcome to claim. She did realize she was lying on something sharp, and even though the pain of that had to be so much less than the pain of her severed hand, it bothered her enough to stir her into action.

She was lying on the broken remnants of the Talish cuff, scattered fragments of quartz. It couldn't have been broken by Tamura's sword, which couldn't possibly have been strong enough. She must have destroyed it herself with that burst of magic, without meaning to. Now she had no source of power, no life force but her own. She was as helpless as she'd been during her first ride as queen to Daybreak Palace, when the dreams had come upon her for the first time.

The dreams from Velja. And Velja had come to help her today, had lent her power when Eminel called. She sent up a prayer of thanks, the only other thing she could think to do as she lay there, emptied out, having done what she came here to do but having no idea what came next.

Then a voice in her head said, *Go.*

Back to Daybreak Palace? I don't want to.

No, said the voice.

It sounded familiar. It wasn't Beyda, though, and it wasn't Sessadon. It wasn't her own voice, though it reminded her of how she sounded when she used her voice of command with the court.

Where? Eminel asked the voice. She was too tired to resist, too tired to care. Probably she was still in shock.

Sestia, came the answer.

Why?

Sestia, the voice repeated, with something that sounded to Eminel like irritation.

She recognized the voice then, when it lost its pleasant edge. There was no doubt in her mind. She knew it from her dreams.

"Honored Velja," she said aloud. It felt more real when she spoke aloud. She needed something, right now, that felt real.

Here, Velja said, and Eminel felt the place where her left hand used to be tingle—not pain, but something else, like a web stretching over the exposed bone and muscle and skin. The ground near her was red with blood, but the stump had stopped bleeding, and when Eminel looked at it, she saw something that stunned her. Chips of the Talish cuff, blue and glowing, embedded in the flesh. Whether those chips were enough to store life force that could power her magic, she didn't know. But from these chips of quartz, she felt the tug of an enchantment, and knew instinctively that the spell she had cast to seal Daybreak Palace was still intact.

"Thank you," she said to Velja, because it seemed the right thing to do. Even though she didn't see the god, she could feel Her, acknowledge

Her, recognize Her. And now, when Eminel needed Velja most, she could even follow Her.

Sestia, repeated the voice, more urgently.

If that was what Velja wanted, decided Eminel, so it would be.

Out loud, humbled, gripping the stump at the end of her left arm with fingers that sought out the chipped, cool surfaces of quartz now one with her flesh, Eminel said to Velja, "Show me the way."

✦ 27 ✦

AFTERMATH

Hayk to Ursu, Paxim
Nebez, Stellari

Nebez stood on the main street of Hayk, staring blankly at the carnage, surrounded by eerie quiet. His nose was still full of the burnt smell of flesh and leather, his ears still ringing from battle's ugly music. He couldn't get used to the silence, even though part of him knew silence was good. Quiet meant the worst was over, at least for now. And in this case, quiet meant they'd won.

Slowly Nebez realized that people were turning to him, looking at him. He had ridden at the head of the fighting force, not just the King's Elite and the men of the Swans but the hundreds of other Paximites, trained separately, attacking together. He had been the commander of every person here. A dozen, then two dozen, eyes stared at him expectantly. Suddenly he realized why. These women and men expected him to speak.

But Nebez was a fighter, not an orator. He had seen and heard and smelled too much death to speak in triumph, even if his forces had won the battle. There was only one person he cared to tell of their victory, and she was hundreds of leagues away. He'd been charged with the sacred duty of commanding this force, but there were many kinds of duty, and he would need to choose.

He chose to go.

He raised a hand, warding off the interest of the soldiers, and backed away from the field. He wouldn't stay. He couldn't. He looked around for Queen Eminel, the only person here he thought might understand, but he didn't see her. For a moment he worried whether she'd made it through the battle, but he quickly realized his worry was misplaced. She'd been protected by magic, he told himself, the only person here who had been. Queen Eminel would be all right.

One more choice to make, then. He'd need someone to entrust with command. He ticked off the possibilities in his mind. Round-faced, battle-hardened Floriana, perhaps, or the capable one known as the Shade? No, the Shade hadn't come, he remembered now. And not everyone here would follow the Arcan queen alone. He needed someone from Paxim, someone already known, someone with rank. He fought the last name but it surfaced anyway. *Jovan.*

Even as Nebez let himself think the name, painful as it was, the man himself came into view.

A year in command of the Swans didn't seem to have changed Jovan; he looked just as Nebez remembered him. Thick muscles on a lean frame, hair worn in curls to his shoulders, the top of his head exactly level with Nebez's own. When they'd served in the Swans together as a bonded pair, they'd been so alike that new recruits often confused them for each other. Fondly, their commander had joked that their love was mostly narcissism.

"Nebez?" Jovan had caught sight of him, was nearing, a look of concern on his once-familiar face.

Nebez froze to the spot. He'd brought the Swans here by written negotiation, sending a swift runner. In the heat of the battle he'd focused on nothing but the victory. Now the walls were crumbling. The man who'd broken his heart stood here, close enough to touch.

"No time, sorry," he mumbled dismissively. Then he turned his back so he wouldn't see Jovan's face. To rise to the head of the Swans, ambitious Jovan had chosen command over love, leaving Nebez behind. Nebez would not open old wounds today. There were fresh wounds to be dealt with, both inside and out.

Instead, he called out, "Floriana!" and gestured her closer.

Without speaking, she came. He told himself she was the right choice anyway. She'd proved herself both a powerful fighter and a capable officer, guiding not just a single trained unit, but Paximites of all kinds, women and men, experienced and novice. She'd kept her head. She could handle this.

In a voice not much louder than a whisper, he said to her, "The army is yours. Take them home."

Her eyes went wide in shock, but the surprise was too welcome to throw her off-balance for long. He saw Floriana swallow and muster herself. To him, she said simply, "Thank you." Then she strode back toward the ground he had abandoned. He wanted to watch her step up to address the triumphant army, to signal his approval, but that would mean the possibility of glimpsing Jovan again. Nebez already felt as fragile as glass. One more glimpse could shatter him.

Even at a distance, he heard Floriana call for the crowd's attention. As she began to speak, Nebez quietly walked away.

In the stable his army had commandeered when they arrived in Hayk, he found the palace messenger. The boy should probably have already been gone, but he was fiddling with his horse's bridle, apparently waiting for someone to tell him what to do. Nebez was happy to be that someone.

"Is this the fastest horse?" asked Nebez.

The boy swallowed and nodded.

"Give her to me."

The boy's gaze darted around the landscape, but seeing no one else to override the command, handed the reins to Nebez.

In the distance, Floriana seemed to have struck the right note with the troops; Nebez heard voices from an untold number of throats roaring approval as one.

No Paximite soldier who had been part of the second battle of Hayk would ever forget this day. If the Scorpicae continued their aggression, Paxim would give them cause to regret it. And the Scorpicae could not absorb losses forever. Paxim could throw thousands of soldiers into battles like this, and would, until the smaller nation's army dwindled down to nothing. This might not be the end, Nebez knew. But it felt like the beginning of the end. And that was news Heliane needed to know.

His journey back to Ursu this time was long and exhausting, much like his previous one, but this time he was buoyed by the knowledge that his news was welcome. Tamura's death would have been better tidings, but it should be enough that they'd set the Scorpicae running. That the combination of the Arcan queen's magic and the military skills of the Paximite army had, as Heliane intended, won the day.

The ride back was long enough that after he stabled the horse, he felt incomplete entering the palace on foot. Perhaps he would ask to command a regiment of horse-soldiers; that would be a good match for his skills, and likely less strain on his shoulder blade, which ached now with the fierce, enduring heat of banked coals. He had built his strength until no one could look askance at his warped back and shoulder and say he had no business with a sword. Years of training had made Nebez not just as good as other men, but better. But between the battle and the ride, he'd pushed his body far beyond its natural limits. Perhaps he would ask the queen for some time to rest before taking command of that force he'd ask her for. He wouldn't ask for command of the Swans, though it had crossed his mind he could do so to punish Jovan for leaving him behind. Jovan had only proven what he wanted more than he wanted Nebez. Jovan was happy now. It wouldn't bring the past back to take that happiness away.

So Nebez would focus on the future. When he told the queen of their victory, there would be a moment where she felt relief, pride, and above all, gratitude. He would make use of that moment.

Recognizing him, the guard at the palace gate not only let him in, but escorted him swiftly toward the queen's chambers. But in the hall outside her door, where the Queensguard stood in their pale cloaks, no one stepped aside. Their expressions were stormy, and he wasn't sure why. Did they not know him? Was he not the conquering hero? One, with thin lips above a prominent chin, moved to block his path. She wasn't the tallest of the Queensguard, though still taller than Nebez, and he knew better than to attempt to pass her by.

"My name is Nebez of Havarrah," he said, forcing his mouth into a broad grin. He couldn't afford to look angry, not now.

Not returning his smile, the woman answered in a voice that betrayed no emotion, "And my name is Tuprah of the Queensguard."

He waited for Tuprah to go on, but she didn't. He tried to hold on to the joy he'd felt, the news he was sure would delight the queen to hear. The Scorpicae had never attacked in such force before, yet the Arcan queen and the Paximite forces under Nebez's command had managed to break their ranks and send them running. Yet this one woman, without even drawing her weapon, could bring him to a dead halt. It didn't feel right.

Nebez went on, still straining to make his voice pleasant, "I am here to see the queen."

"You can't," answered the unsmiling Tuprah, her eyes narrowing, her hand moving to the hilt of her sword. The blade was unusually long, but so were Tuprah's arms, he noted. No doubt she could have its tip against his throat in half a heartbeat.

"She'll want to see me," Nebez said, his voice starting to give away a bit of his strain. "Queen Heliane set me at the head of the Paximite army to reclaim the city of Hayk and drive the Scorpicae from our lands. We succeeded. I've come to bring her the good news."

The woman's expression shifted, and it was different than it had been, but still unreadable. Not warm nor dismissive, not angry, not indulgent. No, if he had to put a name to it, he'd say the emotion on her face was pity.

Still, Nebez didn't understand until the woman spoke.

With a shake of her head, Tuprah said, "I am truly sorry, Nebez of Havarrah. I congratulate you on your victories. But I apologize that the queen will not hear good news from your lips. She is quite beyond hearing. Queen Heliane died this morning."

✦

This time, the waiting was waiting like Stellari had never felt before.

She couldn't celebrate, not yet. How different things were now than when she'd celebrated being raised to consul, wild with wine and ardor, luxuriating in pleasures with Rahul for hours on end. Rahul was not even here, Stellari having yielded to Panagiota's unrelenting complaints that if Stellari herself would not travel to Calladocia, at least Panagiota's grandson could do so, never having seen his ancestral lands, and him how old already? Eight years? So Panagiota, Aster, and Rahul—an odd trio if one had ever been seen—had left the week before on the southward journey. Rahul had said no more about wanting to travel to Arca, seemingly contenting himself with this journey instead, leaving Stellari and Evander here in Ursu to share a household for the first time as wife and husband.

And though the two of them often passed entire days without speaking—with her so busy, and him still apparently timid—they shared pleasures regularly, maintaining a thrice-weekly schedule to maximize her chances of bearing another child. The prospect of the longed-for daughter seemed closer than ever to Stellari. How perfect that would be. Perhaps the watered seed was already growing within her on this, the day of her greatest triumph so far.

But though Evander seemed pleasant enough, and his skills in bed more deft than she'd expected, there was no question of pulling him onto the bedsheets without warning to indulge in exploration. She had no idea how he'd react if she even tried. That alone was reason not to try, not on a day like today. Besides, she could not secrete herself away behind a closed door. What if she missed the messenger? She was finally where she wanted to be. There could be no mistakes.

Stellari paid the cook at the palace good money to keep her apprised of events, and she congratulated herself on having made such a smart decision. Messenger boys always got some kind of treat after they delivered their messages, good or bad. Once a messenger boy wolfed down whatever the cook grumblingly gave—seedcake or cheese, honey-twist or boiled egg—the woman would ply him with a gentle question or two, while he was still in her debt, and information would flow out of the boy like water through a sieve.

So when Paulus had died, Stellari had been the first person outside the palace to know. The same had happened when the second battle of Hayk concluded with a triumph for the Paximites. She'd still been digesting that bit of news when another unofficial messenger brought a note that the queen was dead. And that meant everything was finally, finally falling into place. Just as Stellari had envisioned.

But Stellari couldn't rush to the palace based on the unofficial news; it wouldn't be appropriate, not befitting her new station. She hadn't yet been officially notified that she'd be stepping up to act as regent, making decisions for the nation on behalf of the queen in waiting, in addition to her other consul powers. She had to wait for the news to work its way through the proper channels. There were a few things she could do in the meantime. Not many. But the things she could do, she did.

She sent a coded note to Faruzeh, who had managed to hang on to her position as war minister by the skin of her teeth, and whether or not Heliane had planned to keep her in that position was no longer relevant. Faruzeh was there and she was key. Thank the All-Mother that Stellari had begun grooming her years ago, locking down her loyalty, ensuring that when this day came, there would be no ambiguity about who the nation's army would fight for. Faruzeh was in Stellari's court, utterly. The army would be too.

She would have to play this perfectly. That involved seeing all the things that could go wrong before they happened and making sure she nipped them in the bud. That playmate of the kingling, for example, the one called Ama. She'd been exiled by the queen herself, but if she came back, she would certainly have to be dealt with. Willingly if possible, fatally if needed.

And should Stellari commandeer the Queensguard? Could she? Better not to try. She could establish her own protectors. She knew three loyal women who'd been passed over for entrance to the Queensguard; she'd call them to her side immediately. Three was perfect, as it would show she was not trying to replicate the Queensguard, and would send the subtle message, too, that her guard was so skilled and deft she'd only need three of them. For a moment she considered asking a man to join her guard to send a message of inclusion but followed that thread down its logical path and dismissed it. She didn't intend to win over the radicals; they were probably lost to her in any case. She needed only convey an appearance of continuity. Of return to tradition. There were enough women who had feared the rise of Paulus into a ruling king to cut off the very idea of men's representation at the knees.

First things first, she told herself. She braided her own hair while she plotted. She wanted no one near her. All too soon she would be jostling with people, commanding them, wheedling, convincing, claiming her place at the top of the queendom. In this moment she could still be alone with her thoughts. Her own mind had always been her best company.

Stellari donned her deepest blue robe, one she'd never worn, having worried that it was so close to purple, people would whisper she was attempting to claim herself royal. Now, though, it was perfect. Let people whisper; the ones who really mattered would recognize it as the rightful claim of the powerful. Had Stellari not been consul already, had there been even a single girl anywhere in Paxim the queen was willing to acknowledge as her successor, had the queen's heart not already been weakened by her injury at the hands of that sorcerer at the Rites of the Bloody-Handed and again from the poison, things would not have lined up so perfectly. But they had. And for all Stellari's ability to imagine outcomes, while she had imagined this one over and over, she had always worried something unexpected would prevent it. But now, on the threshold of becoming the most powerful woman in Paxim bar none, nothing stood in her way.

She would be a good ruler, Stellari promised herself. She'd worked so hard to arrive at this moment; not just because she wanted the power, but because she truly believed she was the right one to wield it. She had once been a girl no one wanted, mother dead in childbirth, mother's sisters passing her around between households like a mangy stray dog, no one wanting another mouth to feed. Stellari had fed herself more often than not, and she could still taste the laces of that sandal, feel the leather against her teeth and tongue as she chewed until her jaw ached and her mouth went dry. Finally she'd found a position as servant girl in a ramshackle stable, stealing a few bites of the horses' mash for herself every time she fed them, and fighting her way up the ladder rung by rung over years until she not only ran the stable, but owned it, and turned it from the third-best stable around to the finest in the district. Then she rose to the Assembly, then the Senate, and she would never have to curry, shoe, sell, dispatch, geld, or scrub another horse again.

But enough of memories, she told herself, shaking off the memory of that neglected girl, that desperate young woman who always stank of horses. Now she was not only the head of the elected government of the most powerful of the Five Queendoms, she would run the monarchy too, concentrating the entire nation's power in her own two hands.

She wished she had someone to share it with. The longed-for daughter. Or Rahul, whose absence had struck her harder than she'd expected, who she had not even spoken to the day he left for Calladocia, everything so hectic that she didn't realize until sunset that she'd missed her chance. Only belatedly did she think of Aster, how he was her own child, who she did not miss, and did not see as someone she could share her successes with. How strange. Something had never been right between them. Her own inability to feel, probably. She'd never fallen headlong into loving the child as she'd been told mothers generally did. She supposed it was better to consider herself incapable of love, if she thought about it. Love made people fools. Just look at what had happened to Heliane, in the end.

Finally: the knock on the door.

Stellari rose, brushing down her robe and squaring her shoulders. She waited to hear the servant open the door, listened for his voice, confirmed that the visitor was the one she'd waited for. The near-purple robe swirled around her feet as she walked briskly down the hall. Her heart hammered like a fresh colt's. There, framed by the open door, stood the red-shirted messenger boy she'd been waiting for, breathless.

"What news?" she asked, knowing the answer full well. She would swoon a bit, exclaim, cry out; but quickly she would pretend to master herself, to choke down sentiment. In that way she would immediately establish that she was prepared for anything, that the confidence of the people could be placed, entirely, with her. If asked, the messenger could speak to her manner, the way she'd put aside her fear and concern to do what was best for the country. That was the tale she wanted told, in the days and weeks and months to come.

And now? It was time for Stellari to rule.

✦ 28 ✦

MOTHER

Autumn and winter, the All-Mother's Year 517,
and spring, the All-Mother's Year 518
Three leagues north of Ursu, Paxim
Ama, Vish

I t was remarkable, thought Ama, how no one looked at her anymore. She had been so keenly observed and observing the whole time she'd been guarding Paulus, a figure of interest for all and sundry. Now when she went to the market, swathing her growing body in heavy shawls, she felt no eyes on her whatsoever. Sometimes she accompanied Vish to trade the vegetables they grew for other foods. Sometimes she went alone just to see what was there, for something to do. But no matter how crowded or sparse the gathering, she didn't stand out. She found it both comforting and disturbing. There were Scorpican war parties in Paxim, the love of her life had died without her by his side, and the world had just kept moving on. Any day might be the worst day of someone's existence—and yet for most of the populace, nothing mattered beyond the daily eating, voiding, working, sleeping, then the next day rising to do it all over again. In the scheme of day-to-day living, what did someone like her matter? She was unregarded because she was unimportant.

Ama knew the child growing within her was far more important than she, but she was not ready to share that child with the world. Would it be a boy or a girl? Wondering was not a pastime she enjoyed, but it preoccupied her nonetheless. A boy with Paulus's eyes, equally eager to wrap his hands around a dagger handle and the spine of a book of tales? Or a girl with Ama's own watchful stare, her distrust and wariness? She knew she'd prefer a child who reminded her of Paulus, whatever gender it happened to be.

If it was a girl, she knew, she would have to go tell Heliane. There was no other option. Ama would bear the infant in her own arms to the palace and confess what she had hidden, accept any punishment the queen might mete out no matter how severe, so that Paulus's daughter could one day take her rightful throne. Paulus would have wanted that. Giving a future queenling to Heliane would be the right thing, the best thing, the only thing.

But if it was a boy, thought Ama, she could keep him for herself. Heliane had pushed herself to the limit to pave the way for her son to be king. Had Paulus lived, she would have succeeded, Ama had no doubt. But it wouldn't be the same for a grandson, for a boy no one would be able to prove was even Heliane's blood issue. That was the problem with passing down a crown through male lineage. Ama could not swear on enough gods, no matter which ones, to establish beyond a doubt that the child was Paulus's. She could only prove it was hers, which wasn't enough. For a girl, they might squint and allow the question to pass, but not for a boy. Everyone had to *want* to believe. Things would be cloudier, too, if the child were established as both genders or neither. Ama would love a child of any gender, but she was too practical to believe that the child would be treasured equally by others no matter what. And at birth they would not know. The path would proceed based on the best available guess.

In any case, the child would not make its appearance for months. Ama tried to enjoy the uncertainty in the meantime, to reach a new equilibrium, since she had no other option. It was challenging. She had never been one to enjoy uncertainty.

Today she dawdled at the market, wasting time pretending to inspect ripe plums, juicy peaches. Stone fruits invariably put her in mind of her own state, of the way her skin stretched tight over her belly like a drum, all that soft flesh swelling underneath. The child, she supposed, was the hard pit at the center. As if agreeing, the baby twitched, a fluttering Ama felt under her ribs, and seemed to turn inside her to find a more comfortable perch. Ama had not gotten used to the sensation, but she liked it. She could be alone and yet not alone. She always had unobtrusive, silent companionship, which was the kind she liked the most.

"Hungry for peaches?" asked Vish from next to her, her voice low but clear. "If you want some, I still have berries left to trade."

"No, no," Ama said, stepping back. "Just looking. We probably need cheese more. Or meat. If anything."

"For meat, we can hunt in the morning. A few coneys from the woods will keep us for the week. Or I can go hunting, I mean, myself. If you . . . don't feel strong."

Ama was about to tell Vish not to be so gentle with her, but she'd barely opened her mouth to speak when louder words interrupted.

A piercing voice, almost a bellow, cut through the crowd. "News, news!"

With that, the ordinary music of market day, a merry chatter of barterers and shoppers, farmers and friends, hushed almost immediately. Ama had never lived in a Paximite town before. In the army and at the palace, news had come from messengers, young boys in bright red tunics who scurried from place to place on fleet feet. But here the news was called out by a crier, a bull-voiced woman named Leven, who carried a small gong and never seemed to blink or swallow. Her body was surprisingly small for how far her voice could carry. Leven came to the square every day at the same time to call out whether or not there was news. Now, however, was not her usual time to appear. Which meant the news was urgent. And then Leven struck her gong, its metallic sound an unmistakable signal. Voices hushed in its wake.

Ama felt a twinge low in her belly. She hoped that was only anticipation, not the child signaling an intent to emerge. Ama had added up numbers, and while she was unsure exactly when Paulus's rain had watered her seed, she felt it was too soon. The kicking from within was still gentle. She didn't know much about bearing children, but she'd seen one of her fellow soldiers in the later months of pregnancy back when she'd been under Floriana's command. Toward the end the baby had kicked so hard the shape of its kicking foot was visible, bowing the skin of the soldier's belly outward as if someone were bouncing a brick in a wineskin.

As she waited to hear what Leven had to say, Ama suddenly felt Vish's hand on her arm. She glanced toward her companion. Vish's face was drawn. She moved her hand higher, gripping Ama by the elbow.

"This way," said Vish, attempting to steer Ama away from where Leven was climbing onto her small, high platform, preparing to cry her announcement. The gong sounded again and Leven held it high above the crowd's heads, steadying herself, grim-faced.

Ama planted her feet, frowning at Vish. "But I want to hear the news."

"We won't go too far," said the older woman, glancing around them. "I just don't want to be in the midst of a crowd if the news is bad."

Vish was like this now, overprotective; Ama was both flattered and annoyed by it. She let Vish move her a few steps. She wondered if Vish were just guessing or if she had actually heard whispers of what the news might be.

The crier sucked in a deep breath and shouted, "News! From Ursu! From the palace itself! Terrible news!"

Ama felt a chip of ice lodge in her heart and begin, slowly, to spread its chill.

In that moment, she wished she had let Vish take her not just farther away, but out of earshot entirely. It was too late now. Too many bodies milled around them, paths closed off in an instant as people pressed closer to hear.

At the news that the palace was involved, whispers and murmurs began to ripple through the crowd. Ama did her best to ignore them, her attention trained on the crier. She didn't look away, didn't move. If the news was from the palace, she couldn't.

"Our beloved monarch! The radiant Queen Heliane! Has died," cried Leven, her voice breaking on the last word.

The news made Ama want to curl an arm protectively around her belly, but she didn't move. She was careful not to give any sign she was carrying a child at all, let alone whose child it might be. No one could know.

The crier was going on, talking about the national time of mourning and the ongoing discussions about which girl would step up to take the queenship, but Ama couldn't listen. The chill had spread all the way through her body and numbed her from fingertips to toes. Her heart cried out and not just for Heliane. Now, finally, she allowed herself to look at Vish.

Their eyes met. Vish's gaze was rich with sympathy, with anguish, though she said nothing. She seemed to be waiting for Ama to speak.

"She couldn't live without him," murmured Ama quietly, so no one but Vish could hear.

"Come," Vish said. "Let's go home."

✦

Vish was certain that Ama's time was coming long before it actually came. The young woman's body changed and grew, the bubble of her swollen belly protruding in clean, curved lines from her lean and muscular frame. She was barely any heavier in the hips, only in the belly, and Vish had never cared to watch a pregnant woman's figure closely enough to know whether that was the usual way of things. Ama was similarly in the dark. So as winter waned, they spent weeks thinking any day might be the day, until they finally began to despair that the day would ever come.

"Is it possible to be increasing forever?" grumbled Ama, rubbing both hands in long lines down the sides of her curved belly. She'd stopped going to the market with Vish once her belly grew too big to cover with shawls and cloaks, and she was restless. The mother-to-be paced almost constantly, through the small house and across the yard, making circles around the larger dogwood and the smaller one, day and night.

Vish tried her most soothing voice, but soothing didn't come naturally to her. "Never heard it happen that way."

"Perhaps it's another sorcerer," quipped Ama, but neither of them felt much like laughing when the Drought of Girls was invoked. The last fifteen years had brought so much pain. The Drought had ended but the pain had not. They, and the entirety of the Five Queendoms, were still mired in the aftermath.

Then one spring afternoon, the goat Vish had bought for milk slipped her rope while Vish had gone to a neighboring farm to trade some of that milk for eggs from the neighbor's ducks. Chasing the goat, Ama walked the long way down to the stream, over hillocks and rocks and ground almost as steep as a staircase. Then, having secured the goat, she walked all the way back uphill, pausing regularly to yank at the obstinate creature's lead.

By the time Vish returned, Ama lay sprawled sideways on her pallet, panting hard, staring at a spot on the far wall.

"Ama?" asked Vish carefully, clutching the basket of eggs so she didn't drop them in her growing panic. "Are you all right?"

"I feel strange," said Ama, her gaze still fixed on the far wall. "Flowing and aching and pinching. Is this how childbirth feels?"

"I have no idea," Vish replied.

Then the first bad pain hit her, and Ama made a choking sound. "Oh, I see," she said. "Yes. I think this is it."

Things went steadily downhill from there.

"You need a midwife," said Vish.

"I only need you," panted Ama.

"Your mother had me and a midwife also," Vish pointed out.

"Only you," said Ama again, and then her breath was stolen by the next squeezing contraction and she said nothing for a time, only howled.

Vish said to herself, *Oh, Khara, if only you could see. She is so strong, but she needs you so much. We are not complete without you.*

There was a saying across all five queendoms, probably from the time before the Great Peace, Vish suspected: *The daughter has the birth of her mother.* She prayed it would not be true. The scent of birthing blood brought it all back so sharply: the way Khara had twisted and panted, the terror of finding the child *makilu*, the relief of the safe birth all too quickly followed by the Challenge and the fight to the death that followed. Khara hadn't died that day, but in a way, she might as well have. That day led to Tamura's successful Challenge and Khara's death, Ama's exile. The birth was the beginning of everything; after that, there was no turning back.

In this the mother and daughter had to be different. Because there was no Beghala here, no expert midwife to guide and soothe. Vish could not turn a *makilu* child. She had walked away from Ama at the Orphan Tree, which still pained her even though she knew it was the right thing to do; she had sought to make up for that by guarding Eminel, but the child had been kidnapped from the temple of the Bandit God in Hayk. Even though Vish knew Eminel had not only survived, but become the queen of Arca—unthinkable, nonsensical, that little wide-eyed girl grown into an enormously powerful stranger—she still regretted the moment she'd lost the girl, which had led Vish to walk away from Fasiq, the love of her life.

Vish loved Ama in a different way, the way a mother loves a daughter, less like a lightning strike, more like the wind in a field of green wheat. That was the love that kept Vish at Ama's side, murmuring and counseling, praying and rocking, through the long labor when Ama rejected, again and again, Vish's pleas to bring help, turning only, again and again, to Vish herself.

The labor had begun at midday, but as labor dragged on in a mishmash of pain and panting, stomping and howling, the moments of quiet all too brief, darkness had long since fallen. Ama moaned and sweated, half reclining in a pile of blankets on the floor, the only comfort she could find. Vish murmured praise and mopped Ama's brow, kneaded her back with strong fingers, poured water carefully between her parted, fluttering lips.

"Talk to me," moaned Ama, and the echo of her mother's long-ago words was a fist around Vish's heart.

Vish looked to the outside before she spoke, then said, "It's so dark out. Maybe the sunrise will arrive first, maybe your child will. Or perhaps one will follow closely on the other, like a twin whose head touches her sister's heel. The pain is worse with twins." She thought a moment, then added, "I have heard."

"Did you ever," panted Ama, clearly trying to distract herself as a long pain wrung her out, "bear a child?"

"No," said Vish, so briefly the word could not be parsed for emotion. She didn't want to say more, but the laboring woman's face was an open plea. Vish strove to unearth a few words for her, something else to hold on to.

"My body—" Vish said, then paused, searching for the words. "My body was always my own. I wanted no one else to have a claim."

"A child would."

"Not just that," said Vish, who had never spoken a word of this to anyone, not even Khara. But this was what Ama asked of her. Vish wouldn't refuse her friend's daughter, who had become in turn her own friend. Her only one, really. She owed the girl—it was impossible not to think of her as a girl, though she was fully a woman, the pending child being the proof—both distraction and honesty. And Ama had given her a simple way to do both. All Vish had to do was tell the story.

"Pleasure never tempted me. On my first trip to the Moon Rites, I heard and saw women and men in the throes of passion. They lost all control. Why would I give someone that power over me? I wouldn't surrender."

Ama took a long breath, the pain seeming to have given her back for a moment, and her lips curled up in a half smile. "Do you drink wine? Wine is surrender."

"But to one's own impulses. It's different. Not to someone else."

"Sometimes wine makes one . . . more willing."

Vish shook her head. "Never with me. With you? And . . . Paulus?"

"Yes," said Ama, her eyes gleaming a moment with warm memories, before the pain and the present stole them away. She began to pant again. "But we. Are not talking. Of me."

"True," said Vish, rubbing her throat, which had begun to ache. She was not used to talking so much. Even before her injury she had not been given to long stories. Had it been two years since she'd spoken so many words? Three? But she couldn't think of that. Surely the longest story she'd ever told had been to Fasiq. When she thought of the giant, how her silvered scar gleamed in the flickering firelight, the softness of her bottom lip between Vish's teeth . . . it was too much.

Ama groaned through a long pain, squeezing Vish's hand, until the pain seemed to fade and her grip relaxed. Silence hung heavy. Then Ama said, "Do not. Think. That I. Forgot."

"What's left to say?" asked Vish, evasive, her longing for Fasiq still narrowing her throat.

"Everything. Say everything. No men for you? Ever?"

"Never."

"And women?"

"One," murmured Vish.

Ama turned her head away, a long, low animal moan working its way out from between her lips seemingly against her will. Still, she was relentless. As soon as she could speak again, she said, "Tell me. About. Your one woman."

"Fasiq," Vish said, her voice so husky it was like a hoarse growl.

There was silence, and then Ama said, "More," and then silence reigned again.

Vish spoke slowly, each word a struggle in its way. "She was a giant. So alive. Vital. Witty. Terrifying. Glorious. I was drawn to her and didn't know why. I wanted—I wanted to give myself up to her. To rest."

"To surrender? Like you said you wouldn't?"

It became harder and harder to tell the truth. But something about it felt right. Here, just the two of them, as the tense work of labor went on. "I decided it wasn't so bad. If everything was right. If there was trust. If there was love."

"Yes," said Ama, the single word turning into a hiss, *yesssssss*, clearly not thinking of Vish and Fasiq at all. Her eyes rolled back in her head. Her grip loosened and Vish worried that she might have lost consciousness. But then she squeezed even harder than before.

Vish squeezed back. And without being asked this time, she continued the story. "I trusted her not to break my heart. I don't know why. She could be petulant, sometimes. Arrogant. Careless. But I put my trust in her. Something told me I could. She never gave me cause to regret it."

"And when you finally—let someone touch you?"

"Fasiq wasn't just *someone*," said Vish, harshly, not realizing how close to the surface her pain lay until it burst forth. "She was who I'd been waiting for. I hadn't even known I was waiting. For her, and only her, my body came alive like a torch lit in the night."

And even as she spoke the word *night*, Vish saw the first hint of the sun on the horizon.

Ama saw it too. Its rays touched her hair, giving the tops of her sweat-soaked curls a reddish glow. "Ah. The light came first."

"The light," Vish echoed. She didn't think she'd be able to speak another word, but for a long time after that, she didn't have to.

The growing light highlighted the tracks of tears on Ama's face as she panted, "I'm not sure. But I think. It's now."

Then the race was underway in earnest between the child and the sun. More and more light peeked over the distant horizon; the child's head—thank goodness, the head, the baby was not *makilu* as her mother had been—pressed at Ama's opening and then receded, pushed out and drew back in, giving rise to a new howl of pain each time.

"In the palace. They would have. Surrounded me," Ama panted quietly to Vish in between the final pains, clutching the older woman's hands as if they were the only thing keeping her clinging to life.

"Might've been better."

"No!" shouted Ama. "No lotions or incense. No pomp. Just us two. And soon, her."

"Her?"

"I hope. But no matter what. We honor. My mother. With this birth."

"Khara would be proud," said Vish. Then she was relieved of the need to speak at all by a new, sharp, prolonged howl from Ama, her strong hands squeezing Vish's until Vish was sure she heard a soft snap, and the sound went on and on and on.

And then, in a rush of blood and flesh, there was the child.

"Here. Please?" Ama could barely speak, but her hands reached for the child immediately. Vish maneuvered the slippery body into her mother's hands and supported them, not relinquishing her own grip until the small form lay mewling on Ama's blood- and sweat-slicked chest.

Vish saw the moment when Ama forced her gaze to stay on the child long enough to find out what she most needed to know.

A girl. A small, loud girl, howling at the injustice of cold air on her tender flesh, her skin quickly turning red with fury, her small bud of a mouth open wide. The sunlight touched the black hair on her head, finer than her mother's, plastered wet and tight to her tiny scalp. She was perfect, thought Vish. Messy and ferocious and perfect.

"Hello, Roksana," said Ama. She fell silent for a long moment, tears in her eyes, and when she spoke again, this time to Vish, her voice trembled. "Her father liked the name."

"Roksana dha Amankha," Vish answered automatically.

Ama turned her eyes on the older woman, her gaze a question.

Vish said, "If she chooses to take her place in Scorpica. But let's not talk about that today. It's not up to us anyway."

"I want her to be queen of Paxim," Ama said firmly, looking down into the tiny, squashed face. "When the time is right."

Vish said, "And you think *that* will be up to us?"

"These people love nothing like they love a royal bloodline. Can you make me a promise?"

Vish knew all the dangers inherent in a promise, all the ways it could go wrong. But she didn't hesitate. "Yes."

"Guard her for me?"

"You can guard her yourself."

There was a glimmer of fight in Ama's tired eyes. "When I can't be with her, I mean."

But Vish knew what Ama meant. She wasn't inviting Vish to raise the child alongside her, to be a *tishi*. Ama was asking far more than that. She was asking everything.

The only question was how long it would take for Ama to disappear.

She's not Khara, remember, Vish admonished herself. Ama would make her own decisions. Her mother would never have chosen revenge over love. Khara had killed for the right to know her daughter; a few years later, when death came for her, she chose to face it head-on. The mother had chosen her path. Now the daughter would choose hers.

The next four mornings, Vish woke up in the early dawn, opened her eyes, and saw Ama suckling her daughter. Ama's head hung low, her gaze fixed on her daughter's tiny, scrunched face. Her hand ran over the baby's fluff-covered head, over its curves and soft spot, stroking her with the lightest touch, as if she wasn't sure the child was real.

They were quiet days, long days, and the two women rarely spoke a word. Ama slept for long stretches, then rose from time to time to test her strength. On the second day she circled the small hut several times, shuffling on the first circle but stepping more deliberately and carefully as she practiced. On the third she went outdoors for the first time since the child's birth. By the fourth day, she paced the yard on steady legs, staring up toward the sun with an expressionless face, before the baby's cry called her back. Vish brought her food and drink, the things Scorpicae used to build a new mother's strength; strips of fresh rabbit, warm oat porridge, tea from a plant that the Paximites called *fenigrik* but Vish had always known as milk clover. She left these things next to Ama's pallet like offerings, never disturbing her as she slept but making sure she had everything she needed before she thought to ask.

On the fifth morning, when Vish woke up just as the sun began to tint the sky, she looked over, expecting to see Ama bending over her daughter to feed her, but this time, the baby lay alone on the cot, nestled next to the wall, her tiny chest rising and falling with regular breaths. Ama was already gone.

Vish knew Ama hadn't only gotten up to take care of bodily needs. Her knapsack was gone from its hook, her shoes from their place by the door; every trace of the young woman had vanished, except for the slumbering child she'd left behind.

Lying in her own cot, overcome by disappointment, Vish did not move to wake the baby. Not until Roksana woke of her own volition and turned her cheek expecting the soft flesh of a breast to present itself—and opening her small mouth in the beginnings of a wild cry once she found only cold air—only then did Vishala rise.

She bent over the cot, lifting the small, squirming body and folding Roksana into her arms, murmuring, "Here, here, child, I'm here." She fumbled for the cloth she'd hoped not to have to use, a soft thing soaked in goat's milk, and brushed it to the corner of Roksana's mouth until the baby turned her head and latched on with fiery spirit.

And then Vish sang the words of a long-forgotten song, the tune low and lovely in her tender throat, her heart both aching and full.

When the warrior has brought in the victory
Climbed the road home so rocky and steep
Laid herself down surrounded by sisters
Peace be upon the land, and sleep.

When the Scorpion calls us to battle
Wipe the sleep from your slumbering eyes
When a girl helps a girl helps a girl
Strength be in your arm, and rise.

✦ 29 ✦

TRIALED

The fifth month of the All-Mother's Year 518
The Scorpican camp, Godsbones
Gretti, Ama

Gretti had become so comfortable with the routine of trialing new warriors, she felt like she could have done it in her sleep. Some days, she practically did. She awoke, welcomed any women who had approached the camp, read out the rules, watched them perform, evaluated that performance, and asked Lembi to tell her if their intent was pure. If it was, Gretti asked them to bow their heads all the way to the ground and welcomed them; if it wasn't, she nodded to the smith, Zalma dha Fionen, and she did not think about what happened after that. Gretti hated that she'd hardened her heart. But it was the only way.

Then one morning, a recruiting party delivered five unfamiliar women to the Scorpican camp. It was both an unusually fruitful day and a lucky number; Gretti forced herself to slow down and pay attention. Perhaps today would be different. Though why should it?

Why should she be blessed by the Scorpion with happiness?

She turned to them, put on her ringing voice, and said, "Shall we trial you all today?"

They all nodded their heads in assent. Gretti looked them over with a practiced eye. Two were wiry and thin, one solid and muscular, one tall and bulky, and the last short enough to resemble a small child, though her face was the most deeply lined of the five. Both of the thin ones had cut their hair short, probably hoping that if they looked more like warriors they would be more likely to be welcomed. The tallest and shortest ones wore their hair long, though at least both had pulled it back in simple plaits, two plaits for the taller woman, one for the shorter, whose black hair was touched with gray. The muscular one had hair cut short but not shorn like a warrior's, spraying out like the sun's rays from her face in short, spiral curls. There was something about her features that Gretti liked, though she couldn't quite put her finger on why. Well, it made no sense to get attached to any of these women before they were tested. Each would pass the tests or pay the price.

Gretti went through the tests by rote, testing their martial skills, evaluating them as potential warriors to see where they could contribute. The short one had trouble holding up the heavy sword but was remarkably fast on her feet, so Gretti made a note that she might be useful for other pursuits, anything that required speed. The tall one with two plaits was attentive, with a face that tended to smile at rest, and Gretti thought she could be a valuable asset for recruiting, someone who could bring in more like her to become warriors.

She left the muscular one for last. The young woman had a scar across her cheek, a perfectly straight raised line pale against her skin. This suggested she'd fought before. In her combat trials the young woman moved with obvious effort, as if her body wouldn't quite obey her commands, yet she still beat her first three opponents handily. She seemed to have an unerring instinct for where her enemy was about to move. Gretti threw a fourth and then fifth opponent at the recruit to see what would happen, and though the young stranger's wins grew narrower and narrower, she still defeated both. As the scarred recruit held the tip of her sword to the fifth warrior's throat, her tired eyes sought Gretti and lingered. The question was implied.

Gretti finally nodded and said, "Well done."

The recruit withdrew the sword, handed it to the armorer who had given it to her, and rejoined the line with the others. Gretti had a dozen questions for the young woman, but there was no sense in asking any of them, not yet. Right now only one question, and her answer to that question, mattered.

And so Gretti asked that question of each of the five new recruits in turn, and each answered, and Lembi told Gretti whether her answer was true. Three passed, one failed—the tall one with the plaits, a pity—and then it was the fifth one's turn.

Gretti felt a flutter in her chest as she asked the scarred young woman with the short curls, "Do you truly, in your heart, wish to be reborn as a Scorpican warrior?"

"Yes," came the answer. No hesitation.

Gretti inclined her head as Lembi whispered to her, one syllable's breath puffing against her ear, and she had her answer.

"Bow," she said to the young woman. "Put your head to the ground."

The muscular one had seen the other accepted recruits do this, but unlike them, she hesitated.

"Head to the ground," repeated Gretti.

For another long moment, she thought the applicant wouldn't comply. But then the young woman knelt as she was told, lowering her forehead to the ground. Gretti was able to see what she needed to see.

She asked every applicant to do this, had done so since the very beginning of wartime recruitment. She knew that others thought it odd. She had never shared her reasons. Sometimes during this stage, Gretti tugged on the backs of their tunics to lower them; with this one, whose tunic scooped deeply in both the front and back, she did not bother. She looked at the young woman's upper back. Muscled, like the rest of her. Then, no inflection in the quick word, Gretti said, "Rise."

The young woman raised herself, her eyes meeting Gretti's with a clear question.

Gretti was careful to keep her voice level, to betray no emotion. It would be strange enough for the other warriors to hear words from her mouth they'd never heard before, but she didn't want further curiosity. So she pretended nonchalance and chose her words carefully, her eyes on the young woman's.

"This one needs more training. I will take responsibility for it, and for her," said Gretti. "This one will be my daughter."

✦

All four of the new recruits followed the Scorpican known as Gretti, a woman of perhaps three decades and a permanent crease of worry between her brows, to a cook fire for the noon meal. While they ate, scooping coney stew into their hungry mouths with two fingers or a flat of unsalted bread, messengers fetched the warriors who would be their new mothers. First came a tall warrior who Gretti addressed as Pakh, introducing her to the small new recruit with gray in her hair. Then Gretti presented two of the other new daughters, the wiry ones, to a warrior of middle age whose name Ama didn't catch. There were words of explanation, words of welcome, words of thanks. Then the new families drifted away, daughters trailing mothers like cygnets in a pond.

After Ama had not only emptied her bowl but licked her fingers clean several times over, only two of them remained at the cook fire: Ama herself and the warrior Gretti. Ama, for her part, was utterly exhausted. She stared down into her bowl, trying to gather her strength to speak, to move, to do anything at all. It was clear she had pushed herself too hard too soon. She shouldn't have tried the combat trials when she wasn't fully healed from childbirth. She'd been lucky to pass, especially fighting opponent after opponent with no break in between. As she rested, she swore to herself she'd be more careful. She was with the Scorpicae now. If she made another error this serious, it might be the end.

Then Gretti said, "Is it you?"

Warily, setting down her empty bowl, Ama said, "What do you mean?"

"I mean this," said Gretti, reaching around to the back of Ama's neck, then running the tip of her index finger down Ama's spine a few knobs. Her fingertip came to rest and she tapped the spot. "The mark you have. Your mother loved that mark."

"My mother?" Ama whispered. She'd just promised herself to be careful, but was it possible—had this woman really known her mother? Or was this a trap? Ama was so worn out from the journey and the fighting, from the loss of Paulus, the birth of Roksana. She was scraped raw. To let herself hope for an ally felt foolhardy.

"Your mother," said Gretti, her voice thick with emotion, letting her hand fall. She sat down next to Ama but didn't look at her. Gretti stared straight ahead into the cook fire, which was now burning low. Soon it would be only coals. "When you slept, she would bend over you and plant a kiss just there. It was always obvious that she loved you more than anything in the world, but when she kissed you on that mark between your shoulder blades, that's when it was most clear."

Ama said, gently and quietly, "I'm sorry. How do I know you're telling the truth? About who you were to her, and who you think I am? I could be anyone."

"You could be anyone, but you're not. You're Amankha dha Khara."

Hearing the name she hadn't used in a decade, an identity almost no one knew, Ama felt something shiver inside her. She took a moment to collect herself before she responded, and then she asked her most crucial question. "How do I know I can trust you?"

Gretti's answer was quick, her voice grim. "You can't know for sure, and that's the truth. Just like I can't know whether I can trust you. Maybe you're a living, breathing trap. A girl Tamura found, with the same marking Amankha had, and sent to test me. Maybe I'm sealing my death just saying these words out loud. But you know what? *Mokh* that woman and *mokh* the death she intends for me. I'm sick of holding back. Because if it's you, Amankha dha Khara, the fight is worth the risk. Are you she?"

There was no way forward but to leap. Ama said, simply, "Yes."

Gretti continued to stare straight ahead, but Ama saw a muscle twitch along her jawline. When she spoke again, there was hope in her voice.

"I understand you may not remember me," said Gretti. "I was not your mother's lifelong friend and councillor, like Vishala dha Lulit. But Khara was special to me. She saved my life once. She always took me seriously, even when I was young and foolish. I would have followed your mother anywhere in the world. When she was killed, when Tamura sent her to the Underlands, I wanted to join her there."

Ama closed her eyes, shook her head. "But you stayed."

"I stayed." Gretti finally turned to look Ama in the face. "Scorpica needed me more than your mother's shade did. And deep in the Drought, I pledged my help to Tamura—I thought I could shape her, guide her. I thought I could make her a better queen."

"Did you?"

"Maybe, for a while," Gretti said, and her grief was palpable. "But then, even though the Drought was over, she pushed forward with the attack on Arca. It's strange: she and I both love Scorpica more than anything else on earth, but we differ so much on what form that love should take."

"So you want to end the war?"

"As soon as possible. You?"

Ama nodded her assent. Then, fingering the hilt of her weapon, she said quietly, "I don't know how I can fight alongside these women. Against my adopted homeland. But I have to. I need to build trust with the other warriors until I can choose one strong enough to second me."

"Strike that from your worries," said Gretti. "I will second you any day you choose. If Tamura were in the camp, I would second your Challenge today."

"She's not here?" Ama felt a wave of emotion, mingled disappointment and relief, sweep through her body.

"No. She stayed in occupied Hayk. Troops rotate back here for a week at a time, but otherwise it's mostly a recruiting base right now. And a safe place for those who need safety more than glory."

"Does that include you?"

"I'm being punished. Rightly so, I suppose. And so is Azur."

"Azur?" The name was unfamiliar.

"Tamura's successor, if she doesn't come back." Gretti's tone was unambiguous; she did not approve. "They call her the First Mother."

"First to bear a daughter after the Drought, I assume?"

"You assume correctly."

Ama focused, frowning. "If she's special enough to be Tamura's successor, what's she being punished for?"

"Putting herself at risk." Seeing the confusion on Ama's face, Gretti went on, "Tamura wants things her way, and if someone goes against her—but enough of this. There will be time enough to talk. You need rest. Don't deny it."

Ama was tempted to smile. She had, of course, been about to deny she needed rest, but it was undoubtedly true.

"Your mind moves faster than your body, I noted," Gretti said. "Has that always been the case?"

"No. I was recently . . . injured." Ama hoped Gretti wouldn't guess the precise nature of her injury, which was not exactly an injury. The older woman could probably be trusted with the secret, but Ama had other reasons to hold it close. If she thought too much about her daughter, she might abandon this risky enterprise entirely, go running back to the safety of that cottage with the dogwoods out front. But a safe house in a dangerous world wasn't true safety. Vengeance for Khara and Paulus was only one thing at stake. Defeating Tamura could help end this war. So Ama needed to leave Roksana for now, to make the queendoms better for her—and everyone else—later on.

"Then rest," Gretti said. "And that will give us time."

"Time?"

"For me to tell you everything I know about Tamura."

"Like her weaknesses?" Ama knew she would have days to learn these things, weeks, maybe even months, but she couldn't help her curiosity. Even if she could barely keep her eyes open and her arms felt like slack ropes knotted to her shoulders, she could listen.

"I'm sorry to say she doesn't have any of those," said Gretti. "But I can at least share everything I know."

"Tell me what weapon to use against her."

"She's unbeatable," Gretti said flatly. "No weapon is her weakness—and in fact, no weapon at all is her favorite weapon. You know already—I guess the whole world knows—that she snapped that sorcerer's neck barehanded. She's deadly with a bow and arrow, a sword, a hatchet, a staff. She took a shield, a dull, round, iron-edged shield, and rammed it through your mother's neck."

Ama stiffened.

Gretti rushed to apologize, laying her fingers on Ama's arm, touching her for the first time since she'd pointed out the round birthmark on her back at the beginning of their conversation. "I'm sorry, I didn't mean—"

"No, no. It's not that I didn't know how she died. I just—I hadn't pictured it before. I spent a lot of time trying not to picture it. Now maybe it's time for me to face it. It could help."

"You'll need every last shred of help you can get."

Ama put her hand over Gretti's and said, with a grim smile, "Gretti, it's almost like you think I can't win this fight."

"You have to," Gretti replied, almost without emotion. "There is no other choice."

"Maybe you're only saying that because if you second me, and I die, you'll die too."

"There's that," said Gretti. "But more, too. Scorpica's future. What kind of country we want to be. I think it comes down to your path or

439

Tamura's. I don't know what path you'll choose, but I know hers. I have to believe yours holds more promise."

Ama found herself running her fingers along the leather pocket that covered the sharp edge of her blade, stroking it like a pet. "So she's perfect on every weapon? Truly? I'm good with a staff."

Gretti shook her head. "Staff, spear, dagger, it makes no difference. She's trained on every weapon in the arsenal."

Something occurred to Ama, and she drew the curved blade from its pocket. "Don't happen to have one of these in the arsenal, do you?"

"Can I see that?"

A light came into Gretti's eyes as she inspected every inch of the blade, twisting it this way and that until every corner of it had caught the light. She ran her fingertips along the flat side of the blade as tenderly as she'd caress a lover's cheek.

"Yes," said Gretti at last. "This'll do quite nicely."

"You think there's another one of these lying around somewhere?"

"No," Gretti said. "Not yet."

INSTRUCTIONS

**The Holy City, Sestia, and Daybreak Palace,
Arca Eminel**

As she galloped across Paxim on the back of a dead Scorpican warrior's pony, following Velja's edict to travel immediately to the Holy City of Sestia, Eminel had never felt so alive. There was something intoxicating about setting out across the land like this, telling no one, truly alone for the first time in what felt like forever. In many ways she craved the company of others. She knew that about herself. So she wasn't prepared for the flood of relief that came upon her when she gazed at the far horizon and realized that no one in the entire world knew where Queen Eminel, Well of All-Magic, Master of Sand, and Destroyer of Fear, was at this exact moment.

Of course the rivals she'd scattered throughout Arca could, given time and intent, put in the effort to find her. Every last one was rich and resourceful, or she wouldn't have been at court in the first place.

Any scattered courtier could hire the world's most talented Seekers and send them off in search of the queen. But in order for the Seekers to find her, if Eminel understood Seeking magic correctly—which she did, Beyda had made sure of it—Eminel would have to register in the minds of people along the way. That was something she could do something about. She knew, after all, how to hide. As she traveled, she did her best to interact with as few people as possible. If she absolutely had to interact, she was careful to leave no impression.

Eminel had no way to remove the snake necklace, but she hid it under her clothes, wrapping a scarf high on her neck and tucking the front into her tunic so it wouldn't fly loose in the wind. In the wilds of the country and scattered farmland, she foraged for food and drink. When she made her way through the occasional cities, she found ways to steal what she needed. Creating an apple or a flatbread or wedge of cheese was possible with magic, but Eminel had no interest in learning the hard way how much of someone else's life force that might take. Only the lightest flicker of magic was needed to get a shopkeeper to turn the other way at the right time. Often, no magic at all was required. Intelligence, and a few tricks she'd remembered from her days with Hermei, got the job done.

The pony was a miracle. Smart and tough, a worthy companion over the long miles. When she'd approached the abandoned pony after the battle, Eminel hadn't been sure she could even ride her. But once Velja had made it clear what step she expected Eminel to take next, Eminel found the magic within her to make the attempt.

Hush, hush, Eminel had said, speaking directly into the mind of the pony, trying to make her voice as soothing as a stroking palm would be. The pony tossed her head once but then seemed to settle. Eminel gripped the pony's knotted mane with her remaining hand—the stump moved with it as if to help, but she squeezed her eyes closed against the pathetic sight—and swung herself up onto the pony's back.

"I do not know your name, I am sorry," she said, speaking aloud.

Now that she was on the pony, she could try something besides magic. "Is it all right if I call you . . . let's see . . . Sandstar?"

As if in answer, the pony tossed her mane and began to trot forward, westward, toward Sestia.

It was unavoidable, crossing Paxim, that she would think of how she'd grown up here. Months, then years, hiding inside the covered wagon that played home to the Rovers. Surely she had traveled down many of these same roads. But she couldn't tell what was familiar and what simply felt familiar. She had been so young.

When she spotted her first temple of the Bandit God, that was when her nostalgia turned to tears. Gruesome as it was, she wished she'd brought her hand with her instead of leaving it in the dirt outside Hayk, though by now it would have been rotting. She could have sacrificed it on the altar for the Bandit God. As it was, she had almost nothing to give. Then again, almost nothing was not the same as nothing.

She dismounted from Sandstar, then loosened the thin fabric belt around her waist, which was more awkward with only one hand than with two. She'd wear her tunic unbelted; there was no one here to criticize. But it felt like such a meager offering. She needed to give more, and as the tears welled in her eyes, she realized that was the answer. She soaked the belt thoroughly with her tears until its golden color had darkened to a coppery brown, then wove it through the other leavings on the temple's inner walls. The god was known to content Himself with odds and ends, and she thought this one was probably no worse than He was used to.

While Eminel was focused intently on the wall of the temple, carefully weaving the thin belt above a gleaming black mussel shell, below a protruding knife hilt, above what looked like a desiccated knob of ginger, she felt something moving behind her. Someone. A shadow, in the doorway. Larger than her. Breathing.

In the first moment she turned, an old memory slamming into her with almost physical force, she thought it was Fasiq.

But as she blinked away the rising tears, she saw it was just someone tall, their face unscarred, their body lacking the reassuring solidity of the giant's. Their expression was blank and unthreatening. They seemed to barely even notice Eminel's presence, yet their intrusion felt like a clear sign that Eminel was unwelcome.

She left her task undone, the loose end of the belt dangling from the wall, and ducked out of the temple. Outside she gulped in the humid air and searched for her pony. There, tied to a tree, just where she'd left her, thank the All-Mother. When she mounted the pony in a rush, it was the first and only time she dug her heels deep into Sandstar's sides to urge her forward. Truth be told, she was not even sure she'd urged the pony in the right direction. The only direction Eminel cared about in that moment was away.

After another week in the saddle, when she finally arrived in Sestia's Holy City, she saw the familiar yet unfamiliar shape of the temple-palace on the horizon and turned away. Since she wasn't entirely sure yet what Velja intended for her here, she thought she probably shouldn't attract the notice of the High Xara just yet. Eminel didn't think she looked much like a queen just now, but in certain circles, she was sure to be recognized.

As a first action, she decided to stable Sandstar. Without too much trouble, she found a clean-looking stable near the outer walls that seemed to cater to visitors. If the woman who took her coin thought it odd that a one-handed woman who was clearly not Scorpican was riding a Scorpican pony, she made no comment.

Standing outside the stable, brushing the dirt of the road from her unbelted tunic, Eminel considered what to do next. At some point she would need to find lodging, but that wasn't the right place to start. She'd been sleeping in ditches and fields, and if she had to sleep in an alley, she would. For now, she was itching to get started, ready to search for the resting place of the quartz heart. After all, with enough magic, she should be able to detect its power. She moved to press the fingers of her remaining hand against the stump where the other hand had been, feeling for the chips of quartz. Here in the teeming city she could feel the life force around her like a steady hum. No one would notice having a little drawn off here and there. She could work her magic, achieve her mission, and slip out of the city as unnoticed as she had slipped in.

Wait, came a familiar voice inside her skull.

Then Eminel realized she should have expected this all along. Had she really thought Velja would simply give her vague instructions and then leave her to her own devices? The god wanted chaos, yes, but not that kind of chaos. When it came to getting what She wanted, the God of Chaos was as happy as anyone to establish some kind of order for others to follow.

The god seemed to be waiting for some kind of response, so Eminel sent a word of thought her way. *Yes?*

Then Eminel realized something: not a feeling, but the absence of one. This internal conversation with the god didn't seem to drain her magic. Probably the god's magic took care of everything, or at least that was her guess. All told, Eminel almost would have preferred to use her magic to open and exchange her thoughts. That might have helped her feel more in control.

Wait, Velja repeated. Then, a bit later: *Here.*

Here? Eminel sent back the thought, but there was no response, so she took a moment to get her bearings. With the stable behind her, she saw scattered handfuls of Sestians, separately and together, moving down the wide road in both directions. It seemed like a typical midday in any sizable city. People traveled mostly on foot, with a cart or wagon here or there. As she watched, wondering what it was she was waiting for, she heard the faint creak of the stable door. Suddenly the woman who had taken her coin was standing at Eminel's elbow.

The stablewoman was perhaps forty years of age, about the same height as Eminel, slimmer in the hips, with a blunt nose and deeply cleft chin. Her hair was done in two short, tight braids on each side of her head, not even long enough to touch her shoulders. Eminel hadn't spent enough time in Sestia to recognize the style as either typical or atypical; she only remembered the High Xara in her saffron robes, a matching saffron streak blazing in her long dark hair. This woman was more humble in every way, and though her manner had been friendly enough when she'd taken Eminel's coin, now her genial air was gone. She drew uncomfortably close to Eminel, almost as if she didn't see her. The stablewoman settled her feet into a wide stance, then folded her arms. Though she wasn't quite facing Eminel, Eminel could read her expression, which seemed just as out of place as her stance: equal parts skeptical and expectant.

"Is there something you need?" blurted Eminel, forgetting to be polite in her surprise.

"Ha!" came the reply from the woman's lips. "No."

And even those two short syllables made it clear to Eminel, the familiar voice coming from the unfamiliar mouth. The stablewoman, in this moment, was not actually the stablewoman. Velja had occupied the stablewoman's body, riding perched within it like the driver on the seat of a cattle cart. Eminel couldn't quite identify why she found it uncomfortable, and she didn't suppose it mattered; Velja would hardly ask her opinion.

But Eminel needed to speak with the god, and she couldn't quite keep the annoyance out of her own tone as she said, "So we can speak without my magic if you use yours to steal a body?"

"Steal?" said the woman possessed by Velja, tilting her cleft chin, shoulders rising in an exaggerated, disingenuous shrug, thin lips turned up in a god's power-drunk smile.

"Very well, then. I don't object," Eminel lied. "Let's not waste time. You can say what you want to say, and then you can let this woman go back to living her own life."

"Comfortable," Velja's voice said, the woman's form rolling her shoulders, shifting from foot to foot, almost like a sprinter about to run a race.

"This one worships your sister, not you," argued Eminel, unable to let the comment pass. "She isn't yours to take."

"Sure?"

The shudder that raced through Eminel's body at the thought unsettled her. Was Velja suggesting that everyone belonged to Her, even those who didn't worship Her? Then it unsettled her more that the shudder itself could be Velja's work, a sign that the god could send sensation through her at will. This business of dealing with a god felt unspeakably dangerous. Eminel needed to find out what the god wanted and be done with Her, at least in this intimate form. She would have no trouble finding enough faith in Velja to worship Her like any other Arcan, with a shrine and offerings and a household figure. She just didn't want to meet Her face-to-face again, especially when she was keenly aware that the god was wearing an innocent stranger's face.

Forcing more patience into her voice, Eminel said, "I just need to know what to do. Why I'm here."

Velja let one more word fall. "Xara."

"The High Xara?" guessed Eminel.

"Yes."

"Go see her? Is that what you mean?"

The god rolled Her human host's eyes.

"I'll do it," Eminel hastened to clarify, "but I'd like to know the whole plan. Now, this time, all in one go. So we can avoid you needing to hijack other bodies along the way."

The body Velja occupied cocked her head, fixed Eminel with a glare. "Demanding."

"Not demanding," said Eminel carefully. "Asking. So I can be sure what you want."

"You," responded the god, poking her in the center of the chest, not gently.

Something in her intonation made Eminel venture, "What *I* want?"

"Yes."

"You brought me here," Eminel said, trying not to make it an accusation. "For something. For my own good, I assume, but . . ."

The host body stepped forward. She lay a flat palm on Eminel's chest, where the spot she had poked still smarted. In a low voice, as if she were confiding a secret, she said, "Quartz."

"Why would there be quartz here? Sestia doesn't—" And then the meaning of the palm on her chest came to her. The last time she'd been in the Holy City. Who had brought her here, and not survived to leave.

The host's smile was sly, slanting. "Quartz."

Stammering, Eminel said, "But I don't even—I wasn't—I don't even know what happened to the heart. Someone might have destroyed it. With good reason. How do I know it's even still here?"

"Here." The god had no doubt.

"And to find it, I . . ."

The god threw up her hands. "Xara!"

Eminel persisted. She recognized that at this point, she had no real choice but to persist. She had come all this way. And the stump where her left hand used to be felt heavy, leaden, tingling with want. "So I ask the High Xara where the heart is?"

Shaking her head, the god clarified, "Body."

"I ask her to tell me where the body of the sorcerer is." Eminel couldn't bring herself to say the sorcerer's name, not yet. This was all too much. "And she'll do that? Because . . ."

The god's host body pointed at her own narrow chest, crooking her finger, coy. "Me."

"Because my orders come from you."

"Yes." As if it were the simplest thing in the world.

"The High Xara knows what it's like to have a god telling you what to do," she said, as much to herself as to Velja.

The host's expression was inscrutable, neither approving nor disapproving, but she nodded assent.

"All right," Eminel said. "I tell her I'm acting under orders from a god. And then—I should do what?"

The host body's eyes narrowed. "Yes."

Her head spinning, uncertainty welling within, Eminel asked, "I mean, how far do you want me to go? What should I do or not do?"

"*Everything,*" said Velja, and, human form or not, no one who heard how She spoke the word would have recognized Her as anything other than a god.

✦

Even in the Arcan court, with its magic-augmented beauties, Eminel had never seen a man as striking as the one who ushered her into the presence of the High Xara of Sestia. His dark hair was worn loose and flowing over his shoulders, his short tunic belted high enough to show off a narrow waist above thick thighs. His kohl-rimmed eyes were somehow both intent and warm. She felt a shiver climb her spine like a ladder, a sensation she hadn't felt since one of her potential husbands—Alisher, had it been?—had kissed that spot almost a year before.

But this man hadn't even touched her, and showed her nothing but reverence. Had she been in Arca, she would have suspected an enchantment was at work, magnifying her reaction. Instead, she wondered if her own loneliness were the spell to blame. She had reveled in her solitude the whole time she'd journeyed across Paxim into Sestia for this quest, but she was starting to long for company again. Once she returned to Daybreak Palace and reestablished the court, she should consider taking a husband or two, and not just for the power of alliance. Or a wife, she thought. Had a queen of Arca ever taken both a husband and a wife? Or a spouse that was neither or both? The books hadn't said. She would ask Beyda. Beyda would know. If Eminel could marry anyone as beautiful as this man, whatever their gender, she had to believe their company would add to her happiness. She wasn't sure exactly what she wanted, but she wanted happiness. After everything she'd been through—she glanced down toward her missing hand, though she'd rolled down the long sleeves of her tunic to cover its lack—she felt she deserved it. Would completing this mission for Velja make her happier? It almost didn't matter, Eminel supposed. She'd come too far now to turn back.

"Their beauty is not for us," came a bright, sharp voice, and Eminel turned, heat rising to her cheeks as if she'd been caught at something.

Two women stood before her. The High Xara Concordia's face was focused and serious, the yellow-dyed streak that marked her as a Xara standing out from her dark hair like a beacon, a warning. The young woman next to her had no such streak, but like the High Xara she wore a robe of deepest saffron, obviously fine work. It was the younger one who had spoken.

There was an unsettling steadiness to the young woman's gaze. She looked to be about Eminel's age, and like Eminel herself, carried herself with the weariness of a much older woman. Eminel wondered briefly if they were all like this now, all the young women who bore the burden of being the world's last girls for so long. *The lastborn*, she had heard them called. There were newer, younger girls now, but the pain was still there, all that uncertainty, the survivor's guilt, the blame.

The young woman with the steady gaze said, "You are Queen Eminel, Well of All-Magic, Master of Sand, and Destroyer of Fear."

"I am," said Eminel, because what else could she say? Whoever she was or wasn't, she could not deny that she was the queen of Arca, chosen by the blue snake necklace to rule.

"You travel without a Queensguard," the young woman observed, her voice carrying no clear emotion, neither impressed nor derisive, simply stating a fact.

"I do."

Through this whole exchange, Eminel realized, the High Xara had said nothing. The look on her face was colder even than the marble room that surrounded them. Eminel realized this whole encounter was dangerously fraught; she could touch off an incident, considering the fragility of the current peace, and she'd have no one but herself to blame. She had blindly followed Velja's directions, not doubting that she was the chosen of the God of Chaos. She should have been more thoughtful about what Chaos might want to see. Inside the length of her sleeve, she rubbed the stump where her hand had been.

"And are you a priest as—" Eminel began, but the High Xara cut her off.

"Enough interruption! We should be communing with the Holy One," said the High Xara, brushing invisible dust from her saffron robe. "I don't know why we would waste any time conversing with worshippers of Velja."

"But High Xara," the younger woman said, and Eminel did not miss how she subtly positioned herself between the priest and the door, "the messenger said this queen has come all the way here to ask us a favor. Perhaps it is a favor the Holy One wishes us to grant."

"State your purpose, then," the High Xara said to Eminel. "I alone will decide."

"I wish to know where the body of Sessadon is buried," blurted Eminel, and immediately regretted it. It was indeed exactly what she wanted, but to confess it to another queen? What would this woman do with the information? Other than their brief encounter years before, Eminel knew nothing about the High Xara but the swirling stories, her ruthless dedication to Sestia, the sacrifices she'd made, human and otherwise. And that enigmatic young woman—did Eminel know her? There was something about her face that was familiar, but not her eyes. How could she know someone's face but not their eyes?

The almost-familiar young woman, her jaw tense, said, "Impossible. The High Xara cannot and will not reveal sacred secrets."

Brushing the yellow streak of hair back from her forehead, the High Xara said, "If the Holy One wanted me to help you, She would have said so. The god speaks to me and only me, and I do as She commands."

"You do your god's work, I do mine. The only difference is which sister we heed," said Eminel. "We are alike."

The expression on the young woman's face shifted, but Eminel couldn't quite tell what change her last statement had wrought in the Sestian. The High Xara's expression was easier for Eminel to read. Her eyes narrowed, her brow creased. "We are nothing alike," she said.

"We are both queens, are we not?" asked Eminel rhetorically. "We are both our god's chosen."

The pained look on the High Xara's face only intensified; her body remained frozen for a long moment. Then she said, "Come, Olivi," beckoning to the younger woman with a lackadaisical gesture that took obedience for granted. "We have given the foreign queen enough of our time. The god appreciates our charity, but now She desires proof of our dedication. Let us go provide what matters."

Before she turned away, the High Xara closed her eyes and bobbed her head slightly toward Eminel, a gesture of at least mildly respectful farewell. The young woman whom the High Xara had called Olivi did the same, mirroring her superior's position exactly, a physical echo.

It was when Olivi closed her eyes that Eminel recognized her, all in a flash. The Rites of the Bloody-Handed, the only other time Eminel had journeyed to the Holy City and met the High Xara, that was when she'd seen this Olivi. The young woman—she would have been ten-and-four that year, like Eminel—had been memorable because she'd come so close to dying. Olivi had been strapped tight to the bone bed, helpless as the terrible events unfolded. The boy next to her had been slain, but she'd survived.

Olivi had been the intended sacrifice at those rites, realized Eminel, just over two years ago. And now Olivi worked alongside the High Xara, clearly a trusted attendant at the very least, and at most? Who knew? If a girl of Sestia could go from nearly dying to the highest corridors of power, she must be uncommonly intelligent and able. And as Eminel watched, Olivi's eyes flew open again. Even as the High Xara turned her back with a sigh, Olivi fixed her gaze on Eminel, her eyes searching, uncomfortably intent.

Suddenly she was reaching out. Olivi caught Eminel by her left wrist, encircling it loosely with her thumb and forefinger, as if forming a living bracelet that echoed the quartz one Eminel had lost.

Olivi's lips moved silently, forming the shapes of words without breath behind them to make sounds. She repeated the shapes of the words a second time, more slowly, and looked at Eminel's face to see if she'd understood.

Read. My. Mind.

Without another moment's delay, eager beyond belief, Eminel opened her mind to reach into Olivi's mind. Instantly she heard Olivi's thoughts, clear and sharp as if spoken aloud right next to her waiting ear.

The tombs in the northwest of the city, thought Olivi. *The entrance is hidden; there are no guards. Here is how you open the door. The rest is yours to do.*

An image came into Eminel's mind with such stunning clarity that she almost gasped aloud, barely catching herself. She saw the entrance to the tombs Olivi meant, the trick door with a small hole under the heavy bolt where she'd have to trip a special catch; she saw her own path unfolding before her, to leave this place, to cross the city, to find the secret tomb, to open the door.

Then Olivi was turning her back just as the High Xara had, and with the two saffron-robed women already leaving her sight, there was nothing for Eminel to do but go her own way, following the path Olivi had somehow communicated into her brain.

It hadn't been magic, Eminel realized, not on the Sestian's part. If it had been, Eminel would have felt power coming directly from Olivi. She definitely hadn't. But Olivi had known that Eminel could read her thoughts, had called to mind exactly the information Eminel would need to retrieve, laid it out before her like cakes on a platter.

There was more to this Olivi, to be sure, even if Eminel couldn't spare the time to investigate it today.

Less than an hour later, Eminel found herself at the very door that Olivi had visualized for her, its remote entrance built into a hillside so seamlessly that the Arcan never would've found it if she hadn't known it was there. Eminel slid her finger into the hole and tripped the catch, marveling how easily the heavy door slid aside when she did.

Within moments she was inside a network of tombs. When she saw how dark they were, how narrow the halls, she had a moment of panic that Olivi, motivated by some other loyalty, had sent Eminel here to die. If the door closed behind her, she thought suspiciously, would there be a way to open it again? So before she let the bolt fall back into place, she tested the secret catch and found that it worked in this direction too. She took a breath tinged with relief. She was still nervous, but her trepidation was no match for her curiosity. She was ready to move forward, whatever the cost.

Eminel turned to locate the torches she'd seen in Olivi's thoughts, then called forth a quick fillip of magic using her own life force and the fragmented quartz in her skin to light the nearest. Her gut still twisted when she let the door close all the way, almost soundlessly, leaving her alone in the near dark. Suddenly the torch didn't seem like nearly enough to light her way. But as she made her way down the narrow tunnel leading deeper into the tombs, she lit each torch as she passed it, feeling a bit more at ease as each one flickered into life.

As she moved smoothly down the tunnel, Eminel wondered why the Sestians would bury an enemy in their most sacred place, among the dead of their own country. But in some ways, it made sense. This was a place of great power. Sessadon had been a woman of great power. Besides, that door was thick. Eminel, for one, found that reassuring.

When she reached the higher ceiling of what seemed to be the main part of the tombs, the air stale and the torches too weak to illuminate every corner, she paused. The statues of what must be former Xaras unsettled her again. Were their dead, wasted bodies interred under the statues, or farther in? In the flickering light, at the edge of her vision, she thought she saw what looked like the splayed toe bones of a long-dead foot. She turned away, not eager to investigate. She was here for only one purpose. Without focus, she feared she would not achieve it.

Eminel closed her eyes, gathered her power, and reached out for the feeling of magic. It was there, but it was faint. Eventually she located the weak, flickering signal and followed it until it was just a hair less weak, ducking under an archway into another room within the tombs. The floor of the room was marked every few strides with a round flat of cork, three handspans wide, each with some pattern burnt into it. She guessed that they were buried amphorae. She had seen a similar configuration in the cellars of Daybreak Palace, where they were used to store fragrant, deliciously bitter amber wine. Eminel rarely indulged in fermented drinks, but when she did, she preferred amber, the less sweet the better.

But, Eminel realized with a shiver, she was in a tomb. Whatever was in these amphorae, under those scorched cork plugs, was not wine, amber or otherwise.

She focused again. The call of magic came from below a cork plug with a black *S* burnt sloppily into its surface, not far from where she'd entered. On some level she knew she had a choice, but still, she had come this far, and the next step seemed obvious if she wanted to see this action through. The plug in question was not difficult to remove. Eminel peered nervously inside, holding her torch as close as she dared, unsure she'd be able to see all the way down.

The amphora was only a few feet deep, as it turned out, shallower than the amphorae in Daybreak Palace. Within this one lay a heap of bones that Eminel could only guess would be sufficient to support a human body, and lying atop that heap, the fist-sized quartz heart.

It didn't glow. It didn't shine. It was only a rock like any other rock, as if it had never been more. That gave Eminel the confidence to put her hands on it, though she could easily visualize herself melting into nothingness at daring to touch. That would be an ignoble end, after all she'd been through, she realized. But when she knelt outstretched on the floor of the tomb, extended her arm through the mouth of the amphora, and closed her remaining hand over the knot of quartz, she didn't melt. The ordinariness of it was what she found remarkable. After reaching, she only brought up a solid object in her clutched hand, as anyone might do.

The quartz lump that had once been Sessadon's heart was cold and heavy. She lifted it from the hole and set it on the floor, leaving it there with a shiver of suspicion as she carefully used both hands to replace the loose cork with its emblazoned S. Then Eminel turned to the quartz heart, its slick surface reflecting back the lamp's meager light. And she was uncertain.

"Velja," she said out loud, simply. She didn't need to say more. It was clear what she wanted. Either the god would come to her or She would not.

There was the sound of stone scraping on stone and then, with a final eerie screech, one of the statues opened its eyes. It blinked twice and then the mouth began to lever open, impossible but happening, like so many other sights Eminel had witnessed in recent years, she realized.

Eminel braced herself for the voice, and when it came, it was Velja's.

The God of Chaos, in the form of the statue, said, "Yours."

Eminel looked down at the slightly bluish quartz heart, its weight both reassuring and unsettling in her hand. Slowly she said aloud, "Mine?"

With a sigh of impatience, Velja answered aloud, "Yours."

Swept with dread, Eminel looked at the statue from which the god spoke to her, trying to keep her gaze level with the stone eyes. "I can't," she said.

"Can't?"

"Put this in my chest." She brandished the heart. There was nothing to be lost by telling the truth; if Velja didn't like what she had to say, Eminel wouldn't be long for this world anyway. "I'm not like Sessadon. I don't want to be like her. I can't have a quartz heart."

Velja laughed in that way Eminel was growing to loathe, a condescending, dismissive laugh that made Eminel feel small.

Then the god scoffed, "Heart?"

◆

Two weeks later

The first time Eminel had approached Daybreak Palace, she saw now, she'd done so as a child. Broken, confused, she'd arrived here after the rites in the luxurious wagon half passenger, half prisoner. What else had she been? A limp doll. An emptied vessel. A freshly minted murderer, a hero, a god's unwitting tool. Above all, an unready queen.

This time, Eminel approached Daybreak Palace astride a Scorpican pony, her head held high and her hair streaming behind her in the wind, and the only regret she had was that she couldn't ride forever.

She halted Sandstar in a cloud of dust, their stop sudden but precise. She dismounted in one smooth movement. She'd grown close to Sandstar over the miles. She'd learned to read the pony's moods, and vice versa, so the two moved as one even without the formal need for mind magic. If it had been good as she rode from Hayk to the Holy City, it was even better once she'd completed her task in the Holy City, retrieved Sandstar from the stable, and mounted her to ride for home. She would miss the simplicity of those days: rising, stretching, climbing onto the pony's back and hunching forward with anticipation, making leagues of road vanish behind them.

But she was a queen of Arca, not a Scorpican patrol rider from the time before the Drought, and it was time to set things in order. She had left Daybreak Palace sealed up tight, promising that no one but she could break the seal, and today was the day to find out if that was true.

Some part of her had wondered if the magic had broken apart in her absence, especially when the Talish cuff had been destroyed in the battle of Hayk. But here Daybreak Palace stood, just as she'd left it, its spires and curves as breathtaking as ever, no human figures standing in the shadow of its doorway. If the magic had drained away, there was no immediate exterior sign. And as she neared, Eminel realized she could feel the humming of the enchantment she'd put in place, the current of energy walling off the palace from the rest of the world. A hazy memory swam to the surface as she stood there. Warm sun reflecting off a half-remembered lake of glass.

But this was a time for action, not memories. She raised her covered hand. She snapped her fingers, the gloved fingertips sliding against each other in a near-silent whisper. The sound didn't matter. The magic was there. With that quiet snap, in an instant, the enchantment sealing the palace fell away.

Eminel strode into Daybreak Palace on quiet feet, the building's high entrance arch soaring above her head. These past few weeks, she'd pretended she was not a queen. Here, she could be nothing else. But the realization felt right, somehow. The blue necklace of royalty was hidden underneath the layers of her thin traveling costume. She felt its weight on her chest and savored it. It was neither cold nor warm against her skin. The temperature of the glass matched her own. In this way, as in so many others, she finally felt at peace.

The first to meet her was Vermu, the youngest of her Queensguard, who was charging toward the entrance with her hand on her weapon, ready to defend against an intruder. She stopped short when she saw that the intruder was in fact her queen.

Eminel dipped lightly into Vermu's mind. There was no need for a long litany of questions when she could simply know what she needed to know, and she collected the information she needed. The prisoners of the palace had waited impatiently for her return, but yes, they had waited. Things had happened, of course, disagreements and challenges, but none had been fatal. That was all that mattered now, at least from Eminel's perspective.

Vermu's unsteady voice said, "We didn't . . . this is a surprise. We didn't know when—if—you were coming."

"And now I am here," Eminel said. "Thank you for the warm welcome."

Vermu tried to stammer out the welcome Eminel had already thanked her for, but the queen wasn't interested in holding the young woman's feet to the fire. There were others to greet, to reassure. They'd been prisoners and not known why or for how long. Some part of her regretted what she had put them through. Another part of her had no regrets. It had been necessary. It had been worth it.

"I will tell the others you've arrived!" Vermu turned away, already in motion.

"No," Eminel said. She was ready to use magic to stop Vermu, but her voice was magic enough.

Vermu stopped, turned, bobbed her head deferentially. Finally she took her hand off the hilt of her weapon. "You must be exhausted from your journey, Queen Eminel. Perhaps you should rest in your rooms?"

"Thank you, no," said Eminel. "I have other plans." She gave Vermu orders to give no sign that she'd returned, but to summon the young representatives from the matriclans and direct each of them to pack for a journey.

"There will be questions," Vermu said, clearly working to contain her concern.

"I will answer them, in time," Eminel responded. "In an hour, the representatives are to gather at the lower holding room."

"Not the audience chamber?"

"Not the audience chamber. The lower holding room. I will see them there in an hour. Tell no one I have returned, and if they guess, do not confirm it. Clear?"

To her credit, the young guard took the odd request in stride, nodding her agreement. Though once Eminel's instructions were complete, Vermu did suggest once more, "And now, would you like to rest?"

"Thank you, no," said Eminel, exactly as she had before, and pointed Vermu in the direction of her task. For her own part, Eminel set out briskly for another destination.

When she flung open the doors to her bedchamber, the room had a stale air to it, unused. She found that somehow comforting. There had been a tiny, niggling doubt that her plan wouldn't work, that either the senior courtiers without or the junior courtiers within would somehow find a way to break the enchantment. But that had not come to pass. It must have been quiet here without scheming whispers enlivening the hallways. Well, now that she was back, things would change. But somehow she didn't find that troubling or worrisome. Let things change. She was ready.

She paused just one moment in her bedchamber before taking her next step. Eminel had covered herself before nearing Daybreak Palace. She wore leggings tucked into boots and a long-sleeved tunic tucked into gloves, the tunic's high neck covering her own neck, a cowl covering her hair. The fabric was thin to keep her from baking in the heat, but the impression was of a woman covered, only her face showing through. While she wasn't ashamed, she wanted to control the moment when she revealed how she'd changed. There was a value to that she wouldn't squander.

Lowering the cowl from her hair to rest on her shoulders, Eminel slid open the door to the secret tunnel, its air even more stale. Then, she found herself moving faster and faster through the passageway, taking the last few steps down at a half run. The other residents of the palace were more strategically important to the country, to her reign, but there was only one person here she truly cared to see.

Beyda was hunched over the broad table in the study room, papers surrounding her in a scattered wave. She seemed to have no awareness that the door to the passageway behind her had opened. No part of her moved: not her bent head, not her hunched shoulders, not her elegant fingers pinning a handwritten document to the table. For a long, silent moment, she was so still that Eminel thought she might be asleep. But then her other hand spasmed outward and Eminel saw the stub of pen clutched in her fingers. The quick-moving hand scribbled across a sheet of paper so full of letters Eminel couldn't see where the old writing left off and the new writing began, not from where she stood. So intent was Beyda on her work that even when Eminel shifted, sighed aloud, leaned against the doorway, Beyda kept her back resolutely turned. Finally, Eminel realized she needed to speak.

"Scribe," said Eminel.

"For the last time, I told the kitchen I wasn't to be disturbed," Beyda muttered downward without moving her head, without turning. Her voice sounded scratchy with neglect. "If I get hungry, I'll come to you. Don't disturb my work." All the time she spoke, her hand kept scribbling, nor did she lift her other hand even to wave the intruder away. The tableau—stacks of documents, solitary woman—tickled something in Eminel's brain, and she finally realized what it was. One of the stories of Arcan queens she'd learned in the early days of her rule. The fourth queen of Arca, Queen Alaphene, had been obsessed with the queendom's finances. Consumed with growing her fortune, terrified the money would run out even as it grew and grew, she'd driven herself mad with numbers. In the end even her own matriclan had agreed she needed to be removed and replaced, sending a relative with death in her touch to dispatch Alaphene with sudden and quiet mercy. There had been an illustration in a book that looked almost exactly like what Eminel was seeing now: a woman lost in her work, lost to the world. While she'd been gone, Eminel thought with a sick lurch in her stomach, had something broken in Daybreak Palace after all?

"Beyda," said Eminel, nervous but firm, loud enough the scribe couldn't help but hear her. "I hope my return is worth disturbing you for."

Then the scribe stood so quickly her stool tipped behind her, clattering to the floor, and when her face—drawn and sun-starved, Eminel noticed—turned toward Eminel, she was smiling broadly.

Eminel reached out her arms and Beyda threw herself into her friend's embrace. The feeling of holding someone, especially this particular someone, was so reassuring, so powerful, that Eminel found herself squeezing a little harder than she'd meant to.

"Enough!" said Beyda in a choked voice, but she was laughing.

Eminel whispered in her ear. "I have so much to tell you."

"Tell me what's most important. You survived the Scorpican attack, that much I see. And you returned to unseal the palace. Were you tempted not to? I would have been tempted, I think."

"What's most important," Eminel ventured gently, "is that I'm here. And everything is going to be all right. And you've been busy, it appears?"

Beyda stepped back and chuckled, a bit self-consciously, or was there something more to the way she moved her body to block Eminel's view of the table? "Yes. Been following a thread on something I've been studying for a long time. I may have a breakthrough, the translation, if the words were . . . but listen to me yammer on. There will be time. Does anyone else know you're back?"

Eminel told her what she'd told Vermu to do. Beyda raised an eyebrow. "They'll be terrified."

"Let them be. Fear now will mean gratitude and relief after."

"You're better at emotion than I am," Beyda said.

Eminel said, "You're better at other things," and gestured to the table of papers. "Do you want to get back to your work? I'd like to have you in the room for my conversation with the representatives, but I understand I've interrupted you."

Beyda put her hand on the small of Eminel's back and guided her toward the passageway, saying, "No, this work will still be here after you've done what you need to do. It's good to have you back. Shall we freshen up in your chambers before you meet the representatives of the matriclans?"

Back in her own rooms, Eminel splashed some water on her face and some scent on her neck with one hand, but she chose not to change her clothes, staying in her traveling ensemble for now. When she was done washing, she drew her glove back on and ignored Beyda's quizzical look.

By the time they reached the gathering room, Eminel had decided not to reveal all that had changed, not today; she needed to save the impact of that moment. She could do what she needed to do today without spending that revelation. As Beyda had predicted, the young courtiers Eminel had summoned for this audience mostly looked terrified, glancing at each other with nervous, brittle energy. They looked about as Eminel had expected them to, a varied pack of young women whose age was near hers but with little else in common with her or each other. She inspected the front row of five young woman, each the highest-ranking young woman of her matriclan. She had not asked them to stand this way, but they had.

Of the five, only the tallest one seemed unconcerned, wearing a formal patterned gown of deep blue with a tracery of peacock feathers, accessorized with a bored expression. The one beside her with the thick brows and plump lips had dressed herself in several layers of clothing, wearing one pair of leggings over another and three tunics of varying lengths, the traveling pack on the floor next to her stuffed to bursting. The third and fourth stood close to each other, their dangling hands almost brushing, only occasionally glancing up from the floor where their packs sat in front of them. The last young woman in the front row, her hair rumpled and her expression murderous, carried no luggage at all.

The other young women stood behind them, each clustering with her own matriclan, and they, too, varied in what they wore and how they carried themselves. They'd all been given the same instructions but had clearly reacted differently. Several glanced nervously toward the door, where Vermu and another member of the Queensguard stood between the five young women and the room's only exit.

Eminel raised an eyebrow at Vermu, indicating the second guard, an addition to the plan that Eminel had not suggested. Vermu said quietly, "Not all of them wanted to come."

But then the closest of the young women, the one wearing half her wardrobe, noticed who Vermu was speaking to and gasped aloud. Then she looked around the room, took two steps forward, and fell to her knees. "Queen Eminel! Well of All-Magic, Master of Sand, and Destroyer of Fear! You've returned."

"I have," agreed Eminel dryly, as the rest of the young women fell to their knees around her. Even the angry one, after a glance at the Queensguard, followed suit, her eyes respectfully lowered.

Eminel waited until their frightened murmurs took on a warmer cast, words of welcome, and then said, "Stand and rejoice! I regret that it was necessary to keep you at Daybreak Palace these past months, but that time is at an end. I've asked you all to pack for travel because you're going on a mission."

The tall one in the gown raised a skeptical eyebrow. Others leaned forward with growing excitement.

Careful to make her voice friendly and optimistic, Eminel went on, "You will serve as messengers to your matriclans. There are five carts waiting in the courtyard, one for each matriclan. Go to your ancestral lands. Tell the court they may return."

"May," asked the tall one, "or must?"

Eminel wasn't upset by the question, which was reasonable. "I said 'may', and I meant it, thank you. If any member of your matriclan chooses, she may stay where she is. No censure, no mandate. But make it clear to them what they are choosing. The court will meet here at Daybreak Palace on the evening of the second full moon from today. Only those present for that meeting will still have a place at court."

The young woman wearing three tunics shouldered her pack before Eminel had even finished speaking. "Thank you, Queen Eminel," she said. "I have a long way to go. May I leave?"

"Yes. Velja bless you on your journey."

The others trickled away, the two who had almost held hands heading in the direction of the courtyard together, the angry one stalking behind them without going back for luggage. The one in the gown, though Eminel assumed she would want to change clothes now that she knew what was intended, simply glided toward the courtyard with her head held high. Both members of the Queensguard looked to Eminel for guidance; she gestured that they should go to the courtyard with the hostages-turned-messengers.

In the space of a minute, the messengers had scattered. The younger Eminel would have feared what they thought of her, and how her message would be received. The queen Eminel had become didn't care. They would deliver the message, she was sure of that much, and how it was received, she could not control. Courtiers would return or they wouldn't. Her path forward was the same either way.

After the room had emptied, Beyda reached out and squeezed her hand. "Now what?"

Eminel squeezed back. "Now it's my turn to wait."

✦

The day of the second full moon, the day Eminel had designated for the reassembly of her court, the audience chamber rumbled with voices. From her seat on the throne, wearing her costume of head-to-toe linen, she surveyed the crowd. A dish of dates sat next to her. She left them untouched, not wanting to get her gloves sticky, but after this was over, she'd be eager to savor their sweetness.

The recently returned heads of the clans began to present themselves, giving updates on what had happened in their villages. She listened to them, her face impassive, her manner patient. Over the time Eminel had been gone, they reported, the undeclared war had been won. There had been skirmishes here and there in the early months, but after word spread of the defeat at Hayk, the attacks had dwindled to nothing. Many of the newly trained villagers had not even needed to practice their martial skills. For the past month not a single raid had been reported anywhere in Arca. No scouts had seen a single Scorpican, with the exception of those assigned in the far northeast. They had seen a party riding like mad into Godsbones, and some days later a cloud of red dust had kicked up, again moving north. The assumption was that the Scorpican column had gone north and not come back.

They hoped the Scorpicae would not return, but if they did return, the villages of Arca would be ready.

And the court rejoiced.

There were calls for celebration, but Eminel did not encourage them. "We have triumphed," she said, "but that is nothing to celebrate. This victory is our due. This victory came through hard work. And the one to thank for that is Velja. We will not fritter away the coming days with carnivals and celebrations; instead I would like to see us pass the next five days in prayer. It is Her gifts we have to thank for this. It is Her harvest we reap."

Eminel drew off one glove and reached into the bowl of dates, plucking a fat one from the top of the pile and laying it on her tongue. She hummed with pleasure.

"One more thing," she said, catching sight of the woman she wanted to see. "Sobek, will you approach, please?"

Sobek reacted with surprise but then covered it, putting on a bland expression, slowly walking toward Eminel and standing before her on the throne.

"Every member of court who has appeared today will serve the realm. But not all will perform the same services they did before. I've decided to make some changes."

Sobek said, her voice a purr, "I am of course happy to serve you in whatever way you ask, Queen Eminel."

"Thank you," said Eminel, testing the mental shield she'd put in place to defend against whatever words Sobek might speak. "I have a very special assignment for you. To lead an important project."

"I will build whatever you need built."

"It is not a building," she said, "but a disassembly. I wish the grounds where all-magic girls were once trialed to be leveled to flat ground."

Sobek tried to hide her shock but was unsuccessful; she was far from the only one.

Eminel went on as if she didn't realize she was saying anything remotely controversial. "We have no need of trials. There will be no examinations of all-magic girls, no trials that pit them one against the other, and no sponsorship that leaves them open to exploitation."

"But Queen Eminel," Sobek protested weakly. "The glory of the court depends on reviving the system that has been neglected these past years of the Drought."

"Then perhaps we will have a court without glory. And whoever finds that unsatisfactory is free to leave. I won't run a court that seeks only to reconstruct some fabled past. My court will look to the future."

The whole roomful of faces gaped at her now, watching breathlessly. Now, thought Eminel. Now she must seize her moment.

She'd drawn off her right glove earlier to pluck a date from the pile. Now, with deliberate ceremony, she drew off her left. In a voice that mustered thunder, Queen Eminel, Well of All-Magic, Master of Sand,

and Destroyer of Fear said, "Let Velja's work be done."

An outburst of shock ran around the room once and then fell silent. Eminel let the glove drop to the floor, but not a single pair of eyes followed it down. They were all too busy staring at the hand left bare in the glove's absence, which the queen obligingly raised high.

The queen of Arca's left hand was not flesh but quartz, a bluish-white quartz that gleamed with reflected light. Yet it was not cold and still like any other stone. It moved and flexed and bent just like a flesh hand would, though it was not and clearly had never been flesh.

As they watched, the quartz hand glowed brighter, clearly gathering magic, and those not quick enough to look away found themselves briefly blinded.

If there was discontent, it remained at a low buzz. No one even cut their eyes directly at the queen. She beamed at them, a broad smile on her face. Whatever doubts she'd had along the way, whatever pain she'd gone through as Velja led her through the ceremony to transform the quartz heart into the hand she lacked, now she finally felt right.

This was her country. These were her people. She was no longer the unready queen, but a ready one, in full control. She could feel the magic humming in her veins. She flexed the quartz fingers of her left hand, formed a fist, extended the palm and blew a kiss to the court over her quartz fingertips.

With her right hand, the flesh one, she reached out for another date and savored the sweetness on her tongue.

✦ 31 ✦

CHALLENGE

The Scorpican camp, Godsbones
Tamura, Ama

Queen Tamura would have happily breathed her last on the bloody battlefield of Hayk, closing her eyes forever. But she opened her eyes again, and when she awoke, she awoke among the cursed red hills of Godsbones.

Someone had done this to her, perhaps many someones, she realized. It would have taken more than one pair of hands to bear her, limp and unknowing, across the leagues between the battlefield of Hayk and the Scorpican camp, all the way across that narrow natural bridge into the sheltering caves. Tamura had no idea how long she'd been unconscious, lost in the dark. But she was infuriated both by what she remembered and by what she realized she must have missed.

She had not been allowed to die with honor and glory. And the Scorpicae had failed to hold Hayk, that was obvious. They'd been driven from the field. That was the only explanation for the queen of *mokhing* Scorpica to regain her consciousness flat on her back in these red wastes. She wasn't sure which impulse rose stronger within her at that moment: to die or to kill.

She had no inkling what to do, weak and disgraced, yet still responsible for leading her mighty nation to triumph. Was that even possible now? How could she turn this defeat to victory?

Pain-addled and angry, forcing herself to begin her reckoning with the post-Hayk world, Tamura opened her eyes. Crouching at her side was Azur. Her first instinct, misplaced or no, was to spring up to place her blade against the younger woman's throat. She wanted to punish someone, anyone, for what she was feeling, and the closest was the easiest to reach. But when Tamura tried to move, not only did the pain in her head render her dizzy but she found her body weakened by her ordeal. The hand that would have borne a blade only twitched against her own thigh and lay still. Her head throbbed as if Zalma had swung her massive hammer and hit Tamura so hard on the temple she'd knocked the queen clear off her feet.

"Rest, Queen Tamura," said Azur. "I am relieved to see your eyes open, and your warriors will rejoice at the news, but you still need rest."

Tamura opened her mouth to respond, but nothing came out. She wanted to rail, to curse, to strike. The air rasped in her throat like wind in the trees. Words were out of reach.

"Rest," Azur said again, her voice soothing, honey-smooth. "We will regroup. We are strong. We are still warriors. This is only a setback."

Rejecting the words and the woman who spoke them, Tamura squeezed her eyes tight shut. That movement, at least, was not beyond her.

When she regained her strength, she would make someone pay.

But who and how? Was vengeance even the answer? She was so tired, her head clouded and sluggish.

Tamura forced her clouded mind to work. If they had missed both their chance to take Arca and their chance to squeeze concessions from Paxim, they might as well drag their sorry carcasses back to Scorpica and plan never to leave there again. Now that the Drought had ended, they'd do better to build their strength back up by bearing children. She'd taken steps in that direction, sent those young women to the Moon Rites, but now, months too late, she wished she'd done more. And everything had changed. They could never go back to the way things had been before the Drought. Would the other nations ever trust them again?

Only if she were no longer their queen, Tamura realized. If the queen who came after her played things correctly, she could disavow Tamura's decisions and make some kind of change. But Azur would not be able to make such a claim, would she? Tamura had chosen her, deliberately and publicly, as a successor. Everyone knew Azur was her most treasured daughter, mother of her only granddaughter so far. If Azur followed as queen after Tamura, she would still have the cloud of Tamura's misdeeds hanging over her own reign. Then again, it didn't matter what the truth was, Tamura reminded herself, whether or not the two had cooperated. It would only matter what the other queendoms believed.

She had thought once, before this war, that she wouldn't mind being Challenged. She realized now that she absolutely would. Now that she felt power slipping through her fingers, she would do absolutely anything and everything to fight for it.

But would everything be enough?

As the days and nights passed, one sometimes slipping into the next without her noticing, Tamura had some moments of absolute clarity and others when she could barely remember who she was and why she was here. But no matter how lucid or lost she felt, she showed no weakness. That, she decided, was the most important thing.

Over the course of weeks and then months, as Tamura began to regain her strength, she pretended nothing had changed. Let them accuse her, let them Challenge her, but it would be on them to make the move. She would continue on as things had been in all the ways that she could. Scorpicae would continue to recruit, because there were still discontented girls and women of Paxim and Arca who felt more of a kinship with the Scorpicae than they did with the places where they'd been born. An occasional Sestian even trickled in, the word having spread all the way to their lush green farmland that a warrior's life awaited those for whom farms held no promise. Every recruit faced the same tests, and once accepted into the Scorpicae, each one was sister to the rest no matter her history. This, at least, could be celebrated.

Tamura also gave the order that the raiding parties continue, because she still refused to allow hunting in Godsbones, and fighting or not, warriors needed to be fed. She wanted to see how many months this state of affairs could continue before she was forced to a reckoning. Besides, a dozen of the young women who'd gone to the Moon Rites last year showed every sign of bearing warriors inside their bodies, and if enough of them had girls, it would motivate dozens of young warriors to make the trip this year, which would be easier to do from where they were, instead of trekking all the way from Scorpica. The Godsbones camp, strange as it might have been initially, had become comfortable. Tamura was not in a mood to leave it before she absolutely had to, and she was sure she wasn't the only one who felt that way.

She didn't explicitly take power back from Azur, but she thought of all the ways in which Azur had probably been wielding power during her absence and convalescence, and stepped in to reestablish herself. Once Tamura had the strength, she was first at the cook fires each day, making sure to greet each and every warrior she saw, to show she was well again. She took stock of the provisions, monitored what and who came back from each raid. She visited the armorer, the smith, the woman who repaired the tents, every important person she could think of. She honed her sword where everyone could see.

Still, she wondered if the blow to her head had hurt her in ways she couldn't identify, let alone recover from. She could feel things slipping out of her mind almost as quickly as she put them in. And she hadn't forgotten the searing pain that had struck her the moment before the horse had thrown her so fatefully. Just knowing the world had such pain in it, that stuck with her in a way she wouldn't have wanted to describe to another living being, even if she could have found the words.

It had taken more than a month for Tamura to rise from the tent where they'd laid her upon return from the battle, and she spent months after that making a show of competence and authority, returning to rule. So the next season was already upon the camp—not that Godsbones changed much with the seasons—when she decided to ensure that she met every single new recruit of Scorpica, all the daughters who had joined in her absence, the generation that would decide whether Scorpica as a nation would succumb or survive.

Though she had taken pains to reestablish her connections with nearly every woman of importance in the camp, she had been avoiding one: Gretti dha Rhodarya. Tamura was afraid the woman would notice that something in her had changed. But today, Tamura had asked Lembi to introduce her to every new daughter, and she had for whatever reason not thought about Gretti claiming a daughter for herself until that woman and that daughter were standing right in front of her.

This daughter was clearly a warrior, wherever she'd been born: of medium height but densely muscled, with the defined shoulders that gave away a trained swordswoman even at a glance. More than that, there was something unsettling about the intensity of her gaze. Intensity was good in a warrior, but this girl seemed unable to temper hers, as her eyes fairly burned, her stare unrelenting.

Gretti said, "A moment, please, Queen."

That was when the hair on Tamura's arms stood on end. Gretti had not been polite to her in a long time, not since the day Tamura had given the command to attack Arca, the same day Madazur was born. Gretti must have her reasons now.

Still, Tamura kept her voice calm. "Yes, what is it?"

It was the young stranger with the intense gaze, the woman adopted into the Scorpica as Gretti's daughter, who answered. "I have one thing to say and will say it clearly."

In a flash, mostly by instinct, Tamura suddenly recognized the shape of those sharp eyes. Who they reminded her of. And with that, she knew what the young woman would say a heartbeat before she said it.

The new recruit said, "To you, Tamura dha Mada, I speak the Words of Challenge."

❖

Tamura's reaction to her Challenge, at least at first, was not at all what Ama had expected it to be.

"Lands!" exclaimed the queen, her mouth open and laughing. It seemed she either didn't fear Ama or was doing an excellent job of pretending she didn't. "Do you have any idea what you're saying, daughter of Gretti?"

"I do," Ama responded sharply, giving no quarter.

"First of all, young warrior," the queen said, sobering somewhat, "you do not have the right. No adopted warrior has ever Challenged a true queen."

"I was adopted into the tribe, yes. But I was also born to it."

"Are you sure you're not from the Bastion?" Tamura scoffed. "Only scholars speak in these absurd riddles."

"As a matter of fact, I was raised in the Bastion," said Ama, forcing herself to ground her feet against the earth. It was time for the full truth. She had waited so long for this moment, and it would not pass her by. "I was left at the Orphan Tree, and they took me in. It was the only way I could be safe, after you killed my mother."

The warriors around them were too well-trained to gasp but she felt their shock, their wonder.

Tamura's face was stone. If this revelation stunned her, she didn't show it. "I've killed many mothers. Many people. Over the years."

Maybe the queen didn't understand? Ama faltered. "My mother was—"

474

"I know who your mother was," Tamura cut her off, palm out. "She lost a fair fight."

"And now I'm giving you the chance to lose the same way."

Tamura laughed again, but with no mirth, only mockery. "Lose? Young one, your inexperience betrays you. If you'd been raised in Scorpica, if you'd been in this war, if you'd seen me lead, you would know better than to Challenge me. But I will take pity on you. Give you one chance at mercy. Revoke your words and I will not slay you where you stand."

For a moment Ama hesitated, but the moment didn't last long. "The words have been spoken," she said. "I will not revoke them. Battle or forfeit, Queen."

The silence following her Challenge was deafening.

"You have no second, you child!" cried Zalma with derision, breaking the quiet at last. "Have you even been a warrior for a day?"

"I was born a warrior," answered Ama, loud enough for them all to hear. "And my second is here."

It was time for Gretti to step forward, and she did not hesitate. "I, Gretti dha Rhodarya, will serve as second."

"Your daughter?" Tamura said. "I thought we just heard that she had a different mother, to hear her tell the tale."

"This warrior was brought back into the fold as my daughter," Gretti said, chin high. "But I am not her true mother, and Ama dha Gretti is not her true name."

The long moment that followed was silent but not still. Warriors shifted uncomfortably, some turning toward the conflict, some away. The faces nearest the circle told the tale. This was unexpected, but to many, not unwelcome. This reckoning had been a long time coming.

Tamura's gaze locked on Gretti. Now Ama saw a ripple of emotion across her face that the queen couldn't fully disguise. It was somewhere between rage and disappointment. But when Tamura spoke, she seemed to have total control of her voice. The only emotion Ama could hear in it was disdain. "Gretti dha Rhodarya, you would put your life on the line for this upstart?"

"Yes," said Gretti without hesitation. "I will put my life, my property, and my eternal soul on the line for Amankha dha Khara."

Gretti alone smiled as the steady, watchful faces in the crowd transformed with shock. Those who had not been certain of the challenger's identity now had complete knowledge of just who, and what, they were looking at.

"I see," Tamura said.

Ama said softly, "The time has come for you to pay."

Tamura shrugged. "I took no pleasure in killing your mother, you understand."

"That isn't how I heard it."

"Ahh." The queen's voice changed again. Familiar, lightly mocking. "How is our old friend Vishala dha Lulit? Did you sneak her into our camp as well?" She looked around with a showy, deliberate air.

Ama refused to be baited. "I came alone. I owe my life to Vishala, and I chose not to risk hers on this mission."

"Yet you risk Gretti's?" The queen gestured at her former friend, pointing an outstretched finger, without turning to face her. "She was a loyal foot soldier of your mother's, you know. Always thought Khara affixed the moon to its home in the night sky."

"I'm honored to know Gretti dha Rhodarya," said Ama, still keeping her gaze on the queen. "I'm humbled by her faith and her confidence in me."

"Misplaced confidence, I'm sorry to say. You know how many I've killed? You've heard the story of Sessadon?"

"I have," Ama said, her voice cool. "And today we shall give the gossips a new story to tell, one way or the other, won't we?"

"We surely will," said Tamura, nodding acknowledgment.

✦

"And who will be your second, Queen?" called Gretti, her voice ringing out confidently.

Not missing a beat, Tamura matched her confidence. "I have many subjects. I would be happy to let any of them do me the honor."

But a long pause followed her words, one beat and then another. Tamura sought a face in the crowd and found it: her most favored daughter, Azur. Azur was the one she'd raised to the greatest heights, especially after she'd become the First Mother. A seat on the council, the promise of the future queenship. If anyone should rush forward to second her, it was Azur.

Azur returned her adoptive mother's gaze, full comprehension on her face. She understood what question Tamura was silently asking and what the queen expected the answer to be. But the First Mother's mouth did not open, and her feet did not move.

Then Azur's gaze traveled to a point over Tamura's shoulder. Whatever she saw there made her look down at the red earth, blinking rapidly. Tamura swiveled her head sharply to see what or who Azur had been looking at, and she should have known. It was Gretti. Whatever expression had passed between Azur and Gretti, it was gone now; Gretti's face was all confidence, all challenge.

Feeling unsteady, Tamura turned her attention back to Azur. The young woman was already turning away. As she went, the First Mother muttered something about hearing her daughter crying, though she had shown her willingness to ignore the girl's cries many times before.

Tamura felt like she'd been punched in the throat. What a mistake it had been, to trust that girl who'd come from nothing. Ungrateful. Disloyal. No true Scorpican could be so weak. Once Tamura took care of the more immediate threat, she would find a way to pay Azur back for her betrayal.

But first things first. Tamura continued to let her eyes glide over the crowd, and when she spotted Orlaithe, whose group had split from Azur's as they returned from the rites, the queen let her meaningful gaze linger. This time, she got the response she wanted.

"I will second the queen," Orlaithe said. Perhaps she did not sound excited about the prospect, but excitement was not necessary. Tamura barely heard her actual words of seconding, something about the queen's leadership in the most challenging times the Scorpican nation had ever known. In any case, the requirement was satisfied. This was the last moment before the actual fight, and Tamura found herself wishing it would just be over. Did she really want to fight to keep control of Scorpica? Was it time to lay that burden down?

Ama drew her circular blade and Tamura cocked her head, looking at it curiously.

Ama caught her attention and twirled the blade, dipping it in and out of the sunlight, the metal so highly polished it looked like liquid silver.

"You cannot challenge me with that blade!" called Tamura, derision plain in her voice. "It's not a Scorpican weapon. If you were a true Scorpican, you would understand the rules of the Challenge a bit better. Weapons master, could you share with the outsider the rules of the Challenge around weaponry?"

The armorer came forward. "The principle of the Challenge is a fair fight."

Golhabi spoke too softly, and many of the warriors outside the smallest circle could not hear. "Speak up!" they shouted. "Come on! What was that?"

This seemed to rattle the armorer even more, and she shook visibly as she spoke. But when her voice came again, it was closer to a shout, making herself clear. "The weapon must be one from the Scorpican armory! These are the rules of the Challenge."

Ama's grin remained on her face but something fell away, her cheeks hollowing, the effort of keeping still evident.

"Oho!" called Tamura merrily. "You did not know that? I have a suggestion. I'll let you keep that blade if you want, but if you do, I get to choose a Scorpican weapon."

"It is your choice, Queen," said Ama quietly.

"It certainly is. Does your Challenge still stand?"

"Yes, Queen."

"Are you ready to fight?"

"Wait," shouted Gretti, but almost lightly, as if she were interrupting a toast to pour more wine. "One thing."

"You've already put your life on the line," said Tamura, trying to hold herself back from gloating with only partial success. "It's too late for you to take it back now that you know the woman you have pledged your life to has carelessly lost both yours and hers."

Gretti seemed to ignore Tamura entirely, not even turning her head. She walked toward Ama, but then put her hand out toward Golhabi. "Armorer. Could you please produce the weapon from your stores that you believe to be most similar to the one Amankha dha Khara wields?"

Golhabi ducked her head shyly, but she had an answer ready. "Yes, I can."

The armorer pulled a silvery shape from under her cloak. The weapon she held was the twin of the one in Ama's hands, an exact replica, its handle of wood and leather firmly grounding the arc of sharp, deadly metal. She extended the weapon to Tamura, who took it as if she'd known it existed all along. Her face betrayed nothing.

"Thank you, Golhabi," said Ama.

The older woman murmured formally, "Amankha dha Khara, may the Scorpion bless your path."

"Are you ready to fight, then, Challenger?" asked Tamura, her chin high.

"You have the right to put off our combat, don't forget," Ama called. "Or are you the one who needs to re-familiarize yourself with the rules of Challenge?"

"I know perfectly well I have three days, and I may choose the place and time, now that the weapons have been determined."

"If you need a day or two to practice," Ama said, "I can be merciful."

"I spit on what you call mercy," Tamura answered, and did just that.

The warriors began to walk back, marking out a circle, until only Ama and Tamura remained in the middle of it, their feet planted on the ground, curved blades catching the rays of the noonday sun.

◆

Ama feared so many times that she was lost. Twin fires of vengeance and anger burned in her, but anger was no substitute for skill. Her opponent was older, stronger, more practiced. Only the unfamiliar blade kept Tamura from slashing Ama's throat within the first five minutes of fighting, and even then, Tamura learned as she fought. She watched how Ama twisted her wrist as she brought the blade down, and the next time Tamura slashed out, she gave the slash an identical twist of the wrist. She learned to parry at an angle with the short round blade so her opponent's blade slid off. She got better with every minute. After half an hour of fighting, Ama feared, Tamura's skill with the blade matched her own.

But the intensity of the fight had begun to exhaust both of them, their pace slowing as the minutes wore on. They fought just as hard, but swings and slashes became rarer, more time passing between. Ama's arms began to ache and she suspected Tamura's did too. Their feet, which in the beginning had danced, slowed to an awkward, heavy shuffle.

Ama slashed at Tamura but missed, then leapt back to avoid the queen's counterstrike. In the beginning she had tried to use the borders of the living circle around them, the border formed of warriors' bodies, to contain the fight. But she'd realized, later than she should have, that the circle simply moved with them. As she leapt back now, the warriors behind her stepped back, the crowd easing and shifting. Moving like a single animal, they left plenty of room for the opponents to attack but none to run away. Ama stumbled over a small rock and realized the circle had shifted so many times that they now fought on entirely different ground than where the fight had started. She risked a glance to the side to see if she could place them within the camp, but even that moment was too much to give, and she felt Tamura's blade clang against one of her thick copper bracelets and cut a shallow slice into her forearm. She yanked the arm back and while Tamura's blade was extended, Ama lifted her left hand and punched as hard as she could in the direction of Tamura's face. The blow caught the queen just off-center on her throat, not hard enough to break her windpipe, but enough of a surprise to send her staggering back and give Ama a moment to recover.

And in that moment, Ama realized where she stood. She barely felt the pain of her wounded arm as knowledge dawned. The crowd kept her from seeing any landmarks of the camp, but she could still hear. Before, she'd thought she was only hearing the blood rushing in her ears, the sound of warriors breathing, whispering, gasping in surprise as the fight unfolded. But past all that, behind it, there was one more thing, and she finally recognized what it was. She'd been in this camp for months and the sound was familiar. Only hearing it warped through the experience of fighting for her life had made it strange.

She was hearing the rushing river.

Fighting the entire time, dodging Tamura's slashes and striking out with her own, Ama reevaluated everything. Was Tamura chasing her, intentionally, toward the water? The circle of warriors that protected them might simply step away, and then Ama would be standing on the high bank above the rapids, trapped. But the only way not to get trapped was to rush the other fighter, to get around to her other side, and that would require lightning quickness.

Ama took the risk, feinting toward Tamura's left but then diving toward the right, and nearly managed to kick the queen's right foot out from under her. The blow failed but at least she had angled herself properly. She no longer had her back to the water.

Then Ama noticed something odd about her opponent. No matter how or where Ama moved, the queen's gaze remained locked on Ama's face. This wasn't smart in fighting, Ama knew; one had to be aware of what the opponent was doing, which meant quick glances down at the body. The body could give away an opponent's next move. The eyes rarely did.

But Tamura's eyes held Ama's, and Ama could not look away. There was fierce fire in the queen's eyes, of course, but something else, too. Ama couldn't identify it, not with the need to keep herself alive and at a distance from the eyes in question. What was the queen seeing, and why did she focus so tightly? Was it the memory of a woman with similar eyes that she'd killed, nearly a decade earlier, in a setting so similar yet so different?

Then the idea Ama had been chasing through her mind clicked into place. She assumed it wouldn't work, because she had to make that assumption; she had to try this thing while also anticipating the next thing, while fending off the most capable warrior she'd ever faced, the same one who'd overmatched and killed the two people dearest to her in the world.

Ama began to move backward step by step, dragging each foot sideways in the red dust, keeping her blade hand toward the queen. A different light came into Tamura's eyes, this one easy to recognize: the queen assumed she had finally gotten the better of her exhausted challenger and was driving her backward in a retreat.

But Ama was retreating parallel to the river, the circle of warriors steadily backing up to allow her to do so. She let her eyes dart around, as they would have done in a genuine retreat, and spotted Gretti's worried face in the crowd. The faces near Gretti were also familiar, but Ama couldn't spare the focus to read their expressions. Sound was the most important thing now. She focused as intently as she could on the sound of the river, of its exact pitch as it raced over the rocks, and she continued retreating in the same direction until she heard that sound change ever so slightly.

Then Ama sped up her retreat as if becoming truly desperate. Tamura sped up to match her. Ama took advantage of her opponent's forward momentum to suddenly halt, plant both feet, then raise one in an explosive kick.

The kick hit Tamura off-center on the chest, toward her weapon-wielding arm. Tamura managed to get off a quick slash at the leg with her blade, which was what Ama had expected, but the cut was not deep, which was what Ama had hoped.

The kick did more damage than the cut, and Tamura tipped, twisted, and then sprawled backward into the dirt. If they'd been fighting with swords, Ama could have finished her off then, protected by the long span of metal between the pommel of the sword she held and the tip that would enter her enemy's flesh. But the half-circle blades were too short for that kind of maneuver. That wasn't what she'd intended.

Instead of advancing on her opponent, Ama turned and ran in the opposite direction, toward the natural bridge that arched high above the raging river.

She aimed straight for the line of warriors separating her from the river, and they shifted uncomfortably. Some planted their feet. But luck was on Ama's side, and she saw exactly what she'd hoped to see: Gretti, between her and the bridge, reading her intent, moving. Instead of breaking the circle Gretti extended it, grabbing the hands of the warriors nearest her as she turned her back and sprinted toward the bridge and across. Others nearby quickly understood and followed.

The shape of the crowd pressing the combatants together was nothing like a circle now, but it still bounded the combat. On the far side of the river, blocking egress from the bridge, stood two dozen warriors, plenty to block the narrow strip where the stone of the bridge met the land. On the near side, a larger crowd stood, still forming most of a circle except for the gap at the bridge. Tamura was now rising to her feet now, and the gap in the circle showed her only possible path forward.

Panting, the effort of her breath visible from any distance, Ama stood in the bridge's center. Fatigued arm shaking with the effort, she held her blade high. With the other hand, wearily, she beckoned Tamura to join her.

The queen's eyes were on Ama's again, angry and resolved, as she stalked across the last of the flat land and onto the natural bridge. Then her steps slowed, becoming careful, and a smile spread across her face.

The warriors around them blocked off both ends of the bridge. Others began to descend the steep paths down to the river, lining the shoreline on both sides, and Ama would not let herself think about what they waited for.

Tamura said, addressing Ama with a voice loud enough for all to hear, "You are your mother's daughter."

"Thank you," Ama said quietly, just loud enough to be heard over the sound of the water below.

The queen's smile turned cruel. "And you will meet your mother's fate."

Tamura lunged, sure-footed, and Ama spun to block her with the side of the blade. They could move forward and back, but only a step or two to each side. If human hands had built this bridge, they would have added railings to keep those who crossed it safe, but the natural forces that had created it—water, time—had not provided such niceties. The cost of one step too far to one side would be everything.

Ama remembered sparring with Paulus on the fallen tree, back in that quiet practice yard behind the palace, and tears sprang to her eyes, blurring her vision.

Tamura didn't smile this time, but with her eyes locked on Ama's, she could surely see the tears. The warrior queen twisted her blade hand back and forth as she'd seen Ama do earlier in the battle, catching rays of flashing sunlight.

Ama backed up one step, then two, shaking her head to clear the water from her eyes, turning her face away from the flashes of white light. The river seemed louder now, less a growl than a roar.

Tamura pressed her advantage, matching Ama step for step, raising the blade higher to match the angle of sunlight, sending the light into Ama's eyes again and grinning as the younger woman squinted, flinched away.

Ama's knees were bent, her eyes narrowed into slits. Her back hunched as she folded forward as if in pain. She held up her empty hand with the palm facing toward Tamura, a warning, a plea, both futile.

Tamura pressed forward once more, taking one more step that Ama hadn't taken, bringing their bodies nearer. Ama's outstretched hand lingered dangerously close to Tamura's whirling blade, her fingertips an incomplete shield between her face and the weapon. Tamura lifted her blade a fraction higher to keep it in the path of the light, reflecting the sun's bright rays so they cast half circles of light on Ama's nearly closed eyelids.

Then Ama reversed course and sprang.

All the coiled energy in her hunched back and bent knees exploded outward as she closed the space between them with a leap, twisting to plow her shoulder under the standing queen's arm, fitting her back to Tamura's front, grabbing the wrist of the queen's blade hand between both of her own, and flipping Tamura's body over her own in a short, fast arc.

Tamura's back slammed into the red stone, knocking the breath from her body, her blade dropping from shocked fingers and tumbling down, down through the air to the river far below. Ama spun once more and flung herself to her knees to straddle Tamura's chest, landing hard, using her full weight to press out what little air was left.

Tamura opened her mouth to recapture her lost breath, and in a swift motion almost too fast for the eye to see, Ama slashed her blade deep and hard across the warrior queen's throat.

The breath never came.

Tamura's eyes were still open as the blood gushed from her throat, its vivid red flowing and bubbling, but Ama could not watch as she died.

Ama laid her palm flat on the queen's chest and closed her eyes. She listened to the rushing of the river below. Ama stayed there with her eyes closed and her palm flat for what felt like an eternity. She kept the fingers of her other hand curled lightly around the hilt of her weapon, not willing to let it go, but the palm on the queen's chest was the focus of all her attention. She felt the heartbeat under her hand slow, and slow, and stop.

When it had been silent for a while, Ama struggled back up to her feet, so exhausted she could barely stand upright. A figure approached from the far side of the bridge. With relief, she saw that it was Gretti.

Gretti approached slowly, seeming to both want and not want to rush, her eyes inscrutable. She crouched and lay her fingertips gravely against the side of Tamura's neck. The world waited.

When Gretti rose from her crouch, she nodded at Ama, something like an acknowledgment, and also like a bow. Quietly, she said, "Queen Amankha."

Amankha dha Khara, queen of the Scorpicae, felt the full weight of the moment, even in her exhaustion. Warriors lined the banks of the river below and both ends of the bridge on which she stood. She was surrounded by Scorpicae in all directions. Once her mother's subjects, then Tamura's. Now hers.

Gretti made a soft noise between her teeth to catch Amankha's attention. Once she had it, she looked meaningfully at the blade still dangling in Amankha's hand, then touched her bottom lip with two fingers. *Speak,* said the motion. It was important that the first thing Amankha said be the right thing, and it came to her in a flash, what a true warrior would say, having defeated an enemy.

"Let the Scorpion drink the blood of the defeated," said Amankha hoarsely. "The battle is done."

She swayed but did not fall. Gretti didn't rush forward to help her. In that first instant, Amankha was filled with confusion at the older woman's impassive face, but in the next heartbeat, she recognized why Gretti hung back. In this moment, it was essential for Queen Amankha to stand on her own two feet.

So Amankha wrapped her fingers more tightly around the curved blade in her hand, still wet with the previous queen's blood, and focused all her energy on staying upright. She bobbled again, her head swimming. She stepped away from Tamura's body, taking two and then three steps toward the center of the bridge. Then she turned in a slow circle, surveying the upturned faces of the waiting crowd, and spoke to her subjects for the first time as their ruler.

"I am your queen," shouted Amankha. Her voice was still hoarse, but she strove to make it carry. "I am Amankha dha Khara. And I will take you home."

Not every warrior cheered, yet the cries of those who did rang out loud and clear, echoing up and down the banks of the river, lashing the stone of the bridge.

"We belong in Scorpica," said Amankha. "Not here in Godsbones. Not in any other queendom. We can't build our way back to greatness with death and destruction. The pain we've caused, we must heal. My mother, Khara dha Ellimi, would have wanted it so."

"She would," murmured Gretti. Amankha heard a few answering murmurs from the crowd.

"I will speak with the council. And we will end this war."

Cheers of agreement rose up from the bank below, but a voice from somewhere in the crowd on the far side of the bridge called, "You would have us be weak!"

"No." Amankha shook her head. "No. We are the best fighters in the Five Queendoms, and we must change who and how we fight. The other queendoms are not our enemies."

The same voice called, "But if we retreat to Scorpica, we have failed!"

"Why is it failure to return to the land we love?" Amankha raised the volume of her voice to match the opposing voice, the strain of it making her sore throat ache, but she made sure to speak without anger. "To build our future! We already lost a generation. Now we must build the next generation. That is how we succeed."

Murmurs rippled through the crowd on the far side of the bridge, and the speaker pushed her way forward. Now Amankha could see her clearly enough to recognize her. It was Zalma the smith, her round shoulders dense with muscle, thick fingers wrapped tightly around the handle of her massive flat-faced hammer. Amankha's hand tightened on her own weapon reflexively.

"This will not stand," shouted Zalma, her voice sharp, accusing. "You killed our queen and you stuff our ears with nonsense. You can't force us to march north in defeat; you can't force us to do anything."

Amankha braced herself. Zalma was strong, so strong, and Amankha was at her weakest, at least physically. The moment was fragile. But as Amankha turned over the situation in her mind, one thing stood out. Zalma was clearly a loyalist. But if she was so vehemently in Tamura's camp, why hadn't she seconded the former queen when she had the chance?

So Amankha turned her body toward Zalma and addressed her in an even, loud tone. "You would disobey your queen?"

"You aren't my queen."

Amankha had hoped for that answer. Sounds of disapproval quickly began to wend their way through the crowd. She didn't expect every single Scorpican to respect and obey her immediately, but if there was one thing they respected, it was tradition. They might not like the fact that Amankha was queen now, but she had earned the right to call herself that, and Zalma couldn't change that fact.

So Amankha said, "I am the queen of all Scorpicae, including you, Zalma. If you object, there is always one path open to you. Is that the path you want to take? To speak the Words of Challenge to me?"

Zalma glanced around before speaking. Then she growled, "If I do, you will lose."

Though it cost her effort, Amankha forced her chin up, regal, ready. "If you speak the words, you will need a second. Immediately. Someone to speak for you, to tell the assembled company how your rule will be better than mine. I have just defeated the best warrior in Scorpica to become queen; I will be happy to defeat you as well. Just be sure that your death and the death of your second will be worth it just for me to stretch my arms a bit more."

No one moved. For a moment Amankha thought it could go either way. Zalma's fingers curled tighter around her hammer, her arms so tense the cords of muscle stood out from elbow to wrist.

"Zalma," said a new voice, softer and higher, "do you want me to second you?"

Standing in front of Gretti on the far side of the bridge was a young woman of perhaps twenty years, her facial features more delicate and fine-drawn than Zalma's, but the way she held her small, compact body was exactly the same as the smith's. The same, too, were the thick muscles in the young woman's rounded shoulders and the shape of the flat-faced hammer in her hands.

Zalma looked at her daughter and Amankha kept her eyes on Zalma's face alone. She saw when the woman's resolve crumbled. She saw the tension slacken in her jaw, the breath whistle through her half-closed mouth. Then Zalma spoke.

"I choose not to Challenge you," said Zalma, "for now."

"Now is all I ask," replied Amankha.

The new queen of Scorpica looked out at the sea of faces, arranged in seemingly every expression she could think of. There was a great deal of anger and fear, but what seemed like an equal amount of joy and hope. She thought of her mother and what it had felt like for her, all those years ago, to look out upon her warriors for the first moment after she became their queen. And then another moment, just as important, years later. How had Khara felt when she'd slain Mada, Tamura's mother, just after giving birth to Amankha herself? This tired, this uncertain? Khara hadn't killed to take the throne, but when the choice to live or die presented itself, she'd killed to keep it.

When Amankha looked at her warriors, she saw subjects, but she couldn't ignore the danger inherent in every single one of them. Like Zalma and her daughter, any one of them might Challenge, any other might second that challenger, and then Amankha would be fighting for her life again, losing something precious in herself even if, as today, she managed to win.

How many more times would Amankha be forced to choose like this? How many times would she have to kill to reign?

32

A BURNING

The next day
Godsbones
Gretti

The fire rose high, clouds of smoke billowing above the red stone of Godsbones, black against the darkening blue.

The Scorpicae, as a race, did not hold to any particular burial tradition. Over time, following the Great Peace, certain queendoms had established very specific rules for handling their dead. The Sestians had their boneburners, at whose hands human bodies were burned to return to the soil, the same as any animal's. In their god's eyes, there was no difference: a thing grown and invested with life was a thing that, once that life was spent, served as feed for newer lives still growing. The Arcans buried their rag-wrapped bodies under the hearth, a more sacred and respectful approach, thought Gretti. But there were still rules around what could and couldn't be interred with the body, ensuring that nothing was wasted. No one knew what the Bastionites did with their dead, because no method one could think of made sense for them. Could there be burial caves deep among the other caverns? That seemed unlikely. There was no land to waste on bones, not in those ancient stone halls, forever confined. If they burned their bodies, it seemed someone would have noticed the smoke; if they carried them out, threw them from the parapets, ground them up for a kind of grim mortar—someone, somewhere, over the years, would have seen and whispered. There weren't even solid rumors about Bastion burial practices, no pattern to the occasional conjecture. That alone made Gretti wonder how depraved the other queendoms might find the Bastionite method of disposal, whatever it might be. People did not generally bother guarding secrets that would only make the hearer shrug before moving on.

Though she wished she hadn't, Gretti had seen hundreds of dead Scorpicae over the years, in so many places and so many ways she couldn't and didn't count. What happened to the body of a fallen warrior was entirely dependent on where she fell. Those who died near water were generally left to it, dropped or dumped in if necessary, water being an excellent way to dispose of flesh over time. One of the older warriors had died in that first long march down Godsbones, slipping away in the night, and because there had been loose rocks, they had piled them atop and around the body in a sort of cairn. Those who fell in battle were generally left to be dealt with by the enemy; any such tasks could be a distraction, and the Scorpicae liked to spread rumors that any Scorpican body might be doused with the venom of the scorpion. This made the enemy uneasy about handling the bodies, providing another useful distraction. When a warrior's spirit had already arrived at the battlefield beyond, there was no import to the flesh that remained. Whatever might happen to her earthly body, a warrior's spirit was beyond sullying.

Gretti was not naturally so reflective, certainly not where the ways of other queendoms were concerned, but she was alone with Tamura's body, burning it into nothingness. In the time it had taken, while she was letting her mind wander all over the Five Queendoms, night had fully fallen. She'd come far enough from the Scorpican camp that she could no longer even see its lights. The only reason she knew in which direction it lay was that she could follow the river. She had never been engulfed in darkness so thick and black, and she'd moved quickly to light the pyre for Tamura just as much to split the dark as to be done with the task at hand.

Gretti had set the task for herself, of course. No one had asked her. No one else had as much as moved toward the body after it fell, after the crowd that had gathered to watch the Challenge drifted away. Feet shuffled across the bridge in the red dust, the sounds of murmurs and whispers swallowed by the rush of the river below, as they walked off in twos and threes and groups of warriors. Everyone from the newly minted queen to the smith's apprentice chose her path across the red earth back toward camp, those who craved company heading for groups forming around the firepits, those who craved solitude retiring to their tents and caves. After only a few minutes, of the living Scorpicae who had a choice to leave the spot, only Gretti remained.

And she, of all the Scorpicae, couldn't leave Tamura lying there. The sun was still up when Tamura died, but the dark, Gretti knew, was coming. She could not imagine the once-proud queen's body left out in the middle of that bridge to be eaten by creatures, even if Tamura's spirit had already gone to the battlefield beyond. Burning was the fastest, cleanest way, if a bit Sestian in its ceremony. Still, the hauling of the body and building of the pyre out here in the isolation of nighttime Godsbones was lonely work, and Gretti was eager to occupy her mind as best she could. If she had to catalog the burial methods of every queendom, so be it.

What looked like the shadow of a thin woman moved at the edge of the circle of flame, at the periphery of Gretti's vision, and she whipped her head to the right so fast it hurt. The bright light of the fire had rendered her night vision useless, and Gretti cursed herself for not being able to see more clearly, but she had made the choices she'd made. Now she could only wonder what she'd seen, or almost seen. It was not a warrior, she decided. If a Scorpican woman had wanted to come, she would have been here already. She would have hailed Gretti as a fellow Scorpican. The figure in motion could not be a warrior, and if it was not a warrior, it was an enemy.

Distracted by the task, after she'd cut thongs and a stretch of hide to do her grim work of hauling a body no one else would touch, Gretti had forgotten her dagger on the ground back at the camp. An unthinkable oversight, and one that left her here unarmed. She cursed herself for a fool. Her first thought after the smear of movement disappeared in the dark, the thought that sprang to mind before she remembered where she was and what she was doing, was that perhaps Tamura had finally sent someone to end her life.

But Tamura couldn't have done so, because there was no Tamura. After so long looking over her shoulder, Gretti realized, now she had only to look toward her feet.

Tamura was dead. Her machinations were over. Gretti remembered so well that time in the glade on the way back from the Sun Rites, when Tamura had put the arrow between Gretti's feet instead of into her neck. In a sense she'd been on borrowed time ever since. Even in the years working together she hadn't been secure; in the year since, every time she'd openly opposed Tamura, she'd practically dared the queen to kill her.

And now, if indirectly, Gretti was the one who had done the killing. Her hands had not done it, her weapon had not done it, but she'd seconded and encouraged Amankha, and here they were. Or, in Tamura's case, weren't.

Gretti forced her mind to consider the more urgent matter at hand. But this figure, looming nearby, she could not place her. It wasn't the shade of the departed queen; the shadow's arms and legs were too thin, almost wisp-like, where Tamura herself had been solid and strong. As Gretti rose slowly, pretending nonchalance, she racked her brain for fellow warriors whose bodies looked so insubstantial. Perhaps Tagatha, the aged warrior who drove the carts and guarded the supplies because she was too frail to fight. What would Tagatha be doing here?

Gretti walked slowly, circling the dying fire, as if she were only checking the fire itself and not the perimeter. And there again the shadow went, a faint shape in the darkness, no more.

For a moment, the shape of the figure reminded her of an illustration she'd once seen in the Bastion, an image of the god-sister Eresh. All three sisters had been depicted on the mural, and Gretti remembered thinking at the time that only Sestia or Velja would be able to hide herself in a crowd of human women. Sestia's lush curves and Velja's squared angles would blend in with the range of humanity; it was only Eresh whose shape could not be found among the people their mother had created.

Yet here someone was, with those distinctive, lanky arms, and Gretti wondered if perhaps an enemy who worshipped the God of Death had come here to Godsbones and starved herself in hopes of catching the god's attention. Gretti caught another glimpse of the woman's shape but could not make out the woman's fingers, and she wondered how a person could make herself resemble Eresh in that regard. By tradition the god's fingers were depicted as longer than a human's. She shuddered to think of the ways someone might try to mutilate her body to match, and if someone was enough of a zealot to move to Godsbones, there was likely no limit to what she might try. Religion made people do unspeakable things—one only had to look as far as the Sun Rites to see how easily death and destruction could be made not only palatable, but holy.

Thinking of religion made Gretti murmur a prayer to the Scorpion, *If there is blood spilled, may it honor You,* before she slunk into the shadows after the shape, abandoning her pretense of watching the fire and putting herself into position to fight.

But then there was no one to fight. The night was black and silent, empty as a bucket with a leak. Not even a breeze stirred the red dust of Godsbones, when she was certain there had been a breeze moments before.

The night played tricks on a person, thought Gretti. Especially when the smoke of her former queen rose in the air. Tending the funerary fire was a self-imposed punishment, but a punishment it certainly was. She was breathing death into her very body.

Just how Tamura wanted it, she thought: always on the cusp of death, never allowed to cross over.

Gretti looked at her own fingers, stretched them out. If she starved herself, would she resemble Eresh? How quickly would she die, cross the dark bridge into the Underlands, and see that god for herself?

But she knew she would not do it, not tonight, not in the future. As much as she'd hated Tamura dha Mada, she loved Scorpica. She would keep Khara's spirit alive in her way. Khara's daughter now ruled, and Gretti owed it to both Khara and Ama to stand by her side.

One day her beloved nation would rise to its former glory, thought Gretti as she watched the fading embers, and to die before that day would be the worst defeat of all.

33

THE OPEN GATE

In the Underlands
Dree

As a shade, Dree had no body, and that was as it should be. She was far more comfortable as a shade than she'd been in her second life aboveground, occupying the discarded body of Olan. She worried Olan would come for her here. Did the shade of the other warrior even know that her body aboveground had been inhabited by another woman's spirit? There were only tales and myths about shades walking in the skins of others, no facts to be known.

Dying had not imbued Dree with any mystical font of knowledge. She knew little more than she had when she was alive, either time. She'd only learned what the bone bridge between worlds looked like and how one proceeded through the first gate that separated the Underlands from aboveground. And she knew that the guardian of the first gate, the supernatural Voa known as Nazarave, no longer blocked passage through that gate. Otherwise Dree could never have gone Above, never inhabited Olan's body, never made such a hash of her short second life.

And never found herself back in front of Eresh, God of Death and ruler of the Underlands, dreading the report she would have to give of what had gone on Above. Dree wondered if she would continue to exist in any form after confessing her mistake. She supposed there were worse things than no longer existing.

As She had before, Eresh loomed in front of Dree, seeming both perfectly ordinary and so extraordinary that Dree's mind threatened to melt.

The god glared at her, making no secret of Her displeasure. "How are you here so quickly again?"

Dree decided to put it as simply as she could. "I died."

"Yes," hissed Eresh, tenting her long fingers. It was nearly impossible to look away from those fingers, stretched into almost comically long, thin shapes, a clear sign that Eresh was not nor could ever be human. Still, Dree tried.

"I did not mean to, Your . . ." She trailed off. What did one call a god, face-to-face? She had never worshiped Eresh, only prayed to the Scorpion, as the other warriors did. She had believed in the All-Mother's daughters in a general way, an abstract way, but never expected to speak with any of them directly.

"You may say Eresh-*lah*," said Eresh. "It indicates that I am higher than you and you are lower than me."

"Eresh-*lah*," murmured Dree, dropping to one knee. She lowered her forehead, though she had no forehead, to the earth, where there was no earth.

"I care more for your information than your obeisance," said Eresh. "How did you die?"

She considered how to answer. "I was stabbed."

"You risked yourself in a fight? That was foolish. Though I suppose, as a warrior, you can't help your violent nature."

And whether it was because she bristled at the assumption or simply wanted to be truthful with a god who might have the power to see through any lies she attempted to tell, Dree decided to tell the whole story. "No. I wasn't injured in a fight. I didn't risk—well, I suppose I risked my life, but I didn't know that was what I was doing."

"What did you think you were doing?"

"I wanted—I wanted to tell her I loved her," said Dree, marveling at how the habits of the body were still with her even as a shade. She could feel—how?—her throat constricting, tears welling up. "Since I had a second chance."

"A chance I gave you."

"Yes. And I'm so grateful. But I didn't—I'm sorry, Eresh-*lah*, I couldn't help—"

The god interrupted, "Of course you couldn't. Humans. I know how weak you are. Go on."

Dree did as she was bid. "I didn't do it right. I didn't think about how she wouldn't recognize me. And I didn't know she'd see me as a threat."

"Why didn't you just tell her who you were?" The god's voice was, not surprisingly, without sympathy. Of the three god-sisters, only Sestia had once been a fool for love, or so the stories told; neither Velja nor Eresh had ever let that emotion overcome her good sense. Eresh had had Her consorts, perhaps still did—Dree had no idea—and perhaps She had loved, or did love, them. But on one front there was no ambiguity in the stories. Eresh was not love's prisoner; love was Hers.

Dree measured out her answer. She had no intention of lying to the god, but there were many ways to tell the truth. She picked the simplest. "I couldn't speak, though I tried. The body wouldn't let me."

"Tell me more about this."

So Dree told the god how the body wouldn't entirely obey her. How the hands had felt clumsy, the jaw heavy as iron. How what her spirit wanted and what the stolen body allowed her to do were not at all the same thing. Motions could be forced, with enough effort, but words were impossible no matter what. Dree told it all truthfully, leaving nothing out. There didn't seem to be much point in that.

Eresh nodded her understanding, Her look thoughtful. She'd dropped Her unnaturally long fingers to grip the arms of her throne, and it was possible to watch Her face without seeing the hands. From this angle Dree could see Eresh for a moment as almost human. Seen this way, the god could have passed for a fellow warrior, the sister or mother of anyone Dree knew. Some other person. Someone who could feel understanding or disappointment, excitement or confusion, frustration or joy.

The thought gave Dree a curiously tight feeling in what used to be her chest. She had let Eresh down with her foolishness, she realized now. She should have been smarter, better. With a third chance, maybe she could. Was a third chance too much to hope for?

But just as Dree was about to pour her heart out in apologies, the god spoke again, and not directly to the warrior. "Did you hear all that, sorcerer?"

"A problem that can be solved, Eresh-*lah*," said the new voice, and Dree saw something she had not before. A shade lingered near Eresh's right side, as sheer and human-shaped as Dree herself, but older in form, with white curls of hair mixed in among the black. Not a warrior, not with hair that long, nor did her form wear warrior's clothing. Eresh had called her *sorcerer*. Arcan, then.

"You said you could help, sorcerer," said the god. "This is what you call helping?"

"It is just the beginning. The first gate."

"It was I who opened the first gate," said a new voice. "So what good have you done thus far, Sessadon?"

Dree turned again to take in another sight: a woman no taller or otherwise more distinguished than any of the rest of them, but unquestionably solid in form, not a shade. It took her a moment to realize who it must be, even before the new arrival stood next to Eresh and the similarities in their faces became clear. Sharp gazes, high cheekbones, full lips. Though Velja's jaw was softer and Eresh's cheeks more like shadowy hollows, anyone looking at the two would see the family resemblance.

Something dark flashed in the eyes of the shade who had been addressed as Sessadon, but she mastered herself quickly, lowering her head. "I am honored, Velja-*lah*, by your presence."

"Save your honor," said Velja, the God of Chaos, who Dree could not quite believe she was actually seeing. "Honor is pretty bark on a rotten tree. You want to help my sister, sorcerer? Be useful."

But before Sessadon could respond, Eresh spoke to Her god-sister. "Oh, don't lecture on helpfulness. You can't pretend helping me was your only intent when you opened that gate."

Velja shrugged. "I do what I do, and I did what I did."

Eresh rolled Her eyes, just as any human might have done faced with an empty platitude. "And what you did, you did for you, *sister*. We made a bargain, and I intend to keep my end of it. The people of Arca are safe from me. I intend to punish the Scorpion's warriors for their misdeeds in Godsbones. And perhaps I will go a little further than that. But whatever I do with my shades now that the gate is open, your women will not be harmed."

"Not just this gate." There was a stubborn, sharp note in Velja's voice.

"Yes," sighed Eresh. "This gate and all the gates. Wherever shades may rise through an open gate, they won't rise in Arca. Is that better?"

"Thank you. I will return only if you give me reason to doubt," said the god, and She went from solid to vanished in a blink.

And now Dree remembered what the name Sessadon, the name Velja had used, meant. This was the sorcerer who had been killed by Tamura, her own queen, at the last Sun Rites. A power-hungry woman, this Sessadon, who'd tried to seize control of the entire known world. And here she was as a shade, planning something from beyond the grave. Dree had felt cold when she walked in a stolen body aboveground, but now, she felt even colder.

Sessadon was addressing Eresh. "So what is it you hope to accomplish with the first gate? Do you intend to wait for Scorpicae to die on the soil of Godsbones, then replace them one by one with the shades of your own worshippers from the Underlands?"

The words were near nonsense to Dree. She was, it was becoming clear, only a tiny part of a much larger plan. The knowledge didn't make her feel better about her chances of survival, whatever survival meant to a shade.

But at the moment, the god was directing Her displeasure only toward Sessadon, Dree realized. Eresh asked the shade of the sorcerer, "Who are you to question my plans?"

"Only someone who can improve upon them. I didn't want to say as much while Velja was here. She might not like hearing it."

"I have a greater loyalty to my sister than to you, dead woman," said Eresh. "Be clear or be gone. The waters of the Pool of Forgetting would wipe away your foolish notions quicker than the swish of a fox's tail."

Sessadon's smile was crooked, without warmth. "But aren't you tired of letting all that life go on without you? Up there? You're caged down here like an animal. They have the whole sunlit world."

"Sunlight or no, the reach of my world is far greater than theirs, magician," snapped Eresh. "Have a care how you describe my existence."

"Of course, of course, you are correct, Eresh-*lah*." Sessadon's voice was soothing now, her manner apologetic. "I was in the wrong. But in addition to ruling your queendom here in the Underlands, wouldn't you also enjoy ruling aboveground? Expanding your domain to the very edges of the world, in both darkness and light?"

Now the god appeared interested. "And how would you suggest I do that, magician?"

"With my help. And with all five gates open."

"All five! The Voa would never—"

"But one Voa already has," purred the sorcerer. "Nazarave stepped aside, didn't they? And opened the gate? And with little inducement."

"Because a god asked."

"Yes. But there are other ways. Even a Voa, like the rest of us, wants something. Some need to be appeased, some defeated, others satisfied. We only need to address each one in turn. Fight them or trick them, do whatever needs doing. Then we open each of the gates that close us off from the world Above. One by one."

"You think I haven't thought of that?"

"Of course you have. But you're also busy ruling your domain, as you have ever been. I will handle it all myself. Gather the shades we need to open each gate one by one. After all, we have everyone who ever lived at our disposal. I'm sure many of them would be more than happy to assist."

"You are full of hope, sorcerer," said Eresh. "But hope leads to disappointment. Look no further than this shade here. I raised her from the dead to walk the world once more, and she was useless."

Dree wanted to protest, but the god was not wrong. She had accomplished precisely nothing.

The sorcerer's voice was persistent. "But that is what the first gate provides, yes? According to the stories. A way for the luckiest shades to go aboveground, those who wish to visit their loved ones, and see without speaking. A last glimpse. For love."

Dree had never heard this, and now she realized her mission had been doomed from the start. Then again, it was possible that she could have succeeded, even without a voice. She just hadn't.

Eresh said to the sorcerer, "So this was success, what she did? Rise and die? So what the first gate provides is useless."

"No," Sessadon said. "The first gate is essential. Because now that it's open, we can work to open the second. Then the third. With each, shades will gain more power, and that power will be yours."

Eresh raised Her chin. "You're so sure?"

Sessadon's voice was warm with optimism, the voice of a woman who feels no doubt. "Can one ever be completely sure of anything? We don't need to be sure. All we need to do is go forward."

Eresh appeared to consider this thoughtfully.

The sorcerer went on, a new note of excitement in her voice. "And if we succeed? Above will be as below. All yours. The whole world and all its people. To do with as you will."

Dree didn't want to speak out of turn, but she was too curious. She knew many of the old stories but not all of them. The only thing about the afterlife that most Scorpicae cared about was whether they would awake in the battlefield beyond. So she asked, in a loud voice, "What happens when all five gates are open?"

Eresh's grin was wide and terrifying and made it clear that She was not, in any way, human.

The god said, "With all five gates open? The shades will not need bodies at all; they will wear their own bodies from when they were alive, perfectly recreated, according to what the legends say. They may pass from anywhere to anywhere, not just through Godsbones or the five portals, but anywhere across the entirety of the queendoms."

"Anywhere?" asked Dree in wonder. "How many shades?"

It was Sessadon who responded to her question, repeating it with something that looked like delight. "How many?" she echoed. She took her time with an answer, letting a sly smile settle on her face before she spoke the words. "All of them."

"And the dead shall walk the earth," said Eresh, smiling Her grim, godly smile.

At first, thought Dree, the god of the Underlands had seemed doubtful. But that doubt was gone now. Something else, more like excitement, had taken its place.

As the shades watched, Eresh raised both hands and stretched her long fingers up toward the world Above, indicating, embracing, as if it were already Hers.

✦ END OF BOOK TWO ✦

ACKNOWLEDGMENTS

As with the book before this one—really, all the books before—there are too many people to thank. Words don't become a book without a whole lot of help along the way, and I apologize to all those whose names aren't listed here who provided some of that help.

But a few names do stand out, and we can start with those. Huge thanks to Holly Root, Alyssa Maltese, and the rest of the team at Root Literary for their insight, enthusiasm, advice, and general excellence. At Saga Press, thanks go to Joe Monti for his editing expertise, Jéla Lewter for keeping things humming behind the scenes, and Lucy Nalen for her unflagging optimism and persistence in the world of publicity.

While there were some new faces on the team this time around, many of those who were instrumental in making *Scorpica* the best book it could be were back again for *Arca*. Kat Howard again provided helpful insight on an early draft. Valerie Shea, copyeditor extraordinaire, has again saved me from my own inability to do things like spell my characters' names consistently and keep track of whether their eyes are open or closed. As for the outside of the book, while I was absolutely blown away by the ornate, striking cover art

Victo Ngai delivered for *Scorpica*, I think her illustration for *Arca* might be even more amazing.

I'd also like to thank the rest of the extended team at S&S, in alphabetical order: Emily Arzeno, Jennifer Bergstrom, Chloe Gray, Cordia Leung, Tyrinne Lewis, Lisa Litwack, Jennifer Long, Paul O'Halloran, Caroline Pallotta, Esther Paradelo, John Vairo, and Sarah Wright.

As always, there are many people I'm grateful to whose names I don't even know: thanks to the readers, each and every one of you, for embracing the people of the Five Queendoms. My gratitude also goes out to the booksellers, librarians, fellow authors, and other book lovers who've supported my writing in countless ways. Thank you for all that you do. Can't wait to give you more to enjoy.

A Magic Steeped in Poison
By Judy I. Lin

"I used to look at my hands with pride. Now all I can think is,
'These are the hands that buried my mother'."

For Ning, the only thing worse than losing her mother is knowing
that it's her own fault. She was the one who unknowingly brewed
the poison tea that killed her—the poison tea that now threatens
to also take her sister, Shu.

When Ning hears of a competition to find the kingdom's greatest
shennong-shi--masters of the ancient and magical art of tea-
making--she travels to the imperial city to compete. The winner
will receive a favor from the princess, which may be Ning's
only chance to save her sister's life.

But between the backstabbing competitors, bloody court politics,
and a mysterious (and handsome) boy with a shocking secret,
Ning's life might actually be the one in more danger.

"A breathtaking tale with a stunning magic system rooted
deep in Chinese mythology and tea-making traditions.
Lin's originality truly blew my mind. Love and magic overflows
past the brim in this work of beauty."
Xiran Jay Zhao, *New York Times*-bestselling author of *Iron Widow*

"Beautifully written, from the setting to the magic system, A Magic
Steeped in Poison is sure to enchant both fantasy lovers and C-drama
aficionados. I'll be inhaling whatever Judy I. Lin brews up next."
Joan He, New York Times-bestselling author of
The Ones We're Meant to Find

TITANBOOKS.COM

Nettle & Bone
by T. Kingfisher

After years of seeing her sisters suffer at the hands of an abusive prince, Marra—the shy, convent-raised, third-born daughter—has finally realised that no one is coming to their rescue. No one, except for Marra herself.

Seeking help from a powerful gravewitch, Marra is offered the tools to kill a prince—if she can complete three impossible tasks. But, as is the way in tales of princes, witches, and daughters, the impossible is only the beginning.

On her quest, Marra is joined by the gravewitch, a reluctant fairy godmother, a strapping former knight, and a chicken possessed by a demon. Together, the five of them intend to be the hand that closes around the throat of the prince and frees Marra's family and their kingdom from its tyrannous ruler at last.

"*Nettle & Bone* is the kind of book that immediately feels like an old friend . . . It's creepy, funny, heartfelt, and full of fantastic characters I absolutely loved!"
Melissa Caruso, author of *The Tethered Mage*

"T. Kingfisher solidifies her place as natural and inevitable heir to the greats of her genre"
Seanan McGuire, author of *Every Heart is a Doorway*

"This book is so exciting, deeply wise, sad, brutal and compassionate all at once"
Catriona Ward, author of *The Last House on Needless Street*

TITANBOOKS.COM

FABLE
By Adrienne Young

Trader. Fighter. Survivor.

As the daughter of the most powerful trader in the Narrows, the sea is the only home seventeen-year-old Fable has ever known. It's been four years since her father abandoned her on a legendary island filled with thieves and little food. To survive she must keep to herself, learn to trust no one and rely on the unique skills her mother taught her. The only thing that keeps her going is the goal of getting off the island, finding her father and demanding her rightful place beside him and his crew. To do so Fable enlists the help of a young trader named West to get her off the island and across the Narrows to her father.

But Fable soon finds that West isn't who he seems. Together, they will have to survive more than the treacherous storms that haunt the Narrows if they're going to stay alive.

"An incredible, adrenaline-filled adventure."
Reese Witherspoon

"The salty sea and the promise of something hidden in its depths, had me reading this book at a furious pace. You don't simply read *Fable*, you are ensnared by it. This is Adrienne Young's best work of storytelling yet!"
Shea Ernshaw, *New York Times* bestselling author of *The Wicked Deep*

HALL OF SMOKE
by H. M. Long

Hessa is an Eangi: a warrior priestess of the Goddess of War, with the power to turn an enemy's bones to dust with a scream. Banished for disobeying her goddess's command to murder a traveller, she prays for forgiveness alone on a mountainside.

While she is gone, raiders raze her village and obliterate the Eangi priesthood. Grieving and alone, Hessa – the last Eangi – must find the traveller and atone for her weakness and secure her place with her loved ones in the High Halls. As clans from the north and legionaries from the south tear through her homeland, slaughtering everyone in their path Hessa strives to win back her goddess' favour.

Thrust into a battle between the gods of the Old World and the New, Hessa realizes there is far more on the line than securing a life beyond her own death. Bigger, older powers slumber beneath the surface of her world. And they're about to wake up.

"By turns gripping and poignant, *Hall of Smoke* is a compelling debut." *The Guardian*

"*Hall of Smoke* is a breath of fresh air. The world is unique, the fights are top-notch, and the cast is unforgettable."
Genevieve Gornichec, author of
The Witch's Heart

For more fantastic fiction, author events,
exclusive excerpts, competitions, limited editions and more

VISIT OUR WEBSITE
titanbooks.com

LIKE US ON FACEBOOK
facebook.com/titanbooks

FOLLOW US ON TWITTER AND INSTAGRAM
@TitanBooks

EMAIL US
readerfeedback@titanemail.com